W9-DBN-036

AN ELEGANT WOMAN

AN ELEGANT WOMAN

MARTHA McPHEE

WHEELER PUBLISHING
A part of Gale, a Cengage Company

Copyright © 2020 by Martha McPhee.
Wheeler Publishing, a part of Gale, a Cengage Company.

Wheeler Publishing Large Print Hardcover.
The text of this Large Print edition is unabridged.
Other aspects of the book may vary from the original edition.
Set in 16 pt. Plantin.

LIBRARY OF CONGRESS CIP DATA ON FILE.
CATALOGUING IN PUBLICATION FOR THIS BOOK
IS AVAILABLE FROM THE LIBRARY OF CONGRESS

ISBN-13: 978-1-4328-8055-2 (hardcover alk. paper)

Published in 2020 by arrangement with Scribner, a division of Simon & Schuster, Inc.

Printed in Mexico
Print Number: 01   Print Year: 2020

For Grammy
And always for Mark, Livia, and Jasper

■ ■ ■ ■

PART ONE:
ORIGIN STORY

■ ■ ■ ■

1

"WHAT WOULD YOU LIKE WHEN I'M DEAD AND GONE?"

For as long as I could remember, my grandmother was dying and telling stories. "I'm just a candle in the wind," she would say, and clutch her heart, sighing audibly. "I'm just an old, threadbare mule going round and round the katydid." She grew up in Montana, but a long road had deposited her in Ogunquit, Maine, and into a yellow Victorian she had christened, after my grandfather died and in a moment of virtuosic melodrama, Last Morrow.

My grandmother had snow-white hair that she wore like a crown. Her exacting eyes were a startling emerald. Her large, sturdy frame seemed a fitting home for her strong opinions. She dressed impeccably in tailored suits, wore motoring gloves, netted hats, diamonds from Tiffany's. Her snakeskin pocketbook fastened with a golden clasp, and when opened, the cinnamon scent of Dentyne wafted from within. On the dashboard of her black Lincoln Continental was a golden nameplate that read: Mrs. Charles Mitchell Brown — another name in a long line of borrowed names. She was Tommy; she was Katherine; she was Mother; she was Mrs. Brown; she was Aunt Thelma; she was Grammy. She wanted to live forever, or at least outlive Nancy Cooper Slagle, her great-grandmother, who lived to be 104 years old.

In the scheme of things, Grammy almost made it. She lived and lived and lived, despite all the clutching of her chest, the rolling back of her eyes, the repetition of that *candle in the wind.* Her own imminent demise became another yarn to spin. But she lived on and on. My sister Scarlett, deadpan but admiring just the same, called her *a blowtorch in the wind.*

To protect against oblivion the methods of two ancient Greek historians compete: Thucydides, the dominant example, tracked people down and interviewed them, took notes, recorded facts; and Herodotus, the long discredited fabulist, whose allegiance was to a good yarn, sometimes involving gods walking among the place, giving a nudge to events. The thing about Herodotus is that you don't need paper; you just need to keep talking, and on the backs of a multitude of voices the narrative is carried, like the soft shirt-rustle of an afternoon breeze across eternity.

When my three older sisters and I would visit, Grammy would take us on tours of Last Morrow, showing us "the melodeon that had been around the horn twice," a china bowl belonging to Nancy Cooper Slagle, cousin of James Fenimore Cooper, she would say, telling us how Nancy had carried the bowl over the Allegheny Mountains as she fled the Confederate South during the Civil War. Her husband had died in Libby Prison, leaving her penniless, a Yankee widow with seven children. She carried the bowl — given to her as a wedding present — from Richmond to the safety of her husband's family in Ohio. Grammy wanted us to hear these things. She would pause in her stories, ask one of us girls to get her smelling salts. "I feel faint," she would say. And from her vanity one of us would snatch the small silver container filled with ammonia so she'd keep telling her stories. With a sniff of it, she'd sit up straight again, the bulk of her with those green, green eyes, eyes that could hold a child, midbreath, between the future and the past. "I'm not long for this world," she'd say, like a prophet. "You need to know from where

11

you came and to whom you belong."

That was the sound of history. This is the sound of history. Like the catalogue of ships in the *Iliad,* you are not expected to remember particular names, only the sound of the names rolling along as you listen to the poem. Every history is a song, and this is what ours sounds like.

On her side, we were related to Mary, Queen of Scots and the Royal Stewarts of Nairn; a pair of dizygotic twins; an adviser to Bismarck, Helmut von Keller; and Laura Ann Slagle, a milliner in Cincinnati who made hats for Granny Howard — William Howard Taft's aunt.

Our grandfather, on the other hand, was "eleven generations Lynn," and though I had no idea what Grammy meant, I could tell it meant something. She was speaking about Granpy, but I knew she was also speaking about us — that we were somebody, descended from queens and also from Lynn, Massachusetts.

Granpy was the grandson of Nellie Mariah Breed, who lived at Breed's Pasture, the site of the Battle of Bunker Hill. Nellie used to say it was fought in her backyard, as though she had watched it from the comfort of her porch. Time collapsed that way in Grammy's stories, decades, centuries even, living side by side. Our grandfather was Charles Brown, had been the Buster Brown boy as a child, and Grammy would show us his picture as such, our grandfather's image, a young boy, posing in an advertisement. His family had been prominent shoemakers in Lynn — and for most of my life I believed that the Buster Brown Shoe Company had been started by Granpy's family, a notion that Grammy never disabused us of. Rather more stories filled in what logic and truth left out. Granpy's grandmother had escaped the Candlemas massacre up in York, Maine, when she was just a little girl, hiding behind a rock while the rest of her family was scalped. In the telling, Grammy would roll her eyes the way she did and tug at her own hair, lifting it from her scalp. On Last Morrow's kitchen wall hung a family portrait that included that little girl, grown up and so old her face looked like a dried-up apple. I was a little girl myself then, and it was impossible to imagine that I could ever be that old.

On her ring finger, Grammy wore a diamond from Tiffany's. "Extra-extra river water," she would say, showing it to us so that as she did it caught the light, casting a prism of color around the room. I didn't know what extra river water meant, but somehow it made sense. I could see cold river water flowing over the diamond, shaping it, giving it the power to cast light. Eventually she would ask each one of us, "What would you like when I'm dead and gone?"

At night she would put us to sleep, making us wash our feet, dipping cotton balls in witch hazel and then stuffing them between our toes to keep our feet clean so they wouldn't soil the sheets. She'd have us say our prayers — *Now I lay me down to sleep* — and then with her warm, wet breath and a voice airy and strained, soft and out of tune, she'd sing some horrible song about someone dying, "The Little Black Train's a'Comin'," which seemed a way of staving off her own death or at least normalizing it. She was, as she explained to us, "headed down the path toward oblivion," and what she wanted, I came to understand, was to leave a trace. She was on that path for a very long time, and once she actually did die, at ninety-seven years old, it seemed she continued to live some more, haunting us with her stories, stimulating debate and conversation about what the truth was. "I'm combing my hair with a can opener," she'd say.

If Grammy was our version of Homer, I

was Herodotus. I wanted to tell a history, but my allegiances were more toward providing a sense of character. My sisters, on the other hand, were straight-up historians in the mode and model of Thucydides. They required the documentation, the verification, the proof. They were fully possessed of the world's cynicism, of the fact of realpolitik as the true measure of how things happen in human affairs. Long before she died, thus, they had stopped paying attention to Grammy's tales. It fell to me, therefore, to be the keeper of the family stories, my inheritance from Grammy.

All of which brings us to my childhood home in New Jersey, some fifteen years after our grandmother's death, where Emma, the oldest sister, and I stood with our mother in the dim light of the Rose Hill basement, here to clean out the house, which smelled like mice and mildew, a dumpster in the yard. My eyes itched.

Scarlett was with us too, sort of. She studied the situation with her well-honed appraiser's eye, left eyebrow raised, and her ability to sniff out a fake at fifty paces, even through the glass of a computer screen, videoconferencing from a visit to her in-laws in Bordeaux. Of all five sisters and our lone brother, Timmy, only the three of us had taken on this task.

"It must have value," our mother said to Emma and me. "The" — she stumbled — "how shall I put it?" Mom tried to recall words, the weird conjuring that seemed to occur right behind her eyes. We were studying a trunk that belonged to our great-grandmother, Grammy's mother, Glenna.

"Trunk," I offered, finding the word for Mom. She gave me a puzzled look. Her confusion caught us off guard just as much as her clarity — weird illness, strange prism.

"Say our names," Scarlett instructed. We waited, watched her, tried to will her to say the names. Each time the same. If she said the names she wouldn't have Alzheimer's, she'd only have dementia. Scales, degrees. "Say our names," Scarlett insisted.

"Emma, Scarlett, Celia, Isadora." Our mother was a poet, published two volumes before surrendering to motherhood. Growing up, she would say our names all together like a line of poetry — a refrain. For a long time I was the youngest, Isadora, and fell last. I liked falling last.

"And?" Emma asked. We pressed when playing this game, greedy.

"You've got it, Mom," I said. She looked like a little girl.

16

"Zasu, Timmy," she said. Zasu and Timmy came much later. Zasu had a different father. Closer to the present they were first forgotten, last recalled.

"Brava!" Scarlett said, and Mom smiled, as if she had won something. And just like that she returned.

Who doesn't hope to find a hidden treasure at the bottom of a stack of boxes in a basement — that great repository of junk and time. The trick was not to get lost, to stay focused and on task. Already Emma and I had hauled out sixteen heavy-duty garbage bags of junk. The house was slowly sinking into the ground, the forest waiting like an army laying siege to our lovely childhood home, on its hilltop with views off into sky and distance. Our mother, in her forgetfulness, had spent her inheritance from our father, handing out, among other things, hundred-dollar bills to all the grandchildren for their birthdays and Christmas. All she had left was the house. With the cave crickets and the stinkbugs, the slow advance of the forest, the expenses advanced too.

"The trunk traveled with Grammy out west, when she was a child," I said. Though I was not sentimental about stuff, I liked seeing the trunk, that it had survived — or even just that it existed. But if we could have sold it, I'd easily have let it go.

"It's all nonsense," Emma said with a look of grim determination. "Grammy was a storyteller. And if you find any money here, Isadora, be my guest. No one will buy the house with all this junk."

Emma's plan was to clean up the house, get it ready to sell. "We're selling the house," she had announced to the rest of us in an email. "The money can pay for Mom's care. She may live a very long time, like Grammy." Strong as an ox, Grammy used to say. Grown up with children of our own, plenty of knowledge about our pecking order, we humored Emma's ideas, feigned they were the best ones.

Emma had the same severe silver hair, blunt short cut as our mother, same pale skin. They could have been sisters; it had been noted often enough over the years. Mom was just twenty-three when Emma was born. Often Emma acted as though she was Mom's older sister too. "Let's not be romantic . . . or sentimental. Grammy picked up the trunk in a flea market for a few dollars." Emma let the lid fall shut.

"Wait a second," Scarlett said. "Bring me in a bit closer." Her bob of blond curls bounced around her pretty face. She favored our handsome father: round face, blue eyes.

18

Looking at her, I could see him still. When we were children, she declared herself the beauty in the family. I moved the computer screen closer. "There's a market for restoring old trunks of famous makers." She asked me to run the camera over the details of the trunk. "It's a classic Saratoga, but certainly not a Vuitton or a Goyard," she said with her particular authority. The trunk was another instance — one of a thousand things — that needed to be dragged out into the clear light of day, then hauled off to the dump, its story finished.

"That's wrong," Mom said with a lucidity that always startled us, defending more than the trunk. "That trunk — that one right there — arrived at our house in Hasbrouck Heights when I was a girl. From the west, a few days before Grandmother. It's not from a flea market; it's not junk. It was filled with velvet and sheet music, furs and jewels in hidden compartments. It always contained some bit of the exotic — an arrowhead collection mounted on green felt, a coup stick, a tooled leather shot pouch. She would rest it on its side and open it like an armoire. It came again after she died. I remember that, appearing like her ghost."

"Glenna was poor," Emma said. We referred to our great-grandmother by her name, as if she were another relative living a short distance away. "She didn't have jewels or furs."

"She was difficult," Mom said. "But distinguished."

"That may be," Emma said. "But the trunk, look at it. It's finished." Mice and chipmunks and god knows what other creatures had gnawed away at the interior, leaving behind the debris of their nests — middens of straw, acorns, and scat. The trunk's leather straps were torn — or gnawed — the brass buckles rusted and broken.

In one way or another, since childhood, all three of us had been trying to save Mom. Scarlett liked to say that when our father came apart and our parents' marriage suffered and Zasu was born, that she and Emma stepped in to become the parents. Emma became the mother, cooking for us, while Scarlett became the father, taking care of the bills. "That's sexist," Celia would respond, watching from the sidelines. I, on the other hand, created narratives to make sense of it all, while also organizing and ordering, taking action. Right now what I wanted was to find things we could sell in order to help Mom. All these years later, our roles remained the same.

20

"I wouldn't have saved the trunk if it was worthless," Mom said.

"Celia took it to Europe, to Paris, when she moved to teach at the Sorbonne," I said. Celia didn't come anywhere near Rose Hill these days. "It's the scene of the crime of our childhoods," she said dramatically. And for Celia, the basement was a graveyard.

"There's a scorch mark on the trunk," I said, "from a fire. A stove exploded when Grammy was a girl in Montana and Glenna had left her alone. Turn it over and you'll see." I felt my sisters looking at me blankly. A piece of string hung from a bright bare bulb above us. We all had our own claim staked on the past; the stories were mine.

"Okay, okay," Emma said. Turning it over wouldn't be easy, the way the trunk was wedged into its tight space, surrounded by so much other junk, including a pinball machine from the 1970s. Even so, I handed the computer to Emma and started to lift the trunk to show them the scar. "We believe you," Emma said.

"Let's stay on task," Scarlett said. "I don't have much time." Emma moved more deeply into the basement, carrying Scarlett on the computer. I pulled on another string hanging from a lightbulb and illuminated more floor-to-ceiling stacks of stuff — a basement that seemed to stretch, without end. Being downstairs was like a stroll into the hereafter of objects, labyrinthine turns suddenly revealing vast collections of old vinyl LPs, children's toys, files, tools, household appliances, furniture, framed Haitian art from a gallery that our father had briefly owned, photographs and negatives from Mom's work as a photographer, books and stacks of Dad's research archives, Grammy's nursing manuals, Glenna's music, unfinished lives. Emma and Scarlett joked about getting lost in the Library of Babel. One could vanish down here in the musty silence, the sound of time ticking in the pipes. And here was what happened if you did vanish: you got curious, maybe opened a box, a trunk, and kept looking — one thing leading to another, until you were completely, wonderfully lost. Rummaging down here, I once took the nursing manuals, the music, a long, low plastic box stuffed with photographs of our ancestors — artifacts for my work. I felt like I was stealing.

One always to hope for easy luck, I maintained that maybe enough time had passed that the basement somewhere contained the treasures we needed in order to support Mom. Wasn't that the secret heart of every flea market that ever was?

■ ■ ■ ■

I am a novelist of sorts, using biographies of real people as jumping-off points for the stories I tell. I have written three novels, all of which feature families playing central roles. Families for me are like countries. They both contain and create the subject, while a childhood shapes a life. Jeanne Baret was a subject, an impoverished orphan of an illiterate couple, who grew up to circumnavigate the globe in the eighteenth century dressed as a man; Jane Wilson — ethereal painter of the sky, raised in dust bowl Oklahoma by a poet and an engineer — took long car trips across the country with her parents and her sisters, watching the changing landscape bookended by oceans; and Hypatia, earliest female mathematician, astronomer, philosopher, daughter of Theon, renowned mathematician, mother unknown, erased by history. I made it my job to resurrect this mother, and therefore Hypatia, through deduction.

Now, after years of wanting to, I had trained my work on my grandmother, writing her story. This is what I told myself, what I told people who asked at parties what I was working on. It was good to have a clear, unimpeachable subject — one that was straightforward but admitted, just the same, enough depth and complexity to keep things interesting. It put me at ease, and therefore my interrogator, gave me a sense of purpose or at least a sense that I knew what I was doing with myself. More pointedly, I said, on grant applications, for instance, that I was interested in my grandmother, born in 1904, dead in 2001, because her life had spanned a century in which so much had changed for women, and she, an ordinary, unhistoric person was cast within the flow of big history. Whenever I thought of her life against this backdrop, I felt a vista open up before me — a prairie emerging in the original sense of the word, forest suddenly giving way to the horizon and tall grass blowing in the wind. I felt that distant woman call to me, and so she became my subject, as she had always wanted to be for me.

For years I couldn't see, in the way we can never see the most important things for what they are — most likely because they present themselves in the form of endless rows of dusty basement boxes — that her story was mine. Not the details or the particulars. Not the facts or the fabrications. But perhaps the one big fact — that she once was, and so was I. We were shaped differently by our times, by the ways in which we were raised and educated, of course, but what did my grandmother and I share? There was no way through this, I knew, but through the particulars.

There were the particulars, for instance, of an epic-heroic past — some of it factual, some of it running parallel to fact, some of it orbiting in a broad, elliptical path, like Pluto, around the truth, and some of it like the stories about the gods we give to constellations in the sky. We project the epic onto the sky; to find, in the chaos of the cosmos, the patterns connecting star to star that give a snug fit to Orion's Belt; to place in one's palm the ladle of the Big Dipper; and to receive a few practical orienting tricks: that the Dipper's cup points to true north.

My own true north understood that there was something essential being done in my mother's basement, in sifting through and sorting out truth from fable, though even fables have something deeply true about them that outlasts us, my mother's disintegrating mind, our own unique and individual selves shuttling off into the unknown: a truth beyond the objects we tossed into the dumpster and the objects we held on to, a truth in the stories that would remain, when we were dead and gone.

If Glenna were a constellation, you would see her in her white teacher's smock, striding westward across the dew-wet grass of Montana, a rifle in one hand, *Temple's Notes to Shakespeare* in the other. There wasn't room in the sky for a husband with a wandering eye, but that was where stories came in, to fill out an evening, to ask about duplicity and betrayal, the steady march of self-compromise that led to whatever cul-de-sac of banality one found oneself in — and then to wonder about what a genuine hero would do about such things.

If my grandmother and her little sister, Katherine, were constellations, they would be in another part of the sky entirely. Grammy would be kneeling, facing east with her .43 Egyptian just about ready to pick off a prairie dog. Her sister would be standing next to Grammy, looking west, toward Glenna. The larger truth, the one that would outlast all of us, would be reflected in this constellation, this mise-en-scène.

"I need more light," Scarlett said. "The gems will be small. Look for small objects." Scarlett had already staked her claim to the larger gems. One way or another, all of us wanted something to take away. Even so, Scarlett's brand of hope was more practical, more concrete than mine, based on equations made from the way in which Grammy had lived her life, the way in which Mom had saved everything, the fact that none of our siblings had scoured the basement yet, or so I thought, had separated the wheat from the chaff, the disjecta and dross from the "quality pieces." Scarlett's mission was to preserve, find objects of value, and then keep them. Her home was a museum to our shared past.

"The boxes," Scarlett said, her mind working like a heat-seeking missile, "Find Grammy's boxes from the move and do not throw any of it away or sell it." Grammy had moved from Maine to New Jersey some ten years before she died, not long after our father died. All those years piled up, the contents of her life stowed in the deepest part of the basement storeroom, her red ink scrawl informing us of the long-ago room the contents had occupied and to which ancestor they had belonged. As my sisters zeroed in, I noticed, for the first time, a familiar black metal box, smallish with a handle on top. I remembered it sat by my grandmother's bed, held all of her important papers, letters, cards, certificates of deaths, of births, decrees, marriages, clippings from newspapers — papers that I wanted to sift through, that certainly held some approximation of truth and fact. She would put her glasses on and from time to time, in the dull light of one of her fancy bedside table lamps, she would rifle through the contents. I could easily imagine what was inside, wanted it for my own, before my sisters had a chance to stake a claim. Suddenly I had never wanted anything as much. I wanted this expedition to end right now. I stepped forward, twisted my body so my back turned, pressing up against the shelf upon which Grammy's boxes were stacked, hiding the black box altogether with my body. Deftly, I maneuvered it, sliding it more deeply into the shelf, tucking it behind the other boxes.

Just then, Emma asked me what was wrong. Scarlett too. She raised her right eyebrow suspiciously. And then, coincidentally and very conveniently, my sneaker squished into the soft flesh of a newly dead rat and I screamed, startling Mom and Emma.

"Disgusting," Emma said, jumping back. There was blood.

"The house could be infested," Scarlett said. "Call the exterminator immediately.

Mommy pays dearly for the service. Use it."
Emma slammed the laptop shut and handed it to Mom. Scarlet was gone, sucked back to Bordeaux. Emma reached down, her hand in a plastic garbage bag, and scooped the rat off the ground.

"It's a farmhouse," Mom explained.

"We have to wash our hands, Isadora," Emma said to me, as if I were five years old and she was eleven, holding me with her big black eyes, shining as they did, like precious jewels. Grammy used to say they were Glenna's eyes and before that they had belonged to Nancy Cooper Slagle, Glenna's grandmother.

"Let's get out of here," I said, knowing that later I would return for the black box — no golden nugget for the flea market, just papers. I could almost hear Grammy whispering in my ear, *What would you like when I'm dead and gone?*

2
MAGIC CITY

Two sisters: one beautiful, the other not. Little girls, five and three years old, they wore red velvet Christmas dresses and rabbit furs, waiting on the platform with their mother and her violin, for the train that would take them from Ohio to Billings — "Magic City," as it was called, because it blossomed overnight.

They were running away from Father. It was January. Cold. A black trunk stood between them, brass buckled, leather strapped, more suited for an ocean liner, wheels at the corners, almost too heavy for the three to lift. They didn't bring much: summer dresses, white linen, eyelet and lace, lovely and impractical (which made the girls wonder if it might be warm where they were headed), an iron, rosin for the bow, ribbons for their hair, family keepsakes — a Cantonese wedding bowl, *Temple's Notes to Shakespeare,* belonging to Mother's grandmother Nancy Cooper Slagle, a reminder of to whom they belonged and from where they came.

The eldest of the two girls — my grandmother — pudgy and round, considered herself mostly six. Thelma Madeleine Stewart was named for the title character of a bestselling novel by Marie Corelli. Her middle name was for one of Mother's sisters, who died of sepsis when she was seven — a notion that scared Thelma, afraid that fate might befall her. Thelma had always been called *Tommy like a boy,* as Mother would say, as if that were better, and sometimes Tommy thought it might be. The younger girl was called Katherine, etched delicately as filigree, named for queens.

Way back there at the beginning of it all, Tommy stood with her arms long at her side, shivering, her green eyes studying the dark morning: the lonely tracks shooting out ahead and behind, the gray smoky light and the quiet rectangle of the depot against the widening sky, snow on the ground, her breath making clouds. A tired dog lumbered along, leaving prints in the snow, and Tommy imagined the dog was heading home. She waited for the sound of the train, hoping that her father might just appear in time to stop them, wondering what would become of them if he didn't.

In her purse, Mother held one hundred dollars, had counted it out for the girls, wanting them to know that she'd saved it over the last year, that you couldn't buy anything for a hundred dollars, but that she intended to buy a new life. The money had dazzled Tommy, paper and coins, tucked powerfully now in Mother's purse. She had sewn some extra coins that Tommy imagined were worth a lot, a private stash for emergencies, into the hem of her dress so if thieves tried to steal from them, they'd have insurance. "Quiet," Mother snapped, making Tommy flinch, though she hadn't said a word.

A telegrapher for the railroads, Father kept travel passes, which Mother had stolen from him. She was going to the drier climate to cure her tuberculosis, an illness that she did not have. They had left him at the crack of dawn asleep in bed with his lover. "He has a wandering eye," Mother had said to Tommy.

Mother filched the passes, sent the trunk to the terminal the day before, left a note stating that the drier climate would be better for her health. "I'm strong as an ox," she told Tommy, "but he doesn't need to know."

Glenna Idelia Slagle Stewart, my great-grandmother, was imposing — tall, severe, a vanity that made her appear beautiful — leather gloves and a beaver fur, her violin in its case, her Gladstone medicine bag filled with remedies. She was born in Cincinnati eight years after the Battle of Little Big Horn. A primary school teacher at age sixteen in Gallipolis, she enrolled in Waterloo College, took some classes at Oberlin, and had considered herself a new woman, that is, of course, until she met Lavern.

Lavern was a workingman, hadn't gone to college. They met on a train. Because she was beautiful, and because the train was full, Lavern sat down next to her. He asked about the violin, a French Mirecourt, inherited from her German grandfather as a reward for her talents. Other passengers became their audience. Lavern was beautiful too, with jade eyes and jet hair, tall, strong boned. He told her he played the fiddle, fast bow strides fun for dance, and after some coaxing, Glenna offered him the violin and he played "The Devil's Dream." He thought of himself as a western man, though he too was born in Ohio. He traveled west on the trains when he wasn't working, loved them: the forward motion and changing landscape, the cities becoming prairies becoming deserts, rough raw intimidating, empty spaces where all the world seemed opulence and light. He felt important, part of something large.

For Glenna, who was still young, he was adventure and freedom, allowing her independence of mind and body — sensations of body smarting and eager to spill out and pour through. Her music had enchanted him. On the train, she told him she could play anything: violin, mandolin, banjo, piano, harp. Her grandfather studied with the Polish pianist Theodor Leschetizky, one of the founders of the St. Petersburg Conservatory, friend to Johannes Brahms.

"Friend to Brahms," she would claim, and though Tommy did not know who Brahms was, she knew his name attached her mother, and therefore herself, to something more.

On her violin, Glenna played ballads as well as classical. She played "Sweet Betsy from Pike" and sang of the Shanghai rooster and of sand in her eyes. She played and sang Bach, "Erbarme Dich" — thick, dark smoky color, length and shape and folds to her haunting contralto. Cultivation and wilderness combined in her. Lavern came from a good family, was a Stewart whose ancestors descended from Nairn, Scotland, his blood running downstream from Mary, Queen of Scots, Glenna said to her girls. Ancestors were important to Glenna. Lineage defined the great, unceasing march across time, one's ability to defy it.

Within a year, Lavern and Glenna were married, Glenna believing that together they could make something new and different of marriage, something more equal. If she were a new woman, he could be a new man, and they a new couple. They had their first daughter, then their second, lived in a home Lavern's family had constructed for them, a redbrick, two-story with running water and American Standard bathrooms, set back from the street by lawn. It was pleasant until his wandering eye got the best of him and Glenna's sense of freedom yielded to panic, then to a firmer belief in votes for women. She traveled around town on her bicycle making speeches — an occupation Lavern tolerated and teased about, dimples punctuating cheeks — searching for a new stage and always something more. She didn't know what. Power? Freedom? Release? She had an urgent yearning to do something, be something, make something. She did not love being a mother, her children searching her with their scared eyes for answers she did not have.

Today Glenna fled, in full possession of her own will. Auburn hair rolled in the same loose Gibson girl, beaver hat. She boasted an eighteen-inch waist. She believed her children, and therefore herself, descended from queens. "We are of quality," she told her girls in her exacting tone — everything exact about her, even her temper when it arose, fast and definitive, her face fracturing into knife blades.

The first train of the morning was the Scioto Valley Traction Company interurban to Columbus. It ran hourly, starting at six. Tommy took Katherine's mittened hand. She felt less afraid holding her little sister's hand.

"We are headed to gold country," Glenna had told the girls. Young as they were they knew what gold was. Montana glistened in the advertisements she showed the girls: a plow turning up gold coins from a rich soil. A land of snake rivers flowing nuggets.

The interurban rolled into the station, all screeches and metallic clanging, and the girls and Mother stepped on, Tommy looking back one last time with the hope of seeing Father come to save them. They traveled north to Columbus as light lifted the day on white barren stalked fields and scattered farms. A stove, in the place where a seat should be, kept them warm. There were a few men traveling, one in striped suspenders, picked up at other stations, and Glenna asked for their help with the trunk, cocking her head just so and a little submissive smile perched on the edge of her lips. "Would you?" spilling out softly, fragile seeming because she knew exactly what men wanted.

"Why isn't Father coming?" Katherine asked.

"Shh," Glenna snapped, and Tommy echoed her shush. Tommy understood if they were asking for help it was better not to mention Father.

In Columbus, the conductor raised the trolley pole while the train moved, attaching it in a fast, deft gesture to the network of live wires overhead, and the train continued its winding way through town, ushering them toward Union Station, arcaded and bustling with automobiles and bikes and horses tugging loads and pedestrians, trains coming and going and the busy sound of them, and the acrid smell of them and the energy of ten thousand crisscrossing destinations, people scurrying importantly through their precious lives.

Glenna's men helped with the trunk, carrying it to the street, to a wagon, into the passenger waiting room where she and the girls spent the rest of that full, long day, until the 8:50 p.m. Penna overnight to Chicago. Tommy watched passengers come and go, warming themselves around the big potbelly of the stove while agents weighed out freight on the portable scales, dairy cream in their heavy canisters and crated animals making their particular sounds, baled hides smelling of tannin, and furniture, and machinery, and the clank and clink and heel click and dull lull of voices, bundles of mail in from east out to west. And Glenna's gentlemen, one after the next, smooth-shaven faces or beards tidily trimmed, in business suits and top hats and Prince Albert coats, striped suspenders, took up Glenna's hand, slipped off the glove, and placed a kiss on the back of the palm. She raised her head delicately to ask if they were headed farther down the road.

One man asked her if she'd fancy a coffee, which they drank standing at the counter in the restaurant, heads lilting together conspiratorially. Glenna calculated. This was how it happened. All across America. Tommy observed. She and Katherine were children of a certain time. They knew better than to speak when they could be overheard.

At the counter, Mother got a bread roll

and tore it in half and gave both girls a piece, placing it in handkerchiefs taken from her bag, unlatching it, slipping her slender fingers into the cavernous depths, then handing forth the food to the eager girls. It was easy to forget a lot when you were hungry and to be simply occupied by the warm yeast and softness against the tongue and throat and then by the desire for more, which always came the longer Mother shared coffee with the gentleman in suspenders or the one in the hat or the one with the shining cuff links. She knew how to beg and make it appear otherwise.

Tommy pretended as well that she wasn't a little beggar child, that she was like other fancy girls traveling in capes and muffs and dainty and distant, accompanied by a retinue, trailing behind fluffy-dressed, and she and Katherine, not so different, carrying nothing. She stood tall and proud and eagle-eyed, pretending not to notice, pretending to be no different, pretending that a man of Mother's was her father. Noting. Studying. Hiding in plain sight. This was the start of her pretending and she took to it. She observed the diminishing, then entire vanishing, of these well-cared-for children the farther west they traveled.

The overnight took them through Logansport and on to Chicago, arriving at 7:20 in the morning. The night was solid and black with their faces faintly mirrored in the coal-dusted panes, nothing beyond their reflections but the void filling in with visions of golden country.

They were not alone heading west. The year before, Congress passed the Enlarged Homestead Act of 1909, offering 360 acres of land to those who could prove up within five years. Settlers came. They were called home seekers and colonists, homesteaders and settlers, immigrants and emigrants. They came from the Midwest and the East, from Canada and Europe. They came alone, they came with friends, with their families, with all their earthly possessions, their life savings, sight unseen, lured by the acreage, the reports, clever advertising, the designs of bankers and merchants and land dealers and railroaders, the government. They came on the railroad, purchasing special "home seeker fares" for "home seeker excursions," offered monthly on the first and third Tuesdays.

President Louis W. Hill of the Great Northern Railway began his campaign for a better Montana, sending exhibition cars all across the country to showcase Montana's products: "Turnips as big as trombones!" Slogans touted rich soils and a glorious climate: "Watch Montana Grow"; "Back to the Farm."

The Milwaukee Road and Great Northern railroad companies did not have land grants from the government, therefore they had to buy and lease land. To pay for it they had to populate it. Special fares were offered for those crossing the Atlantic. Contests were sponsored with thousand-dollar prizes for the best-grown crops and livestock. Stereopticon lectures celebrating Montana's spoils were filled to capacity in city halls and opera houses up and down and across the eastern seaboard.

The goal was to create a market, and they did, transforming the perception of a landscape that only a few years earlier had been known as American desert. Now apparently it was flowering and green and capable of producing some eleven million bushels of grain per annum. Apparently it was ahead of all states in value per acre of farm product. From Montana came the best wheat, the best oats, the best barley, the best alfalfa grown in the United States.

The railroad companies wanted a particular type of person, not just anyone: the educated, the well mannered, respected, gentlefolk, upright citizens. "They want elegant people," Glenna told her girls. Upper class, upscale. And they came. The federal government gave away thirty-two million acres, and in just a few years, eighty thousand homesteaders staked their claims. The Cinderella State transformed.

Tommy tugged Katherine along to keep up with Mother, overseeing the trunk as they made their way down the platform loud with the engines, passengers catching midmorning trains. Men in bowler hats and top hats and frock coats, carrying canes, puffing pipes, bearded and mustached — businessmen hurrying. Smoke billowed against the sooty air thick with whistles and steam trumpets. Blasts of engine heat, coal fires pocketed the cold. Katherine dragged, leaden tired. Already they'd been traveling for a day. It was close to eleven, the train scheduled to depart. Tommy encouraged Katherine with a force that she knew wasn't nice, and they trailed after Mother, whose gaze was focused ahead as she maneuvered through the crowd.

Their train was a passenger train, not a mixed train, headed down the main street of the northwest. The trip was twenty-six hours long if not delayed.

Ladies in silk swooshing skirts, hobbled skirts, promenade suits of wool and satin, velvet trimmed, fur trimmed, plumed hats from Paris, stepped into the green Pullman cars. Porters busied with luggage. Boys busied with their tin trays, selling foods and coffee and tea and newspapers, flooding onto and out of the cars, shouting headlines, listing their merchandise, ragamuffin criers not much older than Tommy with clothes that smelled of coal oil.

A swarm of nuns in black habits and capes hovered by the entrance to their coach. Glenna stopped to survey the car and then the nuns; she scanned the long train, looked at the passes in her gloved hand, stuck the tickets behind the ribbons around the girls' hats, and patted them forward. The nuns numbered at least a dozen — Ursulines from Cincinnati, on western missionary work. They'd been chattering and stopped under the sudden pressure of Glenna's eyes.

"I need to look after our luggage," Glenna said to the nun standing closest, looking at her as if she were there to be ordered around. The tight cowl beneath the nun's chin pinched the loose skin there ungraciously. "May I leave them with you?" Glenna asked, indicating the girls. There was nothing contrite or apologetic. Her question was a command that would be obeyed. The nun was warm and ugly with dark blueberry eyes. She held a solid woven carpetbag filled with food and had the eager look of a person who knows only how to give and apologize. Tommy could smell the food and wanted to go with the nuns. She'd been taught this way, to desire for herself what Mother imposed. But Katherine clung to Mother until she released Katherine's hand and distanced the child. "You'll be a brave girl. Go with the nuns now," Glenna said. She understood the natural ingenuity of children; she had taught children for almost half her life already. They knew how to find their way and if they didn't, it was a failure not to teach them otherwise.

Tommy pulled Katherine close to her, feeling protective now, her little sister's body so tiny and rigid against her own. The nuns, absorbing the request, admired the long, bouncy curls Mother had set in rags the night before because it was important to be impeccable when traveling. Katherine had asked why they'd had to bother with the curls. She didn't like the fuss and scalp yank. She repeated her question now, quietly, to Tommy, even though she already knew the answer.

"If we die on the train," Tommy answered,

"we want those who find our bodies to know we were of quality." Tommy knew about death, had been taught that it did not take much to die. In the trunk, they carried a death portrait of Mother's sister, Madeleine, in a gold frame that closed liked a locket. Sometimes Mother showed it to them; sometimes they peeked at it on their own. Madeleine was so elaborately dressed, her eyes incandescent, she looked alive. You should be prepared for death, elegant even. Tommy liked knowing more than her sister just as her sister liked knowing less.

"Come, girls," a nun said, the one with the cowl and the carpetbag. They watched their mother march purposefully down the platform, a subtle layer of terror forming just beneath Tommy's skin. The girls entered the train with the nuns, who fluttered about like a pleasant breeze.

"We're going to gold country," Tommy told them, feeling much older than almost six, as if she understood the intricate, ricocheting maze that was the adult world.

At home, they had not only left their father and the redbrick house, but also all of the aunts and uncles — all of Mother's sisters and Father's brothers — an entire party of family who had so recently come to celebrate Christmas in their fancy clothes, with presents and ornaments for the tree and candy canes for the children. Tommy thought about them and felt sad.

The car was bigger and broader than the earlier trains, but none of the fancy women were in this section. Instead there were two rows of upholstered benches and large windows with buckle locks securing the glass. It was warmer in the car than outside and there was a dim natural light that held dust particles afloat so you could see the air. Other passengers boarded — sad-looking men in soot-smudged denim, a young man and his scared bride, a large family with six children and many small burlap bags. The children were noisy and disobedient, speaking in a foreign language. Tommy noted that they didn't look well dressed enough to die or settle in Montana, and that made her feel superior. The children's mother fixed deep choleric eyes on them, casting disapproval from one child to the next until they were all quiet. Tommy wondered if all mothers were mean. She smoothed the fabric of her flounced skirt, hoping the strange children would regard her with deference, enjoying their eyes on her.

The girls slid into a bench. Katherine turned to the door with her fur muff pressed tightly to her chest, keeping a vigil for Mother. "She'll come," another nun said, taking off her cape with brisk energy and a fast, comforting smile. From her belted waist dangled a rosary and a golden cross. Or it could have been the same nun. They were mysterious, all alike in an ageless zone between thirty and fifty, looking neither young nor old, no past no future. All together they were a flock. The girls had never seen so many nuns before. They were almost scary, like witches, but the girls knew that nuns were religious people and that that meant they were supposed to be good. They fussed about, settling in, taking over seats. As the train began to move from the station and the girls' heads bobbed about continuing their search for their mother, the nun with the heavy bag filled with sweet-smelling food sat down on the edge of their bench. The shrill blast from the engine jolted them.

"I want to go home," Katherine said. There was nothing to say to that. Tommy wanted to go home too, back to the house filled with Christmas and the aunts and uncles and her father ready to bounce her on his knee. But no matter how close to four Katherine was she was still only three and Tommy knew she had to behave more grown up than a three-year-old.

"We're going to have independent lives," Mother had promised, and though they hadn't understood the value or the meaning, Tommy had believed somewhere in her golden fields. "And if they're plowing up gold, they'll be having babies, and if they're having babies, they'll need schools, and therefore they'll need me," she had said. She was infectious, spreading a weary kind of hope. It wasn't possible she had left them alone on the train. It wasn't possible that she had missed it, remained behind in Chicago. Worry stained their faces.

"I'm scared," Katherine said. "Where's Mother?"

A choke-throat quiet hung there. The nuns looked to each other as the city and the river drifted by outside, rolling away irretrievably, vanishing like images on a motion picture screen.

"It's all right," the nun said. She smelled bitter and of wet wool. Tommy felt what it must be to be grown up and alone — a slow, hard pounding in the chest.

They sat still for a while, waiting, as if Mother might just step through the door, appearing from outside the fast-moving train in her taffeta and feather boa. To the girls it was an entirely plausible notion. Their little mouths hung open in an expression of expectation. Katherine gripped the muff, patchouli scented with mother, limp in the seat, her eyes too blue for her wilted face. Tommy wanted to snatch the muff from her sister and throw it out the window. She felt old because she knew so much more, powerful in Katherine's need.

"What are your names?" the nun asked.

Tommy studied her. The nun was a good person. Mother had taught them to study a face, to be sure you trusted it before engaging in conversation. "Thelma and Katherine," Tommy said without indicating who was who.

"Beautiful names," a few nuns said together, eyes darting between the girls as if to understand who possessed which name, as if beauty held the answer. The sharp contrast in appearance was something Tommy had felt from the moment Katherine was born and celebrated for her wide-set blue eyes and her long, slender fingers. "She'll be a pianist," was Glenna's refrain. She had a pride in Katherine's beauty that made Tommy understand her little sister was her mother's favorite. But it didn't make Tommy jealous. She was proud of her sister's beauty too, and somehow it gave her hope that one day she'd attain it, as if

49

beauty could be acquired suddenly like wealth.

Katherine had hair the color of summer and a small rosebud mouth. Everything was round about Tommy: eyes, ears, face, figure. Eyes too close to nose. Big bones.

"I'm named for a Norwegian princess from a story my mother loves. Her name was Thelma and she was poor before she became rich. But I'm called Tommy," Tommy said. "Like a boy."

The nuns smiled at her kindly and then introduced themselves as sisters. They were traveling a long distance, to the Crow Reservation, sent by Archbishop Henry Mueller and charged with improving facilities, hospitals, schools, orphanages, and eleemosynary institutions, and with bringing the gospel to convert and educate Indians and settlers, they told the girls, anyone who needed or wanted it. There were two mothers: Mother Baptista Freaner and Mother Fidelis Coleman. The rest of the sisters remained unnamed.

"Where's Mother gone?" Katherine asked again. Tommy wanted her to stop speaking. She didn't like her particular fear; she was afraid she'd catch it.

The city gave way to telegraph wires and red barns in tufted cornfields. The car lurched on the uneven tracks, rocking into wide-open country, nauseating the girls. The conductor walked the aisle, plucking tickets from hats. Tommy wondered if she should ask the conductor about her mother, but decided the question might cause trouble. She knew that conductors had authority and that maybe he could send them to an orphanage if they had no mother.

A plume of the train's engine smoke trailed past the trackside windows, and even though they were closed, cinders snuck through and caught in their noses and eyes until the gentle nun with the blueberry eyes took wimples from her sack and put them around the girls' heads and draped veils over their faces to keep the cinders out. They rode together with the nuns, their minds emptying then filling with the desolate landscape of Illinois and Minnesota and the notion that their mother had left them. Tommy calculated, understanding that she had twenty-six hours to sort out what to do if Mother didn't appear, weighing if she should get off with Katherine when the train stopped next, worrying that if she did Mother would give her a whipping. She wasn't sure which way would prevent a whipping. With a start, she worried it was her fault, that she hadn't understood

51

Mother and that she could still be in Chicago, waiting for them on the long platform. What if she were waiting for them?

Time passed in this way. Hour after hour after hour broken up by silos or the thrumming of the train over an iron bridge. The prairie opened up, no difference between sky and land. Tommy had heard about children sent off in trains to faraway orphanages. She knew about orphanages and she felt scared, more for Katherine than for herself. Katherine didn't belong in an orphanage. Tommy understood that no matter what, she had to pretend so they wouldn't be captured, so Katherine wouldn't worry.

When it was time to eat, the girls had a sandwich between them, two pieces of bread spread with lard, and a winter apple. Tommy tore the sandwich into quarters and gave a fourth to Katherine and a fourth to herself, saving the other half and the apple as she believed Mother would have done. "We'll have more later," Tommy promised, but then she gave Katherine more anyway because she was hungry. Everyone in the car was eating, making cornucopias from paper to drink water from the tank at the end of the car, near the bathroom tiny as a cupboard with a toilet through which you could see the tracks race by. Lunch pails clanked emanating heady delicious scents of meats and pickles and vinegar, so many mouths greasy with the pleasure of food.

"You look hungry," their nun said when Tommy put away the rest of the sandwich. The nuns conferred in their silent way, a nod, a slight tilt to their hooded heads.

"We are," Tommy said without humility, because it was the truth. Where Katherine ended and Tommy began wasn't always certain to either of them. The carpetbag stood open, and from it the nun pulled a metal tin that held fried chicken and offered the girls each a napkin and a piece. "You'll have our food," she said to the girls. The other nuns encouraged them. From that bag, which didn't seem large enough to hold all that it contained, came baked ham and more fried chicken and hard, pungent cheese and rolls that seemed warm from the oven even if they weren't. Sometimes it was better without Mother. Sometimes you got more.

After lunch they dozed, Katherine's head in Tommy's lap with the muff as a pillow, the train pushing forward, the landscape flat and treeless, scattered farms with grain elevators looming against the darkening sky — the black cloud of an approaching storm collecting on the horizon, eating away at the rosy bleeding light. The farther north and west they moved the denser the frost became on the windows. The hours passed, the nuns speaking quietly and steadily, a murmur of important sound even if Tommy couldn't hear specific words. But she knew they too were calculating, assuaging, deciding what to do with the girls if Mother never returned.

In St. Paul, the train stopped for half an hour. The ice on the windows melted in rivulets and then froze again. The fancy ladies from Chicago descended to the platform from the fancy cars, followed by luggage and activity. Boys again appeared, rushing the cars with their sales songs touting tobacco and hot drinks and food, more impending and sensational news. At the lunch counter in the depot men smoked cigars and had quick meals served by a slow-moving waitress in a smocked apron. The nun and the girls walked the length of the platform to stretch their legs. They were the only girls, apart from one beggar girl with a clean face and matted hair, a scrawny stray. She studied Tommy and Katherine with crinkled envious eyes and a permanent little scared look. "Just one penny," she asked. "Spare a penny. On'ill help.

On'snough." Her dirty hand jutted in their direction, startling them with her un-ashamed determination.

"There she is," Katherine said, recognizing Mother for an instant on the face of a stranger. The momentary glad shock of finding her disintegrated. The hardness in Tommy's chest reappeared and spread. She understood they were alone and far away. The sensation rose in her like a sickness, a broadening sensation she would know for the rest of her life, one that held a simple embarrassment and fear: that she too could, at any moment, become a stray. She thought about her father, how he'd scoop her up and never seem to notice that she was heavy.

"Let's be back to our seats then," the nun said, resting her hands on the girls' shoulders. The whistle hollered. Other trains came and went. An old man with an eye patch trimmed oil lamps. St. Paul was colder than Chicago, sharp and bitter.

"Evening storm," someone said.

"Blizzard I suspect. Again," another said — railroad men with waffle-wool coats and smoke-grimed hands and teeth. Lampposts illuminated their weatherworn faces. Some of them were black and very dark and intriguing to Tommy. Mother had told her never to stare or make eye contact with a black person.

"Let's be fast, girls," the nun pressed. Tommy tugged Katherine. The nun was theirs now and they surrendered, stepping back into the car, and before long the train moved away from St. Paul.

"Nowhere," the nun said to the other nuns. Tommy watched her lips as she repeated the word: nowhere.

"You promised Mother would come back," Katherine said, sniffing up tears.

"Don't be a baby," Tommy snapped. The tears spilled from Katherine. Tommy watched her, wanting more tears, waiting for them, and when there were enough, she said softly, "I promise she will." Sometimes it felt good to be mean and then to be kind. Katherine stuffed her snotty face in the muff.

The night became darker with the approaching storm. The car had emptied and only the nuns and the girls remained. Tommy could see her breath in the cold air. A porter entered and adjusted some switches and lights came on. He announced almost gleefully that there was a storm ahead and it looked like the train would be stopped up at Wadena. Farther west nothing was moving.

That's how it was. They made it to

Wadena, where all the emigrant trains for years had passed and stopped and filled and emptied, and theirs stopped as well to ride out the storm, the blizzard now fully engaged and beating against the side of the car. The nuns made a bed on the floor from their capes and blankets and they put the girls in the makeshift bed and told them to sleep. Two porters stood at the end of the car and spoke about a mail car gone astray. Word from Spokane declared this would be the worst storm Montana had ever seen. "Thanks Almighty we're in a station."

"There's plenty of coal. Five cars loaded in the yard. As long as the engine's alive we're all right."

"It's waist deep out further."

"Shh," a nun admonished, her habit breathing with her movements. "The girls."

"It'll be a good year for farming," the porter continued.

"We're out now to the weather," his companion said. They both slurped their words. They snuck back outside, careful not to let in too much snow, telling the passengers not to leave the car unless instructed.

"What if Mother wants to come in for us?" Katherine asked, eyes on the door. Tommy studied the nun in the dim light, the lull of the engine's long vibration mixing somehow with the blinding quiet of the snow.

"She's safe," the nun said. She was quiet. Some of the other nuns leaned into each other, heads resting on shoulders, perched on the benches. There was nothing that could be done. You accepted what God gave — a storm and two young girls. Now it was time to rest.

"I have my little sister," Tommy said. She wanted to cry, could feel the nose prick. She could cry in front of the nun and it would be all right; she'd still be brave. She wondered how she would take care of Katherine on her own. She wondered about the train and tracks and if she could follow them back to Chillicothe, turn around and follow them — one long, straight, easy line. She thought of her father pulling her in the red wagon along the wide street beneath the flowering trees. She wanted to go home; the desire made her impatient; she could figure it out. Her chest became infested with want, buzzing in and on and in and out with her breath — a long life before her of festering, busy, desperate want never satisfied, for her children, her grandchildren, for us, to be something more, something better, to add up to some equation that would satisfy, worthy of being alive. *We come from good stock,* she would say. We are descended from queens.

Suddenly it occurred to her: All she had to do was get to Chillicothe. She could find her father at the depot. She knew how to find it. It wasn't hard to find. She calmed herself in this way. She imagined her father and mother telling her she was a brave girl. She could take care of Katherine. There was always someone kind to help. She pulled Katherine closer against her chest, ran a thumb over her cheek.

"Promise me?" Katherine asked drowsily.

"Promise you," Tommy reassured. And she meant it now.

"It will be all right," the nun said.

A long slumbering pause.

"What if Mother is waiting for us?" Tommy asked the nun, Katherine asleep now. "What if she's in Chicago, waiting for us? I think she must be," Tommy persisted.

"I'm not sure where she is," the nun confessed. "But you needn't worry. You're in God's hands." The nun studied little Tommy, tiny pudgy girl with her big, broad face and thick brow. "How old are you?" the nun asked.

"I'm hungry," Tommy said, feeling greedy in the kindness. What she really wanted to ask about was the orphanage. "I'm almost six. You're lucky to have so many sisters." She paused a moment and then said, "Fortunate. Mother says luck is for gamblers." She looked at the carpetbag as the sister rummaged in it. Tommy wanted to rummage in it as well and steal the food, hide it in her pockets.

"Do you have a name?" Tommy asked the nun. She wasn't sure nuns had names. Another nun snored and Tommy realized it was just the two of them awake.

"Sister Angela," Angela said. "Sister Angela Abair." She had a gentle voice like a song. She held Tommy with her eyes, beautiful blue, holding secret dreams. As soon as the storm passed, she and Katherine would get on a train heading in the opposite direction.

"Sister Angela," Tommy repeated, just to hear the name through her own lips. "There are so many of you. Are you sisters like Katherine and I?" She wouldn't tell Sister Angela about her plan.

"Yes. In a way, yes."

Sister Angela gave Tommy a roll and some hard cheese and she ate it and thanked the sister and said again that she was almost six.

Angela's teeth were well aligned, the other

kind feature in her soft, loose face. "Where do you come from?" Sister Angela asked. Tommy's head rested on a pillow made from a bag, her cheek against the lumpy roughness of it.

"From Scotland and Germany," she answered simply, factually. She could hear the breath of her sister, the in-and-out steadiness and warmth of her, even though it was cold. "We're princesses." She thought of her mother's stories. She thought of Thelma, the heroine, a peasant become a princess.

"Of course, you're princesses," the nun said.

"We're descended from Otto von Bismarck and Mary, Queen of Scots. She was a Catholic." Tommy repeated sentences often told to her, words memorized so she could speak them with confidence. She was a little princess. She believed it, her mother's elaborate stories connecting her to something distant and better, as solidly as the lengths of track connected her to Chillicothe.

"Yes, she was," Sister Angela said.

"She was murdered for being Catholic. We aren't anything. Mother reads us Shakespeare. She says everything we need to know is inside his words." She tried to remember some of his words so she could sound smart. Mother said you should always sound smart and that the only way to achieve that was to be smart. But Tommy couldn't remember the words, could only see a magician on an island producing food and storms. Mother always said to keep quiet if there was a danger of sounding stupid. "It is better to be dumb than dumb," she would say. Tommy wanted to keep talking about Mother, as if talking about her would make her appear. When the nuns were asleep Tommy would steal the food.

"Are we going to die?" Tommy asked, but that wasn't an honest question; the shape of fear wasn't as simple as death. The winds moaned, a low horrendous bass, pushing against the car from both sides. There was nothing silent about the night or the snow any longer.

"Don't be silly," Angela answered.

"I'm cold."

Angela lay down beside the little girl, the entire bulk of her enveloping Tommy, warming her with her unpleasant yet somehow comforting scent. Tommy pushed closer to Katherine and the three of them lay still.

"Go to sleep now," Angela said. "It will be better tomorrow."

"I'm afraid to sleep." The hushed concern of Sister Angela made Tommy feel safe, like she could be a little girl.

"I promise to watch you."

"We're going to Montana," Tommy said. "Father will come in the spring. We're going to farm." She described the future she wanted to have. It was better than her plan. She was tired. Her knees ached.

"Father is still in Chillicothe," Tommy said. "But he's coming."

"Sleep now."

"Mother says they want elegant people for the farms."

"Sleep, my child, sleep."

Angela was silent, observing the girl. Drool glistened on her chin. A long time passed. Tommy pretended to sleep, eyes shut, darkness pulling her against her will. Mysteriously, the lights went out and a nun whispered to another nun in the darkness, heaps of darkness now against more darkness.

"Are the engines down?"

"Conservation, I suppose."

"It's late yet."

"Quite."

"Are they asleep?"

"They're asleep," Sister Angela said.

"What will we do with them?" another asked.

"We take them with us."

"What will we do with two little girls?"

"It won't come to that."

"God's will."

"This is the will of the mother. Not of God."

"I didn't like the look of her."

They were all speaking now, a chorus of urgent whispers.

"I'm not comfortable with this."

"They have a father. We can find him."

"Why would the mother take them and then leave them?"

"Mothers are known to have done crueler things."

"Shh. Are we certain they're asleep?"

"Of course. The poor girls. Dead tired."

"They've eaten all our food."

"She seemed kindly, the lady."

"Rather imperious, I'd say."

"Don't cast stones."

"Do you think she missed the train?"

"Poor woman. Perhaps she's terrified, worried she's lost her children."

"It is good to be kind, but not a fool."

"We should send a telegraph. At the next station."

"To whom?"

"To the stationmaster in Chicago."

"They'll take the girls then. They were entrusted to us."

"It's God's will," Mother Freaner said, and the nuns were quiet, but the energy of their concern filled the car.

How fast does it take to grow up? Tommy wondered. Her eyes ached from the tears swelling there.

"The mother is on the train," Angela whispered after a bit. "She'll collect them. In one way or another."

"Perhaps."

"She'll get into a mistake out there," another said. *Out there* was the wide western horizon.

Just one straight line, one solid line from here to there. Tommy could see it imposed on the image of a map — a solid black line of track connecting Montana and Ohio, not hard to find at all, attached by Union Depots in small towns and big towns and cities on prairies at the edge of rivers by the sides of lakes, countless nameless faces, with Mother, without her, with her gentlemen and the nuns and strangers. Trains pulling in and pulling out, futuristic cities all steam and billowing noise, the scent of metal, of hot tar, of power and potential: the sharp, pointed noses, giants, plowing across the land — the tracks connecting two distant points, Tommy's past and her future. Her father with his well-tuned ear, of which she knew he was proud; he could hear anything, it's why he could sing so well. He repeated the claim frequently, tall above her with his fiddle beneath his chin, his green eyes loving her.

The finely tuned ear was a requirement of his job, making it possible for him to distinguish and read the *click-clicks* and *clacks* of the two different sounders on separate circuits — the railroad sounder, the Western Union sounder — understand which messages were reporting what facts about railroad traffic on his Virginia & Ohio line, Columbus to Roanoke passing through Clear Fork and North Fork, Pocahontas and Big Stony June, to read the desperate private messages of love and woe and business that needed to be delivered to recipients across town by messenger boys on bicycles. He listened. All stations heard all messages for all stations. He could always hear when his station call letters, dots and dashes, came through the continuously droning sounders, could pry out CHIL, the Chillicothe code, with ease and know all movements toward and in and away from his station, carefully reported along the line of his trains. He thought of them as *his* trains.

In fact, he was legendary. His next job would be superintendent of telegraphers for The New York Central Lines — The Big Four: Cleveland, Cincinnati, Chicago, and St. Louis. Legendary because he could speak with a customer, drink a coffee, weigh freight, send a Western Union message on one circuit, and copy a train order on the other circuit all at the same time. He was able to send and receive Morse code messages at fifty words per minute — the best fist in the district, his code easy to copy and flawless to interpret.

So when his two girls and wife rose early that cold January morning and prepared to leave, wrapping sausage curls around fingers to tighten the spring, dressing in their velvet and rabbit furs to head west, his finely tuned ear awoke and read the sounds more easily, of course, than the code. His Welsh girl beside him in the warm bed, spilling exuberance and her giddy good laugh and her desire to love him, he let the family go. He heard his eldest daughter outside his door, heard her want to open the door, heard her choose otherwise. He let the little girls leave the house. Heard the front door open and shut. Heard their footsteps vanish down the street. He was not a hard man. He was a simple man who enjoyed simple pleasures,

whose ambitions were not for status or
wealth, rather for a good laugh and his
fiddle and a little dancing and cheer and to
do his job well.

*The naked girl beside him with her funny
accent and her easy ways and bubbling ir-
repressible energy . . .*

he would send them ten dollars a
month . . .

she was warm and electric . . .

he could release them . . .

her belly soft and tender . . .

he had friends up and down the tracks
who would keep an eye on them . . .

her lips parted . . .

he would follow their western progress . . .

*she would be completely his now, to enjoy
freely . . .*

he let them go . . .

*and she welcomed him, slightly spreading
at the switch.*

It wasn't that he didn't love his girls. He
loved his girls. Who understands the divi-
sions and compartments of a man's heart?

Tommy had stood outside his door. Her
own finely tuned ear pressed there, the hall
dark, no lamps lit, Mother busy with curls.
She could hear him hearing, she could hear
him listening to her breathing, could hear

68

him hear her thinking, hoping, wishing, dreaming, commanding him to come to her. If he came, if he rose from the bed, if he opened the door, if — she was explaining in code; he was receiving, responding. An insistent rain inside her heart. *I don't want to go. I want to stay with you. You hear me.*

She put her hand on the shiny brass doorknob. She wanted to turn it, felt it cold beneath her skin, wanted to see for herself if the giggly girl with the painted cheeks was inside as Mother said, decide for herself if that were such a bad thing. *Don't let us travel so far away.* The *click-clicks* and *clacks* of code. The knob beneath her hand — want entwined with belief, the unflappable sense of her own power and potential: If she turned the knob and opened the door . . . if only she had. But she hadn't, and for a long time she could believe, forever now she could believe that she had only to have opened the door.

That I stay here, he answered, *with her,* he said, *doesn't mean I don't love you.*

The blizzard settled in for two full days, one enormous windstorm over Montana and North Dakota, spreading from Idaho and Washington, stopping up the tracks in all directions so that nothing moved, the whole entire system blockaded with snow, depths as much as thirty feet and men out in it freezing to death because they couldn't see or find their way, their eyes frozen in the sockets, lids sealed, entire trains buried up to the cupola of the caboose and the whistle of the locomotive — just poking through the heavy drifts. Section hands and snow bucking crews starting too soon had their work erased, the winds filling in what they'd dug out, rotary plows breaking against the ice.

When it was over and the snow could be moved, the land would be littered with wrecks and Pintsch gas fires, locomotives dead and starved for water, paralysis of the tracks, of the entire system. The soft weather would come, then the avalanches and more destruction. The worst storm in the history of Montana, unprecedented snowfall. And despite what the porters surmised and men all across the Northwest said, this year would be a dry one, not a good one at all for farming.

The girls woke and slept and shivered and found warmth and were fed by the nuns and told stories by the nuns about the Ursulines in Cincinnati and their western mission and the nuns sang their mass, the chorus of their solemn choir filling out the lonely space.

The nuns taught the girls to chant mass and hymns. Tommy thought of winter birds in winter trees, incongruous and fierce.

Into the second day the girls were given cutout dolls, taken from an issue of *Women's Home Companion* — beautiful figures with coiffed hair and elaborate paper wardrobes of lace and velvet and fur. Patiently Sister Angela helped dress and undress and re-dress the dolls, folding the tabs so the clothes adhered to the bodies, rearranging the outfits. The girls in their red dresses, a splash of color against the black habits of the nuns. Waiting. The endless waiting that is a life.

When the girls slept the nuns devised a plan, that the group of them would scour the entire train just as soon as they were allowed, spreading through it deliberately. The nuns striking in their uniforms, black and purposeful like bats, a cloud would float over the platform, into and out of the cars.

Tommy did steal; on the second night she pocketed hard cheese and rolls, lifted them from the carpetbag when all were asleep, slipped her fingers into the bag, where they slithered around until they found what they wanted, believing that she was a different person in the night than in the day, relieved that she had food to feed her sister and herself, understanding her transformation — that she was naughty and worthy of her mother's whippings. Her fingers rooted and explored, tipped in and out of little sacks until they found a clasped purse, which they gingerly opened to discover the cold metal of coin, a collection heaped together, and Tommy felt very fortunate. Index finger and thumb worked to extract the larger coins, stealthily and with curiosity wondering how much could be bought, so many coins a few wouldn't be missed. Artfully she justified with the logic of an experienced thief (nuns gave, and with these coins they were giving to two small girls), the exhilaration of being bad shooting through her, making her feel very much alive in the dead quiet of the dissipating storm and the silence of sleep.

One by one, in the dark car the coins came into Tommy's pockets, bodies silhouetted by night. A haunting euphoria and a wish to be certain that Mother was finally gone, as if the coins were insurance that she was gone and that Tommy and Katherine were truly alone in this snow-throttled world. She wanted Mother to be gone, entirely and absolutely gone — like some malevolent god in charge of miserable fates. She was her god, capricious and fickle and mean. The coins jingled in Tommy's fist and so she squeezed more firmly, silencing them as they traveled to her pocket, where she dexterously wedged them into the soft flesh of cheese and rolls.

Then the storm was gone and the passengers were allowed to step off the train, while the snow buckers took care of the mess. It wasn't long before trains arrived and departed and the tracks were busy again. The nuns tucked the girls into their coats and hats and tied waxed burlap around their patent-leathered feet so they could walk through the slush on the platform, the sky crystalline. With Sister Angela behind them, the little girls stepped into the Pullman dining car and found their mother seated at a table playing her violin like a fiddle, singing "Sweet Adeline" in harmony with a gentleman just as she and Father would do: *At night dear heart. At night dear heart. For you I pine.* She was a lovely plumed bird sitting there, slashed by sun cutting through seams in the velvet-draped windows. The man accompanying her had a long hempen beard that spilled from his face, white and stained with tobacco.

Mother didn't stop when she saw the girls. She continued with the song until she finished it. The table was littered with food and glassware, cards, cigars stubbed out in the remains of mashed potatoes, congealed fat around leftover steak. Other men sat around admiring Glenna's song and talents, their suits creased from the travel and the long delay. They seemed all mouth to Tommy, big, wide, grinning mouths, and she imagined they were very rich. It made her warm and terrified being so near them, as if they could have whatever they pleased even if it wasn't right. The compartment was upholstered in leather and velvet. Crystal chandeliers dangled from the ceiling and mahogany paneled the walls, carved in relief. Glenna smiled at her daughters, standing in their crumpled dresses. Sister Angela gasped at the sight of Glenna and her men, embracing the girls in the curl of her arms.

"Who do we have here?" asked the man with the stained beard.

Glenna rested the violin against her lap. "My girls," she said, both answering him and addressing them in one fast, deft phrase. "You found me," as if they'd been playing a game. "My girls found me," she said again. "I knew they would. Come give Mother a kiss." Sister Angela did not immediately release her hold. The pause was brief, but large enough to contain new, unwanted understanding. Tommy felt the pressure at her shoulder, could feel her mother's eyes locking with Sister Angela's in a dare that Sister Angela would never win even had she wanted to — because what was she to do, after all, with two little girls not her own?

"Come eat something, girls. You must be famished." Glenna's audience encouraged the girls, and Sister Angela nudged them forward from where they stood framed in the door. Katherine leaped first, hugging her mother, eager to remain a little needy girl, her need draining from Tommy into Mother. Tommy hated Katherine, knowing that Mother loved Katherine best and because Katherine was so fast to forgive. "We thought we had lost you," Katherine said. And Mother responding, "Do you think I'd ever let you be lost?"

Tommy stood there stubbornly, filled with the sense that she could choose, her new freedom and know-how, that her fate and future belonged to herself; she knew now what had to be done to survive and she didn't mind. She wasn't afraid of Mother anymore. She'd been cured of fear, inoculated. "You don't scare me," she wanted to say. She rooted her feet. She could feel the tug of her heavy pockets, the cheese and bread stuffed with coins.

"Come now. You too," Mother instructed. The swirl of her auburn hair, her angular nose, her slender fingers, the crisp polish of her dress (in spite of the long delay), her Gladstone bag filled with its potions and remedies (headache powders, witch hazel, heroin for complexion and bowels, Pluto Water to pep up the system and rid it of waste poisons — all the mother care they advertised), creams and ointments and perfumes, the contrast of her, the fact of her, the latch of her black eyes, the release and relief Tommy could already feel, a lightness restoring in her chest because she no longer had to be the one in charge. Tommy surrendered because no matter how close she was to six, she was still just five years old; because, really, she had no choice.

Mother asked the valet for food for the girls and thanked the nun, letting her lashes fall over her eyes, slowly and deliberately dismissing the sister with the gesture as if she were an unpleasant servant. Mother introduced the girls to the blur of jolly men who asked the girls about their journey and how they passed their time during the storm, declaring they had been thoroughly entertained by the range of their mother's voice, thanking the girls for allowing them the pleasure of her — as if it had been that simple, a generous loan. Glenna's men. Big men who wanted to do big things, become senators and congressmen, blast mines, oversee the construction of very long tunnels through the heart of the Cascades, enabling big transportation of cattle, horses, Ford Model Ts, entire populations. In return for their efforts, compensation, reward. They wore this entitlement in a hungry gaze, in the intensity of a curling lip. Glenna told the girls to wash up in the lavatory.

They returned to a feast: plates heaped with steak, tender and red, mashed potatoes beaten with cream, and spinach drooling butter. The girls ate hungrily, mopping the plates with bread. "You're not hound dogs," Mother said. "No need to lick the plates clean." She asked the waiter for water for the girls, which she colored pink with claret. "To my girls," she said, raising her own glass. Using her daughters in the charming of men was just another one of Glenna's skills. She was like this, had the ability to shift everyone's mood with the progress of her own, drive opportunity to accommodate her needs. She'd earned now the remainder of the children's passage — from them and for them — in the Pullman car. Tommy and

Katherine had paid for this reward. Suddenly Tommy looked around as if she'd lost something, and only then did she realize Sister Angela was gone.

The train moved out of Wadena, picking up speed, crossing into North Dakota. Makeshift towns appeared and disappeared on the prairie, new and temporary looking, blizzard blown, almost hidden in the drifts, elsewhere entirely revealed. Beyond the towns there was nothing for miles and miles but oceans of unscripted white until, at last, Billings.

Tommy would remember stepping off the train in her patent leather shoes, feeling the crunch of hard-packed snow beneath the thin soles, the quiet midnight pace of yet another Union Station, the broad streets with the smooth, raised concrete sidewalks cast in the yellow glow of electric light, illuminated not because it had to be but because it could be: Magic City. Hay wagons and horses, a couple of automobiles, men loitering about, the midnight lackluster actions of people. Mother negotiated as though she'd been here many times, leading them and the station porter, who wheeled their trunk obediently forward.

A liveryman slowed his sledge and studied

them, his face a gnarled root. He offered them a ride, which Glenna accepted, and they ascended to the bench, where he gently placed hot bricks in gunnysacks at their feet to keep them warm. And though she had only a hundred dollars in her purse for their new life, high from the trip in the Pullman car, she asked the liveryman to take them to the best hotel in town.

Tommy looked for the nuns, but they were nowhere. Her little hands darted to her pockets, feeling for the spiky bulk of coins and food.

3
ORIGIN STORIES

The black metal box, about the size of a bread box, that I found in the basement and that I went back to retrieve once I was alone had originally been used to store tea, a relic from a time when tea was rare enough to be kept under lock and key. Inside Grammy's box little trays with tiny handles lay above deeper caverns and secret drawers now filled not with exotic teas but with lives — with documents and records, a photograph or two, newspaper clippings, bankbooks and letters, my mother's wedding announcement, my Uncle Jet's, my grandfather's eulogy written by my father, describing a calm and quiet man who loved to play golf and whose best days were always the one he was living at the moment. There were stacks of letters from him to his mother, describing his travels west for work, Grammy, a young woman, setting up their home in New Jersey, working to be efficient and frugal and always to get a deal. I burrowed into the box, sitting on my living room floor in New York City, excavating evidence, handling every piece delicately — each a fragment from the past that called to the beholder, like a song, for a through line. In this way stories emerge, myths, and the dot connecting begins in earnest. The black box, what people search for when a jet plummets into the sea, isn't even black, but that doesn't seem to matter — not to us. The box is useful that way, the color an ancillary detail. Duchamp had his Green Box, into which he dropped cryptic notes across his lifetime, to be discovered and puzzled over later. The box, one begins to suspect, is a hoax — an idiot — an idiot box, as TVs were once called. In the dim light of dusk in my living room, if I tilted my tea box upright, I could imagine knobs at its bottom, one for volume, one for the channels, and one for a mysterious UHF channel that broadcast only the snowfall of history or sand spilling from an empty tomb.

So what did the box contain?

There were letters from a woman named Nancy LePine, who had been a project of Grammy's, a person Grammy thought she might transform, another life to save. Grammy liked saving lives; it was a hobby of hers. She wanted to save her life, our lives, the ancestors' lives. She tried to save anyone who wanted the help. I'll get to Nancy LePine, but not now.

There were letters that Grammy had written to her father from Montana, all the way back in 1915, written in pencil, the words nearly faded over time. But I could see enough to understand that she was asking him to send money. She would have been eleven years old, living in some remote Montana town. She also told her father that a pair of bobcats were terrorizing the town.

There were pictures and scraps of paper with her red ink scrawl noting names of yet more ancestors — who'd come from where and when, to Virginia, to Ohio, to Pennsylvania. So many lives tucked away and forgotten in this little black tea box with its broken lock and key.

And then there was perhaps the most important document of them all that I found last, smelling of mildew, flattened beneath the weight of everything else: Glenna's genealogy, written out by her on a typewriter after having hired not just one but two genealogists and having done research in the library at the University of North Dakota in 1942.

"When I shook the family tree," her narrative begins, "I found that not all the fruit was good; however, I did find that I come from a long line of American ancestry. My family has not been an illustrious one, but it belongs to those sturdy backwoods folk who have carved out of a wilderness a great nation. Through several generations of American history, we have fought our way, and are just as strong and willing today to continue that fight. We belong to a class of people some term *salt of the earth.*"

Glenna told the stories, carrier pigeon of myth and family lore with some twig of fact in its beak. Before Glenna, it was someone else of course, now lost to the ravages of time — her mother, her grandmother? The stories tumbled down, accumulating details, attaching the family to moments of big history. Glenna had cared. She too liked to save lives, mostly her own, liked the drama of narrative with its power to resurrect, give shape and purpose to a life, to lives — exigency to the brief interlude. Her favorite novels, Marie Corelli's Norwegian epics, paid homage to the ancestors who got us from there to here. She knew in some religions people even fed their dead. Why do we bring flowers to the grave?

Of her husband's family history, she knew

only outlines, but that didn't stop her from telling the story. It was just thin in details, epic in scope. The vanishing point was a queen: Mary, Queen of Scots — the bloody stuff left out. Mary, Queen of Scots and the Royal Stewarts of Nairn lead swiftly downstream to Lavern Stewart, rolling through time at the speed of light, linked along the way by a fable that went something like this: Maid Marian, somehow Mary's ancestor, free spirit, lovely red hair — the kind you see in such stories — flowing curls, cascading down her back, enough to keep her warm, rode eight months pregnant across the highland moors. She wasn't just riding, of course, she was galloping irresponsibly, feeling the joy of speed, and all that hair pulled behind by the strong force of wind and the momentum of her horse. She fell off, and her delicate neck, the way they are, snapped. Someone was coveniently there to help; a cesarean section was performed on the windblown heath at the edge of Moray Firth. From Maid Marian's womb two babies emerged.

Who knows if Maid Marian was the actual mother of a pair of dizygotic twins, but in the way stories can do, her story and the twins' story exist, preposterously, side by side. The twins, Sir Drummond and Sir

James Stewart, grew up to be learned, educated men — a scientist and a painter, fearless explorers, working together to understand the human circulatory system. By night, they hired unsavory characters smelling of fish and garlic, big messy hands, to steal cadavers from graves because that is the sort of thing people did back then. By day, the brothers peeled off a body's skin to study the elaborate network of arteries and veins, running this way and that, blue, black, red, and a yellow that could also be gold. Sir Drummond described while Sir James drew, rendering precise and colorful diagrams that captured for the first time the blood's flow. Celebrated, knighted, the brothers traveled to America, Sir Drummond settling in Baltimore to continue his pursuit of medicine at Johns Hopkins, Sir James wending west following the trail of the Louis and Clark expedition to illustrate the American landscape. Dates weren't important in Glenna's narration, and certainly her daughters didn't think to ask. Out of all Lavern's family, all his history, these were the figures that Glenna chose to preserve, conveniently leaving out the sweaty, hardworking lot who made their way to America for the same reasons as everyone else. She didn't know their stories, hadn't cared enough to learn. What she took away for her own to give to her daughters, rather, like an heir claiming the finest jewels, was a queen, a maiden, and a pair of historic twins.

And all very fast from there, at the speed of myth, leapfrogging generations and hundreds of years, bypassing sense, logic, and the laws of probability, Lavern appears fully formed and married now, father now — weak of heart and discipline, abandoned by Glenna, Tommy, and Katherine behind his bedroom door with his Welsh whore and her rosy painted cheeks.

Change the channel. Glenna Slagle, her family and offshoots, a sprawling circulatory system all its own. And about this she cared quite deeply. The first of her lot to come to these shores arrived in 1700, a wealthy man from Leipzig, Saxony, here to represent his nation in some commercial enterprise, then to serve as a soldier on the side of the colonists in the French and Indian Wars. His name was Christopher von Schlegel, of a noble family associated with royal houses and court life and "men and women of the highest literary and intellectual attainments."

Christopher had children who had children, crossing the eighteenth century, staying in America for religious freedom and the great hope of something more. Schlegel bastardized to Slagle, and von was lost somewhere in the colonies. Time caught up to Col. Henry Slagle of Revolutionary War days, supposed to have been a colonel under George Washington — of course. Other wars to get to, the Slagles spread out and disappeared into the landscape of the ever-westward expanding country, carrying us more closely to the narrative source with John Slagle, Glenna's great-grandfather. An explorer by nature, he had the broad strength of an aristocrat and a Gallic blade of a nose. He joined a militia force in Mississippi that would come to serve Maj. Gen. Andrew Jackson during the War of 1812. John was a leader, saw to the training of rough, unschooled farmers, preparing them for battle against the Red Sticks at Horseshoe Bend on the shores of the Tallapoosa River in Alabama in 1814. His success there made him a hero, an important figure in the war.

He married, moved to Middleton, Ohio, because the farming was reliably good, had a son named James, who was an intelligent boy educated at the University of Virginia. From there he went to Richmond Seminary, became an ordained clergyman, and fell for a girl from the north — Nancy Cooper from Cooperstown, New York, cousin of the great James Fenimore Cooper, Glenna surmised. Glenna's speculation later became Grammy's fact — the way these things would go. In any case, Nancy was the first female in her family to seek a university degree, which she did in Richmond. She brought her intelligence south to fight immediately and directly as an abolitionist, protesting in slave markets when families were about to be split up. No matter how many genealogists Glenna hired, she couldn't verify any of this. Nor could she verify Nancy's long black hair nor her dark gray insistent eyes. Nancy was a petite woman with slender fingers and a story that contained everything. James fell in love with her. She spoke French and read Shakespeare, was unabashed in her opinions and in having her voice heard. They married, had seven children. When the Civil War started, James enlisted to fight with the Union Army, was soon captured and sent to Libby Prison, where he served as chaplain to his fellow prisoners of war. Stick thin, but jolly, he taught his fellow prisoners to sing "The Battle Hymn of the Republic." A tall reed of a man with heavy sunken eyes, missing his Nancy, missing his children, the baby just a seed in Nancy's womb, James contracted amoebic dysentery from the squalid living conditions and died.

Nancy applied to the government for the pension due a widow of the war, but it did not come and did not come. Nancy, impoverished with her seven children, a northern woman in the South, fled Richmond for Ohio and the Slagle family farm. With her children in tow, the baby born, she crossed the Allegheny Mountains — headed for the camps at Blue Sulfur Springs, West Virginia, a former spa town known for its iridescent waters that cured the ailments of the elite. It was used as a camp and hospital by both Confederate and Union armies until 1864, when the Union Army burned it down so it could no longer be used by anyone. Nancy came before it was burned. Her baby swaddled to her chest, and it's getting late. It's getting to what got played at the end of the broadcasting day, the TV dinners abandoned on their TV trays, cartons of Tareyton 100s stacked in a cupboard, the snow on the UHF channel, the flag and National Anthem, which you believe at the bottom of your heart when you sleep and forget upon waking, the test pattern with its severe profile of a Native American in radiating bandwidth like the God of All Frequencies.

Nancy walked more than two hundred miles, her small children trailing behind. They slept in hay barns and washed in animal watering cisterns. They ate what the land offered, borage and edible tubers and wild herbs and onion grass, the coiling antlers of fiddlehead ferns. They killed grouse and partridges with stones. The people were kind, offering them passage in their wagons, food from their tables, tending sores on the children's feet. Along the way, the baby died of malnutrition and was buried by her mother and siblings in the loneliness of the Allegheny hills — quickly and without sentiment.

Nancy and her children traveled for two months until they reached the Ohio River, the southern boundary of the Northwest Territory, a route to freedom for slaves as well. They crossed a pontoon bridge created from empty coal barges lashed side by side and intended for use only by soldiers. In addition to her children, she carried three things from her former life: a porcelain bowl from China, given to her as a wedding gift; *Temple's Notes to Shakespeare;* and her grandmother's Bible, with its fragrances and soft leather binding.

Nancy's son Albert, only eight years old on

that long journey, was Glenna's father. Glenna's mother was Laura Ann Meyer, granddaughter of Helmut von Keller, adviser to Otto von Bismarck, the first chancellor of the German Empire, and instrumental in the war strategies that unified the German states. Von Keller's daughter, Clara, married a Jew, Salomon Luetkemeyer, who brought her and their three children to Ohio in 1870, shortening their name to Meyer as they passed through Castle Garden in New York City's Battery, America spreading open before them. The two sons, young and full of promise, vanished into history until Grammy picked them up sometime later and gave them names (Solomon and Levi) and careers (pineapple entrepreneur in Hawaii for Dole, and beer producer in Globe, Arizona, for Anheuser-Busch).

Laura Ann was small, a little deformed — four feet three inches high with a congenital hip defect that caused her to walk with a limp. A blip of a woman. Does God exist? Does anyone care? Lifts were designed for the soles of her left shoes, but it didn't entirely correct the problem. Someone is about to shoot himself. Someone else is not. Does anyone care? The family was poor and didn't believe in Laura Ann's prospects for a successful marriage, given the hindrances of her appearance — but if you are patient, if you give in to the howling specificity of the black box — the family sends Laura Ann to work as a maid for her wealthy cousin Lottie Nagle. Off she travels with her scant belongings and the considerable paraphernalia that accompany her short leg packed into a steamer trunk.

Lottie, beautiful, poetical nature, dreamy and romantic, had married up into a family with sugar futures betting on plantations in the Caribbean. Her bodices and hoops were made from whalebone and Paris taffeta. Laura Ann helped her dress and fuss with hair and toilet, but Lottie didn't like having a relative as a domestic in her own home. It restrained her from believing fully in the lady she had become. She set Laura Ann up as a milliner at B Nelson's Millinery to apprentice. Laura Ann discovered that it was her calling, that the serious architecture of a hat's construction mixed with the whimsy of ornament, ribbon, and feather and the daring possibilities of perch angle on the crown of a lady's head inspired her to dare. Nets, feathers, pearls. She became the milliner of Cincinnati. The ladies raved about her. They appreciated the slight accent, remnant of her European childhood. She couldn't make hats fast enough. Her little fingers worked with precision and speed. The ladies would wait, patience indulged because it was her hat, her imagination, her humor. Opening the box was like Christmas. She made hats for Granny Howard, William Howard Taft's aunt; she made hats for senators' wives, for Cincinnati society, for people from neighboring and even distant towns. She made hats for the Slagle family, the widowed matriarch Nancy Cooper Slagle, of tufted feathers and a net veil.

In the process of fittings, Laura Ann surprised herself and later her family; she fell in love with Albert, Nancy's oldest child, two years Laura Ann's junior, down from Middleton for a job with McCall's Fashion by Mail. He wore a thin mustache and a daring smile that he concentrated on Laura Ann, his admiration for her talents, her confidence, the swift accuracy of her fingers, and her fragile strength that at once was independent and in need of protection.

When Laura Ann and Albert married, her steamer trunk was repurposed to hold the beautiful and dainty lace and silk lingerie of her wedding trousseau. They settled in Gallia County and had five children: Albert, Glenna, Theresa, Grace, and Madeleine. Madeleine died of sepsis suddenly. Death portraits were rendered, Madeleine strangely in the arms of her parents, with her siblings, Madeleine alone, come to life again, eyes opened, captured as if now she could breathe again, speak again, resurrected in silver sulfide. One of the marmoreal portraits was preserved in a frame that closed like a locket, which Glenna would open from time to time to contemplate Madeleine, remind herself of the pain.

When Glenna married she took her sister's portrait with her, stowing it in her steamer trunk, protected by the silks and linens and pretty lacy things her mother collected and restored, items more of sentiment than of value — her grandmother's Cantonese wedding bowl, *Temple's Notes to Shakespeare,* a hat with ostrich feather trim. Madeleine's ghostly image remained tucked among the finery, ticking away in darkness among the heat pipes, ducting, and mothballs of the everlasting world.

"See her? She's your Aunt Madeleine, and in this picture she's dead," Tommy said to Katherine, pulling the image from the trunk now and again.

"She's not dead."

"She is. She is dead."

It was Tommy who continued telling the stories, repeating them for Katherine, adding to the details, elaborating and embellishing until it seemed to both children that they had lived a very long time. They had lived not only their brief lives, but also in memories that began long before they were born, and that somehow and even still seemed to be theirs.

"Is she still dead? She doesn't look dead."

4
HOME SEEKERS

Sometimes I can feel that I have lived my grandmother's life too, feel her stepping off the train into the icy cobbled streets of Billings in the severe winter of 1910 with her little sister and her determined mother, head forward, alive to extravagance from having traveled so far in the Pullman car. Grammy's feet are cold in the patent leather shoes, wrapped in gunnysacks the way the nuns had done, but the city is bright and hopeful even in the midnight hour. If Grammy spoke to us endlessly about the ancestors, she perhaps spoke even more about her childhood in Montana, so the towns and the travails, rooted more in fact and actuality, became more vivid and concrete, less legend, more realism than the tales of the ancestors.

Billings, incorporated in 1882, had transformed from a one-road town in cattle country, with a few saloons and dance halls, no church, to a gridded city with monster buildings four stories high, theaters and newspaper offices and a sugar beet factory, brewery, dairy farms, and a butcher doing such a volume of business he was selling meat wholesale all over Montana and into Wyoming, blood running into the unpaved street. It was the sixth fastest growing town in the nation by 1910, the population multiplying from several hundred to over ten thousand in a matter of a few years. Banks abounded along with lumber stores and saddle and harness makers and hardware suppliers. There were department stores with striped awnings and plate windows displaying tortoiseshell combs and suitcases with logos and hats come all the way from Paris, narrow-bottomed skirts and laced boots made from Italian leather — a bounty my grandmother admired in the storefront windows, dreaming of a time when she might be able to freely purchase just whatever she wanted like the mothers and daughters who so easily and confidently entered those stores.

On the banks of the Yellowstone River with the rimrocks looming over town, and the cottonwoods and the sagebrush and the swirling alkali dust, Billings was also still a western town thick with miners and trappers and cattlemen feeling possessive of their territory. They called the newcomers chicken chasers, honeyockers, scissor bills, and sodbusters, and they didn't like them for the damage they were doing to the free way of life. But the cowboys were being outnumbered and time was doing its thing, and because they could, cowboys were falling in love with businessmen's and sodbusters' daughters. Everyone was starting to marry each other — foreigners and citizens, cowboys and ladies. Not the Chinese. The Chinese were only marrying other Chinese, here to work on subsidiary lines of the railroad. The Crow kept to themselves. Everyone, or almost so, understood the profits to be made, and that there was solace in that. Money has a way of softening the blow.

It was into this new world that Glenna and her girls stepped when they descended from their train.

The liveryman conveyed them to the Rebecca Hotel on Minnesota, named for a railroader's daughter — everything out there was named for a railroader's daughter. At the Rebecca Hotel, there were Ostermoor mattresses and springs, a telephone in every room, a bar and barbershop, a billiard hall for men separated from the dining room by a saffron portiere. Steam heated and gaslit. Tommy couldn't quite believe they would sleep in such a fine hotel, in a bed, the comfort of which felt like a distant memory. She worried for a moment about the expense, depleting the hundred dollars.

A little man of a manager ran the hotel, and Glenna presented herself to him, standing there with Tommy and Katherine, the trunk at their side. She asked him kindly if he could offer a good price, that the train was delayed because of a snowstorm. It was late. She had many excuses, many options he could choose from to offer her a better price. She cocked her head and gently cast her eyes downward and toward her daughters. The little man wore reading glasses on the end of his nose, looked over them to examine the girls, who were tired and both astonished and embarrassed by their mother's request, that they be given a room for less than others paid.

"In the light of day, we'll find something more affordable," Glenna said.

"The town's packed," the man said, still looking at the girls. Tommy felt ugly beneath his gaze. "How long?" he asked.

"Three nights," she said. "If you could offer us the three nights for the price of one night," she negotiated. "We don't need a big room. We can share a bed. Since my husband died, we're used to that," she said, sweeping her arms around to encircle her girls, offering a look that pretended not to be asking for sympathy. For a moment, Tommy believed her mother, that Father had died and she went white, but then just as fast she understood that Mother was lying to gain advantage. She studied Glenna to see how it was done, understanding that lying with impunity was an art her mother had mastered, and that she always seemed to get just exactly what she wanted, which made Tommy, in this moment, feel safe.

"It's a rough town," the manager said. "You're respectable people. Are you here for a claim?"

"I'm here to teach," Glenna said.

"We need teachers all right," he said, and offered her a smile. "There're other hotels, but some of them are hard going, not for gentlefolk. You need to know what to avoid."

"I'd be grateful for your guidance," she confessed.

"Three nights," he said. "We can do that."

The manager rang a bell, and a black man appeared to help them with the trunk. The room was big with a big bed the three shared. The mattress was covered in smooth linens and eiderdown fragrant with lavender. Saloon music drifted in through the night along with the smell of cold western air. And Mother, happy with her accomplishment and in a generous mood, told her daughters family stories as she liked to do. The girls listened, loving their mother, the enthusiasm coming from her soft, late-night voice as she told the tale of her grandmother, Nancy Cooper Slagle, escaping the Confederate South with her seven children, hiking over the Allegheny Mountains to freedom in Ohio, her husband dead. Glenna pulled Nancy's china wedding bowl — the simple blue Cantonese bowl with its design of potbellied men — her *Temple's Notes to Shakespeare,* and her Bible from the trunk. "She was an educated woman. She knew French and read Shakespeare. She wasn't scared," Glenna said, and meant that since Nancy hadn't been scared they shouldn't be either. Tommy and Katherine curled into the warmth of their mother.

It was easy to fall asleep in the soft bed with Mother's voice unspooling history. The long, unhappy train trip vanished into the past.

In the morning, all three were dressed in their travel clothes, smoothed out by Mother's strong hand. The manager offered them eggs and toast. He didn't ask for the ninety-five cents. Tommy and Katherine, like punctuation marks in the grand, well-wrought sentence that was their mother, addressing herself delicately to her breakfast, tasted what it might mean to have everything.

In the comfort of the Rebecca Hotel, Glenna listed the towns named for railroaders' daughters and Tommy wondered what life must be like for Lorraine, Edina, Mildred, Ada, Beatrice. The town of Ismay combined Isabelle and Maybelle, daughters of Albert J. Earling, president of the Milwaukee Road.

There were exceptions to this naming practice: Fredrick H. Billings, of The Northern Pacific, recognized the singular, strategic importance of his town, and named it, emphatically, for himself. The more general and gentlemanly enthusiasm, however, was to give voice to an indulgence — that some vast and empty stretch of swollen rivers and buffalo grass might suddenly bear the name of a girl, and in so doing ensure that all who followed in the footsteps of these great men would forever after pay unwitting homage to some distant Shirley, Sadie, Terry, or Laurel.

After breakfast, Glenna left the girls in the hotel to begin her search for work. From the Rebecca manager, she learned of the offices of the superintendent of district schools and made her way there.

The superintendent was a large man with a large mustache, heavy sullen eyes, and a hint of German accent. His name was Frank Schirmer, and he was delighted by her interest. Finding teachers interested in the rural schools wasn't an easy task, and there were so many of them, "Sprouting like mushrooms with all the claims."

He handed her a sheet of ruled school paper and asked her to write her name in script ten times. She obliged, sitting at a schoolchild's desk in his office on the second floor of a building that filled an entire block. Light dappled the room. She took her time. When she finished she handed him the sheet. He studied the script, informed her of a job in Ekalaka, out in the Carter County district, told her it was having a tough time being filled. She could collect her warrant in Miles City. He'd arrange to let them know, informed her of the rules dictated by the state, reading them from a manual: *"Female teachers cannot keep company of men; they cannot marry during the term of their contract; they cannot travel beyond the district limits without permission of the chairman of the board; they must wear at least two petticoats and skirts no shorter than two inches above the ankles."*

Glenna listened, and when he was through said, "That's no fun," flirting because she could read this large man and knew he would welcome her good humor, that his sullen eyes were a natural shape, not an inclination. "What is the list of things I am allowed to do?"

Curiosity made him smile. "Well, let's see," he said. She adjusted her perch on the seat, leaned forward. "Music," he said.

"I play the violin," she said.

"I sing," he said, "and play the harmonica."

They made small talk — from where, how long, why — the type in circulation these days out here. She told him she was from Cincinnati, studied at Oberlin, that her husband was dead. Out here you could make your own truth and one's word was often good enough. "And you?" she held him with her steel eyes.

"Harrisburg. Pennsylvania. Five years. You don't mind being alone out there? It's remote," he warned. Her hand was gloved. She wore her boa. "You're a lady," he said. "There are animals. And these are uncertain days. Not everyone is happy with the way things are going, the newcomers, all the claims."

"I like adventure," she said.

"If you get a copy of your Oberlin diploma you'll have an easier go at the city schools. A shoe-in," he said. "You can write to Oberlin and they'll duplicate it for you," he said.

She picked up the sheet of paper with her neat, steady script, each version of the name identical. "You can tell everything from the writing," she said.

"Yes," he answered. "That's what it takes." She knew the elegance of her script, confident of her talents. "Poor calligraphy shows that a person is trying to hide something," he said, serious now.

By the time she left, he still had no knowledge of her two girls.

The streets were busy. Warm, soft days. Women trying to be ladies lifted their hems off the snow-packed streets. Lumber traveling this way and that rattled in buckboard wagons pulled by big bay horses with their furry feet. Cattle folk and home seekers strutted the streets. Businessmen consulted

The Billings Gazette, rolled beneath their arms, for market quotes coming in from Chicago and Minneapolis, calculating what could be made this year on wheat: eighty-five cents a bushel, twenty-five hundred bushels. The record snows promised record wheat — berries tugging heavily on the stalks.

Feel the air, Glenna thought. It's too dry.

While Mother was away, the girls sat together on the plump Ostermoor bed, flipping through the *Saturday Evening Post,* fascinated by sketches, one of an airplane flown by a baby. The girls imagined what it would be like to soar above the ground, to look down at life, the way a bird could. Tommy admired women in the pages, in their long skirts and furs, in their well-appointed lives, far away in New York.

Mother had taught the girls to read, and it was Tommy's job to practice the lessons. She put her finger beneath the words in the column and sounded them out, asking Katherine to repeat, which she did because she was smart and liked to read:

THE-WOMAN'S-REBELLION.
ADVICE-TO-CHILDREN.

Tommy took this seriously, admonishing Katherine if her attention drifted. Katherine was afraid of her sister and sat up immediately. "You'll be nothing if you can't read," Tommy said, and she looked at her sister — so pretty and earnest in her desire to please Tommy, a notion that made Tommy feel powerful. Katherine repeated the words.

But really, both girls preferred the pictures. The pictures told the stories of another separate world they longed to visit. And when the pictures were thoroughly explored, they turned their attention to the room, picking up the telephone to dial the front desk, turning on and off the lights, running the water in the bathroom, flushing the toilet, smelling the soaps, rolling somersaults across the eiderdown bed.

After a while, bored by the room and their lessons and discoveries, the sisters snuck off to the busy streets, where Tommy bought Katherine a doughnut from a man selling them from a cart — the dough yeasty and rising as it hit the sizzling oil followed by a roll in cinnamon sugar. Tommy paid with her stolen nun money, plucking coins from their position in the hardening bread and cheese. Tommy liked being in charge, liked paying for the treats.

"Where did you get the money?" Katherine asked, her eyes widening as she stared at the coins. Tommy always felt so able in front of Katherine, like she could do anything, and there was power in that.

"Don't tell Mother," Tommy warned. Katherine stuffed a doughnut into her mouth, eyes still on the money.

A sign at a saloon entrance read, Trust and Go Bust. Inside was a dark hole with loud voices and the sound of money and whiskey. Outside everyone was alone, swishing this way and that, and it seemed there was a fever in charge, an undercurrent sending people swiftly here and there.

The doughnut was warm against the January noon.

Glenna's job started as soon as she could get there. Fifteen dollars per month. "But you will have to hide," she told the girls. "You can't teach if you have children, and single mothers can have their children taken away," she explained. Glenna never condescended to age. She spoke in a matter-of-fact way about what had to be done. The girls sat obediently on the bed, feet dangling above the floor. They would be left again, Tommy understood. She learned fast. She learned how to camouflage pain and disappointment. At least her father wasn't dead.

"We'll hide in the school?" Katherine asked.

"Not exactly," Mother said. Tommy thought Katherine was very stupid.

"You're not upset?" Mother asked Tommy against the plush comfort of the Rebecca Hotel, but it was more of a command. Tommy picked up the telephone with an absent mind, perhaps with a secret wish to call out beyond this room.

"Put that down," Glenna said, and Tommy dropped the phone. She swallowed back the heat until it smarted and died. Katherine sat there dumbly. Tommy would learn to swallow her sister's pain so Katherine could remain serene, so she could believe there was no pain at all.

Because that's what children do.

The farther west folks traveled, the easier and swifter it was to get a divorce. Migratory divorce. Women and men flocked west to dissolve what wasn't working, and society was blamed and women were blamed. In Montana, it took six months and just cause. Glenna filed, citing adultery. The girls learned the word and Tommy reminded Katherine of the boarder, Harriet, her painted cheeks and her giggly laugh — and they understood filament and tentacle and subterranean secret pleasures not meant for little girls.

In editorials, upright citizens who put marriage first spoke out against divorce, the westward spreading tide of it: *We're being overrun by petulant, libidinous, ill-fitting husbands and wives . . . with no better cause of divorce than their own depraved appetites.*

"Women should be independent, they should be free, they will be free," became Glenna's refrain.

They headed to Miles City, where longhorns fattened on the free lands. There were soldiers and buffalo hunters and bullwhackers and muleskinners and cowboys and Indians all over town. There were roustabouts speaking German, knowing not a word of English but knowing enough — enough to step off a train with nothing but one's tools wrapped in a leather satchel and walk in the direction of the scaffolding springing up over a prairie town. So strange men found their way forward in these new days. Ranchers owned the town. Cattle owned the town, roaming the streets like pedestrians, kicking up dust. Thirty-dollar men in chaps, lassoes in their belts, riding in and through and up and down Main

Street on their muscled quarter horses. Herds came in and went out, bawling down the left flank of the Tongue where there were no fences, the bellowing roar of them making their way. There were more saddleries than all other businesses combined. There were almost no women.

Until the snows melted, Mother stayed in Miles City, boarding with the girls at Bement's Boarding House, next door to the newspaper office. Bement's was filled with boarders of note, including an officer from the Civil War named Colonel Malone and a pair of buffalo hunters who sat at the bar loose jawed and low browed, talking about the good days being gone and that the world was a corrupted mess that made no sense at all.

In the room across the hall at Bement's lived Theodora and Buster Brewer from Cedar Rapids, here taking advantage of the land grab, awaiting their claim. She was an energetic and efficient woman, tiny in size but appearing big because of her determination and generosity, which came forth from her bright eyes and her offers to help Glenna with the girls, who seemed like two impossible miracles blown in from the badlands. Buster was bald, known as Baldy. They hadn't been here long, but already they were loved because Buster had an easy way with people, knowing how to bring out their good moods and because both always lent an extra hand. He drove a hack, carrying people to towns that weren't attached yet by subsidiary lines, which the Chinese were busy laying, overseen by gangs of Russian bully boys. Baldy too helped with the girls, engaging them in games of marbles, singing cowboy ballads with them and playing his guitar. He made them each a doll from corn husks, dressed by Mrs. Brewer in kerchiefs.

The Brewers didn't have children, a fact that Mother noted, eyeing them, and then used to her advantage, negotiating with Theodora to take the girls, offering their labor and a wage. "They're good girls," she said. "Obedient. Accommodating."

To the girls, alone in their room, Mother explained that those who came before had worked hard to get them here, had endured more. She enlisted Nancy Cooper Slagle, showed them again her china wedding bowl, pulling it from the trunk and reminding them how she had carried it over the Alleghenies, hiking to freedom, her children following close behind, eating off the land, blistered feet and empty stomachs. "She carried it for you. So that we'd have it and know what it meant to endure." Tommy looked at the china bowl, and thought how easily it could break.

Glenna presented the girls anew to Mrs. Brewer, this time as a commodity, cleaned up in smocks with white aprons, their faces scrubbed and hair pulled back with bows, ready to work. Sometimes that's all it would take. "They work hard," she said, and the girls smiled sweetly, knowing how to sell themselves and because their ancestors had worked hard and because they could see that Mrs. Brewer would be kind. Tommy read her face, found kindness in the soft smile.

"You will listen to me?" Mrs. Brewer asked Tommy and Katherine. She offered them a plate of warm biscuits in the dark little room with one big bed and a sagging mattress. The girls nodded their heads. Outside on the street a procession of mourners walked by, black-clad, six men in Stetsons carrying a coffin. "They'll listen," Mother assured.

"Girls?" Mrs. Brewer asked.

"Yes, ma'am," the girls answered.

"I'll have them then," Theodora said. "Glad to be of help." Tommy, in the silence that followed, took a bite from her biscuit even though she wasn't hungry.

■ ■ ■

The thing about end-time, of course, is that it's always upon us, but nobody thinks to ask about that. That year Halley's Comet brushed Earth with its tail — twenty-four million miles long — and with it, for some, came a sense of the world's ending. Celestial collision. Poisonous gases. All-night prayer vigils were held, where just beyond the prayer circle others offered comfort, solace against the anxiety of the times, with comet pills: quick antidote to cyanogen, which was believed to impregnate the atmosphere and kill all life. Oceans would empty. Volcanoes would erupt. Earthquakes would shatter. Solar flares would swallow mankind. Apocalyptic prophecies abounded; believers and doubters, curiosity seekers, everyone stood on rooftops and mountaintops and building tops, heads heavenward, watching as the comet's plume flared full of crystalline import across the night sky.

Spring came. "You be good girls now," Glenna said, turning the girls over to the Brewers. She planted warm kisses on their cheeks. "You're strong girls." She was mercifully fast and efficient in her parting. Katherine told Mother that she didn't want her to go. Tommy took Katherine's hand and stared dumbly at the back of her mother as she moved off down the street in her silk skirts.

"Don't cry," Tommy said to Katherine, but Tommy too wanted to cry.

Mother was gone for close to two years, visiting now and again, like a heart-creasing thunder shot. She taught in a one-room schoolhouse in the middle of seven homesteads near Ekalaka, the town named not for a railroader's daughter but for a Sioux girl, Oglala Lakota, daughter of Eagle Man, wife of a white scout. The homesteaders had built the school. The children ranged in age from eight to sixteen. There were nine of them, most of them girls and most Norwegian with little knowledge of English. Schoolbooks from all over the country lined the bookshelves. Glenna's private room was in the basement, held a bed and a stove.

In the snowfield, twenty yards from the schoolhouse, stood an outhouse. In summer, the snowfield grasses were red and green and thick. In winter blizzards, the children had to follow a rope line to the outhouse, but only if they were desperate. Glenna insisted on accompanying them, the winds moaning, pushing such a volume of snow it snuck into the schoolhouse even with the doors and windows closed. In weather, the children stayed at the school until it passed. Ink froze in the well. On the stove, she heated condensed milk with sugar for a treat, and she made up sing-alongs with the violin and they put all the books away. She did not miss her own children. She wasn't a sentimental woman. She believed in their abilities and their strength and found easy rationalization in that: she sent money; she was not far; they were safe; they were safer than they would have been with her.

Without the girls, she could pretend; she didn't feel afraid. Freedom made her giddy, the thrilling sensation of earning her own money, bills in her pocket. Her past fell away, the burdens and restrictions. Alone in the basement, she heard the world move outside — rhythms of weather and season and land — she in a fixed center of it.

There was a cattleman she met in Glendive who visited from time to time. He came with his rough hands and his delicate flute. He told her that in Europe only the rich had cows; he told her here you must have a cow to survive. His herd was five hundred large, bought at auction, a rich man now, didn't need a claim. He came from Norway, had a ranch at Thirteen Mile Creek, had a wife and sons and he was a good deal older than Glenna — unhappy with the fences and the land rush and the games of the railroad and the government and the stupidity of preached belief, of what would become of the land.

These were not her concerns; they belonged to his wife. In the candlelight she undressed, wore just a boa, wore just a silk slip, wore her gartered stockings. The sensation was pure and complete surrender. She was twenty-six and alive and free.

The Norwegian, as she called him, would sell his cattle in Chicago, transport them by freight train, drive home in a new automobile.

After Billings Glenna wired Lavern. *Divorce final. Send money. Stop.* He sent ten dollars a month. When he could, fifteen.

Theodora and Baldy had the girls call them Auntie and Papa. Auntie scrubbed the girls at night and cared for them and got them clothes from the Sisters of the Blessed Virgin Mary — California pants made for boys — but the girls found them warm. By such repeated measures of warmth and improvement; by the sudden appearance of well-worn but perfectly serviceable riding boots once belonging to dead cowpunchers with little feet — into the toes of which Auntie stuffed cotton so the girls' feet wouldn't slip around — Auntie began to win their young hearts.

There was a lot the girls had never seen. The girls had never seen a Chinese person before. He worked the laundry. His people had come to lay the tracks. Now he had his own little shop on the main street between the organ seller and the carpet seller and the bit maker, emitting a strong, mysterious, scorched-heat smell. The unfamiliar look of him mesmerized the girls. He took a gulp of water in his mouth and then sprayed it through his teeth onto the cloth he ironed with an immense iron heated on the stove. His movements were patterned, a choreography, a skill that hewed to the fit and cut of each part of a shirt or pant, and ended with a flourish. The girls stared until Auntie, trailing behind them like a mother, chastised them and broke the spell.

Along the tracks stray children picked up coal, competing to gather more. Their hands and trousers and aprons blackened, their pockets became filled with coins. Tommy was glad not to be a stray, grateful to

Mother.

Auntie took the girls to the station to watch the trains come and go, the unloading of the luggage on the express, the lowboy wagons pulled by draft horses, hauling luggage to the Olive Hotel. Sometimes an immigrant train pulled through, entire cars filled with families, their animals, all the stuff of their lives. Each freight car, each family its own tableau — livestock on one side, furniture on the other, the family in the middle with bright but weary faces.

Mother could have gotten a claim; the girls knew this. Women were allowed. But she was no fool. "I'm no fool," she would say. "Do I look like a fool?" Tommy didn't know what a fool looked like, but she knew a fool didn't look like Mother. And Mother didn't believe in the farms or the big sale advertisements of the railroaders, farmers plowing up gold, talking in the language of magic and miracles as they tried to populate the desert. She understood the moment she stepped off the train that there wasn't enough water and that the Campbell Method of dry farming was witch potion. "No water means no water," she would say. "I'm no fool. Dry farming is just another comet pill."

Mother had understood that there was

advantage to be had in becoming a part of the apparatus of expansion, a beneficiary of fool dreams.

By the station tracks, Tommy and Katherine watched a new trainload of immigrants step onto the bright sunlit platform. Like a mummer's play, families emerged and you could see intention in their eyes, in their gestures. Having come this far, most had sorted things out, had a system in play, had a strategy with a chain of command — fathers shouting to sons for luggage, sons emerging quickly with handcarts, mothers keeping little ones from underfoot. Possessions that couldn't fit into the hack were abandoned by the tracks — a chair, a table, a pianoforte. You saw that out here, strewn across the landscape, something prized from the old life not quite making it to the new. The process for arrival was the same in any language the immigrants spoke, and in time, the platform emptied, the families having moved to the next act of the play.

"I'm no fool," Mother would say. Tommy and Katherine looked at each other in silence. These people hadn't looked like fools.

In late May, the Brewers took up their claim. They packed up the hack and piled

120

the girls into the top seat next to Papa and they rode the bumpy road for a good long distance, hours following the Yellowstone. Papa taught them cowboy ballads, crooning in his mournful alto:

O bury me not on the long prairie
Where coyotes howl and the wind blows
 free
In a narrow grave just six by three —
O bury me not on the lone prairie.

It was grand with the snows gone and the sun coming up fast and early, a new wash of green upon the land. Miles and miles of buttes and mesas, wind scoured, dust whipped, gullies and ravines and wildflowers and strange, new smells of sticky sweet balsam in the air under an ocean of sky. Scattered trees and thickets in the heads of canyons with steep gumbo cliffs and weird rock formations. All around the fragrance of sagebrush and juniper and the Chinook blowing in lush and warm.

"How will Mother find us?" Katherine asked. She held her corn-husk doll. Every now and then a little girl felt very small, a tiny piece of nothing out there, just like the songs.

Tommy didn't know what to say about that, so she said nothing at all.

Auntie always had food and the girls were always hungry: ham sandwiches and hard-boiled eggs and dill pickles and young onions and radishes. Sponge cake covered with powdered sugar.

The spring rains came and folks dug their wells. The girls were frightened by the men down in the well pit, but in the fullness of time, water was just outside, and each time they fetched water, they understood that Papa knew about things, the mystery of things.

Like how to live in the ground, how to make a sod house. *It was just for now,* Papa said, and the girls believed him. They were proud of their claim numbers, knew it like they knew their names: SW 1/4 20-28-53; S27-T20-R53. Neighbors came and helped. The girls went with Papa to help neighbors plant flax, to build granaries. And everyone helped each other, coming from all over with their unfamiliar languages and customs. The Norwegians stopped to eat their "supper" each day at 4 p.m., formal and complete. Sometimes Tommy imagined she was traveling even though she remained in the same place.

One day Papa came back with a loaded wagon. "Windmill," he said, and sure enough, after a few days of cursing and banging away, and climbing up and down the tower, one morning Papa set the blades of the windmill loose. The water poured into a pond, directed by a series of ditches and controls about which Papa worked with singular focus, and the fields turned a vibrant green. In time, men from neighboring farms helped build their wood-frame house and erect fences. Before the frame house was the dirt house. Before the dirt house the girls and the Brewers had slept on the prairie in tents. Now upon that same prairie a frame house stood. A group of men and the girls had built it in a day.

Papa taught the girls to drive the sulky plow. The mule pulled the plow contraption and the hard wooden handles in Tommy's hands plunged the blade forward and flipped the green sod to black, like a wave breaking upon itself. Papa sat behind her. She could feel the forces of the mule and plow cutting into the ground. She could feel Papa's body bearing the plow's heft for her, and the mule's unruliness, so she would only feel the slightest jostle now and then. He was a kind, strong man and an excellent farmer. Tommy felt safe, like she had a father again. Love worked in an easy way; all it took was kindness.

When there were other children around, Tommy and Katherine didn't let on that Papa wasn't their father. And there were lots of children on the other farms. Women seemed to have babies just so there'd be more bodies to help with the work.

In the mornings, early, Tommy and Katherine collected eggs, warm and a surprise each time. Yolks the color of the sun.

The spring rains produced wild roses and wild grasses and prairie flowers alive with jackrabbits and black-tailed deer, foxes, geese, ducks. Wolves and bear too, though you couldn't see them. At night, the wailing coyotes crawled inside the girls' dreams.

"I don't like that sound," Katherine whispered in the dark of their little bed.

Tommy didn't like the sounds either, but she said nothing, letting the darkness swallow her. Her job was to be strong and she liked her job, wanted to do it well so Mother and Father would be proud, so Katherine wouldn't have to worry any more than she already did.

In the morning: the scent of wild roses and plums and crab-apples and loveliness. Crystallized gypsum sparkled in the sun.

■ ■ ■ ■

Ohio receded in the short memories of the girls. The tall maples and the swooning willows disappeared along with their red-brick house, the aunts and uncles, the air heavy with jasmine and white roses and wet lawns and their father.

Papa taught the girls to ride horses. He taught Tommy to shoot rattlesnakes and warned her to keep on the lookout for hoop snakes, milk snakes, and ghosts — all vipers with inventive ways of sucking milk from cows and rolling like hoops to spike poison into a victim. With the swift chop of a shovel he decapitated a rattlesnake and buried it, the jaw still biting. Papa gutted and skinned the snake, sureness in his hands that made you trust him with your life.

Tommy's gun was a .43 Egyptian, long and brown and gleaming, which Papa presented to her because she was old enough to have her own gun, well into her sixth year, taught her to steady the butt against her shoulder to absorb the recoil. She practiced her aim on rodents, plucking them off one by one. The supply seemed endless. Tommy trained her shot until she was so good she did not miss, and Papa praised her with his toothy handsome smile, saying, "What would we do without you?" He placed a kiss on her forehead. She liked the precision. The finality. Carried her Egyptian like Katherine carried her corn-husk doll.

Papa taught her about horses: the breaking process, the gentling process, working on a snuffy bronc, trust and from the ground, patience.

Papa was a jim-dandy. He had a deep bellowing laugh and was easily amused, attracted love and goodness. The cowboys and the settlers alike came out of nowhere, riding across the fields to gather and share each other's company. They sang their ballads and helped each other with projects, lifted the girls into the air.

Even the girls could sing along. They liked to watch Auntie on her tiptoes kissing Papa on the cheek, her arms wrapped around his neck. They wondered if she'd have a baby.

Auntie taught the girls their numbers and about history and geography. No matter how hard the day, it ended with Auntie gathering them to read and play and sing, the happy rhythms of feet jigging to a tune.

From Montgomery Ward catalogues they ordered supplies of sugar and coffee and flour, which they stored in the root cellar along with hunted meats — venison and rabbit and prairie chickens and coons. Papa was an excellent hunter. The little house filled with edible air: the crackle of juniper kindling in the stove, the rasp of grinding coffee, the sizzling, oily smell of bacon.

Ammunition came from Sears, Roebuck & Company in tidy tiny boxes printed with an image of the Sphinx, the brass bullets in neat rows like teeth.

The days were ordered. Tommy liked the order, liked knowing what to expect, liked telling Katherine just exactly how the day would unfold: Wake at 4 a.m. Milk. Strain milk. Breakfast. Dinner pail for Papa. Laundry: scrub rinse hang fold. Feed the chickens. Feed hog. Feed horse. Milk. Tend garden — Montana sweet peas in their husks, sweet as candy. Churn. Turn out the cattle. Sweep floors. Sow garden bed. Collect water. Wash. Prepare dinner. Feed animals. Lay hay. Schoolwork. Songs. Prayers. Bed.

Soon Mother receded too, just like Father had.

The valley brimmed with flowers and blueberries and cherries and gooseberries. Auntie made pies.

Then, not suddenly but slowly, the good times stopped. The green turned yellow before conceding to brown. The sky remained permanently blue, a splendid mocking hue. Fool faces looked to it for answers.

"Baldy, we're past due," a fellow asked of the skies, looking to Papa for an encouraging answer. Others came from their farms to Papa because he was the kind of man who just seemed to know things. They were believers, the whole prairie lot of them and Glenna's two little girls. The rain, they were told, would follow the plow. "It'll come," Baldy answered.

They waited. One hundred and eight degrees. You could break a tooth on a sweet pea.

Auntie's smile sat loosely on her lips as if it could alight and fly away, as she watched the days amass and the field turn the color of nothing. White cud foamed the livestock mouths. Papa stopped singing.

Women waded through the heat in their skirts, the heat visible like liquid. They gathered at Auntie's house, puny beneath the sun's glare, as if together they could do something, as if their collective will would be louder and therefore heard.

Auntie prayed, collapsing to her knees, and other women followed. "Please," she said aloud. Her beauty drained from her. The girls sank to their knees too, arranging their hands in prayer. Their mother didn't believe in prayers, but watching Auntie's conviction the girls thought it could be so simple — just ask for something hard enough. Tommy prayed first for the rain, but then for herself — selfishly; she knew she was a naughty girl, that it wouldn't always be this way, that she would grow up and that it would not be this way.

Preachers preached in make-do chapels: tents, houses dug out of the grass. They spoke of faith and belief and finding good in pain.

The men stood tall, Papa stood tall, in their dungaree work clothes and sweat, visiting each other's farms to see if there were ways to help. This was just the first year. "There is so much more for us to learn," Papa said, and he meant it as optimism, that they could learn their way out of this predicament.

A swarm of dragonflies sailed away, a cloud of translucent wings and their bulging ironic eyes. Even they were heading elsewhere.

It was too hot to work the horses. They could die. The coulees were dry. It was too hot even for rattlesnakes. You could feel the heat in your lips, on your skin cracked and baked. The girls lay in the house, sunburns thrashing their cheeks. In a quiet, eerie tone, Auntie spoke about how life does this, tests us to see what we are made of because life was a judge of us. Her energetic face was limp now and cast in shadow. "I love you girls. Do you know I've come to love you girls?" At times like this she spooked the sisters, who had no answers for adults. Auntie said flatly, "God gives us gifts." Tommy, looking for an answer, started braiding Auntie's long black hair, dividing it into two sections, and encouraged Katherine to braid too. The three of them sat in the shadows. This was what Papa called an adventure — some weren't like setting up a windmill or riding a plow, not fun like that — more like what you heard preachers go on about in the Bible.

Days passed and nothing changed. A hot stillness settled on the world, rustled by a hot wind. It was biblical.

"It'll come," Papa assured. It would come because God works that way. God can be cruel only for so long. But for now, it was biblical hot and there were no trees for shade and the land smelled of misery.

People stopped visiting each other. There was no help needed. People became afraid that it was the others had the bad luck. But misfortune had settled on them all.

Then the wind shifted, carrying heavy dark clouds. Soft at first, hiding the sun and the heat. The clouds moved across the sky for days like an army forming position, deepening, swelling, hovering high above the ground. Auntie and Papa and the girls and the neighbors — everyone watched the sky. Thunder and lightning ignited inside those clouds, dancing around up there inside the skin of the clouds, acoustic, rumbling clouds. Days passed, abundant with dry thunder.

The blast occurred in the middle of the night, a violence that awakened the girls. Tommy scooped Katherine to her, against her plump body. "This is good," Tommy told her sister. "This is good." They heard the storm, the slash of lightning cut the hard earth, the sudden illumination. They listened for the rain.

"This is good," Katherine repeated. She always believed her sister.

Auntie and Papa were in the yard, hastening with the animals, securing doors they'd already secured. Lightning stitched the night, webbing across the prairie westward

to the mountains, spindly legs of electricity.
But no rain came.

And all across the great state the trains
continued to move, rolling west, then east,
west, then east. Cinders shot from locomotives and ignited timber and grass. A spark
here and there, just a small cinder the size
of a jewel, a little red ruby. A few thousand
small fires puffed to life in the forests and
the fields. The fires added heat to the heat
followed by more hope, a blast of cold air, a
blessing to feel cold again, but it was only
more torment disguised as reprieve. The
winds returned with accumulated energy,
hurricane volume stirring the little fires into
one united and colossal whole, until the
entire western sky was filled with smoke.
Ships well into the Pacific could see the
smoke, the western progress of that smoke.
For days, it looked like night. The air
smelled like a chimney. The people wore
kerchiefs over their mouths and noses. The
cows wore kerchiefs. Two of Papa's four
cows died along with the hog, smothered.

"Are we going to die?" Katherine asked.
Tommy slapped her because it was what she
believed, that the universe was vast and
filled with fire, that they were alone in it, so
far away from Mother and Father and the

aunts and uncles in Ohio. But Tommy would never say aloud what she feared.

At night, Auntie began speaking in tongues. "She's just dreaming, is all," Papa said. Papa stroked Auntie's long and unbrushed hair. Her pale and slender frame collapsed in Papa's arms. She wasn't dreaming. It was terrifying to see an adult cry. Tommy wondered where her mother was. Would she have cried? Katherine began to cry. Pretty soon, everyone was crying in the dark. Tommy stroked Katherine's back, whispered to her that they would be fine, though she could see clearly that they would not be fine.

When the rains arrived, it took more days for the hardened land to moisten and absorb the water, to snuff out the fires and the smoke, and for Auntie and Papa and the girls and the surrounding farmers and families to feel that this was more than a reprieve, more than some dark biblical trick. The creeks and the river swelled. The rains came and then stopped, and then came on again. The girls danced in the rain, bare feet against the tendering earth. The birds sang out in the dark. They had passed through something, and the girls felt strong for having seen it to the other side.

And time did its tricks, pulled away, and the next year brought abundance. There were dances, and learning, and Auntie started cooking her pies again, and Papa raised turnips that the entire county marveled over, and the sweet peas were sweet and soft again, and the people gathered to establish more solid roots, coming out of and off of their farms to find each other. Because they had known such awfulness and fear they became generous for a while, overflowing with the sense their prayers had been answered. They pooled resources for the building of the school, which served as a church on Sundays and a dance hall on Saturdays and a parlor room for card parties and taffy pulls and shivarees on other days, literaries and Bible readings. The loneliness of the terrible year fell away and in its place came the oceanic land poured into the community. The entrepreneur turned his traveling wagon of supplies into the general store near the school and he wrote to Washington, D.C., to file for a post office and a town was made from their efforts. And it was not named for a railroader's daughter, but for the sweet smell after a freshet of rain. A baseball team formed. Their little town, Balsam, rose swiftly.

In the mist of this promise, Tommy asked that she and Katherine be allowed to go to school, bargaining hours of work for hours at school, persuading and convincing until Papa and Auntie laughed at Tommy's cajoling — happy too, because the fields brimmed and there was plenty of work to be done: stack threshing, disking and harrowing, and because there was work too, for the binder and the hay barges and the grain cradle. Golden pyramids of wheat rose in the silos.

A stranger appeared. A lady on a white horse, dressed in summer linen punctured with eyelet, a divided skirt for riding astride and a broad, straw hat secured with thin leather ties beneath her chin. The girls watched her make her way over the fields, a mirage transforming.

"Is that Mother?" Katherine asked.

"Can't you tell," Tommy said. Both were afraid she was coming to get them.

She looked like a queen on the horse, the most beautiful thing they had ever seen and they were proud to be hers, but they did not want to leave. Glenna's auburn hair spooled beneath the hat. The girls stared, were shy, unsure now to whom they belonged. Mrs. Brewer appeared from inside the small house. Her hands seemed to tremble too as she rested them on the girls' backs. The girls looked from Mother to Auntie. Auntie was younger than Mother, but looked older. Auntie's expert hands, which could suture and save a dying calf or throttle a chicken, looked like thick pegs. Her boots were dull brown. They did not shine in the saddle the way Mother's did. Auntie smelled like deer. Mother smelled of lavender. Tommy could see in the thin lines and creases around Auntie's eyes, which had stared so hard into the skies for so long, that her smile was a mask that she wore for Mother's sudden arrival.

"What a surprise," Auntie said. "Come now, girls, a hug for Mother." The girls obeyed.

Glenna had a satchel and a parasol. Auntie welcomed her into her small home, offered her the girls' bed and a bowl of water for freshening up. With Glenna primping like an ostrich, the wood frame house seemed small as a shoe box. "There's just enough room here to change your mind," she joked. Auntie didn't ask how long Glenna would be staying and she didn't offer the information. She made herself comfortable, asked the girls how they were doing, if they'd been studying, spoke with them as if she'd been gone only a short time. She drank her water, then she stood before the mirror for what seemed a long time and fixed her hair. "Now then," she said. "Let's have us some fun."

Mother was radiant in her pressed linen. She carried her silk parasol everywhere. She was welcome news in the area with her violin. Neighbors came to sing and dance in the Brewers' yard. Beneath the tall poplar, in the shade, Glenna sat at the center, surrounded by so many hungry for music, believing her to be from somewhere better because she could play and sing like a country girl and an angel. She made requests of Baldy, asked him to choose the songs, said she could sing anything he chose. "You choose, Baldy," and she looked up to him with eyes that made him believe he knew the answers. Then she sang for the collection of farmers and their wives and children.

When she wasn't singing, she was talking about political equality clubs, creating a local chapter — just casually, like it could be a good idea. "It benefits the greater whole. What are your thoughts on the matter?" She sought out their opinions. A woman here and a woman there asked gentle questions about what was involved, while the men fiddled with their instruments, tuning and then retuning. A man from the music circle gave a long, evaluative glance at Glenna and said, "We've already got a mayor!" and everybody laughed. One woman said, "I trust this business to my husband." Another asked gently, "Perhaps it should be up to the woman to decide?" And yet another: "I've heard of women traveling around the country with men other than their husbands. Now just think about that for a moment. It's unbecoming."

"I see," Glenna said. She knew how far to push, knew how to read her audience.

The women, in their long, aproned dresses, were weather-worn and polite. "It's complicated no doubt," another said. "So many, you realize, newcomers from Europe and so many of them poorly educated and predominantly male. They can vote, but I'm not sure they know how to vote . . . being so new and unfamiliar with our ways. It would seem," she said softly, "that women on the ballot would help strengthen the voice of the educated American man."

"That's a concern," Glenna said. "But it's more that women really should just have an equal right at the ballot box."

"Women are on our side," another man said. "Most of us already agree with that. With women, our numbers can compete, maybe, with the interests of corporations."

Back and forth it went in the warm July breeze. Glenna told them about her school, about the winter, the scarlet fever epidemic, the theater productions she put on — how the children loved to dress up and act. Tommy looked at her mother with curiosity, watched the people listen to her. True, she wasn't the mayor, but if the vote were held today, maybe she would be.

When enough had been said, Glenna pulled her bow across the violin's strings and started up a song. Soon everyone was singing again, and when they paused, talk reverted to the beauty of her Mirecourt violin and the clarity of her contralto. She was a beauty and they were mesmerized.

Tommy studied the control her mother had of the moment, to direct it and steer it just wherever she pleased. Mother liked that these folks believed she was from somewhere better. Tommy and Katherine believed it too — they almost wanted to go with her to wherever that someplace better might be.

But of course, Mother had not come to

take them away. When she left, she kissed the girls, told them to be good, and gave them leather lace-up boots for winter from the Montgomery Ward catalogue, packaged in tissue and just enough too big they'd last. She hoisted herself onto her horse in her divided skirt and just as gracefully as she arrived she rode away.

"She's not a bad woman," Auntie said to Papa late in the night. "She works hard. She does this for her daughters," Auntie continued. "She's a good, virtuous soul. She's been unfortunate, but she's making the best."

"Virtuous?" said Papa. "You don't need to be kind."

"She's a new woman," Auntie said.

"The political equality clubs, they'll create disorder, unrest. She's stirring trouble."

"There's good she's serving there. Come now."

"Don't get any ideas," Papa said. "The order changes, the system breaks."

"The girls are innocents. I love them, Buster."

"Shh," he said.

"They're our girls," she persisted.

Tommy, in the dark with her sister breathing against her chest, heard herself dream.

■ ■ ■ ■

Glenna sent Lavern a picture postcard from Glendive with a one-cent stamp. The caption read: "Picture 8124. Red Rock. Yellowstone National Park. The river roars through the canyon."

On the other side in black ink, fine, articulated script: *We are at school. We are all OK. The children are just fine. We are housekeeping, getting along great. Love to you, Glenna and the girls.*

This document floats to the surface of Grammy's black box, another message from a black tea box, arriving from a distant time.

The news came as it always came, slow yet determined, carried by songs overheard in saloons, told from one homesteader to the next to the next, picked up from a train passenger or someone visiting town, someone with a paper, old, out-of-date, partial or exaggerated, but discussed and parsed and mulled and contemplated. The *Titanic* sank with royalty and eleven from Butte, including the Copper King's grandnephew. Days and days and days of talk, of speculation and rumination and attempts to understand spectacular failure, of wealth drowned, of poverty drowned, and the boy from Cornwall on his way to Butte to mine, filled with dreams of sending money home to feed his family. Something was beginning, a shock and surprise spreading across faces. A threshold was being crossed, a shifting attitude aimed toward fear.

A black man arrived at the farm, showing up on foot. Papa was in the field. The girls were in the garden. Auntie was on the porch. She saw him arrive, shouted for the girls, who came running across the yard. She instructed them to get inside the house. The man strode right up to the porch, took off his hat, and said to Auntie, "Good day."

"What can I do for you?" she asked.

Inside, the girls were scared there would be trouble.

"I've got a claim nearby," he said.

"And," Auntie said with an impatience the girls didn't often hear.

"Well, I'm raising money," he offered. He was carrying a satchel, which he set down on the porch. "I'm wanting to make a moving picture," he said. The girls peeked through the window. The man was tall and very dark skinned. He slipped a book from his satchel and handed it up to Auntie and she took it. "I've written this book. It's a

142

novel, the story of a black homesteader. He doesn't like it much, the homesteading, isn't good at it, so makes art instead."

"And," Auntie said again, as if that were the only word she could offer. She looked him up and down. "Why aren't you on a horse?" she asked.

"I sold it to raise money," he said. He spoke with confidence, as though he were just like her.

"What do you want?" she snapped.

"I'm selling my books here. I'm wondering if I can sell you a copy."

To get rid of him she bought the book, offering less than he asked. As he walked away across the fields, the girls watched him. It took a long time for him to disappear.

Katherine picked up the book and flipped through it — so many words. "If he wants to make a moving picture," she said, astonished. The girls had seen them at the carnivals. "If he can do that, can't anyone?" Katherine asked her sister.

"You'll make a beautiful actress," Tommy said, understanding how her little sister was dreaming. Katherine twirled around the room.

"Back to the garden," Auntie said. The girls obeyed. For a long time, they thought about the dark-skinned man selling his novels door-to-door.

Mother showed up a last time, driving a gleaming green open-bodied Ford Model T on loan from a married senator in Helena, Tom Walsh. They electioneered together, traveling the state in his car to promote the vote for women, campaigning to educate and then elect favorable legislators. Walsh played bass and they made music together, though Glenna was just amusement. He was married and a faithful Catholic.

She arrived in his touring car, long scarf around her neck, and a broad, dismissive smile in her sharp steel eyes. She had no more need for the Brewers. She collected her girls efficiently. They were giddy with the automobile and the idea of riding in it, the knowledge that their mother always returned. She would leave them, but she would always return, and each time reappearing in an even grander, more dramatic way. She was taking them now to Winston, where she had a job that accepted her children.

Auntie packed up the girls' things, embraced them. She too tried to be efficient, but left tears in the girls' hair. She filled a small sugar sack with food.

144

"We're coming back," Tommy told her, and Tommy believed this and therefore Katherine believed this, watching the words come as truth from Tommy's mouth. She trusted what Tommy said. "We won't be gone long," as if it was that simple.

Glenna offered Theodora one hundred dollars for the care of Tommy and Katherine, pulling the clean, crisp bills from the pocket of her dress. The girls stared at the money, in shock. The big car shimmered in the sun. "Please have the money," Glenna said, handing it forth. Theodora's eyes met Glenna's. She was in shock too, with a faint smile of disbelief. Auntie and the girls looked at Glenna blankly, unaccustomed to such things. Glenna knew this, knew that this would happen. The girls watched, suspended between the women.

Then Papa stepped in and took the money Glenna offered. He thanked her, folded the bills, and slipped them into the pocket of his trousers. His lips twisted into a weird shape the girls hadn't seen before. A flicker of affront wafted across Glenna's face, the calculation gone wrong. Tommy studied her mother, the way that children do, to understand how she was supposed to read this moment. She studied Papa, his awful lips. He did not look at the girls.

"Come along," Glenna said, their eyes now on Papa's pocket, replaying the exchange, crisp bills slipping from Glenna's hand to Papa's trousers.

Everything was for sale — easy as when he took grain to market all the way in Glendive, the receipt for the grain to the bank where it was exchanged for cash. A hollowness formed in the center of Tommy's chest as Papa embraced her in a farewell, as he pulled her into his strong arms, the smell of him, earthy and metallic. He released her, planted a kiss on the crown of her head, didn't hold her with his eyes. "You be good girls now." And with that he sent them off.

In the car, loaded down with the trunk and its contents, the Egyptian, which Mother said could be useful, Tommy held Katherine against her chest, the wind on their faces, fields and fields all around a brilliant emerald green; it would be another good year for the farms. Mother sat tall behind the wheel, navigating the bumpy road, heading west.

"They are dreamers," she said of the Brewers. "We are not dreamers." But Tommy didn't listen to her. She thought of fool faces, so many people unloading what wasn't needed, discarding bits of their lives piece by piece by piece. The tracks and the roads littered with belongings that had once meant something, how you'd come upon such objects while traveling, see the old pianoforte by the side of the road and know that there lay another lost life, like a cross marking the spot where a person had died.

"They ate coon meat," Mother said. "You girls will never eat coon meat again."

Tommy's eyes burned. She felt suddenly big and older. She was glad Papa took the money. She thought about that money now and realized if Mother had enough to offer the Brewers, she would be capable of earning more, and Tommy would find it and help herself to it so she could take care of herself and Katherine.

I hate you, Tommy wanted to say to Mother as the farm disappeared, and eastern Montana surrendered to the mountains, and the uncertain future rose. She repeated *I hate you* over and over in her head on the long journey. She knew just exactly what was being asked of her, bought and sold, to love and then to shed love as easily as slipping out of clothes. *I hate you. I hate you.* Until she was screaming it in her mind so loud she was afraid Katherine would hear. She didn't care if Mother heard, didn't care if she got a whipping.

"I'm going to grow up fast and leave

here," Tommy said to Katherine. "I'm going to take you with me. Just as soon as we can."

"Where?" Katherine whispered into Tommy's ear, and only then did Tommy realize Katherine had been crying too.

Their father came to visit once. He came in the late fall of the year Glenna and the girls left the Brewers, and stayed with them for a few weeks in Winston on the lonely northeast slopes of the Elkhorn Mountains, thick with ore. Glenna taught the miners' children, their fathers here to work the Iron Age and Martha Washington mines. The school looked like all the other schools sprouting up across the state — sixteen by twenty-eight feet, spare and tidy, with a seesaw in the yard. Temporary and surrounded by a lot of nothing. The only unusual thing was that this school had an apartment, a little extension off the back that served as their house and had two bedrooms. She told the superintendent that she'd been widowed. "Remember, girls, your father is dead."

Lavern arrived with a suitcase and settled in as though he had only been away a short time. Tommy noted that the suitcase was small and at first she felt shy. He tried to pick her up the way he used to, swing her in the air, but she was too heavy now. She wished she could become tiny again. Katherine was still small enough. "My growing girls," he said kindly and with pride. He was a handsome man; Tommy could see that. He was tall with dark good looks and startling jade eyes, more emerald and defined than Tommy's. "My girls," he repeated, and Tommy wanted nothing more than to be his girl.

Every morning it was the sisters' job to ring the big steel school bell, needing the two of them to manage the weight. Lavern loaned a hand so the job was effortless. Tommy and Katherine were filled with the giddy hope that it could always be this way.

In the afternoons, Father took the girls fishing to Beaver Creek or Weasel Creek. Sometimes he took them hunting. They trailed behind him, following his instructions to be quiet as they tripped over leaves and stones, real still to create surprise, then boom. He taught them how to skin a rabbit, to lift the pelt off as easily as a banana peel. Rabbits were abundant. He promised coats that would be the envy of the mine owners' daughters with their fancy styles and china dolls. At night, Glenna had the girls perform for their father, sing, and play on the piano. Sometimes they recited lines from Shakespeare. Katherine was more talented, braver, liked to stand upon the stage and vanish into herself and the music or the words to bring out a character. Later, Lavern disappeared to Glenna's room.

In the morning, he made more promises, more rabbits, more furs accumulating in a lovely soft heap. For dinner, they ate the rabbit; they were so rich in rabbit meat that they gave it away to neighbors. The girls came to believe that he would never leave. "The West is my land," he said to the girls with his jolly smile, as if that proved he wouldn't go. Glenna snuck her head around his shoulder, planted a soft kiss on his smooth cheek, something kind and appealing about her to the girls, and it seemed that all was right in their world. Sometimes they'd play their banjos and sing songs and then gossip about the aunts and uncles back in Ohio and who had married and who had had a baby and who had lost all his money and who had run off with a man fifteen years her junior — Aunt Grace, the kindest of the aunts, Tommy remembered, always offering the girls candy at Christmas.

At school, the girls showed off Father, walking with him between them, hand in hand in hand. Even though they pretended he was their uncle, his presence offered them an idea of what their lives would have been like with him. Their classmates stared. Tommy liked their eyes on her.

The weeks passed. He said he had to get back to Ohio, his life there. His work. Tommy thought of the lover, her painted cheeks. He left Tommy with thirty dollars and told her to continue doing such a good job with the family. And just like that he was gone.

In Helena, in Butte, in Bozeman and Livingston, White Sulphur Springs and Virginia City, Glenna stood on soapboxes on street corners, outside saloons, and talked to strangers, knocked on one door after the next of row house and grand house, spreading the word of enfranchisement. *Man is man and woman is woman and our natures are different and our voices are different, but both must and will be heard.* If she believed in anything, she believed in this.

At fairs and carnivals and parades, women marching with their yellow banners and white dresses, Glenna participated too: *As teacher, it is clear to me: the slow progress of our movement is lack of education.* Education, education, education. Behind her, twelve little girls dressed up like golden butterflies, followed by a train of corset makers and nurses and social workers and schoolgirls, society women and laundresses, chanting with dignity and conviction: "Our day is coming; join with history."

Tommy was embarrassed by her mother, standing on soapboxes while ladies swooshed by or, worse, spoke out against her, told her they trusted their husbands. Women who did this like Mother, it seemed to Tommy, didn't have husbands. Glenna wanted the girls to stand up too, wanted them at her side, to hold signs and pass out flyers: *Mr. President, How Long Must Women Wait for Liberty?* Later, when women earned the vote, Glenna said, "You see, our voices made a difference."

Fridays the little Irish whores came to Winston and the slopes of the Elkhorn to service the miners, arriving on the evening Jaw Bone from Helena. How many times had I heard about the Irish whores, a story that thrilled me, that I could see vividly, my grandmother as a little girl learning to understand the seedy underside of the adult world. She didn't use the word whore. Rather she simply called them girls and allowed her expressions to carry all the innuendo. My sister Scarlett, though, had no problem using the term later, in our room at Last Morrow, translating for us

Grammy's innuendo, left eyebrow raised. "Whore, as in prostitute. They do it for money."

The girls came up the hill solemn as nuns, wearing hooded blue capes, eyes staring into the dry, dusty ground. Tommy knew they entertained the men at the commercial house in the dayrooms. Across the street was a park with a swing set. Tommy and Katherine swung as high as they could to peer in the windows of the second floor, standing on the swing bench to pump and push and Katherine asking, "What are we trying to see?"

The ugly Iron Age mine shafts, the tailing piles, the smell of arsenic and chemistry and leaching was for a brief moment sweetened by the presence of the Irish girls. Tommy soared on her swing trying to get to the top of it all, a rush that would certainly get her a whipping if Mother understood. The Irish girls colored up the gloom until they disappeared entirely into the rooms to nourish the hungry miners.

Tommy knew what was going on inside with those clean Irish girls and the dirty men. There was something raw and dangerous that appealed to Tommy, that made her want to get beyond this in-between age to be a grown-up woman. In the morning, the

Irish whores filed down the hill one by one to the waiting train.

Glenna warned the girls about these kinds of women, that the same could happen to Tommy and Katherine if they didn't get an education.

They were always leaving. From Winston, they went to Hassle and from Hassle to Virginia City, once the capital of Montana and famous for its gold rush at Alder Gulch that was now all mined out — water-filled holes and rubble piles. It had been called the Social City, cradle of civilization in the wilderness. There were theaters, a music hall, and a movie palace, bookstores, billiard halls and fancy dress shops and fancy food stores, though its better days were in the past. Fourteen miles long, Virginia City lay between the Ruby and Madison ranges thick with coyotes. It was the biggest town the girls had lived in since Miles City, and there was fun in that.

In Virginia City, as it happened, Tommy learned to trap from a boy two years older than she. He wanted to kiss her, but she'd have none of it. He told her the best money was wolves; coyotes were good and you could get something for muskrats, weasels, and rabbits, even skunks found in bottomland brush patches. He told her Virginia City had always been famous for its hunters and the best were the Lemhi Shoshone — the tribe of Sacajawea.

His name was Cane and she met him at school, but he didn't much like school, preferred hunting, and he told her so when she asked why he wasn't there much. "Because I can make money hunting," he said. She asked him if he'd show her and he seemed delighted and curious — delighted by her interest and curious that a girl would want to hunt. He had a broad, goofy, bucktoothed smile through which spilled dreams of easy fortune. Catching a coyote would bring ten dollars. He showed Tommy how to bait the trap with meat scraps from lesser animals, showed her the right weight and tension, to dig the hole she set the trap in, how to find the coyote corridor, to read the winds so the scent of the bait floated on its back right down the tunnel to lure them.

"It's a science," he said. He helped her build and set her traps, doubling the spring on a small catch trap to save money. Cane had sloppy eyes and dirty hands, and he liked to tell Tommy he was smart enough not to go to school. Tommy told him that he wouldn't be anything without an education. At night, they laid their traps, checked them in the morning.

Tommy's hands and pinafore became dirty too and Mother gave her a whipping for the dirt, the back of her hand hard against Tommy's face.

"I don't have time to wash. Do I look like I have time for washing?" All eyes and madness, a look that once had scared Tommy, fractured and cut up as if Mother's features were all independent. Tommy wished her father would come back, but she wasn't afraid. She was going to make money now, legitimate money. All she had to do was sneak off at night.

She caught two coyotes right off the mark — their necks cracked by the spring, both of them still alive when she checked the traps, writhing in pain. Cane finished the break with his hands and showed Tommy how to skin them. The blood didn't bother her. She didn't tell Katherine what she was doing when she disappeared with Cane. The coyote was hung up on a hook in Cane's cow barn and the cuts started at the feet, delicate incisions involving precision and patience. The rest came easily like slipping off a tight dress. Getting over the skull required technique again, to slip the pelt over the head without tearing the coyote's thin skin.

"I skinned rabbits," she told him.

"Rabbits are different," he said. "They're easier and they aren't worth as much. The fur is not as warm or rare." The cleaner, the more valuable. Fur companies advertised everywhere. Almost every boy was a trapper of some sort or another. The skin was salted and dried and resalted and skinned and pickled and sold. Cane did the selling, gave Tommy her cash.

Sometimes at school, Tommy daydreamed of Cane, what the feel of his lips would be like on hers, of his big hands handling death, of his manner sneaking through the night as if it were day, of the two of them alone in those tangled silhouette woods and no one knowing and she a girl, acting reckless. She always wore the dress and pinafore. Never the California pants. A kiss, what's a kiss? She wanted a kiss. She was ten years old. She felt her body at the beginning of change, a blossoming — that's how she thought of it, like a flower opening out. Sometimes she thought that when she did blossom she'd become pretty like Katherine.

"I won't kiss you," Tommy said just as often as Cane asked. "I'm not marrying a cowboy." He looked at her, friendly and with a laugh that made you happy you caused it. She liked the attention of the boy. It made her feel like she had something. "Who's talking marriage?" he said. But he had an uncomfortable look on his lips that indicated disappointment. Tommy knew he fancied her, knew he admired that she didn't mind slitting open the body of a coyote, its blood and innards warm all over her hands as she pulled them out, feeling strong and capable and safe in her know-how. And sometimes she pretended. Sometimes she wanted his lips on hers just to know the sensation — she felt what it could do to her, how it would ripple across her skin.

Glenna said that lazy women, women who wanted it easy, to sit back and watch life — those women were in the East. If it wasn't laziness that stopped them it was fear. Out here, if you had means, it was still hard and you had to fight. Ladies were in the East; women were in the West. Western ladies headed east, daughters of the railroaders and the bankers and the lawyers and the politicians went to New York to find their husbands.

Tommy had a sense of them from reading the *Saturday Evening Post* and *Ladies' Home*

Journal. The fancy women therein stepped off trains in St. Louis and Chicago, like the ones she had seen so long ago, their hands resting limply on the arm of a gentleman in a top hat and a cashmere coat, a man of lineage and money. Those men were found in the East or heading back east once their fortune was secure.

Tommy was old enough to imagine her future. With her coyote business, Tommy knew how to make a living, and her desires swelled all the way to New York.

Evenings, when the children were home and the schoolroom was empty, Glenna sat Tommy and Katherine in the front row of desks, illuminated them with candle glow, and read Shakespeare, performing a scene for them, playing different parts. Katherine would step in, easily becoming someone else. "And you, Tommy?" Glenna would ask. She wished she could tell her mother how brave she was with the coyotes, wished she wanted to share the money with Mother. Glenna directed Katherine, offering her better ideas for approaching her lines. Four small windows opened on the bright star sky. Some nights Glenna had the girls memorize a sonnet. *Who will believe my verse in time to come?*

Virginia City was the last time Tommy went to school. After Virginia City, they moved to Butte. It was a big place, so Glenna could leave them there. She felt they were old enough to take care of themselves, and it was easier to find work as a single woman. There was too much work for Tommy to do, caring for Katherine, to also manage going to school. Tommy told herself that she didn't like school anyway. In Butte, the school was filled with rich girls. Tommy didn't like seeing their advantaged smiles and sense of plenty. She decided she didn't need to go to school, that she would just read Katherine's books to learn, and the newspapers. She would spend her free time trapping coyotes.

Tommy read the catalogues to Katherine. At Sears, Roebuck, you could buy anything: a musical instrument, a Singer, an automobile or a buggy or a horse, food, salted cod (which was soaked overnight and steamed the next day with wild spinach), schoolbooks and clothes and shoes. Tommy bought pretty blue shoes for Katherine before leaving Virginia City, gave them to her as a birthday present once Glenna had left.

Bought them with her coyote money. She wanted Katherine to be like the entitled girls of the shopkeepers and mining bosses and the lawyers and the doctors and the politicians. The catalogues even sold houses, dreams of a new life.

Saturday nights, Tommy took Katherine to the Movie Palace and they watched the newsreels of the war in Europe and then Gloria Swanson or Mary Pickford or Charlie Chaplin. "That's what I want to do," Katherine whispered in the dark of the theater. She disappeared into the movie, transfixed, wishing she were up there on the screen.

Twelve years old, Tommy was the head of the house. Glenna didn't bother finding someone to stow them with when she went off to teach, to electioneer, to fight for women's suffrage, for Jeanette Rankin, engaging senators, negotiating with congressmen. She hid Katherine and Tommy in Butte in the one-room apartment in the Princeton on the Dorothy Block, with a big Acorn cookstove that heated the room, had supplies sent in from Kansas City, large amounts of flour and sugar by the barrel. When it arrived, they were rich.

"Don't be foolish," Mother warned before leaving. "You're responsible girls. I believe in you."

Tommy arranged the trunk like a table, placed Nancy Cooper Slagle's wedding bowl on top, with the *Temple's Notes to Shakespeare* and the Bible inside, reminding herself and Katherine of all that Nancy had endured. She rested her gun in the corner by the window, hung curtains made from some limp burlap from a flour shipment. She liked homemaking.

Butte was different from the other towns. People came to it from all over the country and the world, the town sucking them in with copper promise. You heard different languages on the streets, the gridded city sprawling out north, south, east, west. People scurrying here and everywhere, dodging trolleys and automobiles and trucks and horses, and above it all buildings rose, and beneath it all the dirty streets were paved with granite blocks the size of bread loaves.

Tommy was too busy to be lonesome with Katherine gone all day: there was the laundry, the cooking, the cleaning. She ironed with her hand, warming her hand at the stove and pressing it against the fabric of Katherine's pinafore, Katherine's shirt, pulling it taut with her other hand. The energy of the city, alive and coming through the windows, made her work harder, made her organize and list so she could accomplish and be productive. But sometimes she wanted to just sit still, dreamed of painting the scene outside her window — rooftops stretching like stepping-stones to the hill crowned with chimneys, spewing refuse that slimed down its flanks, inching toward Broadway and Main and Park and Silver and Gold and Copper.

Everyone was here for the copper, of course, taking it hand over fist to feed the beast, taking it and taking it for bullets and lights and telephones and trains and for everything modern and new and convenient. Here, because here money could be made. Tommy understood this and wanted to make her own money too. Pulsing and alive out the window: the Anaconda mine backlit by the snow glow of the distant peaks, the mines puffing as volcanoes do, the smoke cloud shimmering silently, beautifully, above the noisy town.

The most expensive car in town was a Locomobile and was owned by the madame who frequently took her girls for a ride, fancy silks and taffetas sashaying by in a rainbow mirage. The ladies lived in the Windsor Hotel in the Tenderloin, thick with gamblers and rounders, male habitués frequenting the Copper King Saloon. In their thin dresses and fanciness, they posed in the doorways of their cribs like livestock at an exhibition while secretaries and paramours on the arms of executives sauntered by. Everyone here was generous. Money floated around on the air. They gave money to Tommy, who wanted money more than anything. She wanted to buy her way out of here. She jutted her hand out in front of her and magically, it seemed, it filled with shiny coins from the demimonde. It was just a different kind of hunting, is all, Tommy told herself, shoving the coins into her pocket.

At home: Tommy's knees pressed into the floor, her hands in prayer at her chest, little prickly tears in the corner of her eyes, wild horses pounding their feet as they galloped across her heart — growing up seemed so far away, impossible, like scaling a slick iron wall. Butte was loud and dusty with progress, construction every which way. Here, people were too busy to notice motherless girls.

With her earnings, she bought bread at the Iona. Handing over the money to the cashier made her feel grown up. She held the warm oven-fresh bread against her chest.

Home, she was careful to be discreet. A nosy neighbor with a thick English accent, hard to understand, had her eye on the girls, asking them about their parents, and did they go to school.

The winds blew, cold and angry. Women sewed lead weights into the hems of their skirts so they stayed down in the tempestuous air. On the back of these winds, it seemed, news of the war arrived. The nosy neighbor, not bothering to knock, pushed the girls' door open and stared at them, sitting on the mattress, studying beneath the gloom of an oil lamp: "There's the war," she said with her heavy accent. "The war's come to us, a bad war." A notion that was too large for the girls to immediately comprehend. They thought the war was outside on the street.

"I'm afraid you'll get tired and go away," Katherine said. Her eyes glistened, even in the dark shadows of their apartment, lying on the mattress going over the math, *Robinson's Complete Arithmetic.* She dropped her head. Katherine's long golden curls pooled around her shoulders. "Let's switch places," Katherine tried. "I don't want to do this anymore. I'm tired. I hate being in the school with those girls. I hate seeing what they have all the time. I hate them walking home together and not ashamed. I'm ashamed, Tommy. And I don't like to pretend." Katherine felt like a liar, dressed lovely, but living without a mother or a father. She felt like a fake, hiding behind the dress and the studies. The words kept coming, new and familiar, and Tommy hardened, each word making her nastier, cold and indifferent. Katherine kept speaking, words describing girls and dolls and the lips of girls and hair and the ribbons and the pinafores and the families and the stores with all the beautiful things and the books she didn't understand anymore because she couldn't concentrate.

"What about your shoes?" Tommy asked. "You have beautiful shoes. And your clothes are lovely. I make sure they are."

"I'm embarrassed," Katherine said flatly. "I might have the pretty shoes, but I live here. The shoes are just a lie, Tommy. And you don't even go to school." At first Tommy wondered if she could work harder, looked around the room and calculated the more she could do. "This isn't right. This isn't how people live. I see at school how people live. They live as families. Mother, father, sisters, brothers. This isn't right."

"You've got to use this chance, Katherine.

It won't always be this way. This is how we work our way out. I promise you that. We're clever girls. This is how we do it," Tommy said, but saw in her sister a weakness come from the privilege Tommy had provided. She thought again of the more she might do, that it was work was all. She'd work harder. She got a notion they could get a better apartment. There was certainly more she could do. More lodged in her, a compass fixed on the inevitable direction of more.

Tommy went back to the whores and begged. They spoke every language but English, but they understood what she wanted and they gave it to her. On East Mercury, at the Victoria Hotel, the Windsor Hotel, satin-covered sofas and gilt-framed mirrors, plants in brass jardinières, opium dens spilling lethargic men. They gave it to her and smiled and told her to scat. It was easy if you could pretend you didn't mind feeling like you were nothing.

"Have you ever wanted to kiss a boy?" Katherine asked Tommy. Again. Alone. Night. On the flimsy mattress, but enchanted and carried on the back of a soft kiss.

"Who?" Tommy asked.

"He's at school."

"I was almost eleven," Tommy said, recalling the midnight forest. Cane a ghost. He had lifted her chin with his finger to meet his lips.

"You wouldn't tell?" Katherine asked.

"Don't let anybody see you, then it's all yours."

They were silent, imagining kisses. Then Katherine asked, "How is a person made?" For a moment Tommy thought she would need to explain sex to her sister, started formulating analogies and euphemisms. "I don't mean that," Katherine said, understanding what Tommy was thinking. "I mean a life, growing up, understanding who you are and what you want. How does that happen?"

Mother stormed in, acted as though she had never left, yelled at Tommy for eating a box of chocolates given her by a congressman. She inspected for dust, didn't yell at all at Katherine — Katherine was her favorite — made her presence known to the neighbors, gave the girls shoes, took the girls for a drive up to the Anaconda to see, didn't say a word. At first, they just watched: men like hardworking ants, heads bowed, fatigued, so many of them, all over the place, drooping stains. Tommy thought about Katherine's question, looking at these sad men —

how is a life made?

"This is what happens," Glenna explained patiently, her face all eye, the two blurring to one. "You will menstruate, the scarlet flow, some people call it euphemistically. But there's no need for that. Have you started yours yet, Tommy?" she asked. Tommy had blood in her panties. She engineered rags, washed them, dried them. She had figured it out. But she didn't respond to Mother. "When it happens, then men will want you not for you but to relieve themselves. They will smell you and want you. It's an urge that has nothing to do with you. You see these wasted men? These men can't pay for it so they'll try their luck with girls who know no better. You don't want to be one of those girls. Those girls get into trouble, they get pregnant, then cause their own abortions and oftentimes they die, and if they don't, it isn't any better. The way things work, respectable men only want clean women."

Tommy thought of Papa's bull, strutting among the cows in spring, smelling their urine, and come November it was a happy time when the calves were born. She thought of the little Irish women in their blue capes, coming up the hill from the evening Jaw Bone.

Glenna fell silent again as the working-men filed by, a chorus line beneath the iron sky. Tommy wanted to get away, head east and show Mother and Katherine both how a life is made. You make your life. That's how a life is made. Tommy wanted to make a family, marry a gentleman and have children and keep them close to her, tending a house like the women in the magazines, like a book she read about in the newspaper: *Mrs. Beeton's Book of Household Management,* written by an Englishwoman and in which every facet of running an efficient and effective home was described — maids, cooks, butlers, underbutlers even. She wanted to show Mother all that she was capable of, but she kept her notions secret so Mother couldn't criticize them, tell her that she'd raised her to be independent, that she didn't need to rely on a man unless she was the one in charge. Even so, Tommy dreamed.

Then Glenna was gone again, vanished into larkspur and cow country. She left behind ten dollars. Tommy gave it to Katherine to donate to the Red Cross, knowing Katherine would keep it.

The war asked this of everyone:

- Gasless Sundays
- Fuelless Mondays
- Meatless Tuesdays
- Wheatless Wednesdays
- Meatless Thursdays

The upstanding women of the town planted a victory garden, which produced sweet, succulent corn that they shared with the neighbors.

The nosy neighbor with the heavy accent stuck her head inside the girls' door. "Your mother doesn't live here, now does she? You girls live alone, now don't you?" She stood just inside the door, cast in its shadow, the outline of a disappointed woman.

Tommy trapped and skinned another coyote with another boy, this one called Hamlet. She told him she read the play, asked him if his parents were literary. That was Glenna's term. She met Hamlet on the streets of Butte, stirring up pelt traders. She spotted him negotiating with a slick old man, the lovely slide of money exchanging hands, and she knew what he was about. She liked the looks of him — his broad confidence and the keen smarting of his dark, intelligent eyes.

"Why aren't you in school?" she asked, following him away from his trade.

"Why aren't you in school?" he asked.

"That's my business."

It didn't take much for them to talk, both kids who should have been in school, both getting away with something, trying on life too soon. He wanted to be a gentleman someday. For now, he was a trapper.

"I'd like to trap with you," she boldly said.

"It's not girls' work."

"Who makes the rules?"

He looked at her, studied her face. She almost felt pretty in his gaze. She thought of her mother standing on all those soap-boxes. Mother would be proud of Tommy questioning rules — even if she would also give her a whipping for her escapades with a boy.

"I'll be darned," he said, and cocked a smile. "You know how, don't you? I want to see this."

This time she did better, she got fifteen dollars and entranced him with her skills. No one had ever told him a girl could trap. He lived on a sheep farm; his father owned the Metropolitan Meat Market.

"I bet there's a lot of things you don't

know," she said. This was another midnight forest, Katherine asleep at home, unaware; Glenna where Glenna was off to now, living in a granary or in a schoolhouse basement or with a family, telling lies about the husband and children she'd once had, but lost.

Tommy had cut her long hair short. She looked like a boy, but her eyes were emeralds. She wore pants and carried her Egyptian, still good as new, shot rodents for coyote bait. She rode with Hamlet on his mares, slipped off them, and quiet as thieves prepared their traps.

"Can't make money if I'm in school," he said. "And a man can't get anywhere without it." Said he wanted to go east too and make a mine of money, said he didn't need an education to make money, any fool could make money.

"The mines are out here," Tommy told him.

He was like a jackknife, sharp and fast. "Won't you kiss me?" he asked.

"What is it with you coyote hunters always wanting to kiss?"

He read her face, her history in the story of her eyes.

"You don't have to beg," she said.

The wind days: blue and cold. They met

to trap. They met to kiss. Midday, midnight. She was in full bloom, becoming a woman, tall for her age, slimming down. Her round face wasn't beautiful, but it had something — something lovely and smart in its determination, wisdom and adventure in her eyes that served almost as fair exchange for beauty.

She explained to Hamlet that *Hamlet* was a revenge play. She told him she had a sister who could play Ophelia — the twisted, sad pain of her — that her sister was going to be an actress in the movies. Hamlet told Tommy she was smart, and with him she felt smart, and it was more powerful than kisses, which made her arm hairs smart too, the way he didn't just kiss her lips but around her lips and around her nose, and gentle on her eyes, and the way his palms pressed against her back possessively until her body willingly surrendered. This was proof she was growing up and it made her proud.

And then they were all business with the traps and setting them and checking them and slipping off the coyote pelts and selling them to the burly men. Collecting the money and feeling so capable, so eager to see Hamlet again, holding him inside her heart like a secret life, an infinite and expanding universe that was her future. She thought, alone during the days in her apartment, checking the mirror to be sure that she was as beautiful as she felt, that she was in love.

Hamlet too became a ghost.

He was called up to serve, a draftee sent to the war, killed in Gesnes, France, his body decimated beyond ability to identify. But that was later.

All the boys would leave, sucked down by roots. Forty thousand Montana boys, not much older than Tommy, sucked down by roots. You saw those boys; they were abundant rain feeding thirsty roots until there was no water left.

Red Cross nurses blossomed like Indian paintbrush.

The German immigrants kneeled to kiss the flag, demonstrating allegiance, but no one believed them. Will Campbell, the wild-eyed editor of the *Helena Independent,* wrote frequently about German agents: "Are Germans about to bomb the capital of Montana? Have they spies in the mountain fastnesses equipped with wireless stations and aeroplanes? Do our enemies fly around our high mountains where formerly only the shadow of an eagle swept?"

Nuns made quilt squares and sold them to raise money.

Glenna drove in again in her own Model T, summer and hot and dry, traveling the state for Jeannette Rankin. Glenna's effort and enthusiasm made her kind and warm. She told her girls she was opening the century for them, that it would be theirs to do with and enjoy as they pleased. Tommy wanted to tell her mother all about her coyote money, how it helped them get along so well.

"Rankin will be the first female congresswoman, but she will not be the last. Unrestricted universal enfranchisement is certain."

She examined her daughters, asked Tommy what she had done to her hair, said she now looked very much like a boy indeed. "You will grow it."

Then it just started to get worse, one calamity spilling into the next. Headlines shouted all day long, songs about them in the saloons. You couldn't escape it. Tommy wanted to press her hands to her ears to keep the news out. One hundred and sixty-four miners died in the Speculator Mine fire. Fifteen thousand miners went on strike, causing ammunition problems.

Then disaster set its sights directly on the girls. The Acorn exploded, shot out from the wall, and caused a fireball in the apartment. Fire sprayed from the stove, igniting the burlap curtains in the dark hollows of a night, licking up the mattress and the few clothes the girls had. Tommy and Katherine woke fast. Tommy tried to put it out, throwing blankets on the mattress, throwing salt and a bucket of water, but the flames rode the water and spread deeper into the room.

The girls hadn't filled the kerosene properly, had dripped a path of it from the stove to the gallon container holding the fuel.

Tommy worked fast, thinking silly things; she thought she had to get Katherine out of there, that a burn would wreck her beauty. She thought Mother would give her a whipping. She thought the life she had made would be lost. She worked feverishly, hoping no one would hear or notice, hoping she could make it all right. It was hot and terrible, and as one flame ceased another flared to life. Rivulets of fire streaked the floor and the walls.

Katherine stood dumbly by the door in her nightgown, arms long, face beautiful, hair pulled back in a large barrette, sleep still in her eyes as Tommy darted among the flames. But when Katherine offered to help, Tommy shouted for her to stay away, warning her that she'd get hurt.

"But you can get hurt then too," Katherine said.

"I can't get hurt. Not like you. I can't get hurt like you." Somewhere Tommy believed that, that because she wasn't beautiful the fire couldn't hurt her the same as it could hurt Katherine.

"We should run away," Katherine said, speaking fast.

Tommy said nothing. She wasn't succeeding with the fire. She slumped down to her knees, wanting to pray and to cry. The tears came and they were hot, sliding down her cheeks. There was a strange silence in the fire — a calm destruction. In that silence, their lives were suspended, outlines in the smoke. The hem of Katherine's nightdress polka-dotted with flame. "Do you hear me?" Katherine persisted. Tommy had never hated her sister before in this way. The wretched emotion crept in slowly, but emphatically because she could see that Katherine was a coward. She wouldn't fight to save what they had made because she didn't know what they had made. Katherine had made none of it. She'd simply been allowed to go to school. Resentment is not a lovely sensation. "We need to leave now; we need to run away from here."

The smoke was in their eyes and lungs. Their flesh was cut with shrapnel and small burns. The smell of singed hair. "Why aren't you moving?" Katherine took Tommy's hand, dragging her toward the door. "We don't need any of this," Katherine said. She was pulling Tommy harder now. "We must be quick, before they come. We can disappear. Come now, Tommy, be strong." But Tommy wasn't strong. She was a rag doll in her sister's clutch. All of her coyote money, all of her begged money, everything was in the mattress, which burned now with abandon. Katherine pulled the trunk out of the fire's way, grabbed Nancy's bowl and placed it inside, slapped at the flames eating at the trunk until she snuffed them out. "We need to leave. Come now, Tommy." But Tommy was frozen, watching flames devour the Egyptian, standing tall where she had left it near the windows, hating her sister for wanting to run away.

Then the silence was over. Someone screamed from down the hall that the Germans had invaded. More neighbors started opening their doors, screaming about the Germans too.

"Come now, Tommy, don't be stupid.

Don't just stand there. Tommy, act. We have the chance to get away, Tommy. If we stay, we're over — you and I."

"I hate you," was all Tommy said, watching the fire eat up her hard work. She was speaking to herself and Katherine and Mother and the room that had once held everything.

Only the trunk with Nancy's bowl survived the fire. The trustees of the school board up at Helena were contacted and Glenna was summoned, accused of child abuse and ordered not to leave her children or they'd be taken away from her, placed in an orphanage. She arrived in her black automobile, lace to her neck, chin high. She told her daughters that because of her work and her efforts the doors had opened for them and now they had jeopardized it all. In Montana, they could vote and run for office and do better work than the Irish whores, own their own land and be in charge of their own destinies. "You foolish girls," from the whip of her tongue. She told them they would need to find rich men and have babies, terrifying them. She practiced her violin, sitting in the window of a hotel room they couldn't afford. Quiet: just the sullen, arrogant bow strides as she disappeared her

180

upset into music. The girls knew if they disturbed her, she would slap them.

Terror was sowed and grown and breathed and eaten. And the terror of the Germans and of the war morphed and spread into terror of the land and the heat and the parched stubborn sky until all the people were breathing fear.

Sometimes Tommy thought of Auntie on the farm, thought of her warm biscuits and of collecting warm eggs from beneath the hens, thought of Papa singing a ballad with his fiddle, thought of being a little girl in a white pinafore and learning her lessons at Auntie's side, her breath like summer mint.

They left Butte. Glenna carried her black Gladstone medicine bag filled with poultices and herbs. They all carried the trunk, strapped it once again to the rear of the Ford. Glenna was strange to the girls, a distant relative, determined and nervous, her features sharpening, an exactness trying to ward off failure. This was their mother, almost vulnerable.

They traveled south to the Gallatin Valley, east again toward Billings, then Miles City. Glenna looked for work, speaking with strangers, struggling to charm and fascinate, jaw raised, wicked, daring smile, hair swirled in a crown. But there was something new in her eyes, and Tommy almost felt sorry for her. Mother was a proud, diminished woman in her impeccable dress, telling the girls that the money was running out. Without the gun, without the help of a trapper, Tommy wasn't much on her own in the midnight woods.

In Miles City, Glenna took them to a dressmaker and had them outfitted in billowy white blouses and skirts that came to their ankles so they were freer to move about. She had their heads scrubbed and their hair trimmed and curled. On their wrists, she rubbed rose-scented toilet water. She spent her last dollars on their appearance. She relied on kindness for food, in the way she had always done. "If we look respectable, we'll be treated with respect," Glenna said. Tommy almost felt a tenderness for her mother, something giving up inside, surrendering to a will that wasn't hers, to the knowledge that her will, strong as it was, was not strong enough to steer a divine will.

All over town were advertisements for women wanted for the war. They flocked to Europe by the thousands, filled with sympathy for the Belgians and the French. They went as nurses, as canteen hostesses, as ambulance drivers and switchboard operators. They went as storytellers. "We can do that," Glenna told her girls.

Jeannette Rankin had voted against the war, but women nonetheless formed an army. It was in the air, everywhere, all across the country, here in Miles City. Women organized committees to roll bandages, raise relief funds, even to send aid to the suffering French. Glenna understood the historic significance. Women had not been able to help much before. She took the girls to churches and they rolled bandages until their hands ached, learning about the women who had gone, who wrote home, describing their work — amputations, playing games, reading to the wounded as they died. They worked in casualty clearing stations, smelling the stench of filthy, sick soldiers, steamed and etherized and shot to pieces. You could see the images from the letters, shared by a sister or a mother or a cousin here, rolling bandages and everyone listening to the stories, something familiar and specific in the notion of these American women in Europe, working collectively to help, tethered by letters to here and so many other small towns where women worked for the war.

In one such letter, Plasticine portrait masks were described, the labor of making them for disfigured soldiers so they could appear in public without scaring people. *"So many wounded,"* the letter writer wrote, the words coming from the lips of a gray-haired woman, her hand shaking the sheet of paper. *"But I find beauty now in the faces of these noseless men like heroic sculptures from ancient Greece. But it's one thing for me to feel this way, I know. It's another for the man living with a part of his face interrupted, the horror I know he feels when he doesn't recognize himself, the unmitigated hell he endures when he is a stranger to himself."* Tommy thought of faraway Europe, men walking around behind masks and their shattered faces.

Horses dominated the town, more horses than people. The fields brimmed with stallions. Representatives from the British and French and Italian governments came to Miles City, majors accompanied by military veterinarians. Sought were lightweight horses for the cavalry. The immigrant trains filled now with horses, tableaux of a different sort. On the front, the average life of a horse was seven days.

184

■ ■ ■ ■

Millions of grasshoppers arrived as if sent to destroy, scouring the fields of crops, the wool of the sheep, every blade of grass. Vast waves of the insects collected against the fences, feasting for days as they whirred and rasped, a moving screen, their silver wings catching the sun. They lingered until most of the wheat across Montana was gone — wheat the color of pale yellow silk, flowing in wind. Seventy-two thousand grasshoppers per acre, hatching eggs small as seeds, kernels emerging from the soil, popping through, chewing the shock crops, enjoying it all for their greedy selves. They left behind notches in the fork handles, fence posts stripped clean, clothes hanging on the line filled with holes, heads in hands again and again, mothers and fathers crying.

And this was just the beginning. Wheat that survived was leveled by hail, houses blown down, people beaten to death by ice big as golf balls, the grasses diced against the ground. The wait for water was permanent: skies black and ominous and hope filled in with blue again and the land returned to the desert it always had been and wanted to be.

Through a horseman Glenna learned of an opportunity at Lame Deer on the Cheyenne Reservation. She applied and was given the position, given a log cabin and charged with helping the Cheyenne assimilate into white culture by keeping them healthy, teaching them hygiene and educating them in issues of health. They stayed a year. Tommy and Katherine learned Lakota from Mary Shoulder Blade and Louise Big Foot.

And here I must pause again for a moment.

Grammy told us stories about these girls, their names lodging in our minds. Hokum, blarney, fabulation, ballyhoo arrive not on the local but by means of the express, the high-priority freight train, of narration, bypassing the nitty-gritty whistle-stops, where the peculiar knock of fact can be heard, in favor of propulsion and the high drama of self-regard. What are the odds, after all, that my grandmother and her sister *learned Lakota*? About the same odds that a humble tradesman from Nazareth becomes a major world philosopher who never sinned and was conceived by mysterious intercession of a Holy Ghost upon a virgin. It was far more likely that the two girls may have overheard some Siouan variant — Assiniboine, for instance, more common in eastern Montana, repeating phrases overheard to try the language on.

But in the narration to us, her granddaughters, saying that she and her sister had *learned Lakota* is more metrically stable in the telling than *learned Assiniboine*. Lakota sounds like Dakota except slightly more exotic and therefore more believable. They had to sound, to white ears — specifically to the ears of my sisters and me, for whom credulity could be expressed within a wildly elastic range of the probable — both familiar and exotic. "Mary Shoulder Blade" and "Louise Big Foot" came into mythic existence. Somewhere in those two names lurked the Alcotts and their bookish little sister, Louisa May. When our mother heard us recite the names, she would roll her eyes. "Shoulder Blade?" she'd say. "Really?" If we dared rush back to interrogate Grammy with skeptical questions, she would give us one of her looks that seemed to wonder if we hadn't lost our marbles.

"Louise didn't have a big foot and Mary didn't have a strange shoulder," she'd say with calm authority. "This was a Cheyenne naming practice," she'd say. And on she'd go.

■ ■ ■ ■

Katherine and Tommy loved the names. There were others, more, and many more: American Horse, Hiwalker, Beartusk, Braided Hair, Kill on Top, Big Left Hand. The days were dry and the winters cold on the plateau with short hills all around, shallow waters in the Rosebud and Tongue. Mother told the girls history, of Custer's battle at Little Big Horn and the Cheyenne girls told of the men seeing nothing but a big cloud of dust, the women seeing more when the fighting finished. The girls' grandmothers stuck awls in Custer's ears, turning the blades so he could finally hear what the Cheyenne had to say. But Cheyenne was not the name these people had for themselves; they knew themselves as Inke Wicasa — the natural humans, the free of the world. They called Katherine and Tommy the white girls. The Cheyenne girls wore their hair loose and long. It was fine black silk and they held the rain in their hair and they would leave it loose when rain was needed. Rain was needed. All across Montana rain was needed. It was needed today and it would be needed tomorrow.

Glenna treated the new babies with silver

nitrate in the eyes because the women had been infected with gonorrhea by white men, families torn up by their illnesses: traders, river men, voyageurs. The medicine men were suspicious of Glenna in her elegant dress with her swirled auburn crown. At first, everyone was scared, standing long with scared blank faces. But when her work began to heal, the women decided they approved of Glenna — women with the wonderful names: Mary Teeth, Josephine Limpy Stands Near Fire, Annie Medicine Bull. They liked Glenna, wanted her lessons. "You can become medicine women," she told them in Cheyenne.

Larkspur and ether doused on hair and bound tightly in a cloth treated lice, cotton at the edges so the bugs couldn't crawl out. Inhaling sulfur cured a sore throat. To fix broken bones a balm of chewing tobacco moistened with whiskey was rubbed into the arm and then all of it wrapped in rawhide. For unwanted babies an ergot of rye was made: an infusion of molded rye, created by dampening and leaving it in a dark place for several days. The mold was extracted to make an infusion by boiling it with water and steeping it for several more days. Then it could be drunk. "This will bring on menstruation," Glenna instructed the girls. "But don't get in need of it," she warned, the group of them sitting around her in her log cabin thick with the smell of dense coffee. The government issued coffee; there was always plenty. Buttermilk assuaged thirst and relieved constipation. Glenna made poultices from bread drenched in milk and laid them on the open wounds. She practiced acupuncture and cupping — attached a heated cup to the surface of the skin to pull out pulmonary disease — techniques picked up from the Chinese. Glenna always wanted to learn, was always open and prepared to transform. Her patients lined up outside her cabin, barefoot and drooping. With each one, Glenna was patient and tender; she planted a soft kiss on their cheeks, touched them with light fingers. She was deep inside her work. Tommy watched her, saw something she hadn't understood before — beauty in her mother's ability to morph and yield, to become something other, to adapt.

Tommy didn't think about love very often. Love was an abstract notion. She loved her sister. She loved her mother and her father because they were her parents. But what really did that word mean? Here with the Cheyenne, watching her mother's work, her confidence and determination, her knowledge and desire to heal, she came close to feeling what she imagined love should be — an admiration, a desire to protect, to be inspired, to be cared for and safe.

A rattlesnake struck Katherine, playing barefoot in sagebrush and the dried gumbo of cactus and mud. The diamondback was the color of the earth, disguised until Katherine stepped near it. The sound of the snake was followed by its sudden strike, fangs darting into Katherine's calf. She shrieked first in surprise and then horror, then a pain that left Katherine doubled over in agony. Her calf swelled, fierce and ugly. Tommy scooped Katherine up, believing herself strong enough to run with Katherine across the fields. Tommy hadn't wanted her mother's help in a very long time, but she wanted it now. She began to scream for Mother; it was a terror that took her over completely. Mary and Louise ran across the brittle field to fetch Mother.

Katherine turned an ugly blue and Tommy understood she could die. Mother had always warned them about snakes; Auntie and Papa had warned them about snakes. Tommy remembered snakes coming through the floorboards of the long-ago schoolhouse near the Brewers' farm, how a father of one of the students had come to shoot them all, crawling under the school to get the nest.

"Mother!" she screamed. She kissed Katherine, who was unconscious with the pain. The vast desolate land of the reservation seemed to spread in all directions. Now too, Tommy had gone inside fear so she could see and hear and know nothing but the dread of her sister dying, able only to wail, "Mother," who was there now with a crowd, faces and braids and curiosity.

Glenna ripped her Elgin watch off her wrist and smashed the crystal against a rock, used the glass as a blade to scoop out the venom. Blood tore down Katherine's pale and swollen leg as she lay limply on the ground. Glenna put her mouth to the sore and sucked out the remaining venom, spit it on the ground. She chewed on a bit of cactus to clean her mouth, quickly made a poultice from the cactus chew, and mounded it on the cut.

She was magic women.

Glenna held a limp Katherine against her chest, and there too Tommy thought she saw love.

"I thought you would die," Tommy said to Katherine, just the two of them at Kather-

192

ine's sickbed. "I thought you would be stolen and I was so scared." Tommy thought of her mother's sister, Madeleine, the death portrait in the locket frame that they still carried with them. She thought of losing Katherine, of her being gone and no more, out here in this desolate land, taken by a snake. "I love you," Tommy said, and she felt the words spread, coursing from her heart.

"I know you do," Katherine said. "It's the one thing I know."

Smallpox, diphtheria, spinal meningitis, puerperal fever, typhoid fever, births, deaths — Glenna cared for it all. Tommy admired her, didn't understand where she got the courage. The courage, and the success it rewarded, made them happy. The Cheyenne were kind and welcoming, cooking food for them, inviting them to their ceremonies, telling them their legends. Teaching them to keep track of the days with moon-counting sticks, to collect mint for wild mint tea, to bake squaw bread and pemmican with berries and kidney fat, to speak. They smoked red willow bark in the ancestral peace pipe and the smoke went to the spirit world and the spirits were everywhere — in the animals and the land and the stones and the water, and with the rising smoke went fear, and this was how Glenna found her courage, by smoking the red willow bark. She wore her long auburn hair now in braids and they danced on the sacred dancing ground to bring the rains.

Little girls becoming big girls, they were being made, shaped and molded and formed and designed.

Tommy loved to ride. She had a gray pony all for her to use. They rode bareback, fast over the land, into the saffron sky. Mary Shoulder Blade chasing Louise Big Foot chasing Katherine. They rode together, holding on to each other's backs. Speed was in their hair. Katherine wanted her hair to be the rain too. There were ceremonies and powwows and ear piercings and sacrifices. A man died and his horses were killed — heads to the east, tails to the west.

And sometimes the world was just beautiful, a lightning display in the lavender and mauve sky just above the Little Wolf Mountains.

The daughters didn't say it, but they loved Glenna. They wished they had always been here and could always stay. She was important and respected, and the Cheyenne girls were jealous of Tommy and Katherine, and that made them happy too. "You have everything," Mary said to them.

Green frog skin: dollar bills. The Cheyenne girls thought Tommy and Katherine were rich. Their clothes were clean and white and tidy. They drove an automobile. Green frog skin and they wanted to have it. They wanted it to become their own skin.

At night, by kerosene lantern — there were no electric lights on the reservation — Tommy prepared Katherine for her annual exams. "Why does it matter?" Katherine asked. Tommy was impatient with this. She snapped, "You know."

"But don't you like it here?"

"Katherine," Tommy said. The sisters looked at each other. Tommy understood something now, because she was older: she understood her sister needed her and that the need created power in Tommy and that power was tempting, had always been tempting. She understood too that at any moment everything could change.

"And you?" Katherine asked.

And then came what the Cheyenne called The Year of Many Deaths. Glenna and the girls left the reservation. There was a shortage of trained personnel, doctors and nurses, across the state. It wasn't possible for Glenna to remain when her help was urgently needed elsewhere.

Those who helped were promised gauze face masks. Butte was one of the hardest hit towns in the nation, so Glenna returned with the girls. She did not go for the money or the adventure or to risk her children's lives; she went because she had help to offer and it was the right thing to do.

Young men came into town one day, healthy as an ox, and were dead two days later. All remedies were tried: anti-pneumonia serums, blankets for sweating, magic medicines and witch potions. Alcohol was believed to be a cure. There was a run on alcohol. Chairs were removed from saloons so people didn't stay long. Garbage piled up. Mail piled up. Everyone took to their beds. Telegraph and telephone systems collapsed. Quarantines. Laws against spitting. Schools, universities, businesses of every order, theaters and churches — all shut down. Undertakers were doing well, too well; they couldn't keep up. On every porch, there was a casket. Glenna was not afraid. Katherine was sure they would die. She spoke in laments and sorrows for time past and lost lives, irritating Tommy. "I'm scared to grow up. I wish we had stayed on the reservation. I'm afraid we'll die, Tommy. I'm afraid we'll get struck down. Worse, that you'll get struck down and then what will I do? I can't do this alone, Tommy." Tommy understood who she was, defined clearly against her sister's need. Tommy didn't need. She wanted, but she didn't need. She realized she had more in common with her mother. She didn't stop to think and regret anymore. There wasn't time for that and fear warded off nothing. A snake could strike and kill at any time. Sentiment was for the weak. The strong kept moving.

The girls stayed inside in an apartment on East Park in the William Block. Glenna wore a mask across her face and gloves on her hands. "It's my work," she said to the girls.

Germans, the belief spread, were sending the virus in envelopes. In their smart laboratories, they cultured the virus and sent it to America in letters. Over the sick and the dead, they had advantage.

Waves.

Soldiers returned and with them brought more sickness. More died of the virus than in the war. The girls watched from the window, the streets winnowing as people disappeared, wondering if the virus could drift through beneath the door, an invisible shade. Butte seemed like a different town from the one they had known. They waited. The black mine cloud puffed above the city.

The sky refused to behave.

They waited.

Soaring wheat prices, demanded because of the war, tumbled and then fell some more simply because of fear.

They waited.

Drought set in, burrowing into the land, making it crack and crumble and then become hard, and there was nothing anyone could do with the hard, there was no dream that could penetrate the hard. The plow's golden nuggets from the long-ago advertisements promising Montana prosperity vanished like teepee rings.

The flu too was left behind, along with the war and the soldiers and the dead and the land that was to feed a hungry nation.

The home seekers and the settlers and the colonists and the homesteaders and the immigrants and the emigrants and all who accompanied them and their needs — families and children and lawyers and doctors and missionaries and schoolteachers and shopkeepers — evaporated beneath the fat tracks of dry-farming theorists and newly minted

198

millionaires. The clever visions of railroad executives morphed into villainy.

It was desert, known before, known now, known later. And the songs and the dances and the schoolhouses and the claim shacks and the babies. Gone. Topsoil turned to dust that would amass and accumulate and then blow south to smother. Fool faces.

On the prairie a woman's dead body was torn apart by wolves.

"Which Do You Prefer?" read the headline. "The Home or the Street Corner for Women? Vote NO on Woman Suffrage — October 19."

There were other schools, other towns across the state — Glenna bringing Shakespeare to the far reaches of the frontier, to the loneliest towns where work would have her. She brought always the sense that a girl and therefore a woman should be educated. Days, she ran her schools like missions, made sure there were clothes for the children who couldn't clothe themselves, bought dresses for the girls who couldn't afford them, had costumes for boys and girls alike so they could put on extravagant productions. Evenings were filled with the haunting strains of her violin.

And time passed because it has a way of doing that.

In Helena, the sisters stayed in a small one-bedroom on Reeder's Alley meant for a miner, not a good part of town, windows facing other shacks in the dark and narrow streets, cut here and there by shards of sunlight. Tommy, nineteen now, had a real job. She worked as a switchboard operator, six days a week, nine-hour days, varying shifts, for seventy-five cents an hour. No makeup allowed. High neckline finished off with a tie and blazer, long skirts, clean fingernails, she felt like a woman, leaving in the morning for her job. A busy row of neatly arranged girls before a color-coded switchboard, they processed several thousand calls per day. Early, Tommy started with the wake-up calls, which rolled into morning coffee calls followed by business calls, which soon gave way to more desperate calls — so many lives, dreams, hopes, trials, tribulations, fears, and agonies — plugged and unplugged by Tommy's efficient hand. Wisps of lives fluttered by. You could tell the time of day simply by the nature of the call. She thought of her father long ago — his cool remove as a telegrapher, best fist in the business, tapping out the pain of others.

And while Tommy worked, Katherine attended the Helena High School, turreted and dramatic and all cold stone like some Gothic edifice from a terrifying Poe tale. From call to call, Tommy would think of Katherine, about her days at her desk with a teacher teaching her so many things. Already Tommy couldn't understand the math. At night, Katherine no longer needed Tommy's help with the English or the history — even so, Tommy read the texts, trying to keep up. An unpleasant sensation as Tommy watched Katherine at the kitchen table studying for her exams, asking for quiet as Tommy cooked them a meal or washed the dishes in the sink — the unsettling realization that Katherine might know more.

But age had also turned Katherine into a silly girl, as hard as Tommy tried to make sure she studied and repeated her lessons and did well on her exams, and Katherine did — straight high marks, excellent records. Katherine was equally smitten with the allure of her own beauty now. Katherine became Kathy and Kate, like a character in a Russian novel — pet names and more names made her feel like she had more, that she was more, reflected out as in a three-way mirror, so many of her. She was involved with the theater students at school, went to the movies on the weekend, talked more fervently now about making her way to Hollywood. She was pretty and smart and daring. She cut her hair, wore it in a bob and smoked cigarettes and drank when offered a cordial, kissed when offered lips, smiling sweetly and staying out all night with boys and cheer and good fun.

"Katherine!" Tommy chastised, studying her.

"I'm Kate now." "I'm Kathy now." Lovely girl, nearly grown up now, nearly ready to make her own way off, her own adventures. She cast about a sophistication and grown-up mood easily, a new confidence; Tommy wasn't necessary for her survival anymore. Kate was now a woman, seventeen with breasts and beauty and the desire of men who wanted to dance with her and watch movies with her in the dark of a theater. She wore her skirts in the new fashion, revealing ankle and calf and she liked clothes, and not boring school clothes, but silk and satin and tulle and feathery clothes that she bought along with her cigarettes with Tommy's money because somehow Tommy always had money. She dressed to reveal the length of her pale neck, her lovely shoulders. She gave Tommy a feckless kiss of feckless gratitude: thank you, dear. An afterthought. Mother didn't scare her — off in Lombard, in Lewiston, finally into Idaho because they didn't ask for certificates there yet. There was no more pretending about Mother. She herself began to speak of the need to go to a normal school to get a degree. Tommy didn't scare Katherine either, even when she slapped her for staying out and getting tipsy and buying and smoking cigarettes, the long slow inhale, smoke filling her lungs, swelling them and warming them and caressing them. And she felt so wise and mature.

"You don't care?" Tommy said. She didn't list all that she had done, but the sentiment was implicit in her words. In her mind, she thought about lists, the long lists of all that she had done. She could feel impatience grow in her, the starting point of a fracture, could feel the need to be repaid for her efforts even though she knew it wasn't right. She stood in the tiny alcove that was their kitchen, wearing her long work skirts and high collar with tie, very much an old-fashioned woman, seeming years older than her sister. She felt her heaviness against the lightness of her sister's beauty and style.

"Look at this place," Kate said, and swept

her hand around the little, dank room — the slumped bed, the trunk, the rusted sink, stuffing crawling out of the chair's upholstery. "We can do better than this, Tommy. You know it." It was awful; that was true. Sometimes Tommy would think about their long-ago home. It had grown in her mind over the years, the one they left in Ohio when their parents separated. A beautiful house, built for them in 1900. What would life have been like had Mother stayed? She thought of all the aunts and uncles and their children — news coming in from Ohio from time to time: Uncle Albert's son off to the University of Virginia; Aunt Grace's daughter off to Oberlin. Memories and questions and facts flitted across her mind and impatiently she swatted them away because there are no parallel lives.

"I didn't ask you to do anything," Kate continued. And that's when Tommy slapped her. Fast and without thinking. Kate's face became Tommy's hand and Tommy felt like Mother, that knot of anger tugging away in her chest, willing life to yield her way. The sisters went silent for a while.

Then Katherine spoke, patiently. "I want to go to California." She had been thinking about this for some time — Tommy understood that suddenly, in the tiny room of their tiny Reeder's Ally shack. Katherine had her own ambitions, her own mind. Everyone was headed to California. All day long Tommy placed calls to California. People headed there for the sunshine, for opportunity. Los Angeles boomed. Desert gardens everywhere. Oil. Hollywood. Sunshine. Sometimes Tommy stayed on the line just to hear conversations. Something crumbled in Tommy, the belief shattering that her sister would always need her.

Outside on the street you could hear the landlady, Mrs. Laura Duchesnay, called Mrs. Laura, and all her canaries. She sold moonshine and canaries and collected everyone's rent and never asked questions. Children came to her with wounded birds for her to heal. Always there was a swarm in front of Mrs. Laura's home, the young girls in their soot-smudged dresses with their futures spilling out before them, so like the girls Tommy and Katherine had once been, trying mightily to save themselves by saving a bird. Tommy heard the canaries now, could see Mrs. Laura in her mind, swollen with age, an example of what became of women out here.

"Then go," Tommy said. "When you finish high school in June you're free to go." Tommy had composed herself, but inside a vast emptiness spread. Then what happens to a girl? You finish high school and you go to California and live a dream? Tommy had always wanted to go to New York. She heard those conversations too, advancing a call from Helena to New York so that couples could make plans, a grown child could ask a parent for funds, a daughter could tell her mother she was homesick at school. Lives connected, geography crossed. It was something like a miracle.

But here, now Tommy was arriving at the fork in her own road, a point of truth. She was neither a great beauty, nor in possession of a degree. She thought of everything she had given Katherine and not herself, everything that Katherine had that she did not — her beauty and her slender frame. The world could be anything Katherine wanted it to be. And for Tommy?

"I'm going to be an actress," Katherine said. "I'm going to change my name and become a star. I'm taking my middle name. Patricia Stewart. Patricia means noble." Easy dreams. *We aren't dreamers,* Mother had once said. She meant they weren't dreamers because if they had dreams, they realized them, didn't leave them abandoned on the side of the road like all of those pianofortes.

Mrs. Laura's canaries competed with Mamie's Bells from the St. Helena Cathedral, installed by Mamie's father after her tragic wayward death a decade ago. Glenna had told her daughters the story, because Glenna never missed the opportunity to warn her daughters of tragedies awaiting them just behind the next turn. Mamie, of privilege, lost her way because of a man, hid first in drink then finally in suicide.

Helena, the entire state of Montana, the entire West, was filled with missions and homes for desperate women wanting to start over, for lost girls. Tommy didn't want to start over. She wanted to move forward and into her future, but she realized almost futilely now that in preparing Katherine for the future, she had done nothing to prepare herself, and now Katherine was willing to throw it away on a futile dream named Patricia. *We're not dreamers,* Tommy wanted to say, but didn't as she realized, a slight fear flapping across her heart, the limitations of Katherine's drive.

Tommy started to notice advertisements in newspapers and magazines — "Become a Nurse"; "Be a Nurse"; "Nurses Needed" — placed by hospitals in big cities all across the country seeking young, educated women. They were seeking girls of quality, with high school diplomas and of good family. It was an inexpensive way for hospitals to fill out their staff while also providing opportunity. Tommy clipped an advertisement that caught her attention because it was located in New York. She studied it, wrote away to Brooklyn Hospital, inquiring. They wrote back, stated what was needed to apply. Quickly she made the application, using Katherine's name, sent Katherine's records, which Tommy had neatly organized over the course of the years, wrote a letter of interest, used descriptions from the year on the reservation, her mother's remedies, the snakebite that almost killed Katherine, the days of the plague in Butte, that she came from a long line of strong women — Nancy Cooper Slagle in the Alleghenies making poultices for her children's sore feet, Laura Ann Meyer escaping the limitations of her congenital hip defect through the whimsy of hat designs. Tommy's stories told, records in order, requirements fulfilled, she mailed the application to New York. She explained her diploma would be secured in June, upon her graduation. Then she waited.

The further the days receded from the day she posted the application, the more anxious she became, checking for the mailman several times a day whenever she was home, hoping and dreaming, putting money aside for the trip, looking at train schedules, buying new stockings and sturdy if lovely traveling shoes. She was putting together a trousseau for nursing school.

In some scenarios of the daydream, Tommy would accompany Katherine to New York, continue keeping house for her, continue being her tutor. In another scenario, Katherine would simply leave on her own. Then a third scenario emerged, that was there all along, of course, but that Tommy tried to suppress, tried to stuff back into the forbidden place from which it had come: she, Tommy Stewart, would go to New York in Katherine's place. She, Tommy Stewart, would take Katherine's name, Katherine's successful application, and she would claim it as her own. Justifying this plan took only a moment. Tommy had created a future for them. If Katherine didn't like it, Tommy could use the opportunity. Who would know in New York that Tommy wasn't Katherine? Hadn't Tommy done everything for them both for so long? Hadn't she applied to the school, written the essays? Hadn't she been the one to teach Katherine, ensure she would graduate high school?

But then Tommy would shake off the fantasy, almost hoping there would never be a response to the application. *Dreamers,* she heard her mother say. What a wild, senseless distraction. She would peer into their future and wonder for them both. School almost finished. What next for them? The stark unwritten future terrified her. She disappeared once again into the desperate lives of those customers making telephone calls — how comforting to know that she was not alone in torment.

The answer came, arriving in the form of a substantial envelope in the mail announcing Katherine's success, congratulating her on her acceptance to the prestigious program. Her application had been a strong one. A note in a perfect script at the end of the letter mentioned that Katherine was not only a strong candidate, an excellent scholar, but she was also a magnificent writer. She had, the letter said, all the qualities they were looking for in a successful candidate — education, refinement, curiosity, superb etiquette. Her acceptance would be complete upon their receipt of her diploma.

Katherine was a star, created by Tommy. Katherine was a star and she didn't even know it. The letter sat in Tommy's lap, heavy with the weight of desire. Just one of her scenarios took solid root in her imagination. Outside it rained, a lovely patter against the tin roof.

In this way, they arrived at the divide. A fine June day in Helena. Tommy bought Katherine a graduation dress, calf length, lace over a pale blue silk shift, blue as her eyes. She looked almost like a bride in the white dress with the white bouquet and the daisy tucked into French braiding beginning at her temples, roping down to frame her bob.

Glenna came from Idaho for the ceremony, dressed impeccably, acting the part of the mother, the one in charge, just as she had always done until, again, she was gone. She told the girls she had married. His name was Samuel Brown, and for a moment the girls imagined what this man could be like, a little stunned then as they realized that for a long time now their mother had had her own life. Glenna didn't offer any details. She stayed the night, attended the ceremony — the three of them almost a family, like the other families collected on the school's lawn in their Sunday clothes and summer bonnets as Katherine received her diploma.

After the celebration, Glenna came to the apartment and took what belonged to her: the *Temple's Notes to Shakespeare,* a blue velvet gown, some family photographs, her sister's death portrait, placing it all in the trunk. The girls helped her buckle it shut, fasten the straps for its next journey. Glenna stood there, a diminished woman, shorter than her daughters, her dark eyes more tired and weary than anything else. The girls carried the trunk to the street busy with people and cars. They placed it in the backseat of the Ford, the hood down, a summer day that was cornflower blue. She told her daughters she would see them soon, though she wasn't sure where. She told them they were all grown up and that she was proud of them for that. "You're going to make something of yourselves, I'm sure." She settled herself in her car, started the engine, and drove off west.

Tommy had wrapped the nursing school acceptance letter in a box with a bow. Back in the apartment, she gave it to Katherine, who opened it sitting on their single sunlit bed, apples in Nancy's wedding bowl, glistening atop a chair. Glenna had left the bowl, a reminder for the girls to both care for it and to never forget the distance it had traveled.

The canaries sang in the alleyway. Katherine studied the letter. Tommy's eyes and nose pricked, little wells filling in, and she thought of lakes and ponds and rivers and tributaries and water systems and how they worked within a body too. Her sister would leave. They were supposed to stay together. They weren't supposed to separate, grow up and leave. They were not to have made it this far; this day was to stay out there on the horizon in the unnamed and indescribable future — future perfect and permanent. Tommy imagined her sister on a train, heading to the life that she, Tommy, wanted to live. For an instant, she hated Katherine for being the beneficiary of her hard work. She hated herself for her own clever plan, writing to New York for Katherine's reward. Tommy imagined her future, desolate and incomplete. She understood now what she had worked for. She understood what it meant to let a child go, but she also felt what it meant to be a sister. She understood this in a way she had not understood before. She had always been the one with more — more responsibility, more savvy, cunning, money. And now she was the one with less. She did not like the feeling coursing through her, the rough sounds on the street and the biting sunshine, the incessant canaries that actually didn't seem to be singing at all.

Kathy helped her. "This letter," she said. "It's not for me. You applied for me, but this is what you're interested in, Tommy. Not me." She handed the letter to Tommy, but Tommy didn't take it. Tommy breathed. She felt wicked inside. Katherine was right, of course. An anxious smile perched on Katherine's lips, quivering there. Katherine had never felt entitled to criticize or reprimand her sister.

"It's a way forward," Tommy said, but she knew exactly what her sister meant.

"The acceptance is wonderful," Katherine said. She was thoughtful, composing her words. "Dare I say it? I'm even proud of myself." She laughed. "Of you for making me look so good. Can you imagine that? I'd have loved to have seen the application." Her eyes were so light, her words brimming with subtle insults of the kind that sisters specialize in. "But it's for you, Tommy. Come now. You know that." Katherine handed the letter to her sister again. It rested between them. Tommy wanted to take it, but didn't dare. Even so, the rationalizations she had spent weeks listing rushed through her. She wanted to take the letter, and she wanted to take it with conviction. She resisted. Instead she was thinking fully like a sister, not a mother, strategically, older sister that she was. What she wanted was for Katherine to make the offer.

But Katherine didn't. She would not surrender easily. Silence languished between them. Little sisters take their power where they can. Katherine's dress was beautiful, the blue silk sneaking through the cream-colored lace. "Clearly you've been thinking about this for some time," Katherine said finally. "I think you must be aware that had you asked me if I would like to apply to nursing school in New York City, I would have said that I did not. I have been quite clear that I want to go to California. If I had said I didn't want to go would you have dared to apply anyway?" Truth emboldened her and the sense of having been wronged — she almost seemed to like having been wronged, as though it justified the enduring sense she had always had.

"I don't like the implication," Tommy said flatly. She stood up and went to the sink to wash some dishes. The fire came to mind, the one that licked the trunk, Katherine's notion of fleeing, how it had irritated Tommy and now she understood why: Katherine is a dreamer. Fleeing was the choice of a dreamer.

"Implication?" Kathy asked, following her

sister to the sink. "That's your word." She continued, very matter-of-factly. Her eyes cast light on the letter, flopping now in her fingers. "I'm going to California. That's my dream. You're welcome to join me."

"And this?" Tommy said, indicating the letter, but what flooded her was a crushing sense of fear for her sister. Fool faces.

"I didn't apply for this," Katherine said. "It's not what I want. Now is our chance. Now we get to decide. We get to start fresh. I've tried every different form of Katherine and not one of them fits. I want to try something new. Reimagine who I am. I'm going to California as Patricia." She said she had been thinking about this for a long time now. She would leave and find herself, and when she found herself she would let Tommy know.

Then Tommy said, "Let me use this." She dried her hands on a rag and took the letter from her sister's hand. "Let me go to New York. I do want this. You're right, Katherine. I do." She had never really asked anyone for anything of such substance. She felt like she was begging from the whores and it was an awful way to feel. Suddenly Papa came to mind, Mr. Brewer, long ago on the porch, quickly taking the hundred dollars. She could feel just exactly how he had felt, the ugly necessity of the transaction. Is that what they had learned?

"How do you mean?" Katherine said.

"I think you know how I mean," Tommy answered. For Tommy, in fact, this was a simple matter: she had kept up, taught herself. This was a matter of paperwork — that was all.

"That you become me? Head off to New York and pretend you're Katherine?" She laughed.

"I use your application," Tommy said firmly.

"Pretending you're me?" Kathy persisted. She would not make this easy, reveling, in Tommy's eye, in the shift in power.

"I know how to do this," Tommy said. "You know as well as I that I'm prepared."

"To take my name? What's the difference, right? We are sisters. Two sides of the same coin. Is it even legal, Tommy? Do you even know who I am?" This bold defiance startled Tommy — a pent-up-little-sister rage of the kind older sisters are generally incapable of noting before they witness it explode.

"It doesn't have to be complicated," Tommy said. She returned to the sink, wiped it dry with the rag, holding the letter still in her left hand. She felt impossibly small, smaller than her petite sister in her pretty dress.

"Since you were a little girl you've wanted New York, to go there, become a lady as if it were just that simple. Show up in the great big city and become someone. You think that going there as me will give you that?" She sighed impatiently. "You'll be cleaning bedpans, draining sores, and all sorts of awful things." She held ferociously to the power. Tommy could see it and feel it, a cudgel Katherine wasn't so familiar with. The way she cast it about felt dangerous. Tommy was partly curious, partly humiliated. "How far will you go to get what you want?" Katherine asked. Even though Tommy had dried her hands, moisture penetrated the letter at her fingertips. "Become me? Isn't that ironic." She inserted the small sharp point of her words and twisted it.

Tommy understood that even in becoming Patricia, her sister would never surrender Katherine willingly. Tommy would have to take Katherine, take the diploma, take the acceptance. Tommy understood, could see the reasoning trembling beneath Katherine's eyes. She was afraid it would work out for Tommy, afraid Tommy would succeed and that she would not. And if that were the case, Katherine would spend the rest of her life with the consequences of her choice not to go to New York. Tommy would always be able to say that she had applied to nursing school for Katherine and that Katherine chose not to go. It was clear now to both sisters the dance they were in and how it would resolve. Even so, Katherine added, "I'm going to California. You have to choose for yourself which way you're headed."

The Continental Divide: one sister spilled east, the other west. They packed up their little home, Tommy taking Nancy's bowl, Katherine claiming she didn't care — it was just an object. Later, it would occur to both sisters that a certain kind of fate was sealed in that decision. In the moment, Katherine was setting herself free. At the station, Tommy bought their train tickets, gave Katherine more money for her travels, and she had no choice but to accept it. Tommy kissed her sister on the cheek, didn't feel the prick of emotion.

"Write, of course," Tommy said.

"To the hospital," Katherine said. What do you say to someone who has claimed you? *I hope being me works out?* Is that what you say? Katherine couldn't wait to get away, to be free and independent and on her own. In the deepest part of her she loved her sister, of course. But much closer to the surface was disgust — disappointment in Tommy, the suffocating truth that Tommy would always feel as eldest that she owned a part of Katherine.

Trains came in and went out, busy and loud. "Goodbye, then," Katherine said, clutching her bag close so her hands weren't free for an embrace. Unarticulated emotion moved between them, simmered right beneath the surface — that hate that is so frequently described as being so very close to love. They hated each other for where they each were and for the fact that it was now time to part. They hated each other for not wanting to stay together, for having made it through, for having to figure it out alone now. Katherine hated Tommy for taking her name; Tommy hated Katherine for not giving it to her. They were still so young; they could squander love.

"It will all be fine," Tommy said.

"I'm sure of that," Katherine said. The two sisters turned away from each other, making their way to their respective trains.

Katherine went first to Seattle. She stayed in a home for wayward girls, not because she was wayward, but because that's what girls did who traveled alone. It didn't cost anything. She began to call herself Patricia, though she shortened it immediately to Pat. The smallness of the name suited her, as though she had always been Pat.

She left Seattle as soon as she could, booking passage on the HMS *Alexander,* which took her down the coast to California. She carried little, just her pretty clothes and her cigarettes, shedding the weight of Montana with each step forward. She left her mother, her sister, all the accumulated fear of what would happen next. On the deck, she breathed in the ocean air, the rough seas, and the clear blue days. She felt free, in charge of herself for the first time, a little afraid that she could fail, but confident knowing that that failure need only be understood by herself.

From the boat's dining hall, she pilfered a silver pitcher embossed with the ship's name. She took it because there were so many of them, one for each table. She took it because it was beautiful and no one would notice and because she imagined it on her dining table in her new home in the sunshine of Los Angeles where she was determined to become a star.

But how often does that particular dream come true? On the HMS *Alexander,* Pat met a cop from Los Angeles. His name was Hank Bennett, and Hank had lovely, kind blue eyes and a tenderness and concern for her. He thought she was the most beautiful girl he had ever encountered. He let her know. He wasn't a tall man, but he exuded strength, told her that he wanted her to be his — sea spray in their hair. She felt exhilarated and weak all at once, caught by fate and eager to surrender to his confidence and charge. Then suddenly in the weakness she felt strength as she surrendered completely to love. Ten days after arriving in Los Angeles they married. Pat Bennett, she told herself, is the name of a star. Shortly thereafter she learned that she was pregnant, but she would believe, for the rest of her days, that meeting Hank was the moment her dream began.

And Tommy: She slid down the other side of the divide. She didn't think about her name at first, if it was a good idea to take Katherine's name. She could just as easily say her pet name was Tommy. Rather, she looked out the window at the landscape rolling by, the terrain flattening — fields and fields of green broken up here and there by lavender. When her train passed Wadena, she remembered the nuns. It felt so good to be grown up, not at all lonely. For a moment, she worried about her sister. Somehow it would be all right for them. How strange it was.

She traveled first to Ohio to visit her father and his wife in the home she had left behind so many years before. It was unfamiliar, nothing like the house of her imagination, the one in which her parents had remained together and she and her sister had grown up with a father, on a street with other children, in a town and a state filled with relatives, that other life that she had reached for from time to time where it always seemed to be Christmas. Her father and Hattie, as his wife was called, were strangers to her, but they welcomed her kindly. Hattie was crass, loud, and vain — dressed like a tart, looked in the mirror frequently, revealed cleavage. Somehow Hattie made Lavern laugh and she devoted all of her attention to fussing after him. They called Tommy Thelma. Each time they said the name was like a little shock, referencing something long lost, like one of the ancestors. There was no Thelma. Thelma was a heroine in a novel her mother had loved, but long before Tommy could remember her mother had retracted the name, choosing to call her daughter a boy's name, as if Glenna could see that she wasn't suited to being a princess.

Her father gave her the ticket to New York. He gave her money and he too told her he was proud of her. "You've come far, Thelma. A nurse." He didn't ask after the details, the Katherine hiding in it all, and Tommy offered nothing. "I can hardly believe," he said. He was portly now, a bit shorter in stature than he had been. He smoked a pipe and it embraced him with a sweet smell. She loved that he gave her money, that he wanted to provide. She could imagine the father he would have been. "Do you remember writing to me?" he asked. "Do you remember telling me about the wild bobcats in Virginia City, how the folks there hated them because they ate the lambs?"

"You remember the letters?" she asked.

"Saved 'em all. Stay in touch," he said. He left her at the station. She kissed him, made promises, and continued to New York.

On the train, again she filled with a happiness that she had not felt before. Katherine: Her fate was to be Katherine. She loved the name. Katherine, she was Katherine. Using the name merged her somehow with her sister, as if they were still and always together. Katherine. She wore its secret like a prize, a lovely dress. It was Greek and meant pure. It was a strong, firm name, had belonged to princesses and queens and empresses — Katherine of Aragon, Katherine the Great. The name made her feel new and beautiful, and now it would be hers. It took no adjustment, no getting used to. She stood straighter, taller, understood who she was and wanted to be: neat and calm and clear minded, ready to learn and to show. No one knew her anymore, a stranger come to town. She too was free. "My name is Katherine," she said to anyone who asked — the man seated next to her, the man collecting tickets. She responded to the name with no hesitation when called. To her astonishment, no one said, "That's not your name," and this too added to her confidence. The name multiplied and divided, transforming into pet names: Kathy, Kitty, Kay — a whole new wardrobe, so many variations of herself. Katherine became her. In mirrors, in the glass of the train's windows, she saw a beautiful and refined young woman who kept her hair rippled and her cheeks pinched with color. Her green eyes sparkled. Her teeth were straight. She was slender and fit, nothing to do with the girl she had been.

It was this new woman who stepped off the train and into the swirl of New York City.

■ ■ ■ ■

PART TWO:
TINY HISTORIES

■ ■ ■ ■

5
HOUSE OF TRANSPORTATION

The publication date was March 17, 1929, the trip written up in the society pages, Notes of Social Activities in New York and Elsewhere — *The New York Times,* no less. It was bigger than the tight notices of teas, benefits, luncheons, engagements, marriages, excursions — the usual stuff of these pages: *Mr. and Mrs. Walter Ewing Hope of 43 East Seventieth Street sailed yesterday on the* Washington *for a motor trip in Ireland.* Katherine's notice, and she was Katherine now — Tommy mostly buried by time and geography — was distinguished, large, impossible to miss because it included a photograph above the fold and spanned half the page. Pictured on skis on snow-covered Fourth Lake, just near Inlet, she was with the Simmons family, their little daughter, Doris, on a sledge, recovering from polio, too small and weak to ski. The headline read, "When Winter Comes into Its Own in the Adirondacks: Col. Edward A. Simmons of Brooklyn, with His Family and Miss B. Stewart (left), on His Estate at Eagle Bay, Hamilton County." They got the initial wrong, the reporter and the photographer. It had been her fault, but by the time the notice appeared she was all right with that, more than all right with that.

It had been a splendid trip. She'd been treated like a guest. "I was treated like a guest," she told her friends, she told Charles.

And he'd reply, "Of course, you were treated like a guest," with his handsome, thick Boston accent.

And later, when she and Charles were married and had their children, she'd tell her daughter, Winter, "Treated like a guest." And later still, Winter, our mother, would tell us that Grammy had been "Treated like a guest," when asked by Scarlett about the notice that lay beneath glass on Grammy's vanity in Grammy's room — still Grammy's room though she was some fifteen years dead.

We were once again at Rose Hill, helping in the endless task of cleaning the house to prepare it for whatever was next. "Wasn't she always treated well?" Scarlett asked lazily, not giving the notice her full attention, too busy with the job at hand. "They got the initial wrong," I said, taking it from Scarlett. Grammy appeared, flitting across my imagination, her slender arms and hands dressed in black "motoring gloves" that fastened at the wrists with pearls. "They were important people, the Simmons family," Mom said.

"I've never heard of them," Scarlett said, as though that rendered them, in fact, unimportant. With her sassy ski-jump nose and her bouncy curls, her French husband and their impossibly smart and talented brood of four, she was always treated well.

Later still, I would find more copies of the notice in the black box.

At the time, way back in another era of society pages, the notice would have been seen by Banks and Baga, Charles's father and mother, all the way up in Lynn, and by Charles's sisters and the other Brooklyn Hospital nurses and the registry of nurses and even physicians. Katherine would have clipped the notice to send off to Glenna in Nevada, "Just to let you know what I've been up to," and to Pat in California, keeping copies for herself, gluing one to cardboard cut from the Bonwit Teller box that held the gown she had bought for the excursion in case she needed something elegant to wear — saving the notices in duplicate with all of her most important papers. Proof.

Shortly after the invitation, Katherine took the afternoon off to explore possibilities and found herself at Bonwit Teller in front of a mirror in a dress she couldn't quite afford. But it was so pretty in pale red velvet with no waist and no bust and just to the knee where jagged ivory-colored tulle cascaded the rest of the length to the floor, both revealing and hiding her shapely legs. The same tulle peeked just barely from the neck. A cloche hat (that hid her hair) in a deeper red satin accompanied the dress while also daring to contradict it. She bought new shoes as well, kid leather pumps with entwined, jeweled crossbows.

She made calculations, understood what she could give up for a month in order to afford the dress and shoes. They were so fancy and a little less food would help her figure. Part of the calculation was weighing whether she'd need the ensemble at all, but the colonel had repeated, "You're coming as a guest." She understood. It meant she wasn't coming as a nurse, as little Doris's private duty nurse. She wasn't coming as that. Secretly, Katherine hoped the Simmonses would engage another nurse, perhaps a practical nurse, for Doris for the occasion, someone of lesser standing and decidedly not coming as a guest.

Katherine read the society pages. She knew how these excursions worked: a week of adventures and extravagant parties with guests of all variety — the rich, the famous, yes, but also artists, musicians, lawyers, doctors, people who did things. A nurse! She would be slipping into that realm of privilege that churned out desire and instilled longing in less fortunate folk, in smart little columns shored up with advertisements from Bonwit Teller, from Bergdorf Goodman, from the Grande Maison de Blanc, Dobbs the Hatter, Van Cleef & Arpels. Katherine knew each store and where it was located and exactly what it sold, studying the ads as closely as the society notices. All of this luxuriated on the flimsy pages of newspapers, printed, packaged, bundled, chuted, loaded in bays and on docks, into trucks, trains, boats, spreading into the hands of a thousand little beggar boys and from their hands to more hands distributed to reading rooms and taverns, sold on street corners, plopped down on stoops not once but twice a day to be guzzled with morning coffee or an evening aperitif, to be pored over for the latest society news.

It's no wonder then, of course, that when the notice appeared she held it close, folding it into a tight square that she kept pocketed in her uniform. She fingered it often to feel that exhilaration again, touching it, the winning ticket, unfolding it and refolding it until the creases tore and ripped, the entire notice in danger of falling apart, reminding her as she finally glued it to the Bonwit box that she'd made it inside, into the very heart of the system.

Of course, as the salesgirl wrapped up her package, Katherine had no idea she would make the society pages. So, when the time came to surrender her money to the cashier — her savings, her rent, her groceries — a society notice wasn't a part of the equation. Rather, Katherine felt a combination of a nagging financial worry of the spending-too-much variety, and also the soaring sense of exhilaration because she was just like all the other girls shopping at the department store that midday, in their hats and furs and jewels, part of the same social fabric from which they were cut, carelessly, recklessly buying just whatever they pleased. She was one of them. Chin higher. A guest.

Col. Edward A. Simmons had invited Katherine to his camp in the Adirondacks because he was fascinated by the nurse who saved his daughter's life. The Colonel, as he was called, was a multimillionaire, publisher of trade magazines for businesses involved with trains and boats and automobiles, anything that ferried people or commerce: *Railway Age Gazette, Marine Log, American Engineer, The Boiler Maker* — subsidiary companies involved with sawmills, machinery, and tools that expanded from railway supplies to the general exporting of portable sawmills, shingle mills, saw benches, cordwood, and the like to Europe during the war.

Katherine knew the details of his biography. He was easy to read about in the papers, and she wanted to know all about the man who employed her. More than two thousand Simmons machines went to France, helping win battles at Saint-Mihiel and Argonne. He was commissioned lieutenant colonel in the Quartermaster Section of the Officers' Reserve Corps and became regional construction quartermaster in charge of all new army work in and around New York Harbor.

A big, booming man with a voice he controlled as if with a radio volume dial, lowering the volume because he understood the power and fear a strong voice could instill. He wanted to frighten no one. Rather, he was a warm and generous man, robust and tall, carried a permanent smile, and found his pleasure, it seemed, in delighting others. He was clever in finance and advertising, clear on the principle that the message had to be one that was simple and visible — in a spot where it would be seen by those who wanted whatever the message sold. "I'm just a messenger," he often said.

Before the United States entered the war, he helped the British Army, building heavy lathes for turning twenty-four-inch shells. He referred to his empire as The House of Transportation, and with it he became a rich man in the arcane ways of so many rich men. At that intersection of luck and hard work he found himself behind a big mahogany desk on a high floor of the Woolworth Building. And who could have guessed that his desk, his office, his building stood on a cornice overhanging a massive cliff. Rather all anyone could see was the empire stretching as far as the railroads into the distance.

Just a few days before Katherine and the Simmons family made their winter excursion to Fourth Lake, Hoover had taken the oath of office and Simmons had been not too far from his side. Katherine had seen the photograph of him in the paper, standing there with his kind face, his tidy mustache, looking on. The face seemed to belong to her because she knew him, as though she too were on the steps of the capital.

"See, Charles," she had said, showing him the newspaper and pointing to Simmons. "He's the little girl's father, he's the host at Fourth Lake." Charles had smiled his half smile, indulgently, happy that his girl was happy. She had shown the other nurses too. She'd never been this close to something so important.

Katherine had met Colonel Simmons the year before when his daughter, Doris, had been a patient at Brooklyn Hospital, suffering from polio. Katherine had been the attending nurse who, according to Simmons, had saved his daughter's life. She hadn't, of course. Nor had the doctor, Dr. Le Grand Kerr, child specialist in polio among other illnesses. Doris had simply been lucky, one of very few to have nonparalytic polio. But Colonel Simmons gave the credit to Katherine because she was kind and gentle, but also firm with his little girl, not afraid to tell the truth. Most of all she was not afraid of the disease and wasn't worried about catching it and therefore didn't mind being near it. This was not spoken; rather, it was read entirely in her demeanor and actions, in her proximity to the girl. Katherine understood the illness, unlike so many other people (including other nurses), so it did not instill fear in her.

The Simmonses were pale with fear. But what Katherine noticed in them was how it knit them together, his hand on Mrs. Simmons's back, her fingers linked in his other hand, the respect with which they listened to each other ask and answer questions — together somehow larger and more able to fight. The Colonel's love for his wife, there outside the door to the ward that held Doris, was palpable.

Katherine told the family from the beginning that there was hope, described for them a machine that could help if the worst were true. She informed herself and therefore the Simmons family. Up in Boston, back in October, the Drinker respirator had been used on a girl just a little older than Doris. The little girl had been nearly dead as a result of respiratory failure due to poliomyelitis. Less than one minute after being placed in the chamber of the device she was revived. This iron lung, as it was called, could work for Doris too should she need it. Katherine always had ideas. Medicine was her belief. If she'd been born in a different time and into different circumstances, she would have become a doctor.

She was crisp and ironed and all white and starched with her pinafore apron and triangle hat and clean white sturdy shoes, but she wasn't afraid of the mess — of the bedpans, the douches, the sores, the nits, the unsavory thermometer techniques and purgative enemas, the colonic irrigations, the dressing of wounds after massive surgeries. She wasn't afraid of anything, of the violence the human body could endure. The things she had seen — almost beautiful in their horror, astonishing in the ability of a body to mend. No, she wasn't afraid of death, of her own or anyone else's. And for all this she was revered and sought. She faced the conditions of her work with courage and a smile, embraced the order of routine and rule. Parents, doctors, patients — they all credited her with saving lives. And so she'd come up the ranks of Brooklyn Hospital's Nursing Center — started by the civic-minded women of the Fruit and Flower Mission — through probation and capping (was capped ceremoniously by Rev. Howard Dean French of the Congregational Church of Pilgrims) and finally, graduation, earning her whites, the two black stripes to adorn her cap, and a gold pin from Tiffany's emblazoned with The Brooklyn Hospital Training School for Nurses.

The first thing she did upon being capped was send Pat back her high school diploma, spending precious savings to frame it so Pat could hang the diploma on a wall in her house. In the accompanying note, Katherine thanked her sister and told her again how proud she was of her. As talented as Katherine was at peering into the horrors that could be made of the human body, she was not skilled at seeing the possibility of Pat's hurt. Katherine, she preferred moving forward.

Pat wrote back, a brief note updating Katherine on their mother, who was seeking a degree at Pepperdine, a university in Los Angeles, in the summers, living with the family, teaching in remote parts of Nevada during the year. She was working now at a school filled with the children of Basque sheepherders. Somewhere along the way, she had left the man she married in Idaho. Pat signed off generically, letting Katherine know that they were all very well, baby Slim was thriving. She never mentioned the diploma. Her cursive was neat, her signature large: Pat. The short name stabbed Katherine.

Katherine had hoped that returning the

diploma would set her free from the nagging sense of obligation, release her from the feeling that would appear now and again to suggest her life was borrowed, that as hard as she had worked, it was not quite hers — the feeling festering like a stubborn splinter. There was also a large part of Katherine that simply felt clever, the side of her seasoned in the art of justification — the same girl who had trapped coyotes and begged from prostitutes. Obstacles were to be navigated. This ability is what also made her an excellent nurse, an accomplishment that she alone had achieved. But then the truth would taunt her. It wasn't just the borrowed identity; it was also the fact behind the need for the loan, that she hadn't gone to high school. Her mother hadn't gone to college and lied about it across her years in Montana, until the lie caught up with her. So from time to time, Katherine felt that her loan was like a mortgage that could never be entirely repaid. And it was her beautiful little sister who held the deed. All the way across the country, out there in California, her dreams long since devoured by fear, leaving her with little money in a little house flattened beneath the dry, oppressive sun, with a young son and a cop husband who quit going to school after the third grade. Katherine couldn't help but wonder, as she imagined Pat wondered too, would things have gone differently for Pat had she been the one to come to New York?

Katherine put away those thoughts and busied herself with her present. She was a registered nurse, continually in demand because of her discipline and courage. She wore her Tiffany pin with pride. She was the subject of a network that spread word of her talents from doctor to doctor to wealthy patrons, which translated into more admirers seeking advantage with her for her time. They lavished her with presents and offerings and solicitations. A good nurse was hard to find, so when she was discovered, she was prized, bought quietly with a slightly higher wage, a lovely little keepsake, a dinner out for her and Charles, theater tickets.

A. T. Farrell from Escanaba, Michigan, was a commercial artist for George B. Ethridge, specialist in national advertising campaigns and architect of the familiar Bon Ami pictures. He had fallen in love with Katherine, his private duty nurse. It didn't matter that he was married, that he was twice her age, that he was dying. A broken femur led to the discovery of bone cancer. Katherine encouraged him to keep working, keep drawing. She inhabited his imagination with her strength and determination, her seductive beauty. He asked her to pose, sitting on the floor of his studio, her dress inching up her thigh just enough to reveal the garter. She knew what she was doing, with her cocked smile and long legs; she was making him feel young again, alive again. The charcoal rendering was another expression of his gratitude for all that she gave to him. The image rendered her a daring beauty, which both made her blush and made her proud, so it too was carefully carried forward until it eventually settled between the pages of a Winslow Homer art book, hiding there to be found by my cousin, Uncle Jet's son, and that he used as the cover art for a video he made of Grammy speaking about her life on the occasion of her ninety-seventh birthday. "A frisson," Grammy said to the camera.

A. T. Farrell gave her as well a work of his art, the painting of the clock tower in Avignon, a watercolor in gentle Provençal hues, valued at $150 by the Society of Illustrators. It was Katherine's most valued and valuable possession; she hung it in her bedroom, above her bed. The clock tower, the cobblestoned streetscape of the faraway town, reminded Katherine to dream, and then to realize.

The Simmons family hired Katherine when Doris was finally brought home to their mansion in Ditmas Park. For her efforts, for saving little Doris's life, they gave her a Malle Fleurs, a flower box from Louise Vuitton, filled with fresh-cut roses. The little trunk was an exact miniature replica of the bigger versions used for trips across the Atlantic and other exotic travels, and had been given to the Simmonses by the Vuitton boutique as a gesture of appreciation for their good business. Katherine kept it on her windowsill, filling it with fresh flowers whenever she could afford them.

She would stand by Doris's four-poster bed in her square room with bay windows overlooking other mansions, a whole wide street of them surrounded by many trees, Colonial Revivals, windows illuminated in the winter darkness. Listening to the sounds from the street, automobiles driving by, bells of a distant church, Katherine encouraged Doris first to stretch her limbs, guiding them through rotations, then to take steps. Doris wanted to surrender to weakness, her small-girl body folding back into the full softness of the bed. Katherine would take her arms and right her, helping her to stand very tall and very straight, encouraging her to take the steps required to cross

244

the vast wooly carpet to the window.

"You are a strong girl, Doris. Persist. Come now." Nothing much had been asked of Doris in her short life. Katherine could see that just by stepping across the threshold of their corner property: the swirling staircase and high ceilings, the polished floors, the well-upholstered world busy with servants. Katherine, known here as Nurse Stewart, stood tall and imposing before the fragile big-eyed girl: one bit fear and one bit admiration. Doris did as she was told; she stepped and stepped again, all spindly leg and elbow, like a cricket, making her way from the soft eiderdown to the window.

Sometimes Colonel Simmons watched from the door, the room warmed by the soft lemon glow of electric lights. Katherine spoke calmly and clearly, annunciating each word. "Now, Doris, do not use tiptoes. Place the entire sole of your foot on the floor. One small step after the next. Just one at a time." And in this way, Katherine led Doris back toward strength under the benevolent gaze of the Colonel in the doorframe. Katherine enjoyed the paternal gaze. She felt worthwhile, purposeful. This family exuded kindness, led by the Colonel and his sturdy wife, Ida. In their orbit, Katherine felt the magnetic pull of all she had ever longed for, stirring visions of the family she wanted to create, almost as if it were a tableaux, a little doll's house she could populate and design. The exact opposite of the immigrant train tableaux she had studied as a child in Montana, families that could hardly speak English, shedding their belongings because they were too heavy to carry, not enough room in the hack, the slow misery of those lives struggling to make something for themselves out there — how they had terrified her.

When she was with the Simmons family, the idea of happy domesticity did not feel like a dream, but utterly plausible. Seeing Doris struggle and then flop onto the bed with proud exhaustion, watching the down bloom up around her figure, hearing the sisters down the hall, Aline at the piano practicing Chopin over and again — it was as though Katherine had stepped inside a music box smack in the center of the universe.

Observed by the Colonel, Katherine was self-conscious too, though she pretended not to be, pretended simply to be herself, quietly showcasing her education in the careful articulation of her words. Registered nurses were well-bred ladies from elite circles. She posed there in all her crisp cappedness, lording her rank (if even only for herself) over the dime-a-dozen practical nurses desperate to compete for her position, coming in clusters to the doors of the hospital asking for work, to the doors of the homes of the wealthy known for having an infirm adult or a sick child. One had come to the Simmons's door just the other day. They could smell sickness like a hungry cat. They were uneducated, low class, poor scholarship, bad values, disreputable behavior, illegal pregnancies and the like, drunk to the vomiting point, cigarette smokers. Beneath the Colonel's gaze Katherine felt she was being read, and she wanted to control the words of that text.

Katherine maneuvered therefore with extra commitment to refined grace, taking Doris's hand: "Come now. No rest for the weary." Katherine knew how to manipulate, how to sell herself, knew her currency, her value and what enhanced it, and knew wealthy people had a way of buying what they pleased, so she wanted to be pleasing — just as she had been while posing for A. T. Farrell. She was for sale, discreetly. That's how it worked, and she knew what she was selling: fearless, intelligent authority. She too was at an intersection of determination and hard work that perched her at the window overlooking New York society. When Simmons said, "We're going to Fourth Lake, to Inlet for the week, and we want you to come with us, as our guest," announcing this to Katherine, standing in Doris's doorway, she was both surprised and prepared, as if this were the natural next step for her: the invitation made a certain inevitable sense.

They left on Friday morning, early from Grand Central Station in a private car belonging to a friend and Fourth Lake neighbor, Oliver Murray Edwards, a businessman as well — inventor and manufacturer who figured out a design for windows that opened and closed in rail cars, a detail that earned him fabulous wealth. Not only was the car private, opulent — varnished mahogany and velvet and crystal, like a living room, with servants — his standing allowed him use of private tracks straight into Saranac Lake, tracks once laid for Rockefellers back before the war. Om, as he was called (first initials became pet names of these great men, Katherine noted), lived in Syracuse so was not on the train this bright, clear winter morning.

In his car, instead, were the three Simmons girls, bundled in furs and kilts, Colonel and Mrs. Simmons, and the journalist and photographer come to report for those society pages to see how the Simmons family got along in the Adirondacks in the winter. Their names were Burton Keep and Angus Smith. A little rough around the edges with threads coming from hems and well-worn gloves, carpetbags for luggage — goods that endured and were not easily replaced. Taking them in, Katherine could see clearly the divot — sharp, steep, angular — between the journalists and the Simmons family, with herself bobbing somewhere in the middle.

But the journalist and the photographer were jolly enough and conversational, speaking about the news, full up with Al Capone and the inauguration and the Mexican rebel fiasco. Lindbergh was down in Mexico visiting his fiancée and trying to be the hero, opening up new communication routes to Texas and also vacationing in Cuernavaca. Katherine wondered, with all the news, if there wasn't somewhere better for Keep and Smith to be than here on this train, doing magic tricks now for the girls, coins coming from ears and scarves from their mouths. They were young and hungry, given the assignment, Katherine imagined, because they didn't mind being performing seals. She smelled a whiff of desperation on them too, veneered by the obligation of their job: to observe. They were here to observe the patterns and behaviors of the wealthy and then to report back for everyone else. For Katherine, the pair formed two enormous eyes. A new thought occurred to her: she wondered why anyone in the Simmons's position would agree to have journalists along.

The younger two girls were giddy with the attention, even Doris in pale lethargy, although attention seemed to be something they took for granted. The oldest, Aline, offered only a long-distance stare and mature concentration that distinguished her, at fourteen, as too old for all this.

Katherine, referred to not as Katherine and not as Nurse Stewart, but rather as Miss Stewart on this excursion, pinched herself from time to time just to be certain she was really here, looking around the private varnish, a mansionette on wheels, replete with a library thick with books. Ladies from long ago came to mind, stepping into and off of the Pullman cars in Chicago and St. Paul, fur trimmed and hatted, carrying nothing because it was all carried for them.

At the entrance to the terminal, she had been greeted by a red-capped porter. He had taken her bag so she too had been relieved of the weight and nuisance of luggage. She thought of her new dress, tucked away in her bag. The porter escorted her to the hidden tracks of the waiting train, passing other passengers carrying their heavy loads beneath the vaulted dome of Grand Central, raining sunbeams.

Charles had driven her to the station in his coupe, an elegant ride with a jump seat that they took to the country, with friends piling in for summer picnics with contraband wine. The tall city rose as she and Charles drove through — dashing, kind-hearted Charles, who'd honk thrice beneath her boardinghouse window to let her know he had arrived and she'd descend and they'd drive across the city to see what new buildings had gone up — the Woolworth, the Graybar, the Chenin, Metropolitan Life, Manhattan Bank, General Motors, the Chrysler. They rose and rose, forty, fifty stories tall. Scaffolds everywhere, a skyscrapered world with zeppelins flying above and trains soaring below and double-decker buses and taxis and automobiles that swarmed like flies. A few leftover horse-drawn carts dodged people rushing here and there. The city pulsed and she and Charles would see it all.

"The sky's the limit," Charles said.

Katherine had met Charles at a New Year's Eve party at a friend's apartment, a fellow nurse. The place was packed with nurses and businessmen. The friend, Suzanne, petite and pretty and shy with a look of expectation that things should be done for her that she couldn't do for herself, had her eye on Charles, had taken Katherine by the hand, led her into the living room where a pack of men stood smoking. "There's one man in this room I find attractive," Suzanne had said, pinching her lips, holding Katherine with expectant eyes. Suzanne wore pearl earrings; her family was from Connecticut, and she was precisely who she claimed to be, no hidden secrets. Katherine scanned the room. And there he was, Charles, the only man worth noting, tall and slender with dark hair and big brown eyes. Katherine's first intention was to speak to him on Suzanne's behalf, ignite conversation, and then weave in Suzanne. Katherine went to him, poured him some more whiskey, and began asking soft questions that got to the bottom of him — from Boston, an aspiring engineer for Western Union, in New York for four years, two much older sisters. His accent dazzled her; she'd never heard anything quite like it. His family were shoemakers, last name Brown. As a child, he'd posed for the famous ad for the Buster Brown Shoe Company, so of course she thought, assumed even, that his family was the Browns of Buster Brown, but she didn't feel it was polite of her to ask. Eventually for Grammy, it wouldn't matter that in fact they were not the Browns of Buster Brown, but the Browns of Lynn, Massachusetts. The fact that he'd been the model for the ad made him proximate enough to the company to stake her claim. "If I don't like something the way it is," she'd say to us, old and wise, a wisdom possessed of her own logic, "I simply say it how I would like it to be."

Soon Charles was asking her about her, and Montana unspooled — filled with half-truths and lies. Every part of his attention was trained on her. Suzanne vanished into the woodwork and so did the other men and nurses. At midnight Charles kissed Katherine beneath the mistletoe hanging from the chandelier. They left together, walking through the cold night until dawn. Suzanne never spoke to Katherine again.

And now, a year on, they were still young, still in love, had no obligations other than their work, which they both found utterly fulfilling. Charles, as an engineer's assistant for Western Union, conducted line and office inspections, working on the varioplex, which would enable a single wire to carry seventy-two transmissions, thirty-six in each direction — the future. The couple watched the Western Union Building go up at 60 Hudson. They sailed past the great mansions of Millionaire's Row on Riverside Drive. The Paramount Building. The Savoy Plaza. The Ritz Tower. The Flatiron. Through the lights of Times Square. Down the corridor of Broadway with remnants of Amelia Earhart's ticker tape fluttering in their hair. Chinese dragons and Macy's Christmas Parade and a seaside jaunt for a wild ride on the Cyclone. Katherine did not like it at all; it made her stomach jump, but she went back for more because of Charles, because Charles wanted to. She loved that she did not like it, loved the way it made her stomach feel, loved clutching Charles close, the sense that he could protect her, the speed, as if galloping on the fastest, most dangerous horse. Through the Holland Tunnel to New Jersey. Across the Brooklyn Bridge on bicycles. Those sunny Manhattan skies. Jazz at the Savoy and the Cotton Club. The Tiller Girls, in from England, at Madison Square Garden.

It was a particular moment, a time, when

everything seemed possible, as easy to attain as all the steel climbing into the sky.

Mother, Katherine wrote to Glenna in Nevada, an exercise she had adopted from her first days in New York. *We met a magician last night at the Palm Court. Before the evening was up he had all the ladies' diamonds. He calls himself a Scientific Palmist.* It wasn't true. But Katherine had read about him, Dr. Sydney Ross, how he entertained millionaires, dazzled celebrities, stumped politicians at the Peacock Alley Lounge at the Waldorf-Astoria. In one way or another, Katherine and Charles made the city theirs.

On the cards to her mother, she signed off, *Your loving daughter.* With her sister, she signed off, *Your loving sister.* She never signed off Tommy, or Katherine.

Nights, Charles would drop her off. Gently, gently he'd kiss her. Gently, gently she'd lean into him and he'd lift her chin to his and look straight and deep into her green eyes. "Who are you, Katherine Stewart?" he had asked on a recent night, with his thick Boston accent. Of course, he knew she had grown up in Montana, that she had a sister named Pat, that she came east for nursing school, that her father worked for the railroads, that her mother managed their home. He did not know of her parents' divorce, that her mother had left her father because of an affair, taking the girls to Montana, that she had hunted coyotes for their pelts, begged from whores, that Katherine had raised Pat, that Katherine had once had a different name. Charles knew none of that. Sometimes she wished she could just tell him, release herself in a burst of confession. But then she pressed the unwanted fact deeper down inside her, as if it could be absorbed and incorporated by her will. After a year of courtship, the omission felt very much like a lie, a lie encased in her assumed name. She saw Suzanne in front of her, her hopeful expectation: "There's one man in this room."

Charles's parents, Banks and Baga, came to the city to visit Charles, wrapped in fur and cashmere. They were an old, distinguished family up in Lynn, could count back the generations they'd been on these shores: eleven. In the backyard of Baga's girlhood home, Breed's Pasture, the Battle of Bunker Hill had been fought. Charles was a quiet, observant type. Katherine was a talker, energetic and unafraid, but capable of revealing very little. "There's more to you than I know right now," he said. But he loved her because she was a mystery and a challenge and because she had an unstoppable sense of adventure and she never said no. He loved the subtlety of her mind, her imagination fueled by fearless desire, and that made him want to be cared for and cured and held by her, made him want to watch her evolve and transform. There was something about her, active like a yeast or a blossom, swelling before his eyes. He told her all of this, and she could feel it, his love coming from his pulse, consistent and tender. Sometimes she was afraid, wondered what it would mean to him if he knew she wasn't Katherine. But then she would swat away that truth and remind herself of all the reasons she was Katherine. She would think about her sister in Los Angeles, grateful for her own good fortune while also feeling a tug of doubt and sorrow.

"You're my dream," Charles liked to say to her. "I found my dream." Sometimes she was afraid of love, of the unfamiliar landscape.

Katherine had wanted Colonel and Mrs. Simmons to see Charles drop her off in his coupe, but of course, the family wasn't on the street outside Grand Central Station. Apart from the fact of Charles and her profession, they knew nothing of her life.

She was careful to curate the image of the well-bred, educated lady who devoured the most current authors, always a novel in her pocketbook: Wodehouse, Fitzgerald, Dos Passos, Wharton, Kafka, Wolfe, Faulkner, Hemingway. Privately, and for reasons of etiquette, she read Mrs. Beeton and also Miss Manners so she wouldn't make a mistake with the wrong gloves or the wrong fork or the wrong address to a given person.

Now here she was in this car with a society family trailed by their very own press entourage — well, perhaps not quite an entourage, but trailed all the same. As the trip unfurled before her, she felt she could be whoever she pleased. Yes, she pinched herself. "I am here," she whispered.

The Simmons girls held forth, each in her own particular sister way: Aline aloof and distant; Betty prurient and keen, interested in cross-examining Katherine on the gory details of nursing. "Please, not the bedpans. The wounds." Lethargic Doris studied her older sisters to understand how the big-girl world worked. The girls were a bouquet, variations on a theme, echoing each other, much handsomer than their parents, but they were not inextricably intertwined as she and Pat had been. They, rather, were together but independent — able to define themselves for themselves with confidence, understanding that there was a vast, soft cushion to catch them should they fall. They mesmerized Katherine. She appreciated the clean lines of their lives. It made sense that Betty wanted a view of the ugly science.

The Colonel encouraged the prurience of his middle daughter, keen to her curiosity, and every so often he would look up from his paper and peer above the rim of his readers to remind Betty that Miss Stewart saved lives. "She saves lives," he said proudly. "She saves lives."

"I can tell you this," Katherine said to the little girl, holding Betty with her eyes. "Just the other day I was assisting in surgery with one of our doctors, cleaning a gash in the arm of a homeless man. He had live maggots in the wound. I had to pick them out one by one with tweezers."

"That's just awful," Betty said, and asked, "How could you tell they were alive?"

"Because they moved," Katherine answered. "They were swimming in the wound as if it were a pond."

The train jostled and lulled Katherine as the journalists entertained, as Colonel and Mrs. Simmons read their newspapers and kept delighted eyes on the scene that their intelligence and ingenuity had created.

The group was served luncheon by the steward and his white-gloved men with their service of sterling, bone China, linen, chatting about the Mexican rebels and their fight for free elections. Burton Keep held forth on the subject with interjections from the Colonel about the cost of standing up for a cause. It wasn't entirely clear to Katherine if they supported the Catholics or the secularists. Mrs. Simmons added her two bits about Anne Morrow, the daughter of the U.S. ambassador to Mexico, falling for Lindbergh.

"Wait and see," Keep said. "It'll be Morrow who brokers peace."

With the curtains raised, the car was all glass. Fir trees crowded down from the snow-whitened mountains, standing at attention at the edge of the tracks as if to greet the private varnish of Om Edwards.

The afternoon passed, turning to dusk when they arrived. Two chauffeured cars met them and drove them a distance on paved roads. When the roads ended, horse-drawn sledges swept them the rest of the way through deep woods to Fourth Lake and the Albedor.

The Albedor, the Colonel explained, was named for Aline, Betty, and Doris because it had been constructed for their pleasure. The great camp spanned a stone ledge perched above the lake. The house had three floors with a staircase centerpiece, twelve bedrooms all with en suite bathrooms and terraces and fireplaces, the basement with its boiler room and wine cellar with over three hundred bottles of wine, Prohibition be damned! There were many rooms for entertaining in different modes — with books, music, drinks, food. The vast living room had a ten-foot-wide fireplace constructed from thirteen hand-hammered stones that were once part of a very large boulder retrieved from the grounds. The mantel alone weighed twelve tons.

The grounds included more than a hundred acres with twelve other buildings for boats and cars and caretakers and pumps and an electric generator and three life-sized playhouses for the girls with bedrooms and dressing rooms and bathrooms and space and furniture enough to entertain adults if they chose. One of the buildings housed a play store that sold miniature replicas of national brand products, and when the girls played they used real cash for their pretend purchases, secured in real cash registers stuffed, of course, with more real cash.

When the party arrived, emerging from

the dark woods of a cold northern night, it seemed, illuminated as it was, that the Albedor was a small city. No expense had been spared. Seventy men had worked for two solid years, blasting and excavating and raising and installing and polishing and employing — 5.5 miles of conduit, 5 tons of dynamite, 588 tons of electric wire that could stretch out for 16 miles, 145 tons of slate for the roofs, 407,729 board feet of lumber, western spruce for the clapboard, Douglas fir for the supporting beams, native stone for the foundation. Throughout the lodge, the wood ceiling and wall paneling was hand rubbed to a satin-smooth finish. Colonel Simmons described the construction for Katherine and the journalists, delighting in the details. He was proud, but he wasn't boasting. Rather it seemed he was sort of amazed that he had been able to accomplish such a feat.

There was a laundry house, an icehouse, a summer kitchen. The top floor of the boathouse had a stage with curtains perched above a slippery dance floor. "I made this all for my girls," the Colonel said. Like those daughters of Montana railroaders — Lorraine, Edina, Mildred, Ada, Beatrice — girls whose fathers named entire towns for them. Ghost towns now, dust in the desert. Here the Albedor gleamed, alive on frozen shores.

Uniformed servants greeted them, a butler and attendants who showed the guests to their rooms so they could freshen up before dinner. They were told to ask for anything, anything at all. The girls ran around, jumping into the arms of the staff and planting kisses on them. Katherine was introduced around, warm hands and cheeks, nothing formal. All very familiar, Katherine observed.

That evening, late, from her balcony, cleaned of the snow, she sat in a cushioned chair and watched the full moon's intrepid glide above the white expanse of lake.

They stayed just shy of a week. A blur of parties and dinners and dancing and skiing and skating on the lake, a bonfire with meat on skewers, winter picnics, outings with the girls, a magic show performed on the boathouse stage by the journalists, a palm reader in for the afternoon from Lake Placid, a massage, tea daily, breakfasts in bed.

"What would you like, miss?" asked the pretty girl with her white apron who came to turn down the bed. "For breakfast, miss, in the morning?" The fire crackled and the room was bright even if it was late, the flames smarting in the frost on the windowpanes. The maid picked things up and folded them and straightened and stabbed at the fire, asked if Miss would like another log.

"Eggs," Katherine said.

"Any particular way, Miss Stewart?"

"Poached would be lovely. Thank you."

"Coffee or tea?"

"Coffee."

"The New York Times?"

"Yes."

And it appeared as if by magic, carried in the hands of another maid, first thing in the morning, the big silver tray floating across the room to settle on Katherine's fluffy bed.

"Good morning, Miss Stewart." A fire was laid and lit, then Katherine was left undisturbed to enjoy breakfast, the tray arranged with jams and honeys and breads and the two poached eggs.

There was French toast too and always bacon, waffles, sausage, Turkish coffee with thick clotted cream, always a different exotic juice — kumquat or kiwi or persimmon. She didn't miss Charles, not really. Rather she found herself calculating: the items in the room alone added up to more than she had earned in all the years she had worked; could there ever be enough money to stop thinking about money; could a life like this ever be hers? What if she were a daughter of this world? How would it feel? She sat up higher in her bed, feeling the soft ironed smoothness of the sheets against her thighs, dabbing at her runny eggs with the sourdough toast, buttered with butter churned here at the estate, a creamy sweet freshness. She sipped coffee upon which the clotted cream floated, melting islands. Katherine began to feel a subtle urgency, until she laughed at herself and took a deep breath and put away excessive desire. I'm fortunate to be away, is all, she thought. Away from the stench of her work, from the hospital and the hired-out jobs, the frantic busy pace of the streets. And with that she finished her breakfast and rose to dress, leaving her robe on the floor simply to feel what it was like to have someone else care for your carelessness.

Each day at Albedor would bring both routine and surprise, and the combination made leaving the room in the morning easy. First, she'd encounter Ida, shuffling around in wool sweaters and kilt, scarf around neck, managing the staff and the forthcoming parties and their menus, the excursions. Ida had an easy and thoughtful authority, always with one eye to making sure her guests had entirely what they needed and the other to making all systems run smoothly. Katherine kept waiting to feel like the hired private duty nurse, for the girls to treat her as such, but it did not happen.

Ida was no different, of course, with the journalists. They too were treated as guests. Katherine thought of them luxuriating in their beds with their breakfasts just as she had. The thought annoyed her. When they appeared, they were jolly and boisterous, filled with news about what they'd heard and seen in the night — sounds of wildlife and moonbeams on the silver lake. Ida would kiss Katherine on the cheek and ask if she'd had a good sleep, a hearty breakfast. Then the girls would slip in, then the Colonel, arranging with the journalists logistics of camera equipment for the day's outing.

Though the photographer, Burton Keep, took many photographs that week, the one that would end up in *The New York Times* was taken on one of the exercise outings, the first actually. How casual it had all been. The group was on the lake on skis in their plaid ski skirts and hats and gloves and jazzy patterned woolen leggings when Angus Smith arranged them for the picture. Katherine had stood apart at first, not wanting to intrude, but the Colonel had insisted Katherine join the family and so she had. She was pretending that she knew what she was doing on the skis. She'd ridden wild horses, she could maneuver skis — the gentle push slip of it, stepping and gliding. She was a strong woman. The photographer told Katherine where to stand and she maneuvered into position on the skis, at one side of the family. Betty was nearly hidden on the sledge behind a smiling Doris. Ida's gaze was cast downward. Katherine imagined her pondering fortune and life's ridiculous bounty. Aline looked out, intense and curious, eyes trained on the photographer, who hid behind his cape. And the Colonel, with his kind half smile, seemed to welcome them all into the warmth of his family. And so the family and Katherine were frozen in the image, preserved on Fourth Lake.

Then they released the pose. Keep packed up his equipment. As he secured his camera in its traveling case, Angus Smith, the writer, asked Katherine for her name. Just a formality. He knew her as Miss Stewart and had intuited her first name to be Katherine, though she was mostly referred to as Miss Stewart. He asked simply, "What's your legal name?" He stood up and came close to her, a tall man. Something about his approach and the use of the word legal caught her suddenly off guard. He saw her hesitate, explained again he needed the name for the paper, in case her picture was printed in its pages. A normal enough question, easy to answer, but she was caught on legal, the word itself. Suddenly, she hated the journalist. Why was he annoying her? In all the years of being Katherine she had never been asked for her legal name.

It was a warmish day for these parts. The group came apart, Ida beginning to pull Doris on the sled, the Colonel answering a question of Burton Keep's, the other two sisters making off fast on their skis across the virgin snow. "*s-t-e-w-a-r-t,* correct?" Angus Smith had a notepad now, had taken it from the pocket of his coat. He held a sharpened pencil. In this instant, she felt overwhelmed by the unfamiliar, clear prick of fear — small, sharp, persistent. She tried to regain her composure. The Colonel looked over at her and then turned back to the photographer. She wondered if he'd noticed her hesitation.

"The first initial is fine," Smith said.

"*T,*" she said. Many things soared across her mind: the good fortune of being here and then perhaps in the society pages. But with the high came the low: who would see these pages, and if someone from the old life saw her what would they make of *K* as her first initial? So she said *"T,"* but Smith heard *"B"* and repeated the letter. She reverberated. That burst dam of the cliché, one untruth unfurling another and yet another, catapulting forward until she lay bare and exposed in *The New York Times*. Lies always catch you, that's what they say. Later, she wished she had stuck with *T* or even with *K,* finding easily a million explanations for each. Yet in the moment she was caught in the lie, caught by her own self, caught off guard, but with an audience. Her lie snagged her on the frozen shores of Fourth Lake, one simple letter. A lie she didn't think of as a lie, never had. More, it was an alternative truth. She'd swapped lives with her sister. That was all. Even so she saw for an instant — the way our imaginations can do — her sister, now Pat, the beautiful girl with the sausage curls and the radiant blue eyes, like a dead animal by the side of a road, sacrifice to progress.

Keep was a handsome man, tall with black hair, a strong jaw, though his nose was unfortunate — bulbous and red and out of place, as though it had been pasted to his face by mistake. *"B?"* he asked again, holding her with his eyes, stern and accusing even if they weren't.

"B," Katherine confirmed, believing that an initial could be clearly perceived as a mistake by both her past and her present if she were fortunate enough to land in the society pages at all. The exchange took no more than a minute — but it was one of those minutes that can grow into a complete lifetime, pushing backward and forward, spanning the entire arc. Her cheeks burned.

"And so, we're off," the Colonel said, sliding his skis into gear and commanding Katherine to follow. She did, leaving the journalist and the photographer and the awkward exchange behind, hoping it had registered only for herself.

She wore the red velvet gown, her hair carefully shingled with finger waves beneath the cloche hat, to the party at the Edwardses' camp, PAOWNYC — pronounced *pownick,* named for the railroads Oliver Murray Edwards was most attached to and that had made him the most money: Pennsylvania, Ohio Western, New York. Her new shoes, lipstick, perfume, long-ago pearls given to her by Glenna and that before that had belonged to her grandmother, Laura Ann Meyer. She felt like a Norwegian princess, perhaps as close as she'd ever get to Thelma, riding through the woods in the horse-drawn sledge, the forest silhouetted in dusk, branches coated in snow. She wore a borrowed fur from Ida, after panicking that she didn't have a proper coat for the outfit. She hadn't said a word, but Ida had intuited and offered one of hers, telling Katherine the fur was better for the cold. "And what a stunning dress, my dear."

They approached the Edwardses' camp, on a piece of land jutting into the lake from which you could see Dollar and Cedar Islands floating in the Fulton Chain of Lakes. The Edwardses had opened up the house for the occasion, bringing up ice blocks from the lake and logs from their wood lot out near Browns Tract Road, importing the army of servants from Syracuse, bringing even Himmie, the rhesus monkey, because he was fond of his Fourth Lake cabin and always entertaining.

"A rhesus monkey?" Burton Keep asked, the five of them snug with a blanket draping their laps and legs. Keep was trying to be dressed up in a ready-to-wear suit and tie, his lanky frame bouncing slightly with the movement of the sledge.

"They do it once a year, nothing spared," Ida said. A winter party, the most lavish of the week. Anticipation stirred in Katherine, building from the idle chat at lunch between Ida, the Colonel, and the journalists, both of whom seemed all-knowing about the society encountered here, the information a form of currency that bought them intimate entrance to the conversation. They filled Katherine in on the Edwardses. The pair descended from competing kid glove manufacturers, their fathers understanding the fine art of stretching deer hide. "Josephine's a great beauty. You'll notice her immediately." And Om with his train gadgets in trains all across the world, manufacturing money like a Carnegie. Wisps of conversation floated around, the words held in their warm breath as it met the cold evening.

They arrived to music and dancing, elegant people dressed lightly, as though it were summer, polished toenails peeking from sandals, emerging from the dark and silent woods to converge on the camp. Everyone looked at once singular and familiar, fame that couldn't immediately be identified so their faces seemed to be those of old friends. The Colonel's group dispersed, sucked off in different directions, until Katherine found herself alone, watching couples in conversation, wondering how to interject herself, how not to feel awkward. Men in black suits and white shirts and white gloves carried glasses of wine and champagne, passing them to the guests. She helped herself and took a sip and turned to the pair standing next to her, two old men with matching silver mustaches, and introduced herself, *Katherine Stewart,* offering them her hand. She was not afraid of people. She was not afraid. Rather something came over, a sense of opportunity, of daring. She wanted to meet the people in the room. She wanted them to have conversations with her, know her, be dazzled by her just as she was by them.

She kept the conversations light and moved easily from the men to a pair of women who reminded her of lilies, to another set of men, stern looking, talking about the stock market and the blessed gains, offering wisdom and advice, to yet another set of men engaged with Keep and Smith about *The New York Times.* Always she offered her name and her hand and *Pleased to meet you.* The further into the party she went, the more confident she became, until she was having fun, talking about herself: she was a guest of the Colonel's, staying at the Albedor for the week to ski and toboggan, up from New York — *winter in the Adirondacks is a charm;* she was from Montana, her father a railroad executive who worked on the transcontinental back when she was a girl, not entirely untrue. She knew to keep her details vague on facts and specific on description: she went to school in Butte and then Helena in the booming days of copper in which her mother's family was involved. Words like *involved* were wonderfully vague and promising at the same time.

Once the first lie came, the others tumbled out easily, part of the conversation, part of the narrative that built her up right there in the Edwardses' living room, turned her into a young woman of western privilege who came east for her education, engaging others in western speculation and western envy: *I've always dreamed of visiting the parks. How is Yellowstone, really? Is it all that they say?*

Yes, she was a nurse, but not for money. That remained unsaid, of course, but clearly implied. And she was good too at interviewing, plucking out distinguishing facts, who'd been imported for which entertainment, knowing that people love to talk about themselves, knowing too to steer conversations with curiosity and questions. Conversations fluttered across the room, moving and colliding, careening from stocks to talents to introductions. Norma Talmadge was surrounded by sycophants, feeding off her recent separation from Schenck after she fell for her leading man, Gilbert Roland. But Schenck wouldn't give her a divorce because it would hurt the value of their production company, thriving despite her slump. But she was most famous these days for accidentally stepping into wet cement outside Grauman's Chinese Theater, a trend rapidly copied by other stars. Everyone in Hollywood was stepping in cement.

Josephine stood out indeed, gliding into the frame, silver haired and glamorous, flitting from guest to guest, offering herself up equally. "Call me Josephine," she said to Katherine, extending her long-fingered hand. "You came in our car," she said. "Isn't it fun?" She knew exactly who Katherine was. "You're a nurse, friend of the Colonel's." She asked about Katherine's Albedor visit and if she liked the winter camps and the Adirondacks. Katherine noted just how much beauty surrounded her.

"And I hear you have the most handsome, most delightful beau. His name?" she demanded in that way of the entitled, like any information they wanted was their right.

"Charles Brown," Katherine obediently answered.

"His line?"

"Western Union engineer."

"His family's?"

"Shoes."

"Brown. Of course, as in Buster." This was not a question, but a statement — as if there could be only one shoemaker named Brown.

"In fact," answered Katherine.

"I know your hidden talent," Josephine continued, pulling Katherine toward her and then lifting Katherine's hands to admire them. Josephine's black dress shimmered with fringe. A serpentine bangle snaked her arm. Her rhesus monkey snuck through the crowd to whimper at her feet, looking up to her with narrow, expectant eyes. "Meet Katherine," Josephine said to the monkey. The monkey extended its hand. Katherine took it, gnarly and hard and small. Josephine tossed a grape into the air and the monkey caught it in its mouth.

"Our guest," the Colonel said, appearing from the crowd.

"He always brings the most divine guests," Josephine said. "You're a nurse and you save lives. What a find, Eddie."

That's how they moved, from party to party across the week, from camp to camp, everyone bringing whoever was visiting. In New York, they didn't do that, but here it was the nature and the entertainment. And part of the sport was the rarity of the guest. "We've never had a nurse. What a find."

Dear Mother, and she concocted in her head yet another postcard. *Tonight spent with Alice Brady and Norma Talmadge — more beautiful in person with her bob of brown curls. You'd enjoy them. So easy to talk to. Really, all people want is to be asked about themselves. — Your loving daughter*

She felt stunning in her dress, worth every penny she couldn't afford. Katherine wanted to get back to New York and start her life again, and at the same time she never wanted this excursion to end. The dull lights, the candles, the bounty and beauty — Rosenthal china and Orrefors crystal, Tiffany silver and candelabras and lamps, speed and shock and glamour and the swelling explosive quality, all of them hurtling forward in their bejeweled and talented lives. In the middle of all this, in the very center, she stood, explaining to someone about copper valuations, explaining to another the failures of dry farming technique, and yet another the sensation caused by the Enlarged Homestead Act, and to one more the truths of how an eastern girl managed an education in the West. Sometimes it feels good to pretend, she thought, to just act as if it is all yours, to be the person you desire, to believe you can have what you please, that what you say is the truth.

The Colonel, by her side, swept his hand around the room and said, "We have to care for more than money for any of this to be worth it." The entertainments continued, Josephine calling on her guests, choosing them at random for more sport. She extended her index finger toward John Dos Passos, called him to the center of the room. He stood there, jolly eyes and bald pate, the crowd quieting to hear him recite something incomprehensible, followed by quick chatter of various interpretations. A man standing next to Katherine told his companion that whenever he invited writers they always ate so much. "Every single one of them. Even the women. Sometimes I wonder if they're like squirrels, storing food in their cheeks for later."

Josephine called on Keep and Smith to perform magic and they pulled coins and liquor and scarves from ears and mouths. They too had a crowd of the affluent eager to pin them for a visit to chronicle their lives. Then Katherine was asked if she would play piano, which she had not played in years, but even here too she pretended: Bach's Prelude in C Minor played over and over and over in schools all across Montana, the keys slipping away into music beneath the tips of her fingers, her shoulder blades flapping like wings, the rising chromatic pattern studied to learn the difference between music and noise. Silence followed by applause. By luck she got it right, the song coming out of her as if it were an accomplice. She could hear Mother saying for her to be the one to play the piece, to play from within herself, to play it like a violent storm.

Om was called on, of course, for his poetry, followed by a group of young women to sing "Ain't We Got Fun," inspiring more movement and dance. It was hot inside the house with all the bodies. Windows were opened. Food was served on more silver platters, passed by the servants. And there was booze, plenty of it, smuggled across the Canadian border, but only the butler ended up drunk, found asleep in a snowbank late, not far from the front door, to more amusement for the guests.

Then quiet. Back at the Albedor, seated in front of the fire and the twelve-ton mantel. The party was over, and soon the camps would be empty again, guests and hosts returning to the city. There are these defining moments in all lives, when someone leads you unaware to an epiphany. Katherine and the Colonel would orbit on and away from here, carried by the currents of their days, Katherine a warm memory, the lovely young nurse who saved his daughter's life, though his own death was just a short distance away, two and a half years. A shock to Katherine when she heard the news, nursing her baby, feeling the power of flowing milk, sitting in a rocker in her and Charles's home in Hasbrouck Heights, their first home, with picture windows through which the distant city shimmered, the baby whimpering, little Charles, whom they called Jet for the thick mop of black hair so like Charles as a boy. Their lives were shaping into the vision she had for it.

As she sat with Jet, looking across the Meadowlands to the city, a maid straightening up around her, she would receive the call from a nurse for Dr. Le Grand Kerr. The nurse would tell Katherine the news of the Colonel's heart attack, that he folded in on himself in the grand foyer of their Ditmas Park mansion, the girls and Ida swooning over him. She would recall the house, illuminated in the yellow glow of electric light, the swirling staircase and the girls, the servants at work making their lives easy and smooth and soft. How life pushes us forward so fast and furiously and unforgivingly until it doesn't anymore, until it stops and thrusts us off.

But now the group stood by the fire — the epiphany still to come. Brandy was offered and accepted and drunk. Then one by one Ida and Keep and Smith went off to bed, leaving Katherine and the Colonel alone before the embers.

"You made an impression tonight with the Bach," the Colonel said.

"It was nothing," Katherine said.

"Have you played long?"

"My mother. She's a musician."

"Did she teach you?"

"A little. I was just lucky."

"You're humble."

"I'm not."

"No?"

"I have things I'm proud of."

"Where does she live?"

"In Nevada." The Colonel had a generous square face, inlaid with his happy eyes. What a kind man, devoted to his wife and his daughters. She hadn't understood families like this existed. She could tell the Simmonses were different from the moment she met the Colonel at the hospital, the bright sterile rooms making his skin look like paste, possessed by fear — raw, unapologetic

281

fear, fighting to be camouflaged by his kindness.

"What does she do in Nevada?"

"She teaches school out near Reno. All over actually. Wherever there's work." She thought of her mother, a flash of selfishness, driving in the Ford down the long road to the Brewers' ranch, coming to collect her and her sister. The fear she had felt as a girl, having to go back with Mother, unfamiliar and strange, leaving the Brewers. She knew fear, knew therefore it was best to cauterize it. The fields that day had been promise green, sunlight caught in the blades along with a gentle wind. How she could miss her sister sometimes, the emotion catching her unaware, seeing her sister again as a beautiful little girl bitten by a snake.

"Eastern?" The Colonel shifted his position on the couch to better study Katherine.

"Midwestern. I was born in Ohio. We moved west, to Montana."

"Taking advantage of the second land rush?"

"No. But at that time." It felt good to have his attention. She felt beautiful. She hoped Charles would become a man like the Colonel, she a woman like Ida. His questions made her want to speak, to release

282

something she understood was trapped. Already he knew more about her than Charles did. Though she had enjoyed lying so easily and hopefully at the Edwardses' party, she did not feel like doing so with the Colonel. Rather in her beauty, she felt honest and real. Without quite understanding it, the sensation controlled her. She sipped her brandy; it burned her lips. He watched her.

"A farm?"

"I spent time on a farm, but we did not file a claim. It was just my mother and sister."

"And your father?" She thought of him behind the locked door of his room with Hattie, the boarder — the molten undercurrents of life.

"I noticed this evening, everyone seems to have a hobby, some form of entertainment to offer. Am I your entertainment?" She said it in an almost flirtatious way, not accusatory, understanding completely his perception of her.

"Perhaps," he said, matter-of-factly. "Everyone is entertainment."

"It's not the piano you're interested in."

"No. Though you're good."

"But not very good."

"No."

"You're right there."

"I'm in a choir after all."

"Who am I?" she asked.

"I have a hunch," he said. "What about your father?"

"A telegrapher for the railroads."

"Why didn't he go west with you?"

"You find this entertaining?"

"I love people, Katherine Stewart. Don't you?"

"Yes."

"Your father?"

"He had a wandering eye for women."

"Your mother left him?"

"She did."

"What does the *B* stand for? Or was it a *T*?"

"Is this why you bring the journalists along, to offer your lives up to them? A game you play with your friends?"

"That's good. Perceptive. It was our turn. Everyone has a turn."

"At the society pages?"

"At the society pages. There'll be something in the *Eagle* as well, syndication, by the by. That's the way it always runs." And there it would be, the image of Katherine with the Simmonses syndicated in the *Brooklyn Eagle* for all her Brooklyn friends to see. She'd become a star simply for having been entertainment for the Simmons family.

"Who are you?" Katherine asked.

"Who do you think I am?"

"A rich man."

He laughed.

She looked at him, at his tidy mustache, accenting his lips, making them appear to curl even more emphatically into kindness.

"You're rich."

He laughed again at her boldness.

"Do you like money?" he asked.

"Doesn't everyone?"

"I don't think Keep and Smith care too much about it. Look at how they dress."

It was her turn to laugh.

"Did you know that I didn't finish grade school?" the Colonel said.

"I didn't know that," Katherine said.

"You thought I went to Harvard?"

"I hadn't thought much about it, but I suppose I assumed you went to college. You know, just one of those assumptions."

"And that I'm rich creates those assumptions — education, fine breeding. What if I told you that my mother cleaned houses because my father died suddenly of a heart attack when I was a child. She cleaned to make ends meet and I couldn't stand to see her work like that. I dropped out of grade school and went to work as a sales clerk at A. D. Matthews, the department store in Brooklyn, because my Sunday school teacher found me the job. A dollar-fifty a week. What if I told you I looked in the cash books and learned my sales in challis and Turkey red were higher than the head salesman's, that I spoke with the floorwalker to state my case and received a fifty-cent raise?"

He continued describing for Katherine his rise from a poor kid responsible for his widowed mother, working his way up at A. D. Matthews, then at the *Railroad Gazette,* where he got a job because a fellow member of the choir at St. Mary's by the Sea (which was not by the sea) liked the boom of his tenor, thought it could serve in the interrogator's office. He started at five dollars a week and rose there too until he owned the entire outfit. "Isn't that how it can happen too?"

The fire crackled. The butler brought along more brandy and poured the thick amber liquid into Katherine's glass and then into the Colonel's. His cheeks were rosy from the alcohol and the cold.

"I'd say, bravo," Katherine answered.

He smiled. And they were silent for a bit, listening to the fire and the wind pushing at the windowpanes. They were trading secrets, now, though somewhere she understood that his stories weren't secrets. They were facts known about his life, but cushioned by time and obliterated by good fortune. It didn't matter for him now. And he was a man.

"You never hid those facts," Katherine said, more as an acknowledgment.

"Never. They never embarrassed me."

"They shouldn't."

"But you're hiding, and I'm not sure why. You said your first initial was T. Then you said B."

"I was wondering if you'd heard."

"You hoped I hadn't."

"My name isn't Katherine," Katherine said.

"Intriguing."

"Katherine is my sister."

"The plot thickens. And?" he asked.

"Thelma," she answered. "I took my sister's identity. Her name was Katherine, is now Patricia. Pat. Her second name." Katherine: she loved the name. It felt much more horrid to tell the truth than to lie. But she told the truth and it came from her like ugliness, but came all the same, everything she wanted to tell Charles.

"You're most definitely entertainment,"

he said with his square-faced smile. Then asked, simply: "Why?"

"I didn't finish grade school either." She reddened, the color spilling over her face. Before her stood a cadre of practical nurses pointing fingers at her, calling her a liar. Liar. But she swatted them away. She was clever, was all, more clever than they.

"I had a feeling we were kindred. Why?" he asked. How was it, she wondered, that she was sitting here? How did she get from Montana to this estate on the edge of a frozen lake, built for the king of transportation, his house of transportation, this kindly, generous man, how? Why? Montana drifted in front of her, her mother disappearing and all the good people who took them in, the hail and sunshine and the hard work and wanting to get Katherine to school so that at least she'd have a chance, putting her money on the pretty one to succeed. And once when Katherine was furious at her, once, the only time ever she'd been nasty and mean, calling her from Los Angeles with the baby hollering away: "You stole my name. You did it all so you could take my name. And see where I am now, not even twenty and with a kid and husband who makes nothing. We're poor, Tommy. We have nothing, Tommy." The telephone vibrated with Pat's anger. This was back at the beginning, their new names still new to them, their first transcontinental conversation. Talking to Pat, Katherine wasn't sure what to call her, how to think of herself. The truth was that she preferred not to speak to her; speaking with her, Katherine lost the sense of who she had become.

Her nose hurt with the recollection, the days it had taken to forget the pain that had defined Pat's voice. On the phone, Katherine had breathed, stern air, she had breathed. She would not surrender.

"I want to hear you call me Pat. Say it. Say the name. Use it." The words shot out like bullets. "Use it, Thelma. Let me hear you use it." In Pat's hysteria, Katherine calmed again, cooled, seeing her sister across the line with the shrieking baby and the hard-laboring husband, the misery of their lives. "Let me hear Pat," Pat demanded.

Katherine was silent for a moment, a soft rage swelling in her chest. The name Thelma hit her, old, unfamiliar, ugly. She took a breath and calmly uttered the name. "Patricia," Katherine answered slowly and with control. "Patricia," she repeated for emphasis and to be again the older sister in charge, who had done no wrong, the one with the power. "We are sisters. Our job is to help one another. I am always here for you, as I have always been. Patricia, is it money you need? If it is, then please just ask." She could hear Pat's breath now, moistened by tears as any last remnants of Katherine drained away from her, traveling through the telephones lines from Los Angeles to New York.

"Why?" the Colonel asked again, out of curiosity and familiarity. It was late.

"I raised my little sister. My mother abandoned us, let us raise ourselves." She told the story. She was six years old, Katherine four and sweet and lovely and vulnerable. She had thought of herself as a mother when she was six, had thought of it as her duty, became defined by the idea. In her arms and throat and feet Thelma was tough. "I was called Tommy."

"I like Tommy."

"I liked Tommy too. Tommy, like a boy, as Mother would say. I didn't like Thelma."

"Like a boy, right." Then: "Hiding?"

"I suppose." She paused. She thought. "Maybe, or perhaps I just wanted to become myself, the person I wanted to be, not shaped by circumstances that had not been mine to describe."

"You described it all right. You described

it from the moment you could and had to. You don't need to hide, Tommy. You've more than proved yourself. There are many different ways to do this thing." She thought of her sister. What had Pat described for herself? Had she, Katherine, caused her sister's misfortune by taking her name?

"Did you describe your life?" Katherine asked.

"I wanted to be a doctor, go to school, learn, but instead I made money." He paused and looked at her, held her. "Am I your entertainment?"

"In fact," she smiled.

"Here is a lesson I learned a very long time ago. Remember I am in advertising. Narrative is everything. Own your narrative, whatever you want it to be. We create our origin stories, our myths, and we believe them, and then others believe them. And then they are the truth. Do you like it when I tell people that you saved Doris's life? Does that make you feel strong and important?"

"It isn't the truth?"

"Oh, it's the truth. The way I see things."

"Well, the truth . . ."

"Answer my question."

"Yes. It makes me feel strong and capable and lauded."

"See, I made it part of your narrative by declaring it to be. And it is what I see. How does a man like me make a fortune on trade magazines? I didn't get lost in the thicket of nuance. Rather, I tell stories. The stories of manufacturers, of the railroads, of the various tools and parts and pieces that can be used for other things, to fight wars and win them. All of what we report is true, but it is the narrative that matters. You tell a story long enough, it's the truth."

"That simple?" Katherine said. She was descended from a queen. "If I don't like something the way it is I say it the way I would like it to be? I say it and tell it often enough I can be Katherine even if I am Tommy?"

"Yes. Aren't you Katherine? You've already mastered that. But you can also own Tommy. This is what I am trying to tell you. You need to believe the narrative. The narrative needs to be yours. Your story — that you raised yourself in Montana, raised your sister, borrowed her name, and headed east. Your story, as long as you make it yours, as long as you aren't troubled by it." He paused, then returned to the name, "Does your sister mind?"

"There's a lot of entertainment between the two of us tonight," Katherine said. "We could have sold tickets."

"She does mind," the Colonel said.

"Only when she's mad at herself."

"And you're reconciled with that?"

"I no longer have a choice."

"That sounds convenient."

"Are you asking if I still think about using her name?"

"Yes."

"I try not to and I'm good at that." She felt warm in the waning fire, slightly feverish. "If I'd stayed in the west my life likely would have been more like hers. Or worse. I had no formal education. I am not a fearful person, but that notion terrifies me. I want so much. I wanted so much more for myself."

"And Charles? Why doesn't he know?"

"It unfolded this way. How do you go back and say that actually I'm not Katherine. I'm not who I said I was."

It was very late now. The butler came in once again with more brandy and to settle some logs on the fire, then excused himself for bed.

"You are who you are. Katherine is just a name. Tommy is just a name, which I happen to like better, by the by. If you love Charles and he loves you, he needs to know and it will be all right. He won't mind. He'll think you were clever. That he has a clever girl. What can be better than a clever girl? We do what we need to do to survive. You haven't hurt anyone. Goodness, to the contrary. This is your story, your own House of Transportation. Don't misunderstand all of that. What a dear, dear girl you are."

Dear Mother, she wrote on a postcard picturing Fourth Lake in summer — all green and watery. The ride home was fast and white, the train slithering down to the city, through the endless countryside, the day contracting into a vanishing point in the center of herself. *It was Josephine Edwards's party that you would have loved the most. Three film stars and the governor, who was a flirt. Contraband flowing and I played the Bach perfectly — as mine, with tempers and moods. There was a monkey if you can believe, who caught grapes in his mouth. You must visit sometime.*
Your most loving Tommy.

6
AUNT THELMA IN THE EAST

Pat's boy — gangly and keen, filled with desire and big eyes. Tommy had been sent pictures of him, blond and sweet with a smile that lit up the dull sidewalk upon which he stood, right at the edge of a dried-up California lawn. Slim liked this, liked watching his mother slip the photo into the envelope before licking the envelope glue to seal the letter closed, the mystery aunt in New Jersey receiving news about him. Pat's letters told all about him — that he liked toy guns and wanted to be a baseball star when he was older, that he dreamed of heading east so that he could live in New Jersey like his aunt. "He wants to know you," Pat wrote. "He thinks you're something else."

From a very young age, for as long as he could remember, Slim was aware of his mother's letters east. "I'm writing your aunt," Pat would say. "I want her to know all about you, how special you are and also how good you are with your grandmother. Boys your age . . ." And she would drop off. But he would come to know what she meant, that boys his age weren't always so generous with their grandmothers. Pat would tell Slim the outlines of her letters, making him feel important, a hero. He liked that his mother cared enough to tell stories about him to this sister all the way in New Jersey, as if he were a character in a picture book.

Pat wrote about it all — about Glenna, her long visits with the family, that when she wasn't in Nevada teaching the children of Basque sheepherders or the children of Russian railroad gangs, she was in Los Angeles sharing a room with Slim, moved her things right into his room, taking it over with her pretty glass naturopathic jars and her enema cans. "You need to know about enemas," Glenna would say to Slim. "One day you'll be married and you will need to know about these things." Finding this funny, Pat included the exchange in a letter to Tommy. They could be funny in their letters, the way sisters have their own short-hand and bank of shared knowledge. They understood their mother, of course, that now she was imparting to Slim knowledge she'd imparted to them so long ago.

Slim grew up and Glenna grew old in Pat's letters, a solid packet of them tied together with string, and treasured in Grammy's black box.

Pat wrote boldly, with humor and honesty, describing the days of their lives, soft and gentle as though nothing had ever happened between the sisters, as though only distance kept them apart. Sure there were the tiny digs, never stated directly, only implied in the indirect style of little sisters who feel injustice, "Look at what my son is enduring while Mother rarely visits your family." Once or twice, Pat would let Tommy know that it might be a nice idea for her to invite Glenna for a visit in New Jersey.

Glenna would arrive at Pat's home in the summers in her big black 1928 Buick, outfitted with a portable toilet that no one was quite sure how she managed to use. Her arrivals were loud affairs, the car coming to an abrupt halt by the curb in front of the Vermont Knolls bungalow, low and flat against the wide sky polka-dotted with palms. Glenna would honk the horn and Pat and Slim would appear from the house, Glenna in some kind of long and fancy dress, a dog following her from the car, sometimes a cat. Something always exciting was produced from the cavern of her car. Once she brought a cardboard box filled with a dozen baby chicks. Once she produced a snake. Both chicks and snake were used later as food that she taught Slim to kill in the dusty backyard. These were the Depression years and everyone was destitute. Everyone but Tommy, it seemed, whose letters sailed in from New Jersey with recipes for roasts and stews clipped from magazines.

Glenna instructed Slim to unpack the car and he would do as he was told, hauling boxes into the house, always pausing in the living room, wanting to leave them there. "Your room, Slim," Glenna would say. "I'm your roommate, young man." In this way, Glenna took over the small house and Slim's room with her boxes, books, a radio that she would set up in Slim's window so it could get a good reception for her *Amos 'n' Andy* show. She liked Kingfish best and could mimic him, his deep guttural drawl and funny slapstick patter: "Holy mackerel," she'd say in a way that brought Kingfish to life before Slim, as if Kingfish were coming out of her mouth trying to rouse a bit of trouble. Sometimes Glenna would let Slim listen to his favorite show, *The Air Adventures*

of Jimmie Allen, and it would be like winning a prize for him.

Glenna took over the house so completely
that even Hank retreated.

Newly arrived, listening to something,
Glenna would perch on the side of one of
the twin beds in Slim's room and she'd
comb and comb her long auburn hair while
Slim watched her. Glenna would dem-
onstrate, extracting hair from her brush so
she could use it to fill out her thin bun, roll
it into her Gibson girl hairstyle, so it fluffed
out remarkably with all the preserved hair.

"We're descended from queens," she'd tell
the boy just as she had told her daughters.
"From Mary, Queen of Scots, and the Royal
Stewarts of Nairn. We come from a long
line of ancestors who came to America from
Europe for religious freedom and the great
hope of something more. We fought in the
War of 1812, in the Civil War, the Great
War," she'd say as if it were her and Slim
on the battlefield. "You're somebody," she'd
tell Slim. And it was this kind of talk that
made Slim wonder who exactly he could be
beyond the boy he saw in the mirror.

Pat would write to Tommy that she would
watch her son and Glenna together and
sometimes it was like she was watching
herself as a girl all over again. "I confess, I

have to look away." She could be honest with her sister at times, when she was feeling particularly blue — money woes and the like, that Hank worked ten hour days on the streets of Los Angeles, arresting people, keeping order, and still they didn't have enough. Pat didn't want Tommy to send her money, but she wanted Tommy to be aware of the struggle, that on top of it she had Glenna. Pat didn't have enough perspective on herself to understand that her complaints preserved for herself, and for Tommy, Pat's role as little sister. She didn't have enough self-awareness to understand that somewhere hidden inside this was the only role she understood how to play.

Glenna didn't like to be called Grammy or Grandma or Grandmother. She was just plain Glenna, a short, heavyset woman around 150 pounds. She walked with a pronounced limp because her left leg was shorter than her right leg. She had a defective, arthritic hip joint and it caused her a lot of pain. She told Slim it was inherited from her mother, Laura Ann Meyer, who had been a milliner in Cincinnati. When he looked at her with dopey eyes, she explained, "A milliner makes hats. And Mother was a fine woman. Strong and determined. She made hats for Granny Howard, aunt of William Howard Taft."

If Slim was asked to be curious about his dead relatives, he was more curious about the living ones. The letters that sailed back and forth between the sisters, carrying their lives across the country — first by train and then by airplane — told the stories that Slim most wanted to know. In the East he had an aunt, his Aunt Thelma, called Tommy by his mother and grandmother, called Katherine in New Jersey. Tommy made Slim think about a boy and Katherine was his mother's real name, so with the exacting logic of kids he referred to his aunt as Aunt Thelma because that was her actual name and nobody ever stopped him. Aunt Thelma, Slim believed, contained the answer to his mother and his grandmother and therefore to the biggest question of all: Who was he? Why and how was he here?

Pat was a sad woman, had a penchant for feeling sorry for herself, sorry that she was burdened with Glenna when Thelma was not, sorry that she lived in a run-down little house when Thelma did not, sorry that Thelma had her name and she did not. Everything was a contrast that seemed to rise directly from some equation in her past: who Pat was as a little girl. For all of Glenna's stories about queens, she never told stories about her daughters as children.

So Slim gleaned. He was good at it. His whole childhood, Slim heard about his Aunt Thelma in the East. If Glenna and Pat were fact, Aunt Thelma was myth, rising from the contents of her letters, which were shared at the dinner table the same way the family would listen to a program on the radio. When a letter arrived in the mailbox, thick and substantial, Thelma's precise script, there was reason for excitement. And the recipes always promised to be delicious, but the family could never afford to make them.

Aunt Thelma lived in New Jersey in a big house and she had two children. The pictures came in the letters, stuffed in there to show off the house, the children — a boy and a girl, beautiful kids dressed nicely. The girl had sausage curls that bounced around her sweet face. Her name was Winter, a peculiar name. Aunt Thelma had named Winter for a girl the sisters had known in Montana when they were children. The girl had been kicked in the head by a horse and died. "Tommy," Pat would sigh, and roll her eyes, and with the gesture describe her sister as too much. But the information fascinated

Slim because his mother never spoke about her childhood and it was clear to him, just from being her son, from knowing his grandmother Glenna, that there was plenty of story to be told. There was an entire world of his family in the East, in the past in Montana, that he wanted to know about, as if knowing about it could expand his own existence, make it larger than the boundaries of his family's small, tired bungalow in Vermont Knolls.

Thelma's boy was named Jet, for the color of his hair. His real name was Charles, like his father. Jet was handsome and intelligent looking and wore smart clothes, vests and trousers — even as a boy. Slim imagined what their life was like based on the photographs — portraits of the children, snapshots of the family leaning against a shiny black automobile, seated on the front steps of their big house, in front of a Christmas tree twinkling with lights and ornaments. Pictures of the kids on sleds, racing down a hill in fur-trimmed coats. Slim had never seen real snow or felt real cold. Aunt Thelma's family was the kind that made others long for it to be theirs. "Well, look at that," Pat would say, fingering the photograph delicately. "What a rich car they have." Pat was very good at measuring. She could measure perfectly, even at a distance of three thousand miles. Thelma had more, and you didn't have to go too deep to smell a whiff of that injustice, that Thelma's bounty was achieved at Pat's expense.

Sometimes Slim did his own contrasting and measuring, thinking of Aunt Thelma and his cousins receiving the photographs of him standing on the scrappy, dusty desert lawn — actually not a hero at all.

Aunt Thelma and Uncle Charles were in some of the pictures — refined in their clothes and posture. Theirs was a family with plenty, clear enough — house, car, kids, snow even, experience — and they lived in New Jersey, which Slim came to believe was the greatest state in the nation, and when he grew up he wanted to live in New Jersey. It's what he'd say when people would ask him what he wanted to be when he grew up. "I want to live in New Jersey," and they'd always laugh. He'd study it on a map and imagine himself there in the house with his aunt, uncle, and cousins. Slim was four years older than Jet and eight years older than Winter. "Slim wants to grow up and live in New Jersey," Pat would write.

In the dining room of their small home, Slim's mother had hung her high school diploma — framed and behind glass. He knew she was proud of it. His father was too. Slim's father hadn't gone to school after the third grade. Aunt Thelma had used his mother's diploma to go to nursing school because she hadn't gone to high school. He could tell his mother was proud of that fact too, the way she said: "She had to use my degree because she didn't have one." She'd twist her lips in a particular way that indicated she had something more than her fancy sister in the East.

Slim heard it his whole childhood: "There is nothing more than education." His mother said it. His grandmother Glenna said it. Even his father said it. "Do well in school, son." It was like a jackhammer, but Slim had trouble reading, couldn't see the words straight, didn't do well in school.

Glenna tried to teach Slim to read — threw him right into John Henry Titus: *The Face on the Barroom Floor* and Jack London and Zane Grey, made him sound out the unfamiliar words and then spell them, which was impossible for him to do. Nothing looked as it sounded and vice versa in his mind, which trapped the words and held them hostage, refusing to process them. When he'd get twitchy and impatient she'd throttle him with her own impatience, like she was desperate to make something of him, like it meant something about her, like they were on one big ship and she was trying to get them all somewhere better. In her mind, it seemed, and his, it wasn't just his family on the trip to somewhere better, it was his Aunt Thelma in the East and her babies and their babies and his babies, people who came before and who would follow. Slim was the first of Glenna's grandchildren and he could feel the desperate worry with the reading, like if he couldn't carry his weight, that ship they were all on might sink. Glenna's steel eyes gripped him, urging him to get the words right. Slim came from some spectacular family and it would be lost to him if he couldn't read.

Sometimes Slim would wonder how his aunt had such a fine house in the great state of New Jersey and done so well for herself if she hadn't even gone to high school. Sometimes Slim wished that she would come to visit.

She didn't come visit, though, not while he was a child — but even so he hoped. Slim knew enough not to ask to visit New Jersey. They couldn't afford it. When he asked for too much it made his mother nervous and she would list all the ways in which they couldn't afford whatever it was he was asking for. She'd smoke cigarette after cigarette, the smoke curling up around her, the ashtrays thick with butts and ash. His father would look into his hands, turn his thumbs around each other. Slim kept his dream a secret, learning about Aunt Thelma from wherever she was present in his life, the letters most of all, in which Pat wrote about Glenna, loaning her money now so she could get a degree because no job wanted her anymore without a degree. "Time has caught up with Mother," Pat wrote. Thelma responded by sending two crisp one-hundred-dollar bills, which fell from the envelope to land on the warped linoleum dining table. Aunt Thelma paid with money; Slim's mother paid with time. Lots and lots of time with Glenna. It was clear to Slim that his mother's time was nowhere near as valuable as Aunt Thelma's money.

Thelma wrote about Uncle Charles, his work with the varioplex, "how fast it is to send and receive messages," the children growing up, Jet getting so tall, becoming a basketball player, straight As in school, moves from one house to a bigger house and then an even bigger house. Indeed, it was as if the Brown family was growing, swelling, outsized in all of their imaginations. It didn't seem to Slim that Glenna could also be the grandmother of the cousins in New Jersey. Once or twice during his childhood, Glenna visited Thelma, and knowing she was there he wondered if Glenna taught his cousins how to kill a chicken in their backyard.

Glenna used the money from Thelma first for college, then for an advanced degree. She used it on the right things. She enrolled in USC for her bachelor's. She needed her BA so she could get a teaching job again. The teaching profession had outgrown her education. There were no more little prairie schoolhouses for farmers' children — not in the cities or near the cities. The world had blasted open and there were requirements and rules and regulations now, and because of instruments like the varioplex, information was available fast and everywhere. A normal school certification didn't amount to much. Glenna didn't have the qualifications and couldn't lie her way around that fact because proof was mandatory now and documents so easily accessible.

Sometimes Slim would look at his mother and see that she was beautiful, her blond hair and jewel-like features. From the sisters' letters he had gleaned she had wanted to be a movie star, way back at the beginning of her California adventure: "Don't let your dream go," Thelma had written early on. Slim would look at her and think she could have been a movie star, the way she held the cigarette, the way she sucked in the smoke and exhaled it slowly so it almost seemed to speak for her. Glenna had told him that Pat had been quite the actress, a good deal better than Tommy. *Promising* was Glenna's word, but with the hopeful word came so much futility. "Your mother was talented; your aunt was clever."

"Like by stealing Mom's name?" Slim asked, causing Glenna to sit up.

"She didn't steal Pat's name." That's all Glenna ever said on the matter. She was silent for a moment, and then said again, "I told you, she is clever."

Clever Aunt Thelma managed to marry Charles Brown — a blue-blooded Bostonian whose family had been here in America for eleven generations. Gleaned through the letters, discussed at the dinner table. Charles Brown was the one person in the family Glenna thought something of. He had an education. He was lauded. "Now, he's one fine man," Glenna would say.

He had a college degree from Brown

University. When Slim was really little he thought Brown University belonged to his Uncle Charles — the entire university was his kingdom. And he said so at the dinner table. He said, "What a man. An entire university named after him and his family. They must be something." It made Slim feel like he was more important too. He had a relation who owned a university and he wondered if that meant he could go there to get his education. He'd never heard of it, but if Uncle Charles went there it had to be something. They were eating dinner, some thin, bony roast in gravy, sitting around the table with the afternoon light sliding through the venetians.

"Brown University doesn't belong to him, son," his father said.

Glenna stopped eating and looked at Hank, those steel eyes making him smaller in Slim's own eyes, though he didn't want that to happen, like an awful magic trick. The way she looked at Hank diminished him. She was correcting him with her eyes, telling him he was dead wrong, the university belonged to Charles. She didn't say it. She said nothing, just looked at him, and Slim could tell it hurt his father, as if he too felt he were shrinking beneath the pressure of her gaze. Mother didn't say a word. She just folded her napkin and set it in her lap and waited for the moment to pass. She never spoke back to Glenna. But this time when it didn't seem like it was ever was going to pass, when Slim thought they all might get frozen there, that time really could stop and trap them, Glenna asked Dad what he knew about Brown University. She said, "You didn't finish third grade. What do you know about Brown University, Mr. Bennett?" Slim wanted his mother to stand up for his father. Slim wanted her to at least acknowledge that he finished the third grade. Slim thought about his father's accomplishment, that he'd finished the third grade and that that was something because Slim knew people who hadn't even accomplished that.

"It's shoes he owns," Pat said softly. "It's the Brown Shoe Company. Buster Brown." This is what came to be believed, the Brown name and family business (shoes) doing the work, eliding fact so no one thought to question that Brown plus shoes equaled Buster Brown. Charles, pictured in the advertisement as a boy, served as proof, described artfully in Thelma's letter — a story about Charles as a boy. Left out was the fact that the ad was almost coincidental, a campaign by Buster Brown, Charles chosen as the East Coast model because his family name was Brown and their business was shoes. But this would only be understood much later, and not by anyone at this table. For the people at this table, Charles himself was Buster Brown.

Pat stood up and started clearing. Glenna made Pat weak. She too was diminished in Slim's eyes. He wondered how his Aunt Thelma would have responded in a situation like this. What would she have said about Brown University?

"He's in management at Western Union," Glenna said, continuing in her efforts to build Charles up, outsize him against the slight frame of Hank. She had been to visit them recently. She was the authority. "He makes money, real money that can buy big things, and they like to do that." The way she spoke didn't indicate approval, just facts. Charles and Thelma had matching Lincoln Continentals with gold nameplates on the dashboards; they had a home in Hasbrouck Heights across the marshlands from the city and Winter had a bedroom with a view of the Empire State Building. Pat continued to clear as Glenna spoke. Hank took his napkin from his lap and folded it and set it on the table. He stood up to help clear. Slim felt a pain in his chest, sharp and deep.

Not long after, Charles Brown came to visit. He had dinner with the family, in Los Angeles for business. Before he arrived, Glenna and Pat admonished Slim to polish his shoes. "Uncle Charles hires people to polish his shoes and he'll look at yours to be sure they're polished," his mother said. And he was reminded that shoes were important to Charles, reminded all over again that Uncle Charles had been the mascot for Buster Brown, the little boy with the dog, that the family business was shoes.

Uncle Charles walked in, tall in a dark suit, with his silver hair, an eastern man, not a western man, a corporation man. It was as if a god had entered the home with Glenna catering to him and getting him a scotch from the scotch that Charles brought because of course they couldn't afford such luxury. He smoked a pipe and Slim loved the scent of the smoke; it was like being inside a warm coat. Uncle Charles had thick hair and wide-set blue eyes and the funniest accent that made it hard to understand what he was saying. A Boston accent, thick like peanut butter in his mouth.

Slim was at his desk making a radio so he could listen to his own programs, a little desk tucked between the heads of the twin beds and facing out the window so he could watch the kids race up and down the street on their bikes. A big palm tree stood in the green yard, kept bright by water Hank sprinkled on it in the mornings and the evenings every day of the year. It was the little kind of radio that kids made back then, a crystal radio receiver in a cigarette box. Uncle Charles came into the room and stood behind Slim. He was so tall you could feel his shadow pressing onto you in a kind and comforting way. He asked Slim what he was doing and if he could sit down. He sat on Slim's bed. He was glad Uncle Charles didn't sit on Glenna's bed. Slim thought it would make her mad; she'd notice the imprint and think it was Slim who messed it up. He was embarrassed in front of his uncle, that he had to share a room with his old grandmother. He thought of Aunt Thelma and Uncle Charles's big house in New Jersey, the little cousins. He blushed. He had his father's cast-off tools, and Uncle Charles watched Slim work with them. It was sort of peaceful and Slim liked his attention, liked that Uncle Charles seemed to be studying his methods. Slim wanted him to be impressed, kept thinking that maybe he was, and that made Slim feel a certain kind of hopeful inside. He snuck a peek at his uncle's shoes, looking down, and they were shiny, couldn't have been shinier.

"Keep at it, Slim," he finally said in his calm, slow manner. He was never in a hurry. He had his accent, but each word was said with care and properly. He came all the way across the country in a train and he did it frequently throughout the rest of Slim's childhood, showing up for dinner, chatting with them about Jet and Winter — like those impossible kids you see in magazines, happy, with everything, great in school. Eventually times would change and Uncle Charles would fly. Slim would grow up. The Second World War would start and he would enlist, join the navy, move on and out to the South Pacific. Hank would retire from the LAPD and move with Pat to Klamath. Not long thereafter, Hank would die and Pat would have to work, getting a job as a dispatcher for the LAPD, moving back to Los Angeles again, selling Avon door-to-door in her spare time.

But it was that evening at his desk, "Keep at it, Slim," that Slim would never forget. The next night Uncle Charles returned for dinner and he came with his polished shoes and sat on the edge of the bed again and he gave Slim a present: a box with a new set of tools, all his own — a small vise, screwdriver, side cutters, and long-nose pliers, Western Union stamped on each tool. Professional tools. Slim loved his Uncle Charles. He was eleven years old and couldn't help but wonder, had his mother used her own diploma and gone to nursing school herself in Brooklyn, New York, could his Uncle Charles be his father, could he be living a different life in New Jersey?

When Glenna got her degree, she found employment in Nyala, Nevada — the last outpost of the uncivilized world. In a tiny one-room schoolhouse Glenna taught the children of the Basque sheepherders who'd come to America in the 1800s for the gold, but discovered there was more money in feeding sheep to the miners. When Glenna would come back to visit she'd threaten Slim and say he could be a sheepherder's son, live in a Mormon town. "Its first name was Polygamy Wells," she told him. By now he was a teenager, just a few years shy of heading off to war. She had six pupils and the magnificent salary of four hundred dollars a year. In the summers, she continued her studies in Los Angeles, attending Pepperdine for an advanced degree. It wasn't much then and it wasn't in Malibu yet, a small Pentecostal college with about 250 students. It was near the Bennetts' home and that's why she liked it.

The next year she got a better job in Dry Lakes, twelve students, six hundred dollars a year. World War II started. It was 1939. She rented a small clapboard house in a gas station and railroad town on U.S. 91, about fifty miles northeast of Las Vegas. Dry Lakes was named for a large dry lake nearby. In addition to the gas station, Dry Lakes had one restaurant and one motel. Also, there was a Union Pacific Railroad housing unit for the Mexican railroad track gang and a water tower for steam engines to take on water. Dry Lakes had a population of fifty, sparsely populated and inhospitable like the rest of southern Nevada. Dry heat with temperatures over a hundred every summer with day after day in the 110s. The winters were cold, with cold winds blowing, often below zero. The region was famous for its rattlers and scorpions, but Glenna loved it, said it spoke to her insides like the landscape was having a conversation with her soul.

During the war years she was recognized for writing a song about Nevada, and she also became involved with Senator McCarran, helping him understand how to get farmers to grow enough grain to feed the soldiers.

From Dry Lakes, she went to Tonopah, then to Reno, then to Goldfield in 1947 because she was appointed as a teaching principal of a four-year school. Just before the school year started, Glenna died, during her sleep, of congestive heart failure. She was sixty-six.

Pat got the news, called Thelma, asked Slim if he'd go out there and take care of the business that is required when someone dies. Thelma would meet Slim there to help. His mother promised he could have Glenna's car as a payment. She didn't explain to Slim why she didn't want to go herself, but he knew it had something to do with her sister and the past — with wanting to avoid old wounds and even, he knew, retain old injuries. He knew enough by now about his mother to know that hanging on to old injuries worked in her like a salve, soothing something. Slim agreed because he wanted to help out his mother and because he wanted the car. He had recently gotten a girl pregnant and now they were going to marry, so a car would be a good thing to have. Most of all, however, he went to Goldfield because he would finally meet his Aunt Thelma.

Slim took a bus as far as possible, hitching

rides the rest of the way to the abandoned town of Goldfield that had once seen better days. All over town were the tiniest houses Slim had ever seen, not bigger than ten by fifteen feet, enough space for just a person — the abode of the miner. Some of them were on wheels. Glenna had rented one out only days before she died. They punctuated the streets, reminding Slim of what a person could endure. But big hotels and buildings, the elegant town hall and courthouse, spoke to the town's former glory. Easily, Slim found the funeral home, where he waited for his aunt. Eventually she arrived, appearing in a black Cadillac, a 1947 60 Special with the sombrero wheels gleaming and stainless. The shine of the wheels competed with the polished exterior, all of it catching the sun. A black chauffeur in uniform replete with cap and gloves slid the car in front of Mr. Moon's funeral home, a long rectangular building with a false front, just off Main Street and around the corner from the once glamorous yet now defunct hotel. The chauffeur stepped out of the car and walked around the massive hood to Aunt Thelma in the backseat and opened the door. She had flown in on a prop from La-Guardia and had hired the car and driver to bring her out from Los Angeles, had accomplished all this in less than twenty-four hours. She was a superhero. Slim was almost twenty years old and he felt like both a man and a boy, filled with anticipation to meet his Aunt Thelma.

It was July and desert hot and desert lonely in the little limp town. It wasn't quite a ghost town, because there were some bars and businesses and there were still some operational mines, mostly mining elements and compounds important during the war for batteries and transistors, mining cinders used for roads and such. Everything was quiet, alive but quiet in a larger landscape that had already begun hiding big military secrets — Esmeralda County with its Yucca Mountains and Yucca Flats, Groom Lake and the Tonopah Test Range where an aerial gunnery range and hidden landing strips had been used during the war, training ground for bombing and artillery practice. The U.S. government had already come to realize the value of the ability of Nevada's terrain to camouflage necessary if dirty business — stealth projects that would lead ultimately to nuclear testing.

Beautiful in that stark desert way, the landscape seemed to be of a piece with Aunt Thelma's arrival and her Cadillac, which was the nicest thing this town had ever seen, even in its heyday. Just looking at it made you long for the car to be yours and to be driving fast on long, open roads.

And then there she came, Aunt Thelma, emerging from the rear of the air-conditioned car, stepping into this godforsaken town, not the kind of place where the mother of this woman should die. She was regal, and Slim became a little boy again in his mind, believing Glenna's stories about his ancestors, about Mary, Queen of Scots. Here was their queen. Aunt Thelma gracefully swung her legs out of the car, a robust, strong woman, like Glenna had been once, but beautiful. Aunt Thelma's hair was neatly done behind a transparent net, capped with a pillbox hat. On her long hands, she wore leather driving gloves. Her suit was blue linen and fresh pressed, like she hadn't been sitting in an airplane and then a car for many hours. On her feet, she wore sturdy kid leather shoes with a slight heel. She carried a black snakeskin pocketbook and a broad, proud smile and a slow, deliberate manner. She was not in a hurry, not at all, like Uncle Charles, like they owned time. She oozed wealth. The driver stood holding the door open for her while offering her his hand, which she took as she stepped out. It seemed an audience would be appropriate for this arrival. But it was just Slim. She looked him up and down and then hugged him as if she approved, as if he were good enough to hug. He was wearing his Sunday best, but wished he'd been wearing his sailor's uniform.

"Charles has a fondness for you," she said as the driver closed the door. "So therefore, so do I. It's kind of you to do this business for your mother. I thank you for coming along." In the dusty heat, the edges of this short town seemed to be curling up — the town burning in the sun like a sheet of paper surrendering at the edges. You could still smell arsenic, the faint hint of it from the mines. Aunt Thelma: a storybook figure stepping from the pages of a Cadillac, the sister who took Slim's mother's name to get ahead. Here she was, ahead. Slim was struck speechless even as he had so many questions — a reverent speechlessness because he also had nothing but respect. Money has a way of doing that, and besides, she was his, his blood. Aunt Thelma had a handkerchief tucked into the edge of her glove. She wore silk stockings that shimmered silver.

Mr. Moon came outside just then, as if he too were drawn magnetically by the unlikely image of this woman on this street. For years to come Slim remembered the man's name as Moon and found it a comforting name. Every time he saw the moon in the sky — brilliant in the night, a surprise in the day — he'd think of Glenna and feel a softness that she had been alive. As time crept forward and buried the past, he wasn't always sure if his memory of the name was accurate. He'd struggle to recall, then decide it didn't really matter: Mr. Moon. Grammy too remembered the name as Moon, telling stories of Glenna's death to us, to me, in the lonely town, the undertaker a sharp-nosed, obedient man named Moon.

You could hear the door open, the wasted hinges, the click as it shut again behind Mr. Moon. He greeted Aunt Thelma and Slim with condolences that seemed somehow genuine, as though he hadn't done this many times, which made Slim wonder how often he attended to a dead body in this slow town, how he kept in business. Mr. Moon ushered them inside where it was even hotter. They made their way solemnly down a short corridor to the refrigerated room, very small like a meat locker.

Glenna was on a stretcher, covered by a sheet, head lifted just a bit by a pillow, silenced. That's what Slim thought: the woman of the reading lessons and the enema can and hair brushing, the mother who left her girls to raise themselves, was lying there, finished. She provoked no emotion. He wanted to feel tears, but he didn't. He didn't feel anything but the simple fact that we live and then we die and it means nothing to almost everyone. He realized how anonymously people live their important lives. They are born, they breathe, they live, they try, they fail, they die, and essentially no one knows. They creep through unnoticed. In the scheme of things no one knew Glenna, no one suffered because of Glenna, no one cared that Glenna was gone. Yet even so she stitched time, shaped something large or that at least would endure, carried along by him and his cousins, forward into unimaginable generations. He thought of the seed in his girlfriend's womb; he thought of his cousins; so many lives tethered to Glenna's, now a ridiculous heap beneath a threadbare sheet in a freezing room in a hot desert, waiting to be disposed of. Slim noticed his aunt's eyes were as dry as his own.

Mr. Moon was a slight fellow with yellow teeth and thinning hair, but kindly and gentle spoken if nervous, the kind of nervous that doesn't appear at first glance but then becomes quickly apparent. Over the phone from New Jersey he'd been instructed to leave the body alone, to keep it cold but to leave it alone, and he had.

Slim studied Aunt Thelma to see what she would do, watched as she slipped off her gloves and tucked them into her snakeskin pocketbook, watched as she unpinned her hat, rolled up her sleeves and lifted the sheet that covered Glenna. They found a tiny, shriveled woman who couldn't have weighed more than a hundred pounds. A wire, twisted round her little finger, held a name tag that identified her. Her false teeth were on the gurney near the pillow and her head, along with two photographs. She was completely naked, so Slim averted his eyes at certain areas, but Aunt Thelma continued to inspect her mother, the full length of her. Her skin was waxy and her limbs stiff with rigor mortis.

"She drowned," Thelma said, "in her own fluids." She proceeded to describe congestive heart failure, how it had killed Glenna, heart unable to pump to the extremities, struggling organs, swollen legs, a slow rise of secretions filling the lungs with backed-up blood until there was no air to breathe. His aunt was clinical, her face washed in curiosity like she could see beneath Glenna's skin to her insides and could therefore study how the body had betrayed itself. Aunt Thelma was a registered nurse, of course. Mother said that though she paused her career for marriage and children, Thelma had worked during the war when there was a shortage, that she'd filled in for doctors who'd been called to Europe.

Slim thought that he wanted to see his Aunt Thelma cry, but she didn't. Instead now she explained how rigor mortis had set in for several hours and that it would not stop until after they were gone. She tried showing Slim an example of postmortem stain, as she called it, how blood pooled in the buttocks and back, the skin there an ugly purple red, whereas the rest of the corpse was pale and waxy. "We'll just have to negotiate the stiffness," she said.

"Mr. Moon," she asked. "Would you mind asking my driver to bring my bag from the trunk?" She addressed him directly, looking him in the eye.

"Certainly," he said with a nod, and was gone for a bit. While they waited for his return, Aunt Thelma interrogated Slim, but not as a stranger might, rather as if she'd known him his whole life, as if she too possessed a part of him because he was her sister's child and therefore also Aunt Thelma's child. "You loved her very much. I can see, but she was difficult." It was a question and an answer all at the same time. "She shared a room with you, and that must have been uncomfortable, but you were a good boy and are a fine man." Slim smiled, sort of dumbly, because he was eager for her praise but didn't know where to put it.

Again, he wanted to say more. He wanted to ask about Katherine. That's what he wanted to ask most of all because he knew she still went by Katherine to everyone but himself and his mother. Charles called her Tommy, her children called her Mother, but to her friends and those who worked for her and Charles's colleagues she was Katherine. He wanted to ask her about his mother, how she was as a girl, why she wasn't able to make her dream of going to Hollywood work, whereas Aunt Thelma had made her dream of going east succeed. But Slim didn't know how to ask these questions, afraid he might make her uncomfortable or worse, himself. Perhaps he was like his mother in this way, allowing life to push him along the way it would. Aunt Thelma was the director of her life. She seemed to be able to tell it which way to go. Understanding that was almost enough.

Aunt Thelma lifted the false teeth and inspected them, set them back, and picked up the photographs. They were of her father, and of her sister and herself as young girls.

Mr. Moon returned with a cloth bag and gave it to Aunt Thelma. He saw her holding the photographs and said they had been in Glenna's hand when they found her. Aunt Thelma gave him a quizzical look awash in both confusion and tenderness, as if something was going on deep inside her. Slim hoped it would emerge, but it didn't. She put the pictures down and turned her attention to the bag. She unbuckled it and produced a bundle wrapped in tissue paper, which she carefully took off to reveal a long blue velvet gown.

"Come on now, Slim, this will be the hard part. We're going to dress her now. I'm strong, but a dead body with rigor mortis is even stronger, so I'll need you now too." Mr. Moon's nervous countenance flared as they tried sitting Glenna up on the gurney. She wouldn't bend. He hovered, with his elongated face, wanting to interject, but something about the determination of Aunt Thelma wouldn't allow him to interfere. Slim simply helped her with the struggle. They tried sliding the dress over her head, but then they couldn't bend the arms to fit them in the sleeves. It was cold, quiet, and uncomfortable working with the body. Aunt

Thelma was a little impatient that the body wouldn't move as she wanted it to.

There was something about her, big and imposing, that reminded Slim of Glenna's strength, like Aunt Thelma had even more, if that was possible. She worked her arms awkwardly under the body, her eyes scanning the room for equipment that could help. Slim noticed it as she did, the block and tackle, a pulley system. She turned to Mr. Moon and asked if he'd once again fetch the driver. Mr. Moon studied her as he acquiesced, trying to anticipate what she'd be suggesting next. When the driver in his cap and Mr. Moon in his mourning suit returned, she said, "We have to dress the body and we need your strength to engage the pulley." The driver tried to demur, looking polished in his uniform and uncomfortable with the request. Thelma assured him she would pay extra and that was all it took.

The gurney with the body was moved beneath where the pulley was anchored into the ceiling. Aunt Thelma pulled down the fall line, swaddled a sheet loose enough so the rope could move through it. She got the three men to hoist the body. Beneath it she slipped the rope contraption, then she asked the chauffeur and Mr. Moon to pull the fall line rope. Before Slim knew it, Glenna was raised on a slant, suspended above the gurney with her legs resting on it at an angle, naked and diminished and not a person, just pure and simple deadweight. Nothing here at all to indicate a daughter and mother, just business and determination. Slim was afraid the block-and-tackle system would give and the body would fall and bruise.

Thelma asked Mr. Moon for a knife, and with the chauffeur holding the line and Slim standing around feeling useless, Mr. Moon retrieved one, his long face almost scared. Slim didn't want to think about all that that knife might have cut before. Thelma deftly slit the dress down the back, and with Glenna suspended, light coming through the windows in waves, Thelma gave Slim one side of the dress and together they slipped it over Glenna's arms one by one. Thelma took a bunch of safety pins and fastened up the back. When Glenna was dressed, Thelma instructed the body be lowered down to the table, slipped the rope and sheet out, and then took out a hairbrush and combed Glenna's hair just the way Glenna had taught Slim. A small part of Slim thought of that as his job, wanted to take the brush and comb it himself. That's as close as he came to emotion.

Aunt Thelma combed it and combed it, gently, massaging Glenna's scalp with her fingertips as if Glenna could feel her daughter's fingers. The hair was a luxurious brown, thick, not a strand of gray. With the knife, Thelma deftly cut a lock of Glenna's hair, preserving it in a tissue, which she tucked into her bag. Then she rolled Glenna's hair into a bun, securing it with an ivory comb. She put some rouge on Glenna's cheeks and pried open the mouth to slip in the teeth, which was oddly easy. With the teeth in place, Glenna's face transformed, filling out again. Aunt Thelma put a little lipstick on the lips, not too much, just enough to give color. She folded the hands at the waist and slid the photographs beneath them.

When she was finished, she turned to Mr. Moon and said, "She's all yours now to ship back to Ohio." She told him and Slim that Glenna would be buried in a yard near her father's farm, so she could look out over it. At a sink in the refrigerated room she washed her hands and then slipped on her gloves again. Slim wanted to ask: "Aren't you going to cry?" But he didn't.

After paperwork in Mr. Moon's office, after payment (cash), after instructions for

Slim to clean out Glenna's shack and to ship to Thelma's address in New Jersey a trunk that Slim would find there, she looked at Slim and winked. He fell in love with her then. She said, "Well, we're all done here. Time to head out, Slim." She waited for Slim to open the door for her to Mr. Moon's funeral home. Outside again in the bright light it seemed like nothing and everything had changed. That was it. Over. Done. Finished. Her driver had the car idling to keep it cool. He got out and opened the backseat door for her. She had on a pair of ebony-rimmed sunglasses. Boy, did she look like something. She made herself comfortable in the backseat, asked if she couldn't give him a ride back to Los Angeles, patting the spot next to her with her gloved hand. She knew that she couldn't, that Slim had work here, a car to drive back himself. But he appreciated the gesture, believed she would have liked his company for the ride, and that was enough.

"Thank you, Aunt Thelma," Slim said. "I'll manage from here. I'll be in touch and ship you that trunk." She smiled and told him again he was a decent, worthy man. The driver closed the door and walked around to his seat, tipped his hat at Slim, and disappeared inside the cooled car. Slim watched the black Cadillac slip off down the dusty western street.

His mother had followed the rules and she was almost happy in her small house in Vermont Knolls. Thelma had dreamed and she seemed happier than enough. Another thing he knew about their childhood was that Thelma had been named for the heroine of a novel he would never read, but the story was of a peasant who turns herself into a princess. He thought about the girl he'd gotten pregnant, the baby growing inside her, that he didn't love the girl — not really. He thought about how we make our way forward knowing nothing — how it's all hoping, guessing, dreaming, being smart. "Get an education, Slim." Thelma didn't have an education, she'd named her daughter for a dead girl, Winter. Glenna named her daughter for a princess. Watching the car slither away into the high desert heat, Slim thought about the ship they were all on. He started walking through the town. He wasn't done here; he had tears in him yet.

7
LITTLE SISTER

Not long after Glenna died, Pat came to see Tommy in New Jersey. Tommy wired Pat the money for an airplane ticket and Pat accepted, feeling somewhere like she'd earned it. She flew into LaGuardia and was met by Tommy in the Lincoln Continental. Negotiating the roads and bridges, she drove like an expert until they arrived at the big home in Ridgewood, New Jersey, that Pat had seen in photographs. It was fall and the leaves on the maple trees were changing color, and Pat thought this was the prettiest thing she had ever seen a tree do. The sisters were not awkward with each other. It was easy for Pat to return to her role of long ago, of little sister — it was natural, the old familiar pattern. It struck her how time covers over most things, but not the roles of siblings. And how long had it been? She knew exactly, of course — twenty-three years — but she pretended otherwise, to be the kind not to think about that sort of thing. By now they had spent more time apart than together. Even so, those early years were seared into who she was, and that's why she had finally come.

Pat played her part without even noticing she was doing it. It felt comforting; she didn't need to be in charge. At home, with her husband, she was the one in charge. He never questioned any of her choices.

Charles and the two children greeted the sisters, standing on the front porch looking like a family from a magazine. Pat noticed immediately how beautiful Winter was, a perfect doll, the most beautiful girl she had ever seen, prettier than the photographs and with such a winning smile. The children were dressed up as if for church, Winter with her hair in sausage curls. Pat remembered how much she hated the scalp yank of wrapping her hair in rags. It made her smile, that Tommy was imposing the curls on her daughter. Jet was tall and handsome, a younger replica of his father. Both held the same reserved kindness.

Charles took Pat's luggage and Tommy instructed her children to kiss their aunt, which they obediently did. Winter embraced Pat with a big kiss and told her boldly that she couldn't wait to get to know her. "I've heard about you my whole life and now you're here." This made Pat smile too, knowing that Tommy spoke about her enough that Winter was eager to meet her and imagined it had been the same for Slim — he'd said as much after he'd met Tommy in July when Glenna died. "She's some woman, Mother. She doesn't quite seem real."

And now here was Pat after all these years. She wanted to make an impression on Tommy's children, the way Tommy had on Slim. She wished she had brought them presents, but she hadn't been able to think of what to get them that they would like and that she could afford. Winter took Pat's hand and led her into the house and upstairs to the guest room. Tommy followed, instructing Winter to be careful not to brush the walls. Though she addressed Winter, she was really addressing them all.

"Mother," Charles sighed.

"Well, they've just been painted," she said, a nervous energy hovering around her.

The room was clean and spare with white linens. Against this backdrop, the smooth and cleanly painted walls, Pat felt shabby in her worn-out best dress. Jet slipped away, disappearing into his room. Tommy apologized for him, saying that he was studying for exams. "He's a junior, you know. He has to do well for colleges. It's hard to get in these days and he's shooting for Yale." She was speaking in shorthand, a language of know-how that was unfamiliar to Pat. Most of her visit she didn't see much of Jet for all his studying and basketball practice. Folded on the bed was a set of white towels just as Pat had seen hostesses do in the magazines.

The house was filled with antiques, heavy silk drapes in the living room, a room the family didn't use much, if at all. But the first days of the visit, the sisters were hardly at the house. While the kids were at school, Charles off to work in his suit and polished shoes, the sisters toured about, seeing the other homes that Tommy had owned, and then visiting the city in the afternoon — lunch at the Rainbow Room.

There were two previous homes. The first was very small, where Jet was born. It was a little ranch, not dissimilar to Pat's home in Los Angeles and it was hard for her to imagine her sister ever fitting into it with all her things and taste. The second was also in Hasbrouck Heights, and Tommy told Pat that it had a spectacular view of the city that you couldn't quite see from the street. Tommy parked in front of the house, a good deal larger than the ranch, two stories, a basement. Pat's home didn't have a basement.

"That's how it works," Tommy said. She was wearing dark sunglasses. On her ring finger was an enormous diamond that captured the sunlight, spraying the car with color as she gesticulated. "You start with a little house in a lesser town, let it increase in value, and then you buy a bigger house in a better town. The war helped." Stepping-stones, Pat thought. Somewhere inside she felt ashamed that she and Hank had never been able to step across those same stones. They rented their home and so would never accrue the kind of equity Tommy spoke of.

In this house, Tommy explained, they lived during the start of the war. Pat studied the house, big windows, and painted an East Coast white. Tommy had written, and telephoned, during the war. Pat remembered the stories. In particular, she'd been fascinated by Winter, jealous that Tommy had a daughter. As a child, Pat had sometimes felt Tommy was her mother, that she was Tommy's daughter. Further, Tommy's family had seemed so important with Charles doing big things for the government, something to do with radio frequencies. She remembered that Winter, very young at the time, had thought her father was a German spy. He was too old to go to Europe, but he'd wanted to help, of course. His mission was secret and hadn't been explained to Winter. She thought he worked for the Germans because his behavior had been so peculiar. Pat could recall the scene from Tommy's descriptions, Tommy reading Winter to sleep, *Br'er Rabbit, Uncle Wiggily Longears.* "Do you remember those books?" Tommy had asked in her letter, and Pat had, remembered being read to by Tommy. Tommy told Pat that more than once, after the reading was over and it was time to sleep, her daughter would sit up straight and ask if Daddy was a spy, big spooky eyes holding Tommy. Tommy tried to assuage the fear, but worried about the child's imagination, the effects of the war upon it. Pat would tell Tommy not to be too concerned, that it was healthy for children to use their imaginations to contain what scared them. Pat liked offering advice. The letters were a form of pavement, both sisters understood, paving a road for them away from the past with stories of the present.

The war was still with everyone, even now in the car, so close in the rearview mirror, just two years over. In California, in New York, during the war everywhere you turned there had been posters declaring the effects of the war: one of a girl sitting on her mother's lap, looking hungry, an empty table before her. The caption read: Not Enough to Eat. Everyone had had some role to play — even Glenna. Pat wanted to ask Tommy about that, if she'd been aware that Mother had been responsible for getting entire herds of cattle from the range to slaughter in order to get food to starving soldiers — negotiating with Sen. Pat McCarran and persuading him to get Nevada's stock to the hungry men.

Pat thought of Slim off in the South Pacific, how terrifying each day had been for her, that she would receive some awful news. She had heard how people received the news, and if ever there were an unexpected knock on the door the electricity of fear shot through her. At the time, she had written to Tommy, told her exactly where she had been when she learned about the bombs, in her living room, thinking it was the end of the world and Slim so far away. It had seemed impossible that he would ever come home. He had grown up fast, a sweet boy taking care of his grandmother, suddenly a sailor off to war. It had been silly, but all she could do was iron. Iron and iron, making wrinkled things smooth.

Tommy's life had seemed dazzling in the

letters and calls, the recipes falling from the substantial pages filled with Tommy's words. Theater and fancy restaurants high above the city, the opera ("I'm an opera buff," Tommy had written), a country club and golf and so many friends. She hadn't been braggy, just filling in the details of her life. It had seemed impossible to Pat, reading the letters, that the war could touch Tommy. But, of course, the war touched everyone.

Tommy and Winter had been in the city shopping, had been lunching at the Rainbow Room, were to take in a Christmas show when they had learned about the start of the war. As they came down from the restaurant and into the lobby there was a commotion. A crowd of people surrounded an elevator, the doors of which kept opening and shutting. Inside was a man, crouching in a corner. The crowd shouted, "Jap inside. Jap inside." A strong ox of a man pressed against the parting doors, forcing them open. The man in the elevator was a petite Japanese man, elderly, and he was crying as the crowd pressed in on him. A woman approached him and spat on him. That evening the entire country listened to the Pearl Harbor news on the radio.

My mother has fully entered the narrative now, existent, a beautiful six-year-old girl with dark sausage curls and a bold smile, dressed impeccably by Grammy, like a doll — even during the war. She had her own bedroom with a picture window in the house that Tommy showed off to Pat. From the window the city sparkled in the distance, above the dark and barren swamp of the Meadowlands. During the war when Winter inhabited the room, every so often she could hear the alarms sound for the practice air raids. The German submarines were just off the coast. The city would go dark to hide itself from them, the lights extinguishing like dying stars.

What Tommy hadn't known was the depth of Winter's fear, that it lodged inside of her as a monster — her father the German spy. Everyone in the country, it seemed, was afraid of the spies who lived among them. Winter would think about this after Mother had read to her and turned off the lights. Winter would lie awake, afraid in the dark. Sometimes she would recall the Japanese man, how terrified he was surrounded by the mob. She would wonder what had happened to him. Had he been pulled apart? She couldn't just lie there; she had to know the truth about her father. She would slip out of bed to see for herself what her father was doing. Sometimes she would just stare at the darkened city, worry that it could be bombed the way Pearl Harbor had been, that she would see it implode, the silhouetted buildings dropping one by one as kamikaze pilots dive-bombed — how utterly unimaginable that someone would want to die. Sometimes she worried the Germans would bomb her house. Even at six, she knew it was the Germans to worry about most, more than the Japanese, who she knew were being rounded up and disappeared into camps. Her parents spoke about it in the evenings, listening to the news on the radio.

She went downstairs, outside, around the front of the house where there were windows into the basement. She had to lie on the ground to have a good view. She peered through the basement window and watched her father in a dark turtleneck in the black night, illuminated by one dull lamp. When he was down there he always wore a black turtleneck. She loved her father more than anything. The way he'd hold her and make her feel protected, like nothing bad could ever happen to her, the smell of Sir Walter Raleigh tobacco woven into his wool. She lay on the cold ground and watched him, as if she were protecting him. She'd watch him grinding crystals, quietly and with that impeccable concentration. She wondered what he was doing it for. Her mother said he had a job in Washington. But he wasn't in Washington. He was here. She thought her mother must not know that he was here. Why did he wear the black turtleneck? Her mother always spoke of how she admired her father's elegance, the refined way he dressed, those polished shoes. Winter would watch until he turned off the dull light. She was certain he was a Nazi. She was certain he worked for the Germans, spying for them, sending messages to the boats just off the coast. It was the black turtleneck that gave him away. Tommy believed she understood the secret life of her daughter, but already Winter intuited that there were some things she needed to hold close. If her mother knew about her father, perhaps she would report him the way people were doing, telling on their neighbors, their brothers, their uncles, their husbands. It was known to everyone what happened to spies. More than any attack that Winter could imagine at that point, the idea of her father being a traitor and a Nazi made her understand what the famine posters and the mob around the Japanese man and all the blackouts could not: the terror of war, senseless, ripping lives apart right inside your own home.

But my grandmother didn't know any of this, stories my mother would repeat to me and my sisters many years in the future — the notion of her father as a spy haunting her still. "We all knew, everyone knew," my mother said, "what they did to spies. The Rosenbergs hadn't happened yet, but we already knew."

All through the war the sisters wrote and called. How they spoke and wrote and spoke, but really never talked about themselves. The sisters had seen two wars — one together, one apart. Pat didn't much think about Montana, the years there, growing up. Her life began when she met Hank. Reading the letters, she had felt again her abiding jealousy of her sister. Her sister's children were still little, perhaps scared, but still safe at home, still with Tommy, while Pat's boy had been close to Japan. "Won't you let me send you money for a ticket? Please," Tommy wrote. So many offers and each one a reminder of all that Pat did not have, all that Tommy did have. Pat couldn't help but wonder if Tommy was doing it on purpose, showing her, holding up the differences between them so they could be clearly appreciated. Tommy pushed and pushed the money, the offer of airplane tickets, until Pat found a way to justify accepting Tommy's dividend, for that is how Pat eventually saw it — a dividend created by the profits her name yielded. Such a simple truth: everything Tommy had, she had because of Pat. So finally Pat agreed, and here she was now seated in a car in front of Tommy's second home, on a tour of Tommy's upwardly mobile progress that somewhere Pat felt could have been her own.

"Where have you gone?" Tommy said, bringing Pat back to the car. Pat was lighting another cigarette. Tommy unrolled her window.

"I'm here," Pat answered with a smile, hating the memory of her jealous, measuring self. Somehow Pat recognized that she had always wanted to be saved — saved by Tommy, saved by Hank, saved even a bit by Slim. "Just thinking about the war. And Winter. She's so beautiful. Extraordinary, really. It's not an ordinary beauty."

"I know. I look at her sometimes and I wonder how I got her, where she came from. It's hard to believe that such beauty was produced by me. And there's no false modesty there. It's just a fact." She paused. "Your sort of beauty," Tommy said. "Sometimes I've thought I had your daughter. Isn't that strange? Sometimes I look at her and it's as if I have you all over again." Pat liked her sister in this moment. She wasn't pretending. They had been so close growing up that it was entirely plausible that Tommy had had Pat's daughter, just as Tommy had Pat's name. Pat felt for an instant that they could say anything to each other. *What has it meant to have my name?* Winter did resemble Pat. She'd thought that, but hadn't allowed herself to dwell there because of the child's astonishing beauty. Pat was not vain. But somewhere she loved that notion, that Tommy had had her daughter. Just one more thing that Tommy had that belonged to Pat. Pat wondered then, if she had forbidden Tommy from taking her name, where would Tommy be now?

"Beauty is as beauty does, however. And Winter is often very naughty and difficult," Tommy added. "A mind of her own, I suppose. She has a hard time listening and doing as I ask. You really shouldn't smoke so much. It's not good for your lungs. It will kill you. There are studies." The moment passed as Tommy settled in again to improving her sister. Tommy was always trying hard to improve people. They finished the tour of Tommy's homes and off they drove to the Rainbow Room, then to Tiffany's just to have a look around. Tommy spent money easily, as if the more she spent the more it replenished itself.

At Tiffany's, Tommy bought Pat a pair of gold earrings shaped like the flower of a dogwood tree. The salesman knew her and called her Miss Katherine, as did the people at the Rainbow Room, giving Pat the urge to correct, the desire to respond, to declare victory over her name. Instead she allowed the disturbance to flutter over her. She noticed across the days that the help at Tommy's house also called her Miss Katherine. Her children called her Mother, and Charles too called her Mother, though once Pat heard him call her Tommy, which made her both curious and also understand that he knew her story. And she was glad about that. Mostly Pat felt at a remove, like she was viewing a show. She was a spectator, watching herself and Tommy, watching the girls they had discarded long ago in Montana reemerge in the women they were now.

At Tiffany's Pat accepted the earrings, another form of payment, or dividend, putting them on in the mirror offered by the salesman and at Tommy's insistence, Tommy standing behind her. One sister impeccably dressed, silk and gloves, a cashmere shawl casually, yet stylishly, draped over one shoulder. Admiring her reflection, the earrings shimmering from her lobes, Pat could feel the temptation to become something more.

Her visit slipped by in this way, outings during the day, evenings with the family. Winter would nestle into Pat's lap, still a girl, warm and sweet, on the threshold of blossoming. She would tell Pat about her day, that she was trying out for the school play, that she had made the basketball team even though her mother was against it, that she was writing poetry and reading Blake and also Eliot. She asked Pat to tell her about Slim and about Hank and about their California lives. Slim had recently married. Pat didn't announce that it was because he got into a mistake with the girl, that then after all, the wedding and the setting up of a home together, that the girl had miscarried. Of course, Pat didn't mention all that, but the truth inhabited her mind nonetheless as she watched Winter's ease and entitlement.

Tommy would often admonish Winter, telling her she couldn't do this or that — her clothes were mussed, she was slow to clear the table, too fast in eating her food. *Elbows off the table, Mabel.* Pat wanted to warn Tommy, no need to improve this child — the dangers of focusing there.

In the mornings, Tommy hollered at both children for being slow, worried they'd be late. Pat could see fear on her sister's face, pure fear that a simple tardy mark could ruin their lives. Pat wanted to hold Tommy's hands in these moments, remind her that really it didn't matter if Winter was late. Tommy's demeanor made it seem she didn't like her daughter, a quality that reminded Pat of Glenna, of how Tommy could never quite be enough for Glenna. It also made Pat see that Tommy was using Winter to answer something, give her something that Glenna had not been able to achieve. Pat understood this, of course, because Tommy had worked her entire childhood to give that, whatever it was, to Pat: improvement. Pat felt for her niece, because in all that struggle to give, something was missing — the person. Winter was missing as Pat had been missing. Watching Winter, Pat knew unequivocally that Tommy's plan for nursing school had always been about Tommy, never about her, Pat, or her dreams. Either way, Tommy had made a mistake, and yes, Pat still felt the sharp edges of bitterness. Nursing school had either always been about Tommy or Tommy had lied about it.

Pat could see now that Winter carried the burden of her mother's ambitions.

"Basketball won't be possible, Winter. You have a split vertebra. You know that. You heard the doctor," Tommy continued.

"It's not true," Winter snapped back.

"Don't talk back to your mother."

Pat could feel her niece cling just a bit more tightly. Tommy was trying to protect something that didn't need protecting. The girl wouldn't like her much later if Tommy couldn't try to see her for who she was now.

Charles came in every evening at six sharp. He kissed his daughter and then his wife, poured himself a scotch while Tommy instructed him about their social schedule for the following days, dates after Pat would be gone — the country club, dinner in the city, and all the rest of their busy, full lives carrying on. Charles listened obediently and then went to the study to smoke his pipe and read the evening paper. The house filled with the aromas of a roast or whatever delicious dinner Tommy was preparing. She had always been an impeccable homemaker, even way back in Butte when she was just a girl obsessed by a book that she wanted to buy so she could learn even better how to master taking care of a home: Mrs. Beeton's something or other. Tommy's adulthood, though, Pat observed, was the antithesis of her childhood — safe and structured and abundant.

When Jet appeared, skulking into the kitchen, stooped, wane, silent, Tommy would say he could eat in his room because he needed to study. He smiled kindly at his aunt and asked her if she had enjoyed her day, "Mother show you a good time?"

"You have to do extremely well to get into Yale," Tommy explained. Pat could feel the pressure of Tommy's words weighing on Jet as he took his plate and left. But there seemed to be a system in this household and Pat didn't have the confidence to judge too much. She wished Slim had gone to college, sure. She knew it was important, but she could never have seen herself pushing as Tommy so clearly did. Tommy always wanted to be better than who she was. She was greedy, Pat thought, wanting to snatch from life more than it could give. She wanted that for her children, for her sister, for anyone, even if they didn't seem to want it for themselves — even the cleaning woman. Improvements. Pat heard her tell the lady that she should study for her high school diploma. "I'll give paid time off if you do," Tommy said extravagantly. "Really, it never is too late. We're just plain folk," she told the lady. "Education is what got us ahead." Pat could see right through her sister's distorted truths. Pat saw her diploma hanging in its spot on her living room wall in Los Angeles.

Beauty — a generalized beauty to the veneer of the house, of Winter, of the family, a doll's house — was precisely set so at first one simply noticed loveliness. Tommy kept a glass-doored credenza in the dining room in which she displayed an entire set of china and crystal that she never used, backlit like a display in a museum. She spoke of the Haviland and Rosenthal china, the Swedish Orrefors crystal, the Jensen silver. The names had meant nothing to Pat, but she couldn't miss that they were expensive. The guest room had linen blinds and a double bed with linen sheets and an eiderdown comforter. The bedside tables were marble topped, spare and spotless, just a tiny vase with a violet. Pat had never slept in such luxury, thinking briefly of her own home with all the repairs that needed to be done, the cracking ceilings and walls, chairs that needed reupholstering. But she and Hank didn't have the money for a better home so they became blind to the ugliness. Here, in the guest room, she was not blind and could see each flaw in her own home vividly. Looking in the mirror at the gold dogwood blossoms in her ears, she calculated all that Tommy had spent this week, hundreds of dollars, pulling the cash so easily from her wallet — bill after bill — for the earrings, the roasts, the luncheons out, the tolls, the cleaning lady — how much it all cost to make a life beautiful. And when Tommy wanted a deal, boldly she'd find a flaw and ask for a discount, claim that she and her husband were salaried people. And often her ploy worked. Pat lit a cigarette, smoking it next to the window, feeling the cool fall air.

But then Pat started noticing specific objects as she looked around the house, as she and Tommy had tea in the living room with the curtains open to let in sunlight. It was a formal room, with formal furnishings — elaborate figurines and porcelain lamps, the couches upholstered in golden fabrics. Enjoying the formal tea, presented by the maid, silver service on a silver tray, delicate china, fancy sugar cubes decorated with painted fondant pansies, Pat noticed with a shock the oil portrait of their mother above the fireplace, staring at both daughters with her exacting eye. It was as if Glenna were standing in front of them. Tommy was quick to notice Pat's reaction, regaling Pat with the story of finding it discarded in their father's attic, and the expense of having the portrait both restored and framed, staking her claim to it because of the money she had invested in it. Pat didn't want the portrait, but she was still irritated by Tommy's justification. She wondered why Tommy would want their mother's oppressive and commanding eye monitoring her life. *Are you showing off for Mother?* Pat wanted to ask.

Suddenly then Pat noticed all of it, all the loot — yes that's the word that came to mind — from the former life. Nancy Cooper Slagle's bowl was there, carried over the Allegheny Mountains — how many times Pat had heard that story — Glenna's Mirecourt violin, a pair of lamps from their father's Ohio home, a table. As she sat there, it all popped out at her, little stabs of recognition and memory. She wanted to see it and didn't; she was angry that Tommy had it, wished she had not noticed it, was mad at herself for always being the little sister, for her quiet, unarticulated anger smocked over by silence and the appearance of wanting to please. Tommy, Pat could see, was busy with her house, curating possessions and history. It seemed to Pat that Tommy felt it was her right to have these things because she had the nicer home, had the money to take care of them. A wash of hatred and disappointment spread across Pat as she sat there mutely, hands folded in her lap, revealing nothing, as if she hadn't noticed Glenna's watchful gaze, a young, beautiful woman who Pat could not recall and did not want to recall, sitting there quietly as if this were all fine, fine that Tommy take the possessions, take Pat's name, take her life — stepping-stones. Tommy took just whatever she pleased. In two days, Pat thought, she'd be gone. She wanted more than anything to ask why Tommy was so sharp with her daughter, almost as if she didn't like her. She was taking from her daughter too. If Pat wanted to be saved, she understood now, so did Tommy. Tommy had wanted Pat to save her and now Tommy wanted her daughter to save her, wanted her daughter to be everything she had not been, wanted her daughter to be more beautiful, smarter, better educated, richer, in order to prove up Tommy — like a homestead. Improvement. This wouldn't end well for Winter if Tommy kept persisting. Winter would get sick of the stories, just as Pat had, and then she would want something of her own — her own stories.

Then Pat wondered if Tommy had the trunk, suddenly, like a shot. Of course she had the trunk. Hadn't Slim told her that he had shipped it to her? Urgently, she wanted to see it. She wanted to stand up right then and start hunting for it.

"You don't remember Ohio at all?" Tommy asked, lifting the delicate china teacup to her lips, holding the saucer in her hand — the china so thin, transparent like paper. "Anything? Being pulled in the red sled by Father? The neighbor children who would watch us from the window in their house as Father pulled us through the snow?" Pat didn't remember, and the despair was almost crushing. She didn't want to think about that. She had erased that desire when she'd forsaken the stories for her own life. "The train ride west," Tommy continued. "The nuns? The snowstorm? Mother leaving us?" Pat hurt physically inside. She had spent her adult life forgetting. She wondered if Tommy was doing this on purpose. She also couldn't help but register that along with everything else, Tommy possessed the memories too, memories that should have been Pat's as well. She thought of Hank and then of her small house with the buckling ceiling.

"I don't. I was too young," Pat said, still

thinking about the trunk. She remembered the trunk. She remembered saving the trunk from the flames when the Acorn blew up. She remembered the fire. She remembered wanting to flee, to lead Tommy away and out of there, to take charge because Tommy seemed frozen. For a long time Pat had thought that if they had fled that night of the fire, if she'd been able to make that stand, it would have made her more equal to Tommy, stronger, and maybe then things would have been different. Maybe she'd have her own name still. She wanted to tell Tommy all this, but didn't. She didn't want Tommy's memories to interfere with her own.

Alone, she went to the attic because that is where a trunk would be. The steps creaked as she walked up them, but she continued. She felt like a thief. Tommy was in the kitchen, cooking. Pat liked the feeling of being sneaky, of getting away with something. The attic was finished, more like a third story. In the small hall, there were three doors: two facing each other on the sides and one door at the rear. She opened the door at the rear, and right there was the trunk. *Bingo,* she thought. The room was a catchall, dark and dusty and cluttered with boxes. Pat hadn't seen the trunk in years. Seeing it made memory come to life. It was as though the trunk held everything that was her childhood. Pat could hear a car park on the street below, could smell meat cooking. She took hold of the trunk and tilted it to her so she could see the back, and there she saw the black lick from the long-ago flame. She could feel her eyes prick, then pool. She rubbed them dry. She could hear herself screaming at Tommy for them to leave before the neighbors woke up, for them to run off. She remembered wanting that more than anything, the feeling of flight and bravery, the longing to disappear with her sister. She knew that by doing nothing they'd be found out, sent off or, worse, sent back to Glenna. Pat opened the trunk, the lid giving easily. As a little girl, she had thought the trunk was their home. There was nothing inside. Quickly she closed the lid and left.

On her way back downstairs, Pat hesitated in the short hall, placed her hand on the doorknob of one of the other two rooms. Just a peek, she thought, hearing Tommy far away in the kitchen, wondering what else she might find. The first room belonged to Charles — a truth that made her catch her breath. The room was tidy with a tall bureau and a coatrack, a desk, and a bed. There was a shoe stand upon which stood a pair of Charles's polished shoes. Charles had a room on the third floor. The secret room was above Pat's. She understood now that what she heard above her at night was not the house settling, but his quiet steps as he undressed and got into bed. Pat imagined there could be an explanation, that he snored or had trouble sleeping. She had heard about that with couples. She thought about Hank, about how they would never think of sleeping apart, of how even today they still slept naked next to each other. She missed him terribly. She understood clearly and for the first time that she had something that Tommy did not.

The feelings were almost too much for her, exhilarated by the flaw and the meaning, horrified that her sister's veil of beauty could be only just that. Somewhere she had wanted her sister to have created her lovely present out of the miserable past. But there was also that ugly delight that we all know to be wrong, but that we enjoy just the same.

Behind the third door, which Pat also opened, of course, was a bathroom — neat and spare with a single toothbrush suspended in the toothbrush holder, like an exclamation point.

■ ■ ■ ■

The day of her departure caught Pat by surprise. She was so deeply into Tommy's world that as much as she missed Hank, she hadn't realized how fast the days had passed. The children kissed Pat goodbye before darting out the door for school, lovely and fresh — sweet, golden children. Charles had said goodbye the evening before. It was a warm day. Tommy was dressed, never lingered in her robe in the morning the way Pat did at home. The maid had arrived and was going about her chores, dusting and polishing all those objects from Ohio: a silk screen, a chair, a claw-foot table of curly maple. Tommy handed Pat a cup of coffee and asked her to come with her to the backyard, where they sat at a little glass-topped iron table. A big maple canopied them in all its color, a light breeze ruffling the leaves.

"I'm sad you're leaving," Tommy said. "It's flown by."

"Too fast," Pat replied. She was calculating the time of her flight's departure. She took a cigarette from her purse and lit it. She had the sudden urge to look inside Tommy's purse, find her wallet, open it and scan her driver's license, see if the name read Katherine or Thelma, see if Tommy had legally changed her name. The misery and injustice that swarmed poor Pat's brain. And Tommy, did none of this infect her? Why would it? Her deed had served its purpose. Blithely Tommy moved forward, making her life more and more comfortable, correcting, yes, by moving only in one direction.

"I don't want this to happen again," Tommy said. Pat looked at her, and there was a sadness in her eyes. "I don't want us to fight, to go so long without seeing each other. Promise me?" She took Pat's hand and held it. In holding it, it was as if all the years between childhood and now evaporated. They were sisters, after all, but Pat couldn't quite let go, and she couldn't, either, articulate the mess of her grievances without surrendering more of her dignity. So Pat wasn't sure what to say until she found herself saying, "Of course we won't let it. You'll come to California and I'll show you the Pacific Ocean." She squeezed her sister's hand and then tried to release hers, but Tommy wouldn't let go. They sat there for a bit, not saying what needed to be said. "I don't want you to leave," Tommy said. "I like having my little sister with me. It feels right," she said. Then she added, "Will you promise me one more thing? Will you promise me that you will stop smoking? Do you remember the snakebite?" she asked. "I couldn't bear it if you died before me."

When Tommy went upstairs to prepare herself to leave for the airport, Pat's luggage in the front hall, Pat slipped into the parlor, and without thinking much about it and because she could and because it was just as much hers as it was Tommy's and because she wanted Slim to have something from her past, she took Nancy Cooper Slagle's Cantonese wedding bowl down from the shelf, then moved other objects to fill the empty space. Back in the hall, Tommy's footsteps above on the second floor, Pat deftly opened her suitcase and used her clothes to wrap the bowl, protecting it for the journey home.

8
A STRANGER COME TO TOWN

Tommy wouldn't get the bowl back until Pat died — thirty years down the road, life moving on and away and then boiling down to a sister in bed in her Vermont Knolls apartment. Pat was dying of lung cancer. Hank was dead. Their father was dead. Jet and Winter and Slim were all married, all had children, though Slim's were adopted because his wife couldn't conceive. Life was doing its thing — one dose of happiness to three doses of challenge and misery. Pat lay on her deathbed surrounded by pillows, smoking her cigarettes, puffing away, Tommy pleading with her to quit, understanding, because she was a registered nurse — once an RN always an RN — how the cancer worked inside the lungs, eating them from the inside out. She could see the disease's handiwork as if she were inside her sister's lungs.

"Why in the world would I bother?" Pat

answered.

"Because they're killing you," Tommy said.

"They've already killed me." There was no beauty remaining in Pat's face; she was wizened and wrinkled and angry.

How do I know all of this? A stranger come to town, Nancy LePine — the woman mentioned earlier, whom I promised to get to — who wrote a letter to Grammy and that Grammy saved with her important papers stored in her black box. The letter actually didn't say too much, thanked Grammy for the visit to Last Morrow, telling Grammy what a splendid time she had had learning to eat a lobster, picking clean all the little crevices the creature contained, thanking Grammy for the dinner at the Whistling Oyster and the excursion on the *Ugly Anne* — seeing the coast from the water brought Ogunquit to life in an entirely different way. But Grammy had saved the letter, and when I stumbled upon it, it verified something for me: that Nancy had in fact been important to Grammy. By this time, Nancy and I had become friendly. She'd written to me after Grammy died, after reading a piece I'd written on Grammy for a magazine. Nancy had some stories to share with me. It turns out she'd been a neighbor of Lavern's in Ohio, had grown up across the street, the oldest of a pack of girls. Her parents were friends with Lavern and Hattie, his wife. Nancy was several years younger than my mother, but there was something about Nancy that made my grandmother want to take her on, a project. Perhaps it was the way she watched our family, coming and going over the years from her perch across the street, showing up from New Jersey, taking over Lavern's house with East Coast airs and determination. "Your grandmother was a force," Nancy said to me. A stranger come to town, she was invited to insert her life into ours. She knew Slim, Uncle Jet, his first wife, my father, who got her a job at NBC long ago in the 1960s when he was a producer for *The Steve Allen Show*. She knew Pat. Now she knew me.

"Your grandmother, she changed my life," Nancy wrote me. "I wanted to be like her, like your mother, bold enough to take what I wanted from life — the way your mother must have learned from Tommy. Bold enough to marry a novelist, write poetry, have all those babies. It was strange, you know," she continued. "Pat was different. She wasn't like Tommy, or your mother. I visited her out there in California. We were close too. I called her Aunt Pat. But she didn't take what she wanted from life."

Nancy visited the first days of June 1968, a little one-bedroom apartment with a balcony overlooking a busy South Figueroa in Vermont Knolls and a little brown yard that had plastic flowers — daffodils and tulips, sunflowers — poking up as if that was the way flowers grew out here. Inside was dark and there was Avon everywhere because Pat sold it door-to-door to earn a living. Pat was tiny, shrunken, clutching her pack of Marlboros, tugging away on them. Her face was leathery and thick and she'd become mean, carrying on about Catholics and blacks. Deep in a closet within a closet, Pat had a secret arsenal of guns and ammunition for the day, she told Nancy, when evil would arrive to take over. She told Nancy she was a member of the Daughters of the Nile, an offshoot of the Eastern Star, and that they had plans.

A few days after Nancy arrived, Bobby Kennedy was assassinated. The two of them were glued to the television along with the rest of the world, just watching it and watching it, trying to make sense by hearing and rehearing the same information. The reporters got to Jackie Kennedy and she appeared on camera. Pat was lost in an easy chair. "I hate her," she said. Nancy looked at Pat with astonishment, sort of dumbly. "She's had everything she ever wanted," Pat explained.

"Everything?" Nancy asked. "You mean like losing a child in infancy and having her husband killed in front of her?" But Pat persisted. She hated Jackie's privilege, her entitlement — people who got everything they wanted from life. She didn't need to mention Tommy; it was clear Pat was thinking about her too.

These people you meet in childhood, they are hard to let go of. Nancy couldn't let go of Pat or of Grammy, and clearly Grammy couldn't let go of Nancy, and forward we tumble, returning now to Pat's deathbed and the reappearance of the blue bowl.

Nancy LePine was there, hovering in the background, trying to be useful, saying her goodbyes. Tommy had helped raise Nancy, had seen she'd gone to college, had helped her find a job in New York City. Nancy, named by Tommy for Nancy Cooper Slagle, now served as audience as she watched the sisters in their last act. Nancy was helpful, running errands for the sisters, washing dishes — all of them keeping busy with the business of dying. Tommy, expert nurse, straightened the apartment, wiped the counters, placed cool water at the bedside, changed the sheets, bathed her sister with a sponge, fed her sister pulverized and easily digestible food.

In the quiet sleeping hours, Tommy explained to Nancy that when death came it would come fast; Pat would disappear into the morphine haze and would not return. "I'm sorry," was what Nancy knew how to say. "I'm so sorry."

Pat knew this was how she would go too. She had business she wanted to take care of. She had Nancy dig out a treasure from the back of her lingerie drawer and present it to her, a pair of ugly gold earrings that rested in the big palm of Nancy's hand. Tommy knew exactly what they were: her father's gold fillings, plucked from his mouth after his death. Pat had turned them into the earrings, her inheritance. She said that she wanted Winter to have them. Tommy looked at the earrings, knew that Winter would not want them. Nancy seemed to know that too, and not just because they were ugly. Rather they held some hidden, painful secret that both Nancy and Tommy knew — the unspoken that bound the stranger permanently to the inner sanctum of the family. Nancy studied Tommy to see what she would say to her sister. Tommy said nothing.

"And I suppose you want Nancy Cooper Slagle's bowl," Pat continued, eyes hard on Tommy. "But I want Slim to have it. It's the one thing from our childhood that I have and I want him to have it."

"We're not talking about this," Tommy said. "We're going to get you better."

"Please," Pat said. "I ask that you do this for me, that you give this to me."

Tommy took out the ironing board and started ironing a pile of pillowcases, which Nancy then folded. It was mesmerizing to watch as the wrinkles turned smooth and were sorted out. What days women had, ironing and shopping and arranging and caring and cooking — the endless march of nothingness moving toward nothing.

"How do you make a life?" Pat had asked so long ago. Or was it, "How is a life made"? What did it matter? Some take more advantage than others. And now here Pat was at the door.

"Nothing is standing in your way anymore," Pat said. Her eyes were still that beautiful blue they had always been. Of course, nothing had ever stood in Tommy's way and Pat felt, acutely, the pinched nerve of that. Tommy said nothing particular, continued to iron, sprinkling witch hazel on the sheets to keep them smelling fresh.

Pat repeated herself. Nancy watched and listened, fascinated by the sisters, the drama rippling between them.

"What are you saying?" Tommy asked.

"You can be Katherine now. There's nothing between you and Katherine any longer." A few days later Pat drifted into the haze and was gone.

With Nancy's help, Tommy went through Pat's belongings. She found Nancy Cooper Slagle's blue china wedding bowl, hidden at the bottom of the closet Pat once used for her arsenal of guns, but that now was filled with the Avon she'd been selling door-to-door — the products fragrant with their various perfumes. The bowl was wrapped in an old nightgown, intact. There was no equivocation. The bowl was hers, Tommy explained to Nancy, had been stolen from her.

"Slim's children, they're adopted," Tommy said. "The bowl won't mean as much to them."

Not so long ago, Nancy LePine sent me a package. Inside was a piece of jewelry, a tourmaline brooch that had once belonged to my grandmother. Nancy was returning it to me. "It will mean more to you than to anyone I can give it to," she wrote. Along

371

with it, she returned some more stories that she thought should be ours, that she thought I might like to use in a novel one day. Grammy had given the tourmaline to her when she had come to live in New York City, after college. My grandmother wanted her to have at least one thing that would make her appear to be a lady. My father had helped Nancy find the job at NBC, in the television world, where he had worked before he became famous. My grandmother had loaned Nancy furniture for her tiny studio apartment. It was the early 1960s. My parents had three of their six babies. Nikita Khrushchev was in the city on his *Baltika,* which my parents could see from a window in their Stuyvesant Town apartment, floating in the East River. In those days — the Cuban Missile Crisis, the Bay of Pigs — everyone was terrified of nuclear war, and my parents would have dinner parties to celebrate the end of the world, inviting Nancy because she was young and scared. Important to my grandmother at the time was that Nancy have this brooch to wear.

I was glad to have the brooch back, even if I hadn't known before of its existence. It was as though a part of my grandmother had been returned to me after so many years away.

But I've gotten ahead of myself.

9
D-Day

The summer after Pat's visit, the sisters' reunion after so many years' estrangement, Katherine took Jet and Winter to Chillicothe, showing up in the Lincoln all the way from New Jersey. As Pat had surmised, Katherine's marriage was in trouble: Charles was having an affair. Katherine told no one, of course, but somehow everyone knew. Moving forward, direct course to the future, was Katherine's trusted approach. She knew enough to know that all situations sort themselves out, one way or another. The other woman was a void. Katherine knew nothing about her, not even her name or her perfume. Rather than imagine, she told Charles to figure out what he wanted and then to let her know. She packed her children and off they went to her father's home in Chillicothe, just as they did every summer, but this time the length of her stay was indefinite. Just that she could do this was salve enough, that she could go home. She was not a sentimental woman, but this notion of returning home filled her, allowing her to feel normal, the same as everyone else.

She thought about herself, of course, where she had gone wrong, for she knew she had gone wrong. She had enough introspection to understand her role. All very subtle and quiet, and when confronted, Charles did not deny. Everything does not boil down to sex, but even so sex is important and had been enjoyable once, when she was younger. Now it felt more an insistent obligation and she was anxious, worried about the children, that they would have a lovely home themselves, about their education, that they would do well in school, go to good colleges, excel, be better than she had been. How she would have loved to tell Charles of her fear, that her children would not do better than she had. He would have been understanding, loving, as he had been about her name. How she would have loved to seduce him, take her top off and offer herself to him the way she once had. But she hadn't and she couldn't, and time accumulated. Somewhere along the way, the particulars of her marriage, the romance, the friendship had been swallowed up, leaving both her and Charles orbiting independently in their shared universe. It had not bothered her, until finally, it had bothered him.

In Chillicothe, everyone was busy about Katherine's arrival, not with preparations so much as with gossip. Even Nancy LePine was busy, counting the minutes, because something always happened when the Browns came to visit. Katherine was coming for a long time, planned to stay into the fall if she had to. She was telling her folks, Hattie and Lavern, that her house was being sold and they were fixing up a new one, extensive renovations, and had nowhere to stay in the meantime. No one believed the story because come schooltime Jet would be headed back to live in an apartment somewhere with his father. Why couldn't they all live in an apartment together? It didn't smell right.

Hattie wasn't happy about the arrival. She discussed this openly with the ladies over tea in the afternoons. Katherine, whom Hattie called Thelma, was bossy, took over the house, smelled it up with the fried doughnuts she liked to make, set everything into an order that was her order. "Hospital corners," Katherine would say, and instruct

Hattie how to make a bed properly the way she'd learned in nursing school at Brooklyn Hospital. "I know how to make a bed," Hattie would tell her friends. The ladies listened. Hattie had her own reputation. She wore a lot of makeup, spoke loudly, and was extremely vain even if she was stout. She spoke often about sex and her intimacy with Lavern, that he liked sex — still at seventy. She'd been married before, long before, but the rumor was, and it could have been that Hattie herself spread it, that her husband had come home one day to find her in bed with Lavern and threw her out. She'd gone to live with Lavern and his wife and young daughters as a boarder, causing trouble in that household — sending Glenna and the girls all the way to Montana. But that was old news, deep, deep time news — covered over and smoothed out by the consistency of their marriage and the progress of time. There were some who didn't even remember the story. The new news was Katherine, who was not even Katherine, and her visit promised to both entertain and upset in one way or another.

"Why does she use her sister's name," Julia LePine, Nancy's mother, asked Hattie, to remind her, sitting around in the parlor of Julia's home, across the street from

Hattie and Lavern's. Julia had heard the reason a thousand times, but even so she liked to hear it again. Some stories just never lose their appeal. Afternoon, the light dimming. "You just can't start using your sister's name in life. My name is Julia, plain and simple." She wore simple clothes and had big glaucous eyes encased in large dark brown circles like coins overlaying her sockets. She was a kind woman who taught elementary school music. When school was out, she taught private lessons with a stream of young musicians flowing in and out of the house. Her husband, Edward, worked as a guard at the federal penitentiary and also at the veteran's hospital. But he didn't care about that work so much as he cared about his car, a seven-year-old used 1941 Plymouth Try-Me Taxicab repainted gray. On days off and on the weekends, the family would go out just to drive, taking Hattie and Lavern on long country drives. It was their first car; they called it the Gray Goose. While the ladies were in the parlor, Edward would often be in the driveway with his special cloth, shining the car until it sparkled new. Sometimes Lavern would help him and the pair would get sweaty shining the car. Lavern didn't have his own car, but they did have their own world here, with friends and an order all their own. When Katherine came, she upset the order, stared down her nose at it, cast aspersions from her tower — or so Hattie believed.

"Thelma didn't go to high school," Hattie responded, "but she wanted to go to nursing school and the only way there was through. She stole her sister's name because Pat was smarter. Pat had a degree." Everyone referred to Pat as Pat, even though Pat was really Katherine. No one questioned Pat's name, imagined it had been thrust upon her when Thelma annexed Katherine. "Sisters," Hattie continued, as though that one word explained everything. "They didn't speak for years." Hattie was a practical nurse, worked in an old folks home, people suffering from dementia, many of them a good deal younger than she was. She added, "Thelma cheated." Hattie knew well the hierarchy, that in the hierarchy the registered nurse was on top and the practical nurse a good deal closer to the bottom.

On the stairs outside the parlor, Nancy, Julia's oldest daughter — she had three — would perch and listen to the gossip. From her spot she could see both her father outside and the feet of the ladies inside, hear them as she watched him, listening to them talk about Katherine as her arrival date approached.

Lavern's family had lived across the street from the LePine family for generations, it seemed; it was almost as if they were related. When Katherine came to visit on her own she stayed with the LePines sometimes. They were like a large extended family, and Katherine did enjoy coming home to them even if she suspected they all gossiped about her. Katherine understood that people gossiped when they were curious, when another's life was more intriguing than their own, and she understood as well that she had made something of her life. She didn't mind showing it off. Her private failure with Charles, that was hers to navigate and none of their business.

Lavern, who called himself Vern, and Hattie had a nice old brick house on Musgrove Street, 115 — numbered after the second war when the town filled up again with returning veterans, and houses sprouted up for them to make families in. They were called war homes and went up fast like mushrooms. Lavern's house sat on a big plot of land with a shed in the back that Julia and Hattie called the Doghouse because Hattie would send Lavern out to it when he misbehaved. Sometimes they'd send Edward out there too just to get rid of both men. No one knew what went on in that shed and no one really cared, as long as the men were out of the women's hair.

The LePine house, at 120 Musgrove, was bigger and not quite so old. Since Katherine didn't get on with Hattie, she spent time with the LePines, teaching the girls to cook and to wash clothes and to keep order. Nan liked Katherine. Whenever she came she made doughnuts, perfuming the kitchen with sugar and cinnamon and teaching and instructing Nan and her little sisters, putting them all in aprons along with Winter and even Jet when they visited, aprons that were far too large for their frames, letting them get their hands dirty in the sticky dough, cutting doughnut holes. Katherine was a precise woman, and she worked on the doughnut dough like she was operating.

Katherine let the girls know that a woman could be many things, but it was also essential to be a good homemaker. Of the LePine girls, Katherine was closest to Nancy because she had given Nancy her name. When Julia was pregnant, looking for a name, Katherine suggested Nancy — Nancy for Nancy Cooper Slagle, who had marched over the Allegheny Mountains during the Civil War carrying her Cantonese wedding bowl, her seven children in tow.

"You're as good as family," Katherine had said to Julia. "If the baby is a girl call her Nancy." By offering the name, Katherine wove the LePine family permanently into her own.

Katherine was a good thirty-five years older than Nancy. Sometimes she'd treat her like a daughter and Nancy didn't mind that. "The key is education," Katherine would say to Nancy. "Education and imagination and working hard." She regaled her with stories of her life in the West, of sewing money into the hem of her dress so no one would know to steal it, the Indian reservation, Mary Shoulder Blade and Louise Bigfoot, the snakebite, the flu epidemic — stories her own daughter didn't care to hear. Hailstorms and swarms of invading grasshoppers. Winter did not like to think of her mother as a poor child, wearing gunnysacks for shoes, even if her mother was proud of these details. Katherine loved Nancy for listening, wide-eyed and curious about Katherine's antique past. Katherine would tell Nancy that she could do anything she wanted with her life, anything at all, that nothing need stop her dreams. "Hitch your wagon to a star," Katherine was fond of saying. As a child, Nancy hadn't understood that that was another way of saying *marry well.*

Katherine had come with Charles just the year before when they interred Glenna. Julia and Hattie and the ladies had talked about Charles at the time because he had such a handsome style and face and his shoes sparkled. He came from good folks, shoemakers who were famous for their simple designs and craftsmanship, shoes stitched by hand when it was still done that way and then even after it wasn't. His name was Charles Brown, of Buster Brown, everyone knew even if he never mentioned it. "He's eleven generations Lynn," Katherine liked to say. That meant his family had been on American soil for a very long time, and that fact made him better, more American than everyone else. He was eleven generations removed from the smell of immigrant struggle. "The Battle of Bunker Hill was fought in his backyard, Breed's Pasture." Winter's middle name was Breed. But the most distinguishing fact about Charles was the shoes. They were tangible, had apparent market value. Katherine would discreetly imply the connection and then extravagantly promise shoes for all the LePine girls.

Charles only came that once, but the

impression lasted — eleven generations Lynn, it just sounded good. His accent was called Bostonian, thick. He spoke as if the words came out edgewise and slowly, sort of stretched out like taffy. People could see for themselves that he was a good deal more handsome than Katherine was pretty and they spent time speculating on how she finagled him. Some kind of swindling. She always had a deal she was contriving and concocting, like her name, bending reality to her will, and she walked through the Chillicothe world as if it were there and populated just for her pleasure, for her to act East Coast snob in. Breed's Pasture! Some thought she visited just so she could show off. When Charles had come they had stayed in a hotel.

"She has airs," Julia would say.

"There is no doubt," Hattie would respond. "But she does love Vern. It's almost too much, like she needs to fill something that can't be filled. She calls him Daddy like she's still a little girl."

"Do you think Charles knows about her name?" Julia asked as this newest trip to Chillicothe approached. "It may be that it's her name is the cause of his affair. Stealing another's name is no small item."

For the ladies, the lover was no void. She

was fully formed sex appeal, worthy of Charles Brown of Buster Brown, eleven generations Lynn. Katherine's marriage was in trouble and she was fleeing New Jersey for the safety of home and maybe, just maybe she would be brought back down to size. In Julia's parlor you'd hear words cast about, alluring words that combined to titillate: *wandering eye, affair, other woman.* There was so much sex in the air the ladies couldn't wait for these afternoon teas. Katherine strived to be proper. She wore driving gloves and fancy suits and carried pocketbooks with gold clasps, drove a statement car, dressed her children like dolls. But rumors divide and multiply and then feed upon themselves until they're fat and juicy, because Katherine did in fact have a life that everyone else dreamed of, in New Jersey, because she got out, because she called herself Katherine when her name was Thelma. Most of all, what these women really believed was that it is not so easy to escape who you are.

When Katherine and her children arrived in the sweltering dry drought heat, the trees drooping in everyone's yard, Nancy LePine was sitting on the front steps of her Musgrove Street home, waiting. A young musician or two passed by her as they came for their lessons, scratchy sounds of beginners emerging from the parlor. The dust was so bad the streets needed watering by the fire department, the fire engines parading about, spraying water. The neighborhood children ran behind the trucks to get cooled down.

Katherine's black Lincoln slid into Hattie and Lavern's asphalt driveway, coming to a stop beneath the carport, pausing there like a person thinking. Then the front passenger door pushed open, propelled by a single foot in a bobby sock and a saddle shoe. The farther the door opened, the more leg was revealed. A slim ankle and accentuated calf, the foot pushing into the shellacked wood paneling of the door's interior, lazily like the owner of the foot had all the time in the world. From across the street, Nan watched the girl emerge with the eager expectation of a person who had been waiting her entire life for something to happen.

The foot moved to the asphalt and Winter stepped from the Lincoln — a tall, grown-up girl now, so much more mature than the last time Nan had seen her, which seemed to Nan like a very long time ago though it had only been a year. Winter wore shorts and a blouse and looked fresh and sophisticated, arriving in that shiny black car all the way from New Jersey. Her hair was in Shirley Temple curls. Nan came down off her steps, making her way shyly but definitely toward them, passing the Gray Goose, which in comparison to the Lincoln was really just a dull and ugly car.

Winter wore black sunglasses and was almost thirteen. She stared across the street, looked it up and down as if she were judging whether she could bear it here. She slammed the car door shut. She hadn't noticed Nan.

Then came Jet, an advanced teenager, with his jet-black hair, slicked back, unfolding himself from the backseat of the car, stretching his tall body, his arms rising above his head, his back arching happily in collusion with the stretch. He looked in Nan's direction, spotted Nan's eyes on him, and smiled. "Why if it isn't Nan LePine," Jet said, big and loud, calling her Nan the way she liked. Katherine too came from the car and opened her arms to Nan, who ran immediately into them. Then she ran into Jet's arms and he hugged her as well, just a tiny little eight-year old in his enormous embrace.

Jet's name was really Charles and Winter's name was really Winter, but she had recently started calling herself Pete. That's how she introduced herself to Nan as if she'd never met Nan before, Nan whose name was really Nancy. No one's name was as it was supposed to be; even Hattie's real name was Beatrice, because everyone, it seemed, wanted to be somebody else.

"I'm Pete," Winter said, rolling her eyes over Nan, taking her in, deciding if she'd do as a playmate. Winter scanned the street again and then Nan, seeming to realize there might not be a lot of choice.

Nan looked to Katherine for the truth of Pete's name, fine in a summer suit, and swept her eyes off to one side to indicate that her daughter had a touch of eccentricity, and then she said, "We're home." Katherine asked Jet to help her with the luggage and off they went to the house with the suitcases, leaving Pete and Nan behind.

"That ain't your name," Nan said.

"Ain't is not a word," Winter said, lifting up her sunglasses and resting them on her head. Around her wrist she wore the prettiest gold bracelet, malleable like a ribbon but gold all the same with a small diamond clasp. As she moved her arm the bracelet moved too, sort of as an echo. Her eyes were cold, like they could have been blue if they'd tried a little harder. "You say isn't or is not, but you do not say ain't," she instructed.

"Pete *is not* your name," Nan said. She was wearing a raggedy summer dress, too short for her fast-growing legs, dirty from the dust. Her hair was blond and short and straight. Her feet were bare and soot blackened. She sneezed and itched her nose, which she did a lot because of a sinus problem and allergies.

"You will call me Pete," Pete said.

"Why isn't your father here?" Nan asked boldly with the hungry look of a child who wants to know the truth and isn't afraid to ask.

"You're fresh," Pete said and slapped Nan's face, right on the cheek and hard, the gold bracelet an aftershock. Nan looked at her with a dumb little stunned frown, but also some amount of fascination. If Katherine was alluring to Nan's mother and her friends, Pete was just as alluring to Nan, and for the same mysterious reason privilege everywhere is alluring.

The two girls became friends, as much as a teenager can be friends with a child. Winter bossed Nan around a lot and set her straight a lot, corrected her speech a lot, asked her to do her favors and to accompany her on excursions to town when she didn't have permission. Nan followed along, waiting to see what Pete would do next, and soon it got to be ordinary that Pete was Pete.

When Winter was born, Katherine had been terrified — an emotion that surprised her and that she stuffed back into a secret place within her heart, but that she was familiar with all the same. The baby had been astonishingly beautiful. Winter had reminded Katherine immediately of Pat as a girl — the stunning ethereal beauty. In the haze of hormones and recovery, she worried most that she would not be able to protect this child from the horrors the world can bestow on girls. Katherine was greedy; she wanted everything for this baby, for her to grow up in privilege, have a mother and a father at home, be entitled, want for nothing, be endangered by nothing, and in having all of that it was Katherine's hope that Winter would somehow correct her own past. Sometimes Katherine would stare at her daughter, wondrous that within her such beauty had been created.

Her fears for Winter did not subside as Winter grew. Rather the fear grew too. In school, Katherine would not allow Winter to participate in gym. All of Katherine's nursing knowledge compounded the fear so that a minor concern of the pediatrician swelled into spina bifida, which allowed Katherine the excuse to keep the child out of gym class. "I'm a registered nurse," she proudly told the school's principal when explaining why Winter needed to be excused.

Katherine kept Winter in the most exquisite clothes, an armor against Katherine's fear — hand-washed and pressed. She would dress her up from top to bottom with little bow-clips holding back a curl, a ring of lace frill just at the cuff of her bobby socks. Even in Ohio and even though Winter was now Pete and almost thirteen years old, Katherine still selected her clothes. In turn, sometimes Pete would dress up Nan, putting the little clips in her hair, using ribbons as belts to tighten the outsized dresses. Nan wanted more, wanted Pete to let her wear the lovely gold bracelet that dangled so effortlessly from Pete's slender wrist. "Not a chance," Pete said.

Katherine would warn Pete not to get dirty, to watch out for her issue, the spina bifida. "She has spina bifida and can't play like ordinary children. She can't ride a bike and run and play kickball so don't encourage it," Katherine instructed Nan. But Pete did as she pleased, all those things she wasn't supposed to do. And she got her pretty white clothes so filthy that Katherine would yell at her, which was always followed by some kind of punishment. Katherine would holler at Jet too for not studying enough even though that was all he did, pale and gloomy, working to get into Yale or Princeton. Julia would tell the ladies at tea that fear possessed Katherine. "They don't go to church," Julia said to her friends.

All summer, Pete dressed and undressed, discarding filthy clothes, leaving them on the floor and stepping into a new outfit. Katherine scrubbed the clothes clean, hung them on the line, ironed them so they looked new all over again.

Pete had no problem announcing to Nan that she had made the varsity basketball team at her junior high school, intended to continue in high school, played point guard. "It's a leadership position," Pete said to Nan, then added, "spina bifida," and shook her head in a way that said all at once that her mother was crazy. "There's nothing wrong with me."

Nan followed Pete everywhere like a pet and she grew on Pete. Pete liked having Nan around, although she didn't like the sniffling and the sinus stuff. "It's annoying," she'd say. "Blow your nose." But they chatted about everything, about sex even. "I bet you don't even know anything about sex," Pete said once.

All summer the extended family came and went. Glenna's sisters and brother came to see Katherine and the children, Katherine showing them off, letting them know that Jet was headed to an Ivy, which meant next to nothing to these Ohio folks. Mostly, evenings Katherine made family dinners and invited Julia and Edward to join, the big table filled with people and a meal.

Days the girls moved at their own pace straight across that summer while Nan's parents worked and Katherine cooked and cleaned and set her father's finances straight, writing checks from her own checkbook to pay off expenses, fixing all that was wrong so the household ran efficiently. Prodigal daughter, she'd made something of herself, she'd gone far for the family and could help them out. Hattie and Lavern politely conceded to Katherine's management, Hattie in her nurse's whites going off to the old folks home. She had been a practical nurse for years, back when they were still used and there was the need for lying-in when a baby was born. She had helped the babies come out, had helped the mother adjust to the baby. She had been there for Nan's birth and all of Nan's sisters' births too. But now babies were born in hospitals, so Hattie's work migrated to the old folks home.

Lavern had circulation problems, spent a lot of time in the doghouse because this way he avoided his bossy daughter and wife and could have some peace. Katherine would let him drive her Lincoln and he'd take it to town, take Nan and Winter for ice cream, sitting tall behind the wheel. Katherine liked that she could give her father moments that made him feel bigger, glad she'd made something of herself and that it reflected directly back on him. "Daddy, take the car," she'd say — the car, not my car, as if it were their collective car.

After a while, it felt natural that Katherine was here, that her name was Katherine and not Thelma. This was her family. She declared that a lot, like it didn't matter that things weren't perfect. Katherine would make them perfect with her cooking and her cleaning and her checkbook, her outfits even for Pete and her studying for Jet. She was manifesting perfection. It was part of what was mesmerizing about Katherine; she was going to have exactly what she wanted from this life. In the evenings, she called Charles, reported on the day, asked nothing.

Pete was no different. When she set her sights on something there was no dissuading her. She set her sights on her grandfather. She decided he needed spying on, to see what he was up to in that shed all day. "I bet he drinks and sees women in there," Pete said to Nan.

"For sex," Nan added, and the first time she said it Pete chuckled. "Mother and the ladies say that Hattie's a loudmouth, wears too much makeup." She spoke as though she liked knowing stuff about Pete's family that Pete didn't know herself, those overheard secrets the ladies spoke about in the parlor, and that sharing them could give her currency, make her feel a part of Pete's family.

"Well, anyone can see that," Pete answered. It was true, easy to see. Hattie's aging face drooped under the weight of the makeup, big circles for the rouge on the cheeks like she couldn't see well enough to rub it in. The bright red lipstick leaked into the lines around her lips. Clotted mascara turned her lashes into spiders' legs. But she walked with her head high and as though she were the greatest beauty alive. The Ohio relatives weren't the same as the Boston relatives, which Pete let Nan know. The Boston relatives were rich.

"We have to get into the doghouse when the dog isn't there," Pete instructed, twisting her index finger beneath the gold ribbon bracelet, an affect she had when she plotted. By this point in the summer, the weather had turned. The drought was over and now it rained at some point every day, a heavy pounding monsoon, and the trees rioted, grass thriving with dandelions everywhere and everything always wet, which made Nan's allergies and sinus issues even worse.

"Stop sneezing," Pete instructed.

Mornings Hattie would leave to walk to the old people's home, all dolled up in her starched nursing whites and sturdy white shoes. She'd even wear a fancy white hat that had nothing to do with being a nurse, shameless flirt ready to engage the inmates. She walked even though it was two miles away, striding with importance. Since Lavern couldn't walk much she wanted to walk for him, take his share and use it for herself. "I'm going to grow very old," she'd tell the girls. "You watch and see." The notion scared the girls, that Hattie could know her future.

But the future was far away and now everyone was young, or at least not very old, and Pete had a plan to get into the doghouse and catch Lavern doing something bad. Pete wanted something exciting to happen, she wanted a murder. "We need a murder to solve, Nan." Pete, with her big gray eyes, would look at Nan, and it would seem that Pete actually could produce a murder.

"Ain't gonna be no murder," Nan declared rationally.

"Is not going to be," Pete corrected, then added, "but yes there is, because we need one to solve." Even though a crime had yet to be committed, Pete decided grumpy Grandpa was the suspect. "He's not the victim, that's certain," Pete said as Lavern trudged across the lawn to the doghouse in his bathrobe.

He was a nice enough grandfather, if in fact a little grumpy, always sighing a lot and filled with an apparent expectation that Hattie, and others, should meet all his needs. But he was kind with the girls. He'd pinch Pete's cheek and tell her she was a beautiful girl and that he liked the length of her shorts and that she was fast becoming a woman. "You'll drive 'em wild," he said more than once, slipping her a piece of the butterscotch he always kept in the pocket of his robe.

Nan warned Pete once not to correct him, that he had a temper. "I'll do as I please," Pete responded. "He's my grandfather." But Pete never did correct him and he never revealed his temper to the girls. He wore slippers a lot and shuffled about. Red veins laced his cheeks. In the evenings, he would have a whiskey on the back porch beneath the shade of the tulip poplar and Katherine would tell him that he shouldn't drink so much, that it wouldn't help his heart.

"Daddy, please," she'd say. She didn't want him to die early.

"He doesn't seem like much, but he is," Pete told Nan. "He's heir to the throne in Scotland, but he doesn't care to claim it. His great-grandmother was Mary, Queen of Scots. He's royalty. He prefers America, staying here. He was a railroad man, opened up the West."

Nan gave her a suspicious, dumb little look, but Pete didn't care.

"We'll go in early before he wakes up and set a trap," Pete said.

"But no one's been murdered," Nan said.

"You're so literal," Pete responded impatiently.

"Who gave you that bracelet?" Nan asked. "It's pretty."

"Someone special," Pete said. "It is pretty." But she didn't say who gave it to her.

Lavern's shed stood blatantly in the backyard. No disguising it. No trees to hide under or around. "The only thing that will cloak us," Pete said, those bright gray eyes widening with mischief, "is the darkness of night."

"What if someone sees us?" Nan asked.

"It's a fact," Pete said, "that children can see in the dark, like cats. Adults can't see, so even if they're looking out the windows they won't spot us. We'll go under cover of darkness."

It seemed they spent forever planning, so long it appeared that the planning was the goal, more than actually getting into the shed. The planning involved stealing things. Pete liked to steal. She stole paint and paintbrushes and tools, hoarding them in a secret spot beneath the carport, stuff she said they'd need when D-Day came.

"But why? What do you need all that stuff for?"

"It's going to be an invasion and we're going to win."

"Why don't you just ask him permission?" Nan said.

"Are you completely stupid?" Pete responded with such force it seemed she might slap Nan again. "Where's the fun in that? And if he knows we're coming he'll hide the evidence."

So they studied him, watched him trudge across the yard, unlock the door, "There's a key involved," Pete said, tightening her eyes. His trudge was more like a pull, like he was pulling his heavy body across the yard. He was portly and smelled of old person, kind of musty, but he had the greenest eyes and a head of thick silver hair.

"He sure doesn't look like royalty," Nan said.

"How do you know what royalty is supposed to look like?" Pete asked.

Those eyes of his were always on Pete, like he was possessive, maybe proud, of his granddaughter.

In this way, summer rolled into September and Jet left on a train for high school back in New Jersey, his senior year, and Katherine admonishing him still to keep studying, to know his future depended on it. He kissed his mother and told her not to worry, put his finger to her reprimanding lips and told her he loved her. He was a kind, good boy. And he left. The girls started school. Still Charles didn't come and still Charles didn't say what he wanted when Katherine called him in the evenings to report the day, listening to him puff on his pipe, swirl the cubes in his glass of scotch. Instead of talking about what needed to be talked about, Katherine described the girls, colluding, sneaking about, Winter calling herself Pete, acting like a big sister.

Then just like that, D-Day arrived. Strange how that is, you wait and wait and it seems what you're waiting for will never arrive. But the day always does come whether you want it to or not.

Pete snuck into Nan's house, up the stairs to her room where she slept with her little sisters. She came to Nan's bed and gently woke her, whispering in her ear. It was late September but hot, Indian summer hot. Pete wore just the golden bracelet and a thin white nightgown that you could see right through even in the dark. Quietly Nan slipped out of bed and followed Pete downstairs, outside, across the street, and into the yard. Pete had been right; both girls could see perfectly in the dark. When they got to the doghouse door, they stopped. Pete looked at Nan, readying her for the invasion. Pete's light eyes glowed like a cat's. Nan was expecting to see the hoarded supplies but she didn't see anything other than

Pete and her eyes and thin white nightgown. Pete was beautiful. She was truly beautiful. You could see the outline of her figure, of her panties, of her little breasts beneath the gown, the shiny bracelet dangling from her wrist catching light from the stars. The nightgown had a pocket and from it Pete produced a key, holding it up for Nan.

"How did you get that?" Nan whispered.

"Do you really need to ask? Shh," Pete admonished. With her hand on the knob, the key poised to enter the lock, Pete turned the knob, and just like that the door opened. No need for the key after all. Pete's disappointment was palpable; she'd been a sleuth, gone to considerable effort to procure that useless key. The unlocked door surprised both girls, who sighed until Pete gripped Nan's arm hard, indicating that she should shut up.

Inside was pitch-black. At first they could see absolutely nothing, truly black. But then the weird vision of children settled in and the contents of the room revealed themselves, coming into an outlined focus, a small crowded room but organized and devoted to a U-shaped table upon which lay an elaborate model train. The girls squinted to see better as mountains and bridges and tunnels and towns all connected

402

by tracks emerged from the darkness. The mountains were snowcapped and the white snow stood out more definitely against the darkness. What they could see invited them to want to see more. Even cloaked in night, a lovely precision was evident — a miniature replica of a life somewhere, replete with rivers with actual water that glimmered silver through the darkness, people, animals, lampposts, depots, a constellation of equipment that made the trains run. The girls leaned forward for a better look. Pete reached out to touch something and then so did Nan. It was a world a child would want to play with, like a doll's house but grander. As they snuck their fingers toward the tracks, just like that the landscape illuminated, startling the girls. A steam trumpet sounded and the trains engaged, chugging this way and that. The only light came from the trains' headlights and the streetlamps in the various towns. Trees pushed down from the snowcapped mountains meeting mine shaft heads and tailing piles and other mining equipment.

"What did you do?" Pete asked, and again violently grabbed Nan's arm, forgetting to whisper.

"I didn't do nothing," Nan said, remembering to whisper.

"Anything."

"Anything."

But this little western world captivated them and they stopped arguing and looked at the tracks and the magic towns and the little figured people in hobbled skirts and top hats and long coats waiting on the platforms for the trains that were coming around — some passenger, another mixed, and yet another only for freight, the cars loaded: coal and wood and boxed supplies.

"See, I told you there wasn't anything to fuss over in the doghouse," Nan said.

"It's so intricate," Pete said. And their eyes followed a train as it wended its way around the track, forgetting to worry about how it had turned itself on. The station of the biggest town was at the end of the U and set against the mountains. Above the depot a sign read Butte. Nan coughed a little and sniffled, but Pete didn't notice. The train made its way toward the town, rising on a grade to a long, tall bridge crossing a river filled with the real water that lapped with the train's vibration at the shores of a smaller town. The other trains continued running too, on parallel tracks, on another side of the tableau — zooming along, horns blowing, crossing other bridges, crossing-gates closing and opening as the trains moved past. The girls lost time then to the story; they had no idea how long they stood there, but as their eyes followed the trains eventually they stopped on Lavern, sitting alone in a comfortable armchair maneuvering the controls in a back corner of the room. It was Pete who saw him first and got such a fright she jumped back, crashing into Nan, who stumbled to the ground and then fell into a fit of allergic coughing that this time did annoy Pete. "Stop that," she urged, as if the cough were to blame for the sudden apparition, as if stopping the cough could disappear Lavern.

"They're something, aren't they?" Lavern said with his rattly old voice. "I've been wondering when you girls would make it over here. I've been wanting to show this to you since you first arrived, Pete, and to your little friend too."

"You ain't mad," Nan managed to say through her coughing. Pete didn't correct her.

"Why would I be mad?" Lavern asked. "This is just the kind of thing a kid should enjoy." He sat forward in his armchair, making himself a little taller. He had some chew in his mouth that he kept wadded there, in the corner, and it pushed his left cheek out a bit. His eyes were their gorgeous emerald, holding the girls with an amused smile that brought him to life. He didn't look so old in this light. He invited the girls to come to the controls. To get there they had to sneak around the world.

Buttons and levers and switches and a big electric box stood on a low table near his chair. "This is what makes that tick," he said with a sweep of his arm. "I'm the Wizard of Oz." He chuckled at his joke, but the girls remained solemn. He flicked a switch and the trains all stopped. "First let's fix that cough," he said to Nan, who was wheezing again. He pulled out a little silver box of snuff, a reddish brown powder that he scooped up a bit of with his thumb and forefinger, held it to his nostril and inhaled. He then instructed Nan to do the same and she did, easily like she'd been doing it for a while. She breathed in deeply. He told her to do it in the other nostril. She did. The coughing stopped. "It works like a charm every time. Anytime you get the allergy cough come to me and I'll fix you up."

The girls stood there in their nightgowns not sure what to do next. He smelled sweet, of whiskey and of tobacco.

"Now you, little miss," he said to Pete. "I bet you want to drive these trains."

"Really?" she said.

406

"By all means," Lavern said.

"Can I?" Nan asked.

"You next," he said practically. "One at a time."

"Come over here," he instructed Pete, and she made her way to his chair. Before it lay the long panel with the controls, little lights twinkling. He told a story about all the time it had taken him to make this scene, that he'd been working on it for years and years. "More years than the two of you combined. It means a lot to me and I want to share it with you. I'm so glad you're here. So glad." His eyes glistened. "You know, Thelma wasn't always a proper lady. She was a girl once, lived in a world like this one here."

The girls were quiet.

"Now, this is complicated stuff, to drive them carefully so as they don't crash," Vern continued. "With all the trains, it's complicated and requires some skill, so listen carefully," he said to Pete, patting his knee to indicate she come a little closer, and she did. He adjusted his bulk in the comfortable chair.

Nan watched, paying close attention so she could learn for her turn. Lavern's eyes were on the tracks and one hand was at his granddaughter's waist as he showed her how to maneuver the levers and buttons to make the trains run, intersect and ride up the bridges and through the tunnels without colliding. "My daughters grew up out in Montana and here I've re-created some of the towns they lived in. I was a railroad man," he said. Pete worked the controls, the enthusiasm growing as she speeded the trains along, even as she was admonished for moving them too fast. "Whoa, whoa, not so fast," Lavern told her, but she seemed completely confident in her abilities. Lavern instructed Nan to go back to the end of the room, near the door, so she could have a good view of the tracks. Nan obliged.

That end of the room exposed a broad and comprehensive view of the trains chugging about, passenger and freight running this way and that. Above Nan was a large iron latticed bridge rising to span the tables, uniting them and making an oval out of the U.

Pete set off the steam trumpets and whistles, racing the trains up and down those tracks, one careening past another, blowing through Butte, making the water in the stream ripple. What a world. Pete sat in her granddaddy's lap, the two of them illuminated in shadowy light, Pete listing forward from him with her eyes on the tracks. Nan at the back, watching grandfather and granddaughter, tapped her foot impatiently, awaiting her turn. It seemed Pete was driving the trains forever, would drive them into the next day and the next and the next and no one would ever stop her from driving those trains. The girl got just exactly what she pleased. The screaming steam trumpets echoed annoyingly around the room. Then the light of a locomotive trained itself on Pete, caught Pete's expression, a weird, ugly expression, her torso hiding her grandfather's face. She was making the trains go faster and faster and it was as if the urgency on her face made them follow her will. The glow of the panel too shined right up from beneath her, lighting her like an actress in some weird old-fashioned movie, all light and dark, so that Pete looked both scared, like terror, and also peaceful and serene and excited all at the same time, her body moving rhythmically in a slow consistent dance — a weird little look that didn't know what it wanted to be or what it was doing. It carried on for a long time as Nan stood at the back of the room, mesmerized as Pete transformed, mutating with the power of driving the trains.

"That's right," Lavern said softly, stroking Pete's hair. Nan almost yelled out that it was her turn now. She was seized with impatience. It seemed that Pete was as selfish as ever because she should stop and let Nan have a go. It felt loud and hot in the room, and just as Nan was about to yell out, the door sprung open and there was Katherine with her hair down, catching in an instant the whole scene, her daughter in her father's lap.

"What's going on in here?" she said, switching on the overhead light. The magic drained, everything becoming bright, dull, and ugly. Katherine was in her nightgown too. She had her eyes on her father and her daughter, frozen together in his big and comfortable chair. "Daddy?" Katherine said, puzzlement adding up fast — the spinning wheels of a slot machine just settling into position. "What are you doing with my daughter?" Winter sprang from his lap and then, terribly, Katherine understood everything.

"Get to bed girls," she said, something sticking in the back of her throat. "Now. Get to bed, I said." And for the first time all summer Pete hopped to attention and listened to her mother. She flew out the door in her summer nightgown. She didn't bother to wait for Nan or say her good nights or express apologies or explanations. She disappeared into the house and was gone. "But, Daddy," Katherine said. She repeated it twice, weakly. Even so it was impossible not to hear the long, thin indelible fracturing.

This was a story that my mother had never told me. When I asked her about it, she looked at me, puzzled, thought for a moment and then said, "Why would Nancy LePine tell you that?"

In the morning, Winter was crying, carrying on about her bracelet, which had somehow gotten lost, that lovely gold bracelet, while Katherine was busy filling the car with all their things, reassuring Winter they'd get another bracelet, Winter helping her mother with the luggage — the two of them the way a mother and daughter should be, though Katherine's determined look was broken. By 9 a.m. the black Lincoln slithered into the Indian summer heat and down the road to New Jersey. Just like that they were gone and they never did come back and Katherine never did see her father again.

In the middle of the night, Katherine had called Charles and had told him that she was coming home, that there was no more room for choice or contemplation, they would move back into their house all together just as soon as she could get there. A weight crushed itself against her chest, heavy and insistent. She wanted to speak with Charles honestly, tell him what she wished she could unknow. Winter had crawled into Katherine's bed, was lying there herself trying to unknow. And where do we go from here? "Is everything all right?" Charles had asked. How could she answer that; she thought of his family, then hers, thought of Glenna with the photographs clutched in her dead hands — that last futile hope. There were not many times that Katherine felt the hot prick of tears. "I'm waiting for you," Charles said to the silence.

Katherine held Winter across the night, close to her chest so she could feel her daughter's heartbeat against her own, so Winter could understand that she was not to blame. In the morning, behind the steering wheel of the Lincoln, Katherine sat tall, composed, eyes forward.

"Who knows what to believe," one of the ladies said at one of Julia's gossip sessions, Hattie not present, shortly after Pete and Katherine left.

"Nonetheless, it's better to take care," another said. "I wouldn't be letting Nan do just as she pleases around there."

Julia sat quietly.

"It's the rich ones always inviting the most drama," another lady said.

Nan, sitting there on the hall steps, listened, watched the ladies' feet while her father shined the Gray Goose.

10

A WEDDING DRESS

Here's a story my mother told me, sitting in
my living room, drinking a glass of wine.
Somehow we'd gotten on the subject of
wedding dresses. This was after Grammy
had died and before Mom developed dementia, before the discovery of Grammy's
black box, which contained the newspaper
notices of Mom's wedding and also of Jet's.
The notices paid particular attention to the
brides' dresses, details I found mesmerizing.
As so many stories are, this one my mother
told me was about more than the ostensible
subject, the dress. It was about my father,
about Arthur and how Mom fell in love with
him. I knew the dress well. It hid underneath the bed in Grammy's room, the
creamy satin yellowed now, the vacuum seal
of the Verbyst Dry Cleaning box long since
broken, so the dress was stiff with damage
caused by the elements. Emma and Scarlett
had both worn the dress at their weddings,

contributing to its demise. It languished there beneath the bed, both forgotten and cherished, no one having the nerve to toss it — a skeleton or a ghost.

The wedding years begin with Uncle Jet, who as it happens introduced my parents. Jet went off to Yale in 1953 — so much promise. Winter was relieved for her brother to be heading to college, that their mother would finally stop pestering him about his studies, happy to have the house to herself now. But Katherine didn't stop pestering Jet. She called him almost every day to see if he was keeping up. Late in his third year, he dropped out. Too much pressure. Too many calls from Katherine. Her nerves infecting his own, her doubts becoming his truth. Katherine told herself that eventually he would finish, and though eventually he did not, she ignored that fact and so did he, returning even so for reunions from year to year.

Instead of graduating from Yale, Jet became a corporal in the army, and there was much in that choice to make his parents proud, he at the ready should there be another war. He married a local girl from down the block in Ridgewood. Her name was Nancy, and she seemed young and strong the way that Nancy Cooper Slagle would have been. So many Nancys. And he thought about her, his great-great-great-grandmother. He thought about her crossing the Alleghenies with her children, hungry, poor, determined to get to family in Ohio. He remembered the bowl that she'd carried the distance — or so the story went. He listened to the stories, stored them in the back recesses of his mind, this cast of characters that preceded him and that, his mother often reminded him, made him who he was.

Nancy down the block was pretty and kind and smart and determined. He wanted to marry someone strong who would help guide him away from the failures he had allowed himself to suffer. Weakness countered by strength. They married at the First Presbyterian Church of Ridgewood at a candlelight ceremony in a setting of palms, ivy, and white gladioli and chrysanthemums. Nancy wore a gown of candlelight satin trimmed with frosted appliqués on the bodice. The gown was fashioned with a chapel train. A pearl crown held her fingertip veil of candlelight (yes, of a theme) illusion and she carried a lace-covered Bible topped with a white orchid and sprays of sweet peas. The wedding was a tableaux and it was created by Katherine, who made it her business to manufacture moments.

For Winter, maid of honor, Katherine placed her in a raspberry-colored gown of tissue taffeta, studded with pearls at the neckline. Her silver crown headdress was trimmed with pearls and sweetheart roses, and her cascade bouquet was an arrangement of matching roses, pink and white gladioli, snapdragons, and ivy. Like a master of theater, Katherine had orchestrated and directed the event, which unfolded flawlessly to usher Jet and Nancy into adulthood. And it was something to have accomplished the good marriage of a child.

Now, just a few years later, it was Winter's turn.

All the girls were getting married. Senior year at Wellesley, the girls returned from summer vacation flaunting diamonds. A season later with conveyor-belt propulsion, one by one, little Noh play ceremonies unfolded, dramatic and expensive. Size mattered, of course. The girls enjoyed saying that. But even the glitter from a smaller stone caught the heart with an exactness, a jeweler's precision. Out came the hands, palms down, fingers splayed, sleeves pulled back from the wrist.

Katherine sat across from Winter in the backseat of the Lincoln as they sailed into the city, driven by Samuel — the driver they used on occasion, when display mattered more than pocketbook. He was black and wore a uniform and his name was pronounced Sam Well — with the pause. Charles used him from time to time for business events or when he was tired and didn't feel like driving to the office or taking the train. Katherine's hands were folded in her lap, white gloved, and her black crocodile purse stood erect at her side, between them. They were headed to Bergdorf Goodman to select the dress. The wedding was planned for February ("winter for Winter," Katherine liked to say, and Charles would repeat it), but a good seven months was needed for fittings and design. Katherine had ambitions for the dress. She wanted a Madame Grès or Karen Stark. Jacques Fath was, unfortunately, dead. Ann Lowe would more than do — dressmaker to the Rockefellers and the Vanderbilts; she had made Jacqueline Bouvier's wedding gown, and she hadn't minded that Lowe was black.

The dressmakers' names meant nothing to Winter. The dress, the wedding, were a means for Winter, a passage to the other side — the Lincoln Tunnel from the bland

418

repetition of suburban dreams to the pulsing ambition of the city. Winter loved entering the city, the buildings rising from across the marshes, an Emerald City of noise and chaos and hope. It made her feel important.

Katherine didn't like Timothy. Though he had gone to Yale with Jet, his family was from Queens, his parents still with accents, and she suspected that they could be Jewish. "Mother," Winter said, as if that were corrective enough.

"What's their religion then?" Katherine asked.

"They aren't particularly religious," Winter responded.

"I see, then," Katherine said with a sense of triumph.

To make matters worse, Timothy Fine wanted to be a novelist, and he wasn't stable. He had been sick and Katherine knew it, had had him investigated, had hired a private eye.

"Mother," Winter would reprimand when her mother would make a reference to Timothy's instability. "He has a job, Mother. He's ambitious."

His job was at NBC, a junior producer for *The Steve Allen Show,* while he finished his first novel. The other day at the Hudson Theater, Elvis Presley had been a guest, singing "Hound Dog" to a basset hound in a top hat perched on a pedestal. Timothy told Winter about it over the telephone, described girls throwing themselves at Presley.

They had met when Winter was sixteen, still in high school. Timothy had come down from Yale with Jet. Forty years later, Timothy could still tell her what she had been wearing, still see her as though he were walking through her family's door all over again and there she was coming down the stairs from her room: "The pale pink sweater set with pearl buttons, one closed at your chest." Winter was the point guard of her high school varsity basketball team and she also liked to write. Timothy was Yale's point guard and an aspiring writer as well. They were soon naming titles of novels they both loved — or hated. When she said that she considered herself more of a poet, something seemed to line up in the universe — here was a rare and exotic beauty with a powerful, even alarming name, Winter, but a sweet smile and impeccable taste. Katherine kept an eye on the two of them as they spoke all evening, easily like kids with clear ideas that their futures would be just as they imagined them now. Timothy had the kindest dimpled smile, a broad distinguished jaw, and a mane of black curly hair.

"She has a split vertebrae," Katherine told Timothy at the end of the evening as he was preparing to leave. "She will not be able to have children."

"Mother," Winter said, aghast, the heat of embarrassment spreading through her.

They met again at Yale, at the off-campus party to celebrate Yale's win against Harvard. Winter had come for the game and was now standing in a cramped corner of the apartment, Timothy towering next to her. Others bumped into them, pushing them closer together. Then Timothy leaned down to her like a cascading answer to a question that went without saying. When she spoke, it was to a person and also — they both felt this and would remember this too — it was as if to something between them, her voice acknowledging its sudden, inevitable arrival. She kept her eyes open, watching his lips descend.

"Hello," she said.

He had his hair then. He lost it in England, as if it could be found there, as if he could just go back to the hospital and ask for it. The way he said this, later, implied that perhaps his hair might still be there, carrying on respectably without him.

■ ■ ■ ■

"I remember when the Vanderbilt mansion stood here," Katherine said to the saleslady who greeted them. She had been expecting them, a slim woman with a broad face and startling violet eyes shielded by lengthened lashes, the happy expression of a person seasoned in the import of today's expedition. She ushered Katherine and Winter to the escalators, which they rode up to Mrs. Goodman's apartment above the store where all wedding gown fittings occurred.

"You will see Mrs. Goodman today," the saleslady said. "You're very lucky because she isn't always here."

"Aren't we fortunate," Katherine said, correcting the saleslady's use of "lucky" in her underhanded way. She gave Winter a knowing look: luck is for gamblers. There was the hint of an accent and of the woman covering it up. Later, Katherine would identify it — the outer borough and neighborhood to which it belonged, and she'd note to Winter the impossibility of ever being able to truly camouflage. "You can't hide from who you are." Winter took this as a direct reference to Timothy; she, of course, could translate her mother's slights with ease.

Like Jet's wedding, Winter's would be another tableaux that Katherine would produce and direct, one over which she would have even more control as the mother of the bride, responsible party in footing the bill. Most of the guests would be Charles's business associates, neighbors, and the families of both Winter's high school and college friends. It was for this crowd that she wanted her efforts to shine. But Timothy, his family, always butted with her notions of sophistication. Timothy's family were recent immigrants who ran a candy store and spoke with thick, sticky accents, uninterested in properly learning English. "They're Jewish," Katherine would say. "It's common for them to hide their faith."

"Oh, Mother, you don't mean that. That isn't you speaking. And besides, I don't believe they are Jewish."

Winter had been to their house for the East West College Showcase, both brothers playing against each other for their schools: Timothy for Yale, his brother, George, for Harvard. They'd invited her to come celebrate in their narrow apartment above the candy shop that was filled with much more than candy: newspapers and cigars and the soda fountain. It was a community center of lively attitude on the wide, dreary street lined with crumbling buildings and faded signs advertising long-forgotten products: breweries and sugar companies and shoes. Timothy's mother, Natalia, was a large woman, black abundant hair and searing eyes, in constant motion as if she might run out of time. The family didn't have a television, but they'd arranged for a meal at the candy shop and then to visit a cousin down the street who had a television. The cousin's apartment was tight too, with a buckling couch and limp lace curtains and the enormous television set, smack in the center of the room like a stage. They were a quarter of the way into Timothy's game when the reception went out and the screen went black and hissed, followed by "The Blue Danube" coming forth from the set's speakers the way it did when the network went down.

"Will their guest list be long?" Katherine had asked. Winter thought of all those friends and relatives who'd come to see the game, but ended up listening to "The Blue Danube," the strong aromas of food and smothered smoke while Timothy's father jammed his fist against the back of the television trying to force the picture of the game back onto the screen, a desperate urgency, the only time she'd ever seen him act with passion. All the heavy accents. Winter had felt more like a voyeur than Timothy's girl, a witness to some small but insurmountable pain.

Because of Winter's choice of Timothy, Katherine, deep inside, very privately — she would not even share this thought with Charles — wondered if there was something wrong with her daughter. And she wondered if it had to do with her father's act in Ohio, buried so long ago. Why else would she choose to marry a sick man who wanted to be a novelist and whose family was rough and unschooled. With her marriage and the lovely home and the good school and the money, Katherine had wanted to set Winter free. And yet freed, she had chosen Timothy.

There were secrets Winter wished she could tell her mother, longed to have a mother who would listen without being afraid. Fear crippled her mother, that much Winter understood. Katherine lived in terror of being forced back into her miserable childhood — an abstraction for Winter, but she understood it all the same. In that unspoken way, Katherine gave Winter too much power, and sometimes she wondered if her choices were designed as a punishment.

Winter wanted to be conscious and authentic, but the paradox was that with her mother she could never be. Had it been different, Winter would have described for her mother the secret contours and conflicts of how she could feel and care and seem, the ugly shape of her concerns and their equally perplexing contradictions, her own fears that hid in the crevices of longing that reached back to Timothy in London, to his best friend, Arthur.

Arthur had been with Timothy at Cambridge, an undergraduate on scholarship from Kingston, Jamaica. They played on the basketball team, Timothy in his second postgraduate year. Winter had been in Paris on her junior year abroad when she'd received the news that Timothy was sick, that he'd had a nervous collapse and was in the hospital at Cambridge. Immediately she'd gone to England. She knew of Arthur, of course, from Timothy's calls and letters — of their Italian road trip in the tiny MG, of the team, of their postgame lagers. The idea of him that came through the letters deepened Winter's love; Timothy didn't care about the rules.

Arthur picked Winter up at the station. He wasn't hard to distinguish. He met her in the midst of the throbbing city crowds, a desperate look on his dark face. She didn't know what to say to him. He embraced her, held on to her, and she could feel both the tenderness of his compassion and the eyes of many strangers. She was a white American college girl, in bobby socks and bell skirt with a tight sweater that accentuated her lovely curves. Saddle shoes. And though she'd been traveling she was fresh and her short curls were secured with a wide black bandeau. The contrast of the two of them in the station drew attention, and she did not want to care. She wanted this to be perfectly normal, and this gave her a delicious jolt. She wanted to be like Timothy, driving through Italy with a black man. She let Arthur hold her as long as he needed to.

"We're in a mess here," he finally said. "He's come undone." He pulled away, continuing with the story she had heard over the telephone from Natalia in her chopped English, speaking fast from the candy shop, afraid of the bill and for her son and the embarrassment of the situation. Natalia's was authentic fear, not imagined and embellished fear, and thus she wanted her son to stay away, stay in England until the problem was solved. "We need care of zis," she said, and that meant, you need to take care of this, somehow. All the decorum and privilege that they, the Fines, knew Winter possessed could somehow be put to proper purpose, resolving this blight for them. Winter saw the ugly side of Natalia emerge, and a further, deeper tenderness for Timothy enveloped Winter, a desire to protect him from the world and himself.

Winter heard the story again from Arthur as he led her from the station to the little convertible he'd bought with Timothy at the start of the summer, before their second year. Timothy had sent her a photograph of the convertible, the two of them driving down to Italy in June. A Shakespearean tour of Italy: Venice, Verona, Padua, Rome. Timothy had seemed all right then, describing the convertible as a romantic notion that hadn't quite worked out: "We're basketball players," he'd written. "We don't fit." She liked the image of them, stuffing their long bodies into the car in pursuit of Shakespeare. Timothy never spoke about Arthur's being black, only once said that in Italy people didn't pay attention to race in the way they did in England and America. He said America was the worst.

In the car now, she too was cramped and feeling a tightening, constricting really, the car a vice as Arthur described Timothy falling apart in the Old Vic, there to see Burton as Hamlet, directed by Sir Lawrence Olivier. They saw it twice. It was the second time when he'd had the fit. All the gold brightness and the chandelier and the perfect horseshoe of the seating closing in on him, Burton on the stage playing the crazy-man-not-crazy to such echoing intensity, the words seemed to catch inside Timothy — that's what Arthur said — they got inside and they couldn't get out. "He started squeezing his neck. I hadn't thought about how big Timothy's hands were until he wrapped them around his neck." She could see Timothy's neck like a stem. The more Arthur spoke the faster his words came. At Cambridge, he was a star — on the court, in the classroom, stories continuing to be published in important places. Winter listened to Arthur, pity rising inside.

"I'll never be Hamlet," Timothy had whispered ridiculously. "My writing means nothing." At first Arthur had laughed, thinking Timothy was making a strange joke, but then he saw Timothy cowering in his seat, shrinking before him, his eyes glistening. Hamlet was confronting his mother, pretending to be crazy to see if she were guilty, playing the line between sanity and insanity, fully in control of the logic. And Burton on the stage, handsome and dangerous, making you believe every word, making you understand the tightrope he walked, peering into his blistering eyes both sane and insane, playing his family for fools. "I am Hamlet, yet I will never be Hamlet," Timothy said again to Arthur. They were told to be quiet, but Timothy couldn't be quiet. He started rambling, attempting to keep a hushed tone, explaining that if one had any depth at all he must be both sane and insane, always negotiating the precipice. "My brain is like an egg that needs to be cracked open. I need to crack it open." *Hush. Quiet. Please be quiet.* Arthur tried escorting him from the seat, but Timothy resisted, calling him names — all very quietly but enough to cause a disturbance. "You have no depth so you can't understand. It's the miserable, bottomless depth. You're free of depth. Your mind has walls. Mine doesn't. There's no end, no stopping point." Ushers appeared. Burton kept on though half the theater was now aware of two crazy men — one on stage, one in the audience disrupting the play. The basketball players dwarfed the ushers. "Don't do this to me, please," Timothy said. "Stop. Please. Stop." Arthur finally lifted Timothy up and carried him from the theater to the loneliness of Cornwall Road, apologizing as he exited, worrying that he would be blamed for the disturbance, as if he were the cause of Timothy's madness because his skin was black.

Winter had read that this was how it went, people afflicted with brain fever. They start to ramble and have a mad gleam in their eyes. They become feverish and philosophical announcing their views of life, speaking about god and beauty, carrying on nonsensically, making confessions, creating scandalous scenes. She'd known from the moment she'd heard about Timothy's break what would happen to him, what he would face. She'd wanted to call her mother. She'd wanted to ask her mother, with her nursing knowledge (*I've seen everything; nothing scares me*) if he'd be all right. She'd wanted to fold into her mother's arms and be a little girl all over again, hear her reassuring voice, feel her warm hand on her back, in her hair. For the first time in her life Winter understood her mother's anxiety, how terribly wrong the world could go, and how quickly.

In the English language library at the Sorbonne she did her research to understand the treatment. She knew what she was looking for, a specter of the electric chair, originating with pigs, a way to ease them into death, to numb them before slaughter so they wouldn't make such a fuss, all the sounds of their fear, an entire chorus of pig terror: transcranial electric shocks inducing epileptic comas so they wouldn't feel their necks being slashed. This was the origin of electroshock therapy.

Winter was twenty years old, on her junior year abroad, living with the Moral family, three children and a widowed mother, Madame Moral, widowed by the war, a woman who had absorbed her grief. They lived at 11 Bis Rue César Franck, an Art Nouveau building squeezed between 11 and 13, *bis* meaning half. From the balcony of the apartment you could see the Eiffel Tower. When Winter had arrived in June she was finally independent, a woman of the world, in charge of her own choices, freed from the shackles of her mother's fear. The bis was like a secret all her own, a trapdoor between the buildings, that held her private ambitions for her life as a grown-up: to marry Timothy and lead an adventurous, literary life.

The apartment was in the fifteenth arrondissement, adjacent to the seventh — a calm and quiet neighborhood that seemed to have existed for centuries just as it was. The bakery on the corner, Le Moulin de la Vierge, had existed since 1356 — *depuis*

432

1356. History surrounded Winter — signs of not one but two recent wars, German assaults from the first and Allied assaults from the second. Big empty plots overgrown with weeds and cranes that carried progress. She lived inside a lesson on endurance that felt urgent and truly foreign.

Timothy came up from Italy to see her on his return to England. He proposed to her on the Place de Breteuil, beneath the sculpture of Louis Pasteur, at the axis point of the two broad avenues, two arms reaching out, it seemed, to grasp the Eiffel Tower in one hand and Les Invalides in the other. You could see both in one glance like two vectors converging upon them, the latticed tower and the golden dome beneath which Napoleon lay in his grave. The notion of seeing both monuments at the end of long boulevards had delighted Winter, and Timothy knew it. He dropped down to his knee, his thick gorgeous curls bowed to her feet and then his eyes lifting to hers. "Will you marry me?" He presented her with a ring that he had been holding on to for some time, a solitaire diamond seated in a blue velvet cushion. She was indeed in charge of her own destiny, her own history.

"Yes," she had answered in a burst. "Yes." No pain. No fear. No concern or worry or dread or ugliness. Convergence. Yes. Life spilled out before her, the future hers to determine. No mother to ask.

And now with a phone call all was changed; her first adult decision threatened; her first stand of defiance and ownership and belief in self. Now here she was in November, beneath a cold and lowering sky, with electroshocked pigs in her brain underscoring the daunting task of facing a life with this . . . what to call it? It wasn't an illness, was it? Wasn't the word *sick* a euphemism designed to camouflage? Winter, once again at Place de Breteuil, looked down the avenue of sculpted champagne oaks to Napoleon. She tried to remember being here with Timothy, his black curls, his sweet smile, the offering of the ring. The pain caught at her throat. For a moment, she thought about picking up and leaving, straight for the airport, escaping into the quiet morning sky. Who would blame her harshly, really? Her mother and father would welcome her in their wide embrace. They would tell her they understood. She could feel the warmth of her mother's relief.

Winter heard a radio playing a jubilant song, a woman selling something softly and insistently. Otherwise it was quiet. A grand French backdrop of endurance — *depuis*

1356 — mocked her. How many wars and terrors had this neighborhood endured since 1356, and all along the way people needed their bread and pastries, and all along the way Le Moulin de la Vierge had provided them. People had gone crazy — *depuis 1356* — and here she was, *A girl's life,* she thought. The extreme irrelevance of it, her little life, yet important to her, to Timothy — falling through now, in free fall, her little moment of history.

In the convertible, zigzagging through London (which Winter had never visited before and saw nothing of now and would remember nothing of later — the buildings and buses and stores and clock towers — except for the momentary scare of being on the wrong side of the road, of that oddity turning her around completely, adding to the disorientation) telling the story again, Arthur tightened. He was taking her to the hospital, the loony bin, as Arthur would later describe it — in lighter times, there would be lighter times.

They drove for a while toward the hospital and Cambridge. He apologized for being emotional. "I shouldn't upset you," he said. She loved the way he spoke, like a lilting song, each word catching on to the next in a rhythm of long vowels. He pulled over before they reached the hospital. She knew they were close even though she had no idea where they were. The rural given way to town again, tidy streets and tidy signs and quaint pubs beneath a dazzling sky.

"He won't be the same. He'll be different." Arthur paused. She could feel a different sort of predictable language at work now between them.

"Lace reflects an appreciation of European tradition," the saleslady said.

"Perhaps something along the lines of Charles James," Katherine interposed. "Don't you think Charles James?"

"Of course, his work is divine. Understated American elegance," the saleslady answered, and crimped her lips in thought, as though her mind were scanning the inventory of dresses.

They were seated comfortably now in Dita Goodman's living room. Views up and down Fifth Avenue stretched outside the windows. The room had a French elaborate fussiness to it. "Very Versailles," Katherine would say. A large mirror stood against a wall, rising from floor to ceiling, repeating the room in the glass. Centered in front of it was a floor-length triptych mirror, a stage for the bride.

To one side of the room was an enormous bathroom draped in marble. A girl served tea while the saleslady and a seamstress brought out gowns. Mother and daughter were the only customers. "It will be a private fitting, of course," Katherine had explained earlier to Winter. The seamstress didn't speak English. She was surprisingly young and pretty, sharp, pointy features. She carried a pincushion covered in pins, like a porcupine.

"I imagine business increased after Princess Grace," Katherine said. The comment sparked happy gossip about the wedding invitations and what they'd looked like, the hue and weight of the paper. Then, of course, a turn to her dress — not from Bergdorf's — with the bell-shaped skirt, the ivory peau de soie, supported by petticoats, the high neckline of Brussels lace accented with seed pearls.

"A contrast to Charles James simplicity," the saleslady said.

The dresses arrived carried by a retinue of help, each appearing to have its own escort. Even Winter began to take a genuine interest, perhaps more so than her mother. Each one more resplendent than the last, big puffs of hope, exquisite petit fours that were meant to be admired and then consumed.

■ ■ ■ ■

The hospital was called Fulbourn, an asylum such a brutal word, the way it caromed in the mouth. Winter thought there was something prescient, or perhaps caustic, in the name: Fulbourn, like newborn or reborn. Here you'd come to be full born — like the monster or unicorn you had become.

The Victorian buildings, the jutting water tower, sprawled on spacious grounds, gabled and turreted, rising from a large green upon which patients played a form of cricket, their version — a kind of paralyzed version. Some of them stood frozen, drained of life, staring into the distance. Winter averted her eyes from a man dressed in a white cricket uniform, seated in a wheelchair wearing a helmet. The wheelchaired man was holding a paddle. Others on the green looked crestfallen, some as motionless as if they'd turned to salt pillars, others in some approximation of a cricket defenseman's position, but twitching weirdly, still others looking rather professional and competent. One fielder was in distress. He was crying and soon began to rant. Staff members went out to console him and pull him back into the spirit of the game. You could see them encouraging the man; you could see the shaking of the man's head. He was upset about a previous play. Winter's body stiffened. She was afraid that she would see Timothy among the weird athletes. *It would all be worked out. No one's life is without event. They would sort it through,* Winter repeated to herself. She turned her eyes back to the manicured gardens edging the green, dressed and floral, a disguise so it would seem you were entering a country estate.

Arthur pulled the car to the front, the tires crunching the gravel of the drive as they came to a stop. His knees bumped the steering wheel. She did not want to enter the hospital alone. Suddenly she didn't want to leave Arthur. She was scared. She wanted Arthur to walk through the gate with her. She could see him look at her though she looked straight ahead at the massive structure that housed Timothy.

They sat there for what seemed a long time. She looked at him, this handsome man with onyx skin she had never seen before, only because she had never really looked before so closely at a black man's skin. The jolt — she felt it again.

"You can't be ashamed," he said, looking

down to her. "Don't let that win." Shame had a temperature like a fever invading a body. She could feel it spreading in her, concerns for herself and her parents, for Timothy, how it could surely take him over or would take him over, any confidence supplanted by the humiliation of his brain, his meal ticket, the reason for his rapid rise, the basket in which all his eggs were kept — all the metaphors cracked in a country whose king's horses were real, but a mind, his mind, had gone off the rails. She knew how people thought about the mentally sick, knew the fears of danger and the exile into which one would be plunged hereafter. She imagined all her college friends, powdering their noses, reducing for the big day and their happy lives, whispering The News.

"You're going to think of this as an illness like a bad pneumonia. Nothing more," Arthur instructed. Maybe it was true, but it sounded like a hollow truth, a truth as consolation prize.

"But is it an illness? Shouldn't he be able to control it? It's his brain," she pressed, urgent now.

Arthur looked almost confused, as though he were sorting something through. He stumbled with his words. "No, no. It's an illness. Just like that, think like that, an illness. That's how we must see this."

"But then what caused it? Illnesses are caused. Is it the writing? Is that what this is about? Too much pressure?" She wanted to be good and make it all go away.

"Don't think too much," Arthur said. It was as though he had known her for a long time.

A cool sunshine pressed on their skin. Arthur took her hand. She welcomed his touch, its warmth and familiarity. She had long pianist's fingers, but her hand was dwarfed in his. She imagined him playing ball, striding down the court in a few swift steps.

"I'm afraid that he'll be wiped clean," she said. It was all this that Winter wished she could tell her mother, longed that they could have a real conversation and that she, Winter, would be understood as Winter and not as some idea of what she wanted in a daughter.

"I don't know if I'm prepared for this. I'm afraid," she said to Arthur.

"You came," he said simply. "He asked, and you came."

Before leaving for Europe for his second year, Timothy had driven to Ridgewood to meet with Charles, bringing along the ring.

Choosing the ring, he'd thought more about Charles, wanted the stone to be worthy of Charles's admiration to show the seriousness of his intent. Charles and Timothy had a friendly relationship. They played golf together sometimes, and there was an understanding that they didn't need to speak. Charles, in fact, said very little. Once, on the golf course, his ball went into a forsythia bush and he went in after it. When he emerged, he was followed by a swarm of bees that proceeded to attack him. Charles swelled up like a balloon but wouldn't go to the emergency room. He continued playing the round, saying nothing about the pain or the swelling, though he complimented Timothy's game.

"No, he doesn't say much," Winter agreed when, later, Timothy told her about asking her father for her hand. She wished she could have been there, in the silence of the parlor, with Timothy serious and solemn and a bit scared, staring down at Father's polished shoes. She loved the old-fashioned formality of the gesture.

"I would like to marry your daughter," Timothy had said. "I love her and intend to make her happy for the rest of her life." The parlor was dark because Katherine didn't want the sunshine bleaching out the silk upholstery. She had antimacassars on the twin Victorian couches.

Charles allowed life to pass over him with a slightly bemused smile and concern, as if he were watching an enjoyable film. But when Timothy asked for his daughter's hand, he sat up, elegant as always with his starched pressed shirt, his pipe, the curling scent of its smoke.

"So you do," Charles responded. He was thoughtful for a moment. And then he spoke, instructing Timothy, briefly, with his thick Boston accent, on how he and Winter would proceed, aware of the importance to a girl of entering senior year engaged. She would take her junior year in Paris and Timothy would go back to Cambridge. He could propose as he saw fit over there, and if after this year all remained strong, then Timothy would have his approval to set a date. If, on the other hand, the year got in their way, as years can do, well then no need to say a word; they could go their separate ways.

"The year won't get in our way," Timothy said.

"My blessings, son," Charles said.

"I know Katherine is concerned about my religion," Timothy boldly added. "I want to assure you, we aren't a religious family."

"I'm not religious either," Charles said.

Now, in Dita Goodman's living room, standing before a seamstress in a wedding gown, a pale pink silk with fifty round silk-covered buttons running down her back to a bustle, admiring herself in the very tall gilt mirror, she imagined slipping it off before Timothy, feeling the anticipation of Timothy, she heard her mother's voice interrupt. She was speaking of the midair collision over the Grand Canyon, telling the saleslady how she often jetted out to Los Angeles, had been since '47. That was her route. She had a sister out that way.

"Terrifying," the saleslady said. "They say one of the pilots was on a sightseeing expedition, showing the canyon to the folks on board, showing off really. I can't imagine how you fly." Then Winter was before them. "It's lovely," the saleslady gasped.

Katherine had tears in her eyes. But she quickly composed herself. "Too much cleavage," Katherine said, staring at the apparition that was her beautiful daughter.

"Hmmm," the saleslady said, examining Winter as if she were part of the dress, her large bust swelling beneath the fabric.

The seamstress with the cushion of pins

and very little English, offered lace. She said, "Lace."

Katherine looked at the seamstress as if noticing her for the first time. Thick curls tight and springy around her pointy face, emphatic with steeply arching eyebrows. The woman disappeared. Katherine whispered, "Romanian." The Romanian returned with a square of hand-embroidered lace and tucked it into Winter's bosom, slipping her fingers between the silk and her skin, again as if Winter weren't a person, but a part of the dress.

The inside of Fulbourn was not white, though it was sterile. Wood beams straddled the ceiling and the walls. Large desks for intake lined the entrance hall. The smell of antiseptic hung in the air. Nurses in their white uniforms, tidy hair tucked under white caps, walked briskly. A receptionist directed Winter toward Timothy's ward, to which she was led by a male orderly who seemed younger than she and too eager to make conversation. He held a pack of keys that he jangled nervously when he wasn't using them to lock and unlock doors — so much locking and unlocking. Long corridors of silence then noise, coming in waves, and then a cry from somewhere that could easily have been created by her own imagination.

"Are you the sister?" the skinny orderly asked, leaving her at the door to Timothy's room, where she could see him lying limply on his side, facing the window overlooking a glade dappled in a waning sunshine. Otherwise the room was spare. No electrical apparatus. Just a chair and a sink. She walked slowly to the bed and sat down on its edge. He was sleeping, the calm rhythm of his breath. There was something helpless about him, like a wounded animal by the side of the road. She noticed his head was bald. Perhaps she had the wrong room, perhaps this wasn't Timothy. She wanted this not to be Timothy. She didn't want him to be sick, to care for a sick man. She turned to check the name on the door outside, almost relieved as if this meant she could leave the hospital altogether, get back in the convertible with Arthur and drive away. Her sudden movement jostled Timothy awake.

"Winter?" he asked. She turned, smiled. He was ugly without the hair, but she kept beaming. Just features: nose, bigger now; eyes, bigger now; lips thinner now, pale, almost blue.

"What happened to your hair?" she asked.

"It was stolen," he said. Slowly he smiled.

"Who stole it?" she asked.

"It's a long story," he said.

"I have time," she said.

"I don't," he said. "Let's leave this place. It's boring."

"There's a mop outside," she said. "We could use that."

"A disguise," he said. "We'll just slip out."

"Where will we go?'

"Back to Paris." She liked that. It gave her courage to continue with this strange man.

"Can I shut the door?" she asked.

"Naughty!" he said. A nurse poked her head into the room, looked at Winter, assessed her, then left. "I worried the doctors wouldn't let you in," he said. Of course, he'd been waiting for her. She felt Arthur's embrace, standing in it at the station, his warm hands on hers in the car.

Timothy's face was all eyes and insistent gleam. He was searching for what to say next, then asked, "Did they hurt you? Did the doctors, did they hurt you?"

She caught her breath. The floor was soft and rubbery, which gave her a start, an actual rubber room, no sharp corners, no laces on any shoes, no electrical cords anywhere, no outlets, and she was standing in the middle of it, in a locked ward with her betrothed who, because he was a shattered man trying to keep up appearances, was pretending that *she* was the patient. She understood what he was doing. She looked up, at him.

"They — they didn't hurt me," she said. "Not at all. I don't think."

"You don't think? What do you think they did?"

She thought about pigs, applications for transcranial electricity, helmets attached to electrodes shooting sparks into the brain, convulsing the body, whipping it into submission. Her talented man. That brain upon which they'd build a life, her life: It was in pieces. What would be left? Could it happen again?

"I think they've tried to help me?" She would be him for him, his mirror.

"How?" he asked.

"With electricity."

"Yes."

"Like turning on a switch, flipping the light."

"Yes."

She could feel the tears pricking. Her eyes leaked. She blinked them back. "It's a pretty view," she said at last.

"And the weather's nice too," he said.

"Don't be angry with me," she said.

"I'm not angry with you," he said. "The

weather *is* nice."

"I don't like this game," she said.

He shut his eyes and was quiet for what seemed a long time.

"Then shut the door," he said.

She shut the door, sat attentively on the edge of the bed, and listened as he described his brain fever that wasn't a fever at all but a big, slow barge pushing through a river of ice, he said — the crinkling sound of the ice breaking with the current and the metal of the hull, he said — folding in and over itself, into itself. "I'm the barge," he said. "The slow, slow barge and the ice is the inescapable future." He looked at her suspiciously now and again.

"But that can be a good thing," she said, knowing it was wrong of her to speak the moment she'd spoken. Logic wouldn't help her, Arthur had warned. Just listen, she reprimanded herself. She didn't know how to act. Winter couldn't get a purchase on the scale of the darkness she was dealing with.

"Oh no," he had replied. "Oh no. It cannot be a good thing." What terrified him was the future of lies, all the lying that produced a lifetime — he could look down that span and see it, what had to be done to live, how a life was invaded from every

449

direction and what had to be done to keep those invasions at bay, the cost and expense of that sacrifice, and if you didn't have the qualities or talents required to create the life you wanted, a life of no lies, then you were a blasphemer to yourself. He spoke carefully until she stopped him and he assured her that he was simply trying to explain.

"But I need you to understand. I'm waiting to catch up. I need you to know this, for your future. I'm waiting all the time for the future, to catch it, catch up and be ahead so I can stop running. You know that? How will I manage if I can never get ahead, get up there and into it, that future always in front of me and never with me? Winter, listen. It's simple, Winter. When I catch up to it, I'll be dead."

"Shh," she whispered. She took his hand and held it. It was cold. He rested, but she could feel the passion of his beating heart.

"I was afraid you wouldn't know me," she said. "But you know me."

What he did not tell her in his rant was that what scared him most was the truth, this truth: that Winter would spend the rest of their life loving him, trying to love him in order to prove her mother wrong. And he did not like her mother. Her mother was not the truth. Her mother was a collage of pretensions.

Instead: "I've adjusted," he said, but he was thinking about Charles, how he'd cleverly worked in an escape hatch to his blessing, an off-ramp for his daughter.

Timothy wore a pair of cotton pants and a T-shirt and Winter noticed now that he was very thin, a diminished man. She noticed too that a wall had gone up to keep out whatever might make him fall again, and she was assessing on which side of the wall he wanted to place her. She could see him calculating. This was an interview, a trial. But he was not the judge. Rather, it was up to her to decide which side of the wall she wanted to be on. She saw it then, clearly. On trial was fear — her mother's fear, her own fear, Timothy's fear, the fear of everyone, of all her friends, of life. But here was something else: Arthur was right. No one back home needed to know about this, none of their friends. It was that simple. Her business, not theirs. She had secrets no one knew, not even Timothy. She could help get him home and she would do that, arranging the passage, seeing him to the ship. She understood what had to be done. At home, he would be all right, himself again. They would do this together.

She felt a sudden and practical conviction. No one had to know a thing; you just marched on. If her mother had taught her anything it was that you just marched on. She felt a tendering of herself, a softness that made her malleable. All she had to do was tidy him up — and she could do that. She could see the way through that.

Dita Goodman had a reputation, and anyone who knew anything about the store knew of her reputation, that she was the "Strumpet of Cuba," vivacious and vociferous, swirling into all situations with confidence and the knowledge that she would get her way. She didn't mind the moniker because it was the cornerstone of her creation myth, earned when she was young, the majestic goddess of Cuban society, Spanish come from Spain with her long dark hair and her lovely swirling ways. The kind of girl who spent time in bathing suits on yachts in sun and money with her refined eye for luxury and life.

All of this could be seen when Mrs. Goodman eventually arrived. Stout with age, though still glamorous, her hair, now white, piled on the crown of her handsome face, dressed in a dark summer suit to match her dark eyes — all gold and perfume and tanned skin. She approached Winter, a small weather system, glanced over Winter, then tugged the lace from her bosom and admonished Katherine not to ruin the dress . . . or the girl. "Both are beautiful. She has a beautiful breast. Don't hide it."

Katherine could speak endlessly about whatever was on her mind, telling the same stories of her life over and again, as she had that day as well to the obedient saleslady from Queens, but she fell silent before the apparition of Dita Goodman, reverent and diminished. It was only an instant, but that was all it took for Winter to absorb the contrast — understand her mother's longing and also her mother's calculating, calculating where her advantage could be found. Katherine too was stout if tall, her hair too was white, her fingers and ears and neck and chest jeweled with Tiffany treasures given to her by Charles. But none of her affect was authentic. It was pretend, as Timothy would say. She had always wanted to be someone other than who she was, a poor cowgirl from Montana who raised herself, something better, more — as if who she was could never be enough for this world. Winter felt sad, a wafting of sorrow for her mother as she stood next to Mrs. Goodman, who knew exactly who she was.

The attendants in the room now were in the service of Mrs. Goodman. Her ideas about the lace were addressed, orchestrated by her very being and radiant presence. Katherine retreated, just a little, but enough, a baffled look about her broad face as she ceded her authority. But then with a strength so particular to her, she emerged again, using her new, inferior position to her advantage: "We will take the dress." She looked at Dita Goodman. "You can bill it to my account. Mrs. Charles Mitchell Brown. We are salaried people." She paused, held Dita Goodman with her eye. And Winter knew, mortification spreading across her as her mother continued, "You can make us a good price," she said, taking hold of a swath of satin, raising the dress for Mrs. Goodman to inspect. "There is a small tear." And with that Katherine reclaimed the sense of self she understood best and was rewarded with a discount.

Winter stood in front of the mirror, regarding her image in the dress. Behind her stood the triptych and her reflection in the three mirrors, positioned so she could see the back of her dress, see herself coming and going. Her mother and Mrs. Goodman haggling while Winter admired her figure, the dress, the confection. She noticed that the triptych was hinged, and she adjusted the panels, just slightly, until suddenly the mirrors were at such an angle to catch the image of herself in the gorgeous gown, a bride — an infinite number of brides — repeating into the distance. She touched one of the mirrors and a chain of linked brides seemed to bend off into a greenish, smiling endlessness, as if all of history converged upon a single moment, which it does, she thought, listening to the swish of fabric on the floor, before she moved again — and the moment moved too — and became part of the past.

■ ■ ■ ■

Part Three:
Future Perfect

■ ■ ■ ■

11
AN ELEGANT WOMAN

When I was three weeks old, my parents brought me and my three sisters to my grandparents' rented summerhouse in Maine, in Ogunquit on the Marginal Way, overlooking the Atlantic, close enough to feel the sea spray. We arrived in the early evening, summer light lingering in the sky. My grandparents were in Adirondack chairs waiting for us on their little lawn, edging the public path that itself edged a cliff that crashed straight into the ocean. "Here," my mother said, my sisters swarming at her legs. She handed the bundle of me, swaddled in a receiving blanket, to my grandmother. "You can have this one. I have the three others." It was meant, of course, as a joke, and it was a joke, one that became, over the years, a reliable aperçu, announcing a truce — perhaps the recognition of a truce if not the actual fact — between mother and daughter, who otherwise seemed at odds with each other most of their lives. In this way, I became my grandmother's baby rabbit. I was her girl.

Grammy, with her crown of snow white-hair, her emerald eyes, her motoring gloves and rules for dressing, her detailed stories about her life and the ancestors' lives, her deep convictions about the ways things should be done, her aspirations to be proper — she had a funny perch on life, for me as a child. She could see in all directions — deep into the past and far into the future. She knew what it meant to be poor, to wear gunnysacks for shoes; she knew what it meant to be sophisticated, to wear a Tiffany diamond, to be an opera buff — and she understood, or so it seemed, how one got from there to here.

I grew up listening to her for some thirty-five years. My earliest memories are of her, a registered nurse, correcting my flaws: pigeon-toed, by placing me in shoes that pointed my feet outward and that were attached by a metal bar to lock the feet's position in place; finger sucking, first with bitter iodine rubbed on the finger, and when that didn't work she bandaged the fingers together so I couldn't access the desired finger, and when that didn't work she wrapped the entire hand in tinfoil. Eventually she won. If she noticed my flaws, she also noticed my beauty: my perfect rosebud mouth, my high forehead and wide-set eyes. I loved her very much.

My father, on the other hand, did not.

After I was born, and it had seemed my parents would have no more children, Grammy took to saying to my mother, "You've got the babies, now you can get rid of him." The animosity had been there from the beginning. When my mother announced that she wanted to marry our father, Grammy said to her, "Do you really want to wake up to that face every morning for the rest of your life?"

Our grandfather died in 1967 of lung cancer, and Grammy moved from New Jersey to Ogunquit, Maine, into the yellow Victorian she christened Last Morrow. In the summers, she would drive down to New Jersey to collect us. We would be waiting for her, dressed alike in Liberty prints, our hair combed and braided and ribboned by Mom. We knew to look our best. She had taught us that if there was an accident and your body was discovered you would want those who found you to know that you were of quality. Our mother and father would see us off. We'd pile into the vast boat of a car, squabbling over who got to sit in the front

461

seat. My father was reserved with her, a smile that tried to hide his eagerness for her to be on the road again. Departing, she would say to him, holding him with her eyes, "I thank you for taking such good care of the girls," as if we weren't his girls: Emma, Scarlett, Celia, Isadora in order of our age, each two years apart. When my grandfather died I was three years old, Emma was nine. Zasu and Timmy were not even distant glimmers on the horizon.

On these long trips back to Ogunquit, she always entertained us. On one trip, after our father disappeared, she told us that she had had him investigated and that she had long predicted trouble. Dark shades covering her eyes, she looked like a fading movie star from one of those noirs we watched on television on the late movie, deep in the night while our parents fought. She knew things that we wanted to know, secrets about our world, still out of reach of the child's mind. What had our father done and where was he? And who was she to have the power and authority to have him investigated?

For our father she had airs, she was a snob — in the true sense of the word. She turned up her nose at him, a boy from Queens. "She has a Tiffany complex," he said more than once, because she thought a lady should have diamonds and those diamonds could only come from Tiffany's. She would hold her ringed finger to the light and a prism of color would spray the air around her. "Extra-extra river water," she liked to repeat. I would later discover, writing a piece on diamonds for a magazine, that the phrase came from a Tiffany ad campaign, and it spoke to the grading clarity of a diamond. As a child it was just another thing my grandmother knew.

For our father, she was all veneer. She wasn't the truth. She didn't know what the truth was. She disliked our father because he was a novelist, and the fate of a starving artist was not what she had wanted for her daughter. "Hitch your wagon to a star," she was fond of advising. And our father, at least as a young suitor, appeared to be no star. If Grammy was concerned about the past, she was equally concerned about the future, worried that a match of her daughter with our father would do irreparable damage to her legacy. "You've got the babies."

Liar, fabulist, however Grammy managed it, she provided a sense of purpose, of telos, to the family line. From her stories, our family reached out across time and geography, across to Europe, deep into America.

She had a sister in Hollywood who sold Avon door-to-door whose identity Grammy had taken, adding to her mystery, a mother in the ground in Ohio, a lout of a father also in the ground. "He had a wandering eye for women," she'd tell us. Their rough-hewn ways demonstrated the distance she had come.

The resurrected ancestors roamed the halls of Last Morrow. Nancy Cooper Slagle and her seven children crossing the Alleghenies lived inside her Cantonese wedding bowl atop the melodeon that had been around the Horn twice. She wanted us to know not just where we came from, but that we were part of something long that did not start with our birth or end with our deaths. Everyone is connected to that continuum, she seemed to say. And if, through fate or bad luck, you didn't know where you belonged on it, then you would be forgiven for making a way to hitch your wagon to it, by means of stories from the deep past, stories that were probably not true, or that had just enough of the spark of the probable to seem mostly true, or true enough to satisfy her audience, which was usually us girls. Her sense of detail, of verisimilitude, was deftly practiced, with just enough distance between us and the recognizable historical names to which she connected our family to lend the air of the factual.

Mary, Queen of Scots, the Royal Stewarts of Nairn, Sir Drummond and Sir James Stewart, "the dizygotic twins born to Maid Marian on the moors" — she let these phrases roll off her tongue. Like the catalogue of ships in *The Iliad,* you need not remember their names, just the sound of them thundering along as you listen to the poem.

Even so, names were important details — and there was an art to their deployment. One strand of Grammy's fables — a kind of European variation — featured obscure-sounding, often hyphenated surnames to suggest just the right sort of European register. We were descended, she said, from the Luetkemeyers of the Grand Duchy of Mecklenburg-Schwerin, children of Otto von Keller, adviser to Bismarck and architect of Germany's unification. What child would doubt that? And there was Laura Ann Meyer, small blip of a woman with a congenital hip defect and in need of a shoe wedge to balance her — made hats for Granny Howard, aunt to William Howard Taft.

The shoe wedge, the grave-robbing dizygotic twins, the hats for Granny Howard —

it was impossible for the details to all be true, but there was enough truth hiding in there to prop up the rest. And the point was, it seemed to me as a child, that if you just believed it enough you became it. I could feel like a royal Stewart from Nairn and then be it. My middle name is Stewart.

Maybe that's why Grammy lived so long. Maybe there was some practical virtue in her fables — like the way you could find Polaris if you could imagine the great bear in the stars of the night sky. You could navigate the world. The real suckers in life were those who believed they were the realists, who didn't have heroes, who went without a grand sense of their place in the continuum of time.

Nancy Cooper Slagle was cousin of the great American novelist James Fenimore Cooper. I can still hear Grammy's particular cadence saying the Cooper name, collapsing the two *OO*s to create a *U,* a truncated vowel. "James Fenimore Cupper." So it goes. Playing cards with Dad as children, a game called Authors, I announced to the group that we were related to James Fenimore Cooper, that Grammy had told me so. I had wanted to impress our father; he too was a famous novelist. The author's image was there on the card on the table, the first time the author was someone real for me, *The Last of the Mohicans.*

"No, you're not," my father snapped. He loved me very much; he hated my grandmother.

For me, Grammy was a steady, reliable compass point, even when she and my mother stopped speaking, when she dragged her luggage down our long gravel driveway threatening to hitchhike home, vowing to never darken our doorstep again, our den of iniquity — something that happened with regularity and for a long stretch after Zasu's birth. Even then, Grammy always found her way back to me. She would write letters in an elegant hand, her envelopes scented with pine trees, sea air, and Chanel, instructing me to read, offering me five dollars for each book. She paid me to wear undershirts, a dollar a day. She sent me a pack of five with lace at the neck.

At our house, life was just plain weird and Grammy knew it, and she did not approve, worried something would happen and something eventually did. When I was twelve, I started stealing. I stole a lot from the local mall, the one near Rose Hill. Walked into Sears, tried stuff on, and wore out what I wanted beneath my clothes.

I was a kid in the seventh grade. Zasu was two and Dad was sad. You could see it in his eyes and drooping height. We all knew what he was enduring. We spoke of it at night, my sisters and I. He loved Mom. That was the truth, but she didn't love him. She loved Arthur and she was only pretending with Dad. Emma said Mom had never loved Dad, she'd always been in love with Arthur, that Mom had confided in her when Dad had vanished. One day Dad had just up and left, three years earlier. We thought he had died. Mom had searched, brought in the police, Arthur came to town. Dad didn't return and he didn't return. Grammy said it was because he was unstable, was having another episode. It was for this affliction that she had had him investigated. She'd been right. Dad had vanished out west for a few months to write his second novel, calling home only after he had finished the book. But it was too late. Mom hated him by then, was pregnant with Zasu, Arthur's baby. But Mom took Dad back, sent him to Jamaica with Zasu when she was ten months old so Dad could introduce Zasu to her father, so Dad and Arthur could make peace. Dad would spend the rest of his life apologizing for his breakdown.

Zasu was there between them to remind

them all the time. A year after Zasu's birth, Mom was pregnant again, with Timmy, the boy. My sisters and I, lying in bed late at night, would speculate: Would the baby be black or white? You could tell as soon as they were born: Zasu had been pink. When Grammy came to see baby Zasu in the hospital, she had known the truth immediately the way mothers always seem to know the truth about their daughters. It was as if it was the final confirmation that my mother had failed entirely to carry Grammy forward in the way she was supposed to. After Zasu, that job, it seemed, became mine. Of the sisters, I was the most unlikely candidate, but I loved her most, and I listened and I cared. I preferred her rules and her sense of order, the long histories of our ancestors, the daily niceties of tea parties and heirlooms over the mess that was my childhood home. I was her apprentice, loved the frills of her imagination, the soft cushion against reality, believed I could be a lady if I wore velvet and patent leather only at night. I didn't mind that she would wrap my hair in rags, that across the night the hard combination of hair and cloth bit into my scalp so in the morning I'd have sausage curls bouncing around my face.

White babies weren't pink. Baby Timmy

was white. For a while that convinced the sisters, and therefore me, that Mom and Dad were in love once more and that Mom and Grammy would make peace.

But Grammy and Mom had stopped speaking again. Screaming matches in Maine, then over the phone, finally gave way to a long, slow silence. The silent treatment; we knew it well.

I was protective of my father. I wanted to make him happy. His bald head wasn't a lovely one; it was scarred and rough with patches of thin hair that he usually kept shaved, but sometimes he forgot or was too tired and then he just looked strange. He was the kind of man, smart and funny, who lit up a room when he entered it with his curiosity and his gossipy interest in the love lives of others, his brilliance. But in these years, he was caught. You could almost see it, like he had glass in front of him that prevented him from coming into the real world.

Stealing helped me feel I was in charge of a world that kept growing stranger, that I was controlling something bigger than myself. I did poorly in school, Cs and Ds. Emma was at Yale, and Scarlett was a senior on her way to Yale. Celia was a straight-A arrow on her way there too. Yale, Yale, Yale.

What tripped me up? I was sitting in the shopping mall wearing stolen clothes under my coat and sweater, marijuana hidden in my purse, and it occurred to me that I needed bus fare home. The fountain in the long store-lined alley of the mall glittered with coins. I was reaching into the shallow water when two uniformed security guards and an undercover female detective with very serious glasses approached me. I looked up at them. They looked down at me, a fistful of quarters in my hand.

"What do we have here?" said the woman. She was wearing jeans and sneakers and a stiff ironed oxford.

"I think we have a thief," said one of the security guards.

"We definitely have a thief," said the other.

We were living at Rose Hill, had left New York City for a change, so Zasu could be normalized. I know that sounds awful, but it was true. Dad and Mom didn't say it like that, but in New York too many friends asked too many questions. It would turn out that people would do the same in Rose Hill and then we'd move back to the city again, but that was later. We kept the apartment. Emma was off at college, but the rest of us made new lives at Rose Hill, attending the public schools. The kids were mostly farmers' children and had special schedules during harvest season. In November, they canceled school for the first day of hunting season. Definitely no uniforms. A few writers too had houses out there, country retreats from the city. Weekends there were always cocktail parties, people always drinking too much, then asking questions.

I liked the change. Mom and Dad seemed less stressed. Dad stopped writing; Mom started taking people's photographs to bring in extra money. Dad liked to joke with his struggling writer friends. "If you had books that sold like *The Common* and *The Neighbors,* would you bother to continue writing?" Dad, with his soft charm and kindness, could get away with saying that. It would be taken as self-deprecating. With Mom, he became involved with EST and other find-yourself seminars. They hosted training sessions at Rose Hill, would send us off for the weekend so Rose Hill could be taken over by quacks — all these middle-aged people seeking something life hadn't given them. A pair of nuns even attended one of the retreats, hosted by a guy who specialized in dolphin therapy. Only there were no dolphins at Rose Hill. No matter. It was Scarlett who filled us in on the specifics. With Emma gone, Scarlett was now completely in charge of the children.

Grammy would call and ask questions too. "Dolphins don't need therapy," she would say. "I do not approve," she would say.

Despite Dad's defection from writing, *The Neighbors,* his second and final novel, the one he'd written while vanished, had recently been published to rave reviews, instant bestseller. It was being turned into a movie. Locals in the area knew us. Actually, a lot of people knew us. Dad was famous, which always caught me up short as his child. Our family didn't seem like a famous kind of family. Dad didn't even speak to his parents after the way they treated Zasu, exiling her and Dad and us because she was black and also because she wasn't Dad's. But even here among the farmers, he was known. Everyone had seen the movie of *The Common.* It had terrorized a generation of moviegoers. But we didn't feel famous. I didn't feel famous. I never thought anyone was watching.

"Fine?" the bug-eyed woman asked, looking at my library card, the only form of identification that I had. "Isadora Fine. Rose Hill. Any relation?"

That's the way they said it, always. Always it was understood.

"He's my father." And I was always a little

bit proud, like being his daughter meant something, that it was almost enough. It was a currency. Grammy used it unabashedly, introducing us to her Ogunquit friends as Timothy Fine's daughters. There too I was always surprised and proud that the mention of Dad attracted interest.

"Really?" she said, softening. I thought she might let me go. "The novelist," she explained to the guards for whom the name Fine meant nothing. They shrugged at her, at each other. "You know, *The Common* — the movie?"

"Oh right," one of the guards said.

"Really creepy," the other said.

"No lie. Made me suspicious of everyone. After Manson."

"Yeah. It worked in you, you know, like *Jaws* made you suspicious of the water." The security guards laughed. I laughed. They had to let me off. I was sure of it, but then came a slow unfolding set of moments that turned the atmosphere from jovial to polite, to silent, mutual embarrassment: they asked me to unpack everything I'd stolen, piece by piece, all the merchandise, all the different stores, and I did. When I was finished I was just a dumpy-looking kid with braces and a damp, pink face. The security guards didn't know which way to look.

Protocol was to turn me over to the local cops, and they followed protocol. The police arrived and I was escorted to the squad car, driven to the station, booked, released to my parents, and eventually given a date to appear in court. The stores pressed charges, plus I was charged with possession of pot with hash. At trial — I can still remember sitting there before the judge, the stupidity of a child's brain rattling around, trying to make her own kind of logic. The judge in his robes looked down at me over his readers and said a lot of stuff I didn't understand, but I knew I was in big trouble. I knew that. Even Zasu knew that. "Isadora's in big trouble." I hated her. I wanted my old and normal family back. Grammy hated us now. That's what I thought. She hated us because Mom had ruined our family. Mom was still in love with Arthur; I had a black sister. I was too young to understand that I was a racist. Mom and Dad, though, walked around making promises disguising lies. Even the way Mom carried Timmy around on her hip, like an image of Mother Nature from *The Whole Earth Catalogue,* baby gurgling happily, seemed like a charade.

It turned out the judge was tired of all the

white kids getting off while the black kids served sentences. I'd done enough damage at the mall and was carrying enough marijuana to make me eligible for a corrective stay. My father went berserk, worrying about a record. "I'm not visiting my child in a detention center."

Only then did that possibility sink in. It sank and sank and sank.

My father pulled some strings with a fan of his work, a congressman of influence, and my sentence was reduced to making a visit to the juvenile detention center, located in the bleakest part of Trenton, barbed wire snarled with plastic bags. All the inmates were black. I wasn't allowed to speak to them. No one wanted them to know that I had been relieved of a similar burden because of a privilege they didn't share. I was just supposed to look. What I saw and felt and understood was the huge divide. This was something that my older sisters would never know concretely. It was something Zasu would know, would live.

I was told I would have been sentenced to a year, but been let off after a few months.

My grandmother drove down from Maine that March just after the trial. She showed up in her black Lincoln Continental, her crocodile purse by her side. She and my mother weren't speaking, but Grammy didn't care. Their episodes of silence seemed more in keeping, somehow, with the way in which they loved. She came into the house, ignored my mother, and found me in my room. She sat down next to me on the bed. She lifted my chin so my eyes met hers. "I stole too. I came to tell you myself, Baby Rabbit. I stole too. More than once. Sometimes you need to steal. That doesn't mean it is right. It is wrong, decidedly wrong. But there are many ways to learn." I cried then, falling against the softness of her, feeling the gentle catch of her love. She ran her fingers through my hair and held me. "Here is the lesson," she continued after a while. "This does not define you." She looked at me with those exacting green eyes, the most astonishing eyes, and once again she pulled me into her embrace. "Know this, Baby Rabbit: You can lie, cheat, steal, murder, even, and I will always stand by you. I will always love you. But that's not what you're going to do, because this episode, it does not define you."

She would not give up on me. Perhaps that's why I never gave up on her. Later, when it was time for me to apply for college, when it looked like my options were few and even my guidance counselor suggested community college because I had blown freshman and sophomore years, Grammy told me where to apply, an excellent school near her. She helped me see my narrative of transformation, told me what to do, how to approach the application, how to reveal my best self. By this point I knew Italian well. It was offered at my high school because my town had a large population of Italians. I'd taken to Italian, had a knack for it, and doing well in that subject led me to do well everywhere else. I had turned my grades around. She suggested I write one of the essays in Italian. I applied only to that school and was accepted. She called to congratulate me. "I just knew it, Baby Rabbit. I just knew it. Don't ever take no for an answer. Everyone has her arc."

I first visited Grammy alone when I was five, landing at the Portland jetport where she met me with her dark glasses, her white bun. She drove us to Ogunquit, stopping in York Beach for saltwater taffy, homemade at the Goldenrod, a long narrow store with lots of windows through which I could see big machines pulling the taffy in a rainbow of colors, glistening and slick. From there we went to a petting zoo and watched billy goats with their long beards cross a small suspension bridge. She had all the time in the world for me. She took my hand in hers and we walked in this way through the Goldenrod, through the zoo, along the beach with the crashing waves and sea spray. She was dressed in a stylish suit for summer, cool linens in dark colors. And when she spoke to people they deferred to her, and thus to me. With Grammy, there was time and I felt it, long days stretching into more long days. She took me to Portsmouth, New Hampshire, and bought me a new wardrobe, white panties because ladies only wore white panties, patent leather Mary Janes, and taught me the importance of keeping clean and dressing like a lady. I felt like her china doll, Pearl Honeydew, with all her pretty clothes and accessories stored in Glenna's trunk in the attic. We had tea parties with little porcelain pots and silver tongs for the sugar cubes decorated with painted fondant pansies.

"You come from good stock," she'd say, and she'd let me know about all the ancestors so it didn't feel like just the two of us, but a crowd. The stories emerged from the walls, the photographs, the furniture, the melodeon, the Cantonese bowl, Glenna staring at me from above the mantelpiece, her eyes narrowed and watchful, making me afraid even though she was long since dead. Grammy would tell me remarkable things about Glenna, that she'd been an itinerant schoolteacher, that she'd fought early for emancipation, that she'd written the state song of Nevada. Glenna was described as a beautiful woman, but the oil portrait of her was more haunting than beautiful.

Inside Last Morrow I inhabited the past — the Royal Stewarts, the eleven generations Lynn, Grammy and her sister as girls. Grammy never mentioned the story of her own identity, of how she transformed from Thelma to Katherine, but that story was there too, within the walls of Last Morrow — in the Avon her sister sent from California, packages of honeysuckle perfume and Skin-So-Soft, that overflowed from cabinets and drawers in the bathrooms. Great-Aunt Pat's name was really Katherine, Grammy's name, and it had belonged to Pat before it belonged to Grammy — really as if names could just be passed around like that.

"You know your grandmother," my mother would say in explanation when my sisters and I asked about the name. Stolen identity? What was it? How does a sister take her sister's name? Could I become Celia if I chose? Switch lives? Great-Aunt Pat, I knew, had a hard life, was a smoker, died of lung cancer when I was a child. But the story of the stolen identity lent an aura of mystery to Grammy's past that only served to imbue her journey with a sense that real history was so often about desperate times, and hard times provoked hard measures. At Last Morrow, the present receded. Grammy didn't have much narrative control over the present. She could be suspicious of Dad, fight with Mom, stop speaking with Uncle Jet, but she couldn't rewrite their stories.

Before Mom made a mess of her own life, her brother, Uncle Jet, had made a mess of his — running off with his secretary, leaving our Aunt Nannie and our cousins. The secretary, Grammy told Mom, had stolen Aunt Nannie's sable fur right out of her bedroom closet and had worn the coat into Jet's office with nothing underneath it. Oddly, her name too was Nancy — nineteen, from Queens with a thick accent that she spent a long time trying to hide and then get rid of.

"Never use sex as a weapon," Grammy would say over the years.

"Leave him be," Mom would say to Grammy in those early days of Jet's affair. "We don't know what goes on in the marriage." Grammy was distraught. She had wanted her children's lives to be better than hers. You could see it in her, her steely will confronting the unbending realities of the present. Our past had heroines. Our present had thieves and lowlifes and children who willfully, it seemed to Grammy, threw away the advantage and opportunity she crawled her way out of the West to give them.

Jet was a handsome man, tall and slender with black hair that he kept his entire life. He wore a half smile and didn't speak much, but when he spoke with us kids it was always with kindness. One summer in Ogunquit, after both of our families had blown up, he took us to the summer stage theater to see *The Boyfriend.* Cool Maine summer smelling of pine and all of us dressed up and perfumed with Grammy's Chanel, a normal, generous family and Uncle Jet so tall and dark and handsome and kind. There was something romantic and hopeful in the musical that I would long associate with Uncle Jet's quiet kindness and the promise of a man. Days with him treating us to lobsters at Barnacle Billy's, a trip on the *Ugly Anne* to watch lobstermen pull up lobster traps, thick with the creatures crawling all over each other, their claws caught in the ropes and the seaweed. Mom said Jet was like her father, and through Jet therefore I had a sense of who my grandfather had been. It seemed we were an ordinary family — even if Dad rarely accompanied us to Maine and Uncle Jet's children wouldn't speak to him anymore.

Uncle Jet went into the medical device business and did well. Around the time of the Nancy affair he had an idea for an invention, a device he called a Gait Maker, a more comfortable prosthesis that relieved pressure and friction. Grammy invested in the company, but she didn't trust him enough to make the loan without collateral. She took out a life insurance policy on Jet's life, owning it herself.

"You're his mother. Believe in him," Mom had said.

"I'm doing this to protect you and the girls," Grammy had said. "What if he dies?"

"You can't think like that."

"Nancy would get all the money."

"Mother, I don't care."

Jet brought Nancy to Maine and the vast Ogunquit beach. We hadn't known any family yet to have divorced and Jet's divorce made us sad for Aunt Nannie and the cousins, but Mom told us to be nice to Nancy. Mom dressed the four of us all alike in red-and-white polka-dotted bathing suits. Nancy wore a black bikini, had a huge bust that pushed from the cups, and wore big dark sunglasses that offered a startling contrast to her bleached hair. It wasn't hard to be nice to her. She played tirelessly with us, digging holes and building sandcastles and laughing. Except for her body, it seemed like she was just another girl playing in the sand and I didn't understand why Grammy didn't like her. Then she'd take a walk with Jet and they'd kiss and splash in the ocean and sidle up against each other. "Sex," Scarlett would say, lifting her left eyebrow the way she could do. And it was exciting to look at them. We knew the stories about the fur coat. Watching them was like watching sex.

Grammy ignored Nancy, hardly spoke to her. Grammy made big lobster feasts with bibs and nutcrackers at a picnic table beneath Last Morrow's pines and she let Nancy set and clear the table and run about trying to help, trying to service her way into approval. Grammy treated her like the help. To us Grammy said, "I'm combing my hair with a can opener."

The thing about Nancy, it turned out, was that she was a kleptomaniac. She stole and stole and stole. She stole the fur, she stole Jet, and later, at Scarlett's graduation from Yale, she stole a cashmere blanket. Nancy and Jet and their new baby had stayed with a friend of Mom's, a very wealthy woman. Nancy swaddled her baby in the blanket and took it home. Mom knew exactly where it was when her friend told her it was missing.

Mom, Dad, Zasu, and Timmy, nine and eight years old, drove to Jet's house outside of Boston for a surprise visit. They told Zasu what she had to find while they distracted Nancy, who was so easily distracted by questions about Zasu. "Is it true what they say? Her skin looks like it's true. You're a good man, Timothy." All spoken with that strange accent, trying to hide its origin but not quite getting away with it. Zasu found the blanket, Timmy her shadow and obedient accomplice, and stole it back, hiding it beneath a rain jacket she was wearing though it wasn't raining. Jet and Mom stopped speaking and never did speak again.

Eventually Grammy moved from Last Morrow because she was too old to keep up a house. She moved into an apartment in town near Rose Hill. She was eighty-six years old. I was twenty-nine and Dad had recently died. Grammy thought it would unsettle Mom too much to lose her husband and then have his space taken up by her mother. Mom and Emma had helped

Grammy sell Last Morrow, had packed her up, had rented her the apartment in town, had invested her savings. Grammy had given Mom power of attorney. We didn't think much about this, but Aunt Nancy did. Age had not been kind to Nancy. Everything that had been curvy and bountiful was now droopy and ample. Her hair was yellow from too much bleach. When she appeared at Grammy's door one afternoon, she wore a kilt miniskirt with stilettos, spooking my grandmother.

"Does Jet know you're here?" Grammy asked.

"Of course Jet knows I'm here," she said. "He wanted me to see the new apartment." She went into the kitchen and made the two of them some tea, setting up a silver teapot, sugar cubes, tongs, tea biscuits. "We were wondering, Jet and I," she said, "what you'll do for our girls when you die." Nancy's teeth were lovely and straight, but otherwise everything about her was too strong — hair, perfume, accent. "What are your plans, I mean, to leave them, if I may?"

Grammy stared at her. This was not the kind of thing a person should ask. But it turned out Nancy's question was just a formality. In short order that afternoon, she emptied Grammy's jewelry box, taking all that was there — diamonds, pearls, gold. Nancy poured the loot into her gray leather sack right in front of Grammy, daring Grammy to stop her.

"Winter has the life insurance policy. She has access to your accounts. My girls deserve something too."

"This isn't right," Grammy said.

Nancy took the silver tea service, dumped it into her bag.

"So now you want to speak about right and wrong?" Nancy asked.

"I'm calling Jet," Grammy said.

"Call him," Nancy dared. "But you won't get him. He's outside. He's here. He's waiting for me in the Lexus."

"You said he wasn't here."

"I lied. He's here all right."

"He can't be."

"Look out the window."

"I will not. He's not there. He would never do this. If he is there, he has no idea what you're up to. I'll speak to him."

"He knows that his daughters matter. If you won't think about them, he will. I will. He's not a fan of that child of Winter's. Winter is a disgrace, that's what Jet thinks. Go ahead and speak to him."

Grammy's face reddened. "Zasu is my grandchild. She's Jet's niece, your niece."

"You walk around with your airs. And just look what your own daughter does." Her gray sack hung heavily on her shoulder.

"I'll call the police." Grammy wouldn't look out the window, though. She was afraid she would see Jet.

"Go ahead and make the call," she said. Nancy blocked the hallway. She stood in front of Grammy and then slowly but deliberately she took Grammy's head in her hands, as if she were going to kiss her, but then she turned Grammy's head to one side. She unscrewed the post at Grammy's ear, turned Grammy's head the other way, removed the second diamond, then dropped them both into the ugly, heavy purse. She grasped Grammy's wrist and, prying the finger straight, slipped the emerald off Grammy's finger. Grammy worried for a moment that the ring and earrings would get lost in the bag. It all happened soundlessly, in less than a minute. The knuckle of Grammy's ring finger was too big, protecting the diamond solitaire from Nancy's grasp. All that Nancy left behind was the emptied black felt Tiffany boxes, which Scarlett discovered when she came to visit Grammy. Scarlett liked to keep an eye on things, know that everything was where it should be.

"Go ahead, call the police," Nancy said again. "But you know you've told stories your whole life. No one will ever believe you. You with your Queen of Scots baloney. It's just as likely as anything, you know, that you willingly gave this all to us. And, you know, if you really wanted to stop me, you could have."

In fact, when Scarlett announced that the jewelry and the silver tea service and flatware were gone, Mom asked Grammy why she hadn't stopped Nancy. Grammy did not respond.

"You wanted her to have them, didn't you? Just tell me," Mom said. "You know I don't care about all that stuff. Just tell me."

On the second floor of Last Morrow there was an interior balcony that overlooked Grammy's living room that rose two stories high. Sometimes at night when Grammy and Mom thought we were asleep, my sisters and I would sit on the balcony's ledge to watch them. We felt like we were watching a play, that Grammy and Mom were actors in a drama that illuminated our lives. Soon after Zasu was born, Mom and Grammy sat down there in the dim night light, their images reflected in the tall gilt mirror. Mom was always trying to get something out of Grammy, an understanding, an unconditional love. It was as if Mom was testing Grammy: how far could she push, how unconventional could she be, how much damage could she do to her own life before Grammy would stop loving her. It seemed a part, if not a requirement of their love. And we were simply bystanders.

The room had big bay windows overlooking a lawn that tumbled down an incline to the road. You couldn't see the road, so it was almost as if the room were floating. Mom and Grammy were sipping crème de menthe, an astonishing electric green, and having a lovely time until Grammy said, "She's illegitimate. Not so long ago she would have been illegal. In some states, she might still be illegal."

"What are you talking about, Mother? We're having a good time." It was true. Grammy could only endure happiness for a measured amount of time. If it lasted too long something would come to end it, so in her twisted logic she preferred ending it herself. Perhaps she had the same thing that Mom had, that desire to see how far she could go and still be loved.

"That child."

"What child?"

"You know which child."

"Oh, Mother, please. You don't believe this. This isn't you talking. You know how life works."

"I don't like this. It's wrong and I'm going to be honest. She's an embarrassment."

"To whom?"

"To my friends."

"Oh, Mother." At first Mom was patient. "That's my child and therefore your child and you love her. I know you do."

Grammy was silent. We thought it would be that easy. Of course, Grammy would love Zasu. She loved us; she'd love Zasu. As little kids you sort of accept, in a baffled way, interrogating for yourselves with your own kid logic. But really you have nothing else to compare your experience to. You don't think too hard or too long about the complications. They are abstractions, words tossed into the night from your beds, hanging there to make what you will of them. Life gives what it gives and therefore it is ordinary. Life gave us Zasu and we loved the baby, dressed her like our doll, fought over who got to change her and burp her . . . well, for the most part.

Discomfort comes out sideways. I was always jealous, because her arrival meant that I was no longer the baby; I thought her name was ugly and more proof of how strange we were. "It's a nickname," I'd tell my friends. But it wasn't a nickname. It was Mom trying to be different, trying to test Grammy — Zasu for Zasu Pitts, a silent film star no one had ever heard of. But my jealousies of Zasu emerged later, as she grew older. We didn't think coherently about Arthur, what he meant. Dad was her father; she was our sister and she didn't look black to us. She was light skinned, at least for someone clearly of a black father. When she was surrounded by white people she seemed white. Sometimes I wondered if it would have been different for us had she been dark skinned, if we would have had to think more about her. When she was a teenager there was a period when she wouldn't speak to Mom. She hated Mom, accused Mom of pretending she was white. "You never made any black friends. You never even tried."

We all hated Mom at one point or another, but Zasu's pain came from a point so unfamiliar to us it was like a foreign country. We wanted, my sisters and I, very much to understand it, but no matter how close we came it would always be foreign. One half of her was descended from slaves, from a truth most white people relegated to history, to having happened so long ago they didn't have to think about it. And she didn't look black, but was black; she was American and she was not American. She was camouflaged, but the insults and assumptions that one hears just walking through the world made her quiet, quietly and exactingly aware. When Zasu stopped speaking to Mom I realized consciously what I had known unconsciously all along: that she was different, separate from us, the original four. And of course it was the different father compounded by the fact that she was black, and that carried with it a burden and a history that would never be ours no matter how much we tried. All of us were guilty of not trying hard enough, of believing too easily in easy truths — that she didn't look black and therefore she wasn't black and therefore we didn't have to notice or feel how the insults (that we'd heard since the fights between Mom and Grammy, that we'd heard just from being alive) were tethered to a system whose immediate ancestor was slavery. Even Mom separated Zasu, referring all the time to her four daughters — then, oops, I mean five. But that was later. Now she was a baby asleep in a crib in Mom's room and we were young girls. From the balcony, we watched Mom and Grammy navigate.

"She's black," Grammy said. "And a child of sin."

"Oh please, Mother. You're not even religious."

"I'm smart enough to know that you've made a mess of all the chances Daddy and I gave to you. Timothy is a weak man, he's always been weak, and you've thrown away a lot on him and I warned you of this a long time ago."

"Please," Mom said. Then added, "Leave Timothy and Daddy out of this."

"Bless Charles that he's dead and doesn't have to see this."

And then they were fighting. Mom slapped Grammy. She took a French porcelain lamp, sculpted with a frolicking girl in a hoop skirt and bonnet, and threw it on the floor, shattering it. She was shouting now, so loud we couldn't understand what she was saying.

It was winter and there was a lot of snow on the ground. Emma led us away from the balcony and toward a window at the end of the hall, next to the melodeon upon which sat Nancy Cooper Slagle's Cantonese wedding bowl.

Emma dumped sheets from the linen closet at our feet and the four of us started tying them together in a long rope that we used to slip out the window, shimmying down the sheets until we fell into the snow. One by one. Scarlett went first so she could catch me, then Celia, then Emma. I don't know what Emma attached the rope to, but she attached it to something. She was clever that way, and our rope held. We left the window open with the rope dangling from it. The snow was high and we were in our pajamas with blankets for coats and slippers for shoes that the snow snuck into. I was worried we'd left Zasu behind, but I didn't say anything. Then I was glad. I liked it being just the four of us again.

"Now what?" Celia asked.

"We run away," Scarlett said. She was always matter-of-fact. It didn't seem to matter where. We were taking a stand. We were defending Zasu. We were forging our own path forward. We headed down the long hill of Pine Hill Road. Grammy always told us we could not walk on that road alone, that someone might steal us. "Raped and killed," she'd say. From the outside, trudging across the lawn, we could see Mom and Grammy still fighting, lit up in the living room like inside a snow globe, a little private world that we stole away from into the dark night. I was cold, but I followed my sisters.

We found ourselves shivering at the bar of the Whistling Oyster in Perkins Cove. The restaurant was closing for the night. A bartender, a waiter, the manager, all glum and tired, loitered, hoping we'd be claimed, while Emma and Scarlett tried to come up with our next plan. In a corner, the light of a Christmas tree twinkled on and off. Eventually, the manager looked up Grammy's number in the phone book and called Last Morrow. Mom and Grammy hadn't realized we were gone.

After the fights, Last Morrow would be silent in an eerie way, like it was forcing us to listen to the lingering reverberations of the arguments. We'd slink off to our beds, pretend we'd been asleep, and eventually my sisters would fall asleep. I'd sneak out of my bed and into Grammy's bedroom, into her single four-poster bed that really didn't have much room for me. I didn't care, nor did she. I snuck in next to her, the sheets still cold, no time yet for her body to have warmed the space. It was as though she expected me. She let my tiny body find its way against her. "You're my Baby Rabbit," she whispered, and kissed my hair, and I held her hand and we fell asleep like that. I knew she didn't mean the stuff she said. Sometimes I wasn't even sure if she had actually said the words Mom accused her of saying or if maybe Mom had just assumed she'd say them, that Mom, out of what she feared, had put the words into Grammy's mouth as a way to excise them from her own.

And Grammy would come to love Zasu just the same as us, seeing the funny little girl Zasu was. Perhaps this is how a life is made. "You know," Grammy said to her once. "You're related to James Fenimore Cooper." And she told the story of Nancy and how Nancy was related to the author of *The Last of the Mohicans.* Zasu, not yet five years old, replied: "I should read that book then."

How does this story travel downstream? Distilled to its essence, who then takes it and transforms it to legend? *Collective learning* — isn't that what it's called, ideas stored in a collective memory, accumulating across generations.

In the morning, my sisters and I would rise early and make breakfast to bring to Mom and Grammy in their beds. Grammy had breakfast trays because elegant people had their breakfasts brought to them in bed — coffee and cream, hot cereal melting with brown sugar, drizzled with milk, a flower in a vase, the paper.

We climbed back into the dream, Grammy's tableau.

We all had boyfriends, we all married, started having children. Grammy would study our mates. She didn't like Emma's husband, Claude, because he was old, nineteen years older than Emma. On her wedding day, Grammy looked the groom in the eye and smiled that *you're-about-to-be torpedoed* smile and said, "I do hope you have a *long* life." Her comments, which found the fault lines of vulnerability, came like heat-seeking missiles. The older she grew the more rapidly they were deployed, and with unimpeachable flair — she was an old woman, after all, who could and would say what she pleased; she would zero in and strike. To Scarlett, announcing the news of her third pregnancy, her French husband by her side, Grammy asked, "Who's the father?" She didn't like Jacques because he was too interested in himself to be at all interested in her. She once zeroed in on a boy I was dating — making a comment about the acne scars on his neck. "It looks like you got caught in a rope," she said. I boxed her ears right then and there, right in front of him. No more comments about ropes after that. I married Sam, a man she loved because his family came from Glendive, Montana, where she'd had a happy time on a farm.

In 1992, fifty-eight years old, Dad had a stroke and died. The days in which we boomeranged from hope to despair, Mom lay in the hospital bed with him, assuring us that it would be fine, all fine, Grammy asking us repeatedly, "Is he dead yet?" And when he did finally die, Arthur invited us to Jamaica, all of us, and we went to his compound by the river and the sea, behaving as if he were just Emma's godfather, Dad's friend. Grammy came too and we cried and tried not to think this was strange. It just was. Grammy taught all the little children how to make ice cream and they came out of nowhere to watch her and listen to her while Mom and Arthur fell in love all over again even though Tasmin, Arthur's wife, was right there.

There's obviously a difference between history and fable. Glenna never wrote the actual state song of Nevada, but she had written a love song to Nevada that the governor at the time, Edward P. Carville, had admired and bought the music. Grammy had the letter, stored in the black box. What became of the song in the state is unknown, but Grammy never tired of saying that Glenna had written the state anthem. My mother was a Brown, but I was never related to the company that started Buster Brown Shoes — even though that was just a fact I took for granted most of my young life. It wasn't until after having told friends, after having written articles in which I claimed lineage to Buster Brown Shoes, that I learned — by searching the Internet — that the company was founded in and still resides in St. Louis. Not Lynn. It was all fabrication. Glenna never had love affairs with congressmen and senators. An acquaintance informed me not so long ago that she was a descendant of James Fenimore Cooper, that all his descendants were known and catalogued, and that if I were one I would know that I had been catalogued too. The wedding bowl, the *Temple's Notes,* the dizygotic twins, Maid Marian who fell from her horse eight months pregnant had, of course, all been fabrications. It had been Grammy's job, like one of the singers of the *Rig Veda,* to sing the fables so the world would continue to cohere, and she sang those fables to me.

Grammy said that Nancy Cooper Slagle had lived to 104 because she had wanted to keep receiving her pension due a widow of the

Civil War, the one that hadn't come and hadn't come, forcing her to flee Richmond for her husband's family in Ohio. Grammy's motive was simply to last the longest. But it didn't work out that way.

She began to die on August 11, 2001, the hottest New Jersey day on record — a heat dome, it was called — at our little brother Timmy's eleventh annual pig roast. He'd been having them since he graduated from high school — T-shirts, a tent, an enormous pig rotating on a spit. Over the years of the pig roasts, he'd grown from a full-haired, slender, athletic man into a balding father, carrying extra weight and more and more bluster. He was a showman, and thus Wall Street suited him. Once he hired hot air balloons to rise from the front yard at dusk. Once he hired a huge crane, lifting people a hundred feet in the air so they could bungee jump. At night, laser lights lit up the tulip trees. Every year there were fireworks, late for those who remained, who shut down the party or camped out on the lawn. Each year was bigger and more resplendent than before, and this year's pig roast was Wall Street-financier-and-lobbyist resplendent. He invited friends and colleagues and his wife Adeleine's family, a small group of brothers who sniffed at Mom's rambling, threadbare house with its seventies-era decor, leaky roof, duct-taped patio screens, and intermittently clogged toilets. They thought they were important because they'd made some money.

This was the year Emma had a new job at Dunbar, legal counsel to the hedge fund, which specialized in the kind of arcane financial instruments that nobody wanted to think about. Something about mortgages. Seemed like a sleepy backwater — a horizontal career move for Emma — but, as she kept saying, business was booming. Timmy wanted Emma to invite her friends because they were rich and could be useful with his lobbying interests. Emma always indulged Timmy, ever since he was born, so this year she, boss of the sisters, insisted everyone come home.

We arrived, taking over Rose Hill as though we were returning to our younger selves, claiming bedrooms, declaring our terms and conditions for the visit, making comments on the house and the various ways in which it was falling apart. The four sisters, a variation on a theme, and Zasu with her height and olive skin, her calm remove, spilled into Rose Hill: Celia with her scarves, arriving late from Paris; Scarlett pregnant again; Sam and me pregnant for the first time; Emma on her BlackBerry, dealing with work; all the children slipping off into the yard — our generation taking over. We picked up a conversation that had started long ago and that never seemed to stop, a way of speaking with each other that was about our shared past, present, future — one that, when we were together, submerged the new lives we had created for ourselves.

Later, Adeleine would say that it had been a lucky thing that we'd all come. It was fate aligning so we could all say goodbye. "What a send-off," she'd say. Even Arthur was there, briefly. We'd long since accepted that Arthur and Mom were lovers, though it was never explicitly stated. When he visited, he always stayed in the room next to hers, sneaking into her room at night like a teenager. It made me happy that she was happy even if he was married, his wife in Jamaica.

Timmy wasn't anything like the rest of us. With Timmy, everything was exaggerated and ebullient and he never cared to revisit the past, hear the truth from the sisters about Arthur. Rather, he was a high roller, a big spender who wanted to live in the whirl of forward momentum. Not one of us had any idea if he was actually wildly successful or completely in debt. He loved Rose Hill, wanted to buy it from Mom one day and tear the whole place down and then build it back just exactly as it had been but new and clean and fresh and everything working. "All it will take is money," he'd say.

Adeleine, with her small eyes and big smile, concurred. He liked the notion of having money, said it felt good to make everyone's dreams come true. "Every girl should have a pony," he'd say. He liked to think of himself as Santa Claus, especially before his daughter, Kara. Kara wanted it to snow in July at Rose Hill for her fifth birthday, and Timmy had made it happen. He was not like our father. He was not pensive and cerebral, self-deprecating. He was the opposite of that, though they did share a deep and abiding kindness. Dad had made lots of money, but not the Wall Street kind, not the Santa Claus-snow-in-July kind. And since he had only written two novels, the royalties had been drying up. Dad would have cringed at Timmy's extravagance.

"You can make anything happen, Daddy," Kara had said when the snow fluttered down to dust the Rose Hill lawn. It was eighty degrees and snowing — those machines pumping it out — and Timmy must have felt invincible, standing there watching it all, the gaggle of girls celebrating his daughter with their birthday party tiaras, the snowflakes settling into his hair.

For the pig roast of 2001, Grammy was dressed in a long satin skirt with a sash and a ruffled blouse, sheer white tulle gloves with a seam running around the fingers and up the insides and outsides of the arms, all the way to her elbows — transparent, barely there, but definitive all the same. A white beehive tulle hat perched on her head. She wanted to look like Edith Wharton. Her hip gave her trouble so she remained seated in an armchair covered in a golden fabric. It resembled a throne. For the heat, Timmy had rented giant fans that churned out cooled air. They were placed strategically in the yard, near the tent and near the house.

Party chatter thickened with the Wall Street types who spoke about maneuvering the tech bust to their advantage — chauffeured down from the city, a long line of black Suburbans and Tahomas and Denalis, mountain-sized cars in the driveway, idling, attended by waiting drivers. They were winners. They conversed as if in code. They went on vacation with each other, lived in their own gated communities, stayed in their own circles, and, quietly, busily, made more money than any writer or semiotics scholar or doctor would ever make in three or four lifetimes. I watched them for a time that summer day, huddled together over the crudités, eying our father's house with something that one could mistake for shyness or deference, but that began to resemble superciliousness. They were laughing with each other, and I began to see that a joke was being shared among them. And I remember being irritated. Who were they to look down their noses at Rose Hill? The funders, as Sam and I referred to them, were taking note of the house, its eccentricities — Haitian art everywhere from Dad's years researching his first novel, partly set on a commune in a fictional Haiti. Dad and Mom had loved the raw style. It was pure, they said. The funders thought the house an artist's lair. "Authentic bohemian," they said. Their worlds were sleek and whitewashed and everything chrome and Carrara marble. The only chances they took, it seemed, were with other people's money. Rose Hill was wooden beams and glass and wood-paneled walls and iron carvings of beasts and naked virgins breast-feeding and Eve eating the apple in front of the snake. Everything a little wilted. But Rose Hill had been created by books, the production of art, an author who had taught the next generation to read and write with precision while scaring the daylights out of them. What concrete products could the funders show for their work? How was it possible to make money, to so thoroughly run up the score, without at the same time doing something terribly, fantastically, fundamentally wrong in the process? And how in the world had Timmy and Emma — two of ours — ended up with them?

Grammy sat in her chair and eyed them right back with a stare that could have derailed a freight train. "The more I see of other people, the more I like myself," Grammy said.

"Oh, Mother," Mom said with a roll of her eyes, adjusting candlesticks on the dining room table. We were sitting by Grammy's throne, ignoring her, Zasu and I, then indulging her.

"You're a tumbleweed," Grammy said, turning her sights on Zasu, "and you can't do that forever or you'll get caught in a fence."

My sisters and I knew better than to pin Zasu down. She was a tumbleweed, but she always got caught somewhere interesting — volunteering in Mali with Doctors without

Borders, teaching for Teach for America in Memphis. She wasn't afraid to work and give. She worked hard and she loved. She loved Grammy and understood her admonitions were simply theatrics. She loved Mom and Arthur and accepted that they were lovers even if she wasn't keen to be around them much. Arthur's wife, Tasmin, had been good to Zasu, adored Zasu, treated her like a daughter when she'd gone to live with them, welcoming Zasu as one of her own children. Tasmin was an abstraction for the rest of us, not a real woman married to Mom's lover — even if we had met her. That Zasu had this entire life that wasn't shared with us, that she had another family, essentially, always contributed to her mystery, always lifted her out and away from us. And though she was ten years younger than I, she seemed older, maybe wiser. She was tall and ethereal, a different point of view.

The day stretched into evening and the party crested and then ebbed. Outside the light faded. A pair of couples sat in deck chairs to watch the early evening sky, white wine sweating in their stemmed glasses, Timmy's fans losing the battle with the heat. The couples — neighbors of Timmy's — told each other stories. They were talking about Timmy's house, which was being renovated, how they'd been away and an important package had been delivered containing a stuffed animal, a rabbit, that their daughter had left behind on vacation. She was helpless without the bunny. The hotel had FedExed it and it arrived while they were still away so FedEx delivered it to Timmy's house. The workers accepted the package, which was damaged, so the bunny escaped, falling onto the unfinished floors. As a dark joke, the bunny was staple-gunned to an unfinished wall. "And yes, yes. You're right. It was Easter," said Timmy's neighbor. "How absolutely awful."

"It's dreadfully hot," Grammy said. "I'd have some water." Her face glistened with sweat. She pulled her gloves off. These are the things you remember.

"I'll get it," Zasu said.

I was interested in the bunny somehow, in overhearing the conversation, what was important to these people. Zasu got up and went to the kitchen.

"I'm not feeling well," Grammy said, and grasped my shoulder with her cold fingers. "My heart feels fast."

"You're just an old threadbare mule," I said. Her face lit.

"Going round and round the katydid," she said. "A Home Run Haggerty."

"Do you know how we found the bunny? When they returned home the couple and their kids ran into Timmy and Adeleine. Adeleine asked if they wanted to see the work in their house, how it was coming along.

"That long ago and it's still not finished?"

"Zasu is a tumbleweed," Grammy said. "It's time she settle down."

"Zasu's fine, Grammy," I said.

"I don't feel like I can breathe well," Grammy said. "I feel dizzy, Rabbit." She put her hand in her mouth and pulled out her teeth, setting them on the arm of the throne.

"Grammy," I said to indicate that her teeth should stay in her mouth. I had once hunted for those teeth in a restaurant dumpster late at night after a fancy dinner, through the remains of other people's dinners and the kitchen's scraps. Grammy had wrapped the teeth in a napkin and forgotten them on the table. I found them.

"We wanted to see the house, of course. You know, real estate porn." They were speaking so loudly it was hard not to hear what they were saying.

"Their renovations bring up the neighborhood."

"Which is already up."

"Would you mind pouring some more? This is a lovely Sancerre." I couldn't see them without turning, but I could picture them vividly. They went to see Timmy's house, the little kids and the parents. The little girl who lost her bunny in Bermuda. They walked into the space that would eventually be the kitchen and the little girl burst into a fit. "Hysterics. I'd never seen her cry like that. I thought she'd been attacked. 'It's Bottom,' she cried. 'Mommy, Bottom's been murdered.' " All in an instant the mother saw the bunny stapled to the wall.

"Literary toddlers."

"Absolutely astonishing."

"Was he fired?"

"Who?"

"Someone? The construction worker? The contractor? They're all illegals. Was someone fired?"

"The wine is delightful."

"The heat," Grammy said. "Why are they talking about rabbits, Rabbit? What in the world are they carrying on about? Isn't it time for them to leave?" Zasu returned. She took one look at Grammy and told her to put her teeth in.

"The fireworks, Grammy," Zasu explained. "They're waiting for the fireworks."

I could feel the baby move, just a little, as if adjusting herself in sleep. I loved being pregnant. It made me feel omnipotent.

"The teeth hurt," Grammy said.

"Put them back, Grammy. We have guests."

"My breath smells like the inside of a motorman's glove." Taillights began to illuminate the dusk, the parade of Denalis pushing down the long driveway.

Outside everything was limp, wilting even with the fans. More stragglers splashed in the pool. Celia flirted with Scarlett's husband in French. Earlier she had been flirting with Sam. No one flirted with Emma's Claude; he was too old. Emma stuffed garbage into plastic bags even though there was a staff to do that. The kids, oblivious to the heat, started a football game at dusk. A few fireflies alighted from the grass.

"I want to know if the contractor was fired," the deck chair couples continued.

"I was married in Jersey City," Grammy told Zasu. Zasu had a cool rag that she had put on Grammy's brow. Scarlett waltzed in and lifted her left eyebrow and examined us. "Is something wrong with Grammy?" Scarlett looked like a queen with her ski-jump nose and her perfect curls, studying Grammy. "Put your teeth in, Grammy."

Then: "Did you hide Mommy's silver, Isadora? I told you to hide it. With all these strangers . . ."

"Fired his ass."

"All of them should have been fired."

"The wine is making them aggressive," Zasu noted.

Arthur came inside and smiled at us, carrying plates with remains of the pig roast dinner, followed by Emma with her arms filled with plates too, and the garbage bag dangling from her wrist.

"Will you help me to bed, Rabbit?" Grammy's hand was now at her chest, where she so often placed it, but she'd been dying so long, nobody noticed. Zasu and I helped her up, helped her walk toward her room. We passed Arthur in the living room, holding forth now with Sam and Claude, truly believing that we had no idea he was still involved with Mom, that the secret was theirs alone.

Zasu and I helped Grammy undress, the hat unpinned, the silk shirt, the long sashed skirt, until she was naked, rolls of fat and her long, drooping breasts. A short scar cut horizontally under her clavicle where a pacemaker had been inserted. Her white hair hung long and stringy as though it had, in fact, been combed with a can opener.

Zasu and I shimmied a nightgown over her head, covering her up. Her room — the room that became hers after she moved to Rose Hill from her apartment in town — was filled with remnants of Last Morrow: a dressing table, a rocking chair, stacks of hatboxes, a couple of baroque lamps, a pastel portrait of me as a child that she'd commissioned because important people did that. I remembered where each item had lived in that long-ago house that seemed would always be hers. Nancy's bowl peeked from a high shelf. Under glass protecting the surface of the vanity were snapshots of Grammy as a girl, holding her little sister's hand, holding a gun. There was the clipping from *The New York Times* that had been there all along: a young Grammy on skis by a frozen lake and a group of other skiers: "When Winter Comes into Its Own in the Adirondacks: Col. Edward A. Simmons of Brooklyn, with His Family and Miss B. Stewart (Left), on His Estate at Eagle Bay, Hamilton County." I asked Grammy about the clipping and she said only that she'd been treated like a guest. "And the *B*?" I asked. She twirled her hand in circles at her temple and then took my hand. She held it and she took Zasu's too, then plopped herself down on the bed with our support.

"Are you all right, Grammy?" Zasu asked.

"She's fine," I said.

Adeleine burst into the room with her small smile, her mouth like a Popsicle. She kissed Grammy and said goodbye.

"It was a lovely party," Grammy said.

"Timmy outdid himself again, didn't he? Now the fireworks. Won't you see them? The children are asleep in the car," she said, and was gone, Zasu following her to kiss the kids goodbye. Timmy and Adeleine had parties at Rose Hill, but they never spent the night. There were too many bugs.

Grammy lay back into the pillows. Her bed faced a sliding glass door that overlooked a small garden and the woods. Now it was pitch-black. I turned off the light, snuggled next to her. I could feel her heart beating fast, but I didn't think much about it. Rather, I was thinking about the baby in my belly, that the little creature, due in October, was a life between us. The creature was a girl. I knew that already. As I settled against Grammy, the baby started to kick. I placed Grammy's hand on my stomach and she felt it for a while.

"She's strong," Grammy said, and then added, "Know this: I always loved your mother. Every second of every day I have been alive. When she was born I couldn't believe my good fortune. I never stopped."

"Grammy, don't be silly, I know that. She knows that. Where do you think you're living, after all?"

"I dreamed something different for her, but she did well. I was afraid. Very afraid. It's no way to live."

"You're being morbid, Grammy," I said, because I knew just how she was thinking. A dim outdoor light turned on and a menagerie of bugs quickly fluttered to it.

"This is it, Rabbit," she said bluntly.

"Oh, Grammy," I said. I kissed her clammy forehead and told her to feel the baby who, for emphasis, kneed her palm, making Grammy laugh. "I've died and gone to heaven," she said, another refrain. After a bit, Zasu returned and lay down on the other side of Grammy in the big bed and the three of us fell asleep listening to the sounds of Timmy's firework display zinging and popping away in the night sky. I hadn't meant to fall asleep there.

It was still very dark outside when Zasu woke me, telling me Grammy's pulse was too slow, that she was calling an ambulance. Everything happened fast from that moment. The ambulance arrived. Zasu and I explained to Sam, who would carry the news to Mom and the sisters. We rode with

Grammy in the back while the EMT gave her oxygen. Beneath the bright lights of the emergency room she was attached to machines, stabilized. It was quiet and empty, a rural hospital. After a day, she was moved to the ICU. The sisters and Mom came and went. Jet was notified, arriving too late, told she'd been discharged. Believing her all right he drove home. Celia had to return to Paris, Scarlett to her children's summer plans, Emma to Dunbar. No one thought Grammy would die. Zasu postponed her departure. Grammy was lucid one moment, confused the next. She said things that were clear and understandable but that when strung together made no sense. Then with clarity she told us that she had written a novel, *Sweet Peas and Rattlesnakes.* We sat up taller, asked where it was, the manuscript. "You have it," she said. "You have it all." We asked her what she meant, but then she reverted to gibberish. The doctor initially assured us she could be stabilized, that the heat dome was causing this all over the country, that we'd done the right thing admitting her. Then clarity again: she asked to feel the baby kick, asked me the name of my baby.

"I don't have one yet."

"Grace," she said. "Grace was one of my

mother's sisters, a favorite aunt. Call her Gracie. I can see her; I will know her if you call her Gracie. Imagine all these great-grandchildren."

Then she'd disappear again and hours would pass in this way, Zasu and me trying to make sense of the words coming from her, catching the familiar as it hit up against the strange.

"Take my ring," she said to me on the second day. We were alone in her hospital room. "I know enough to know that I shouldn't die with a diamond ring on. Someone else will get it." She insisted, and I tried twisting it off her ring finger, but I couldn't get it over the knuckle. I forced it, feeling afraid someone would walk in the room and think I was stealing it. But I confess I wanted the ring. It was the diamond solitaire from Tiffany's, the one piece of her jewelry that Nancy hadn't gotten. "Extra-extra river water," as Grammy would say, showing it to my sisters and me. "Would you like it when I'm dead and gone?" But she'd stopped using her euphemisms. She told me to get some baby oil and rub it around the knuckle. I did and the ring came off. "Wear it, Baby Rabbit."

When the ring was successfully on my finger, Grammy looked at me with her sharp eyes and said: "Your mother, she always loved your father. Very, very much. You should have seen her as a teenager. She loved him. Know that. She loved him. And, boy, did he love her. He asked her once to have her portrait taken, send him the many copies of the photographs of her face. He wanted to wallpaper his room with her image."

On the third day, the doctor told us that the only hope was an emergency angioplasty and that his hospital didn't have the technology to perform that. Later we'd learn that hospitals don't like it when people die in them; it's bad for business.

"We need to get her to a hospital that can," he said. Hot potato. The nearest hospital for this service was in Lehigh Valley, he explained to Mom, Zasu, and me. "We can transport her there. We need speed. We'll medevac her." We looked confused. Grammy was sitting up in her bed, sort of regally, her hair swept up in a clip, feeble, but lucid. She wore a pink silk robe over her hospital gown.

"A helicopter ambulance," the doctor said.

Fear spread across Grammy's face. I felt the baby kick, kick hard like it was trying to get out. "It's all right, Grammy," Zasu said. "They know what they're doing."

"Imagine you're flying in a helicopter, Mother. How funny," Mom said.

"What does a helicopter have to do with saving my life?"

I remembered being a little girl with her, at Last Morrow, kneeling for prayers, her crazy songs. *We're just plain folks, your mother and I.*

The helicopter came, landed on a little helipad, and Grammy was rolled to it on a gurney, her pink robe gone. They slipped her inside, secured her in place for the ride. We were able to kiss her, tell her we'd be following on the road in the car, that we'd get there very soon. The helicopter was small and red with the white cross emblazoned on the sides.

"I want to come with you," she said. She offered me a fragile smile.

"It's faster and safer this way," Mom explained.

"Stay with me," she said, clutching my hand hard. She didn't want to let go of my hand.

"I'll be right there," I said.

"We'll be there," Zasu said. The paramedics shut the door and then the helicopter holding Grammy lifted straight up from the ground.

Zasu drove Mom's car — recklessly and

520

fast. We arrived at the hospital two hours later, found her floor, her nurse, her room. She was lying in the bed attached to machines. The one that registers the heart wasn't flatlining and relief spread through me.

"I'm so sorry," the nurse said.

"What?" I asked.

"There's a beat because she has a pacemaker. It's the pacemaker. We couldn't help her. I'm sorry."

I took Grammy's hand and lifted it to my face. It was cold. Her mouth was agape. Somehow, to me, she didn't look dead. "She's not dead," I said. Zasu held me and Mom held Zasu.

"She came in incoherent, speaking gibberish. There was nothing we could do. I'm sorry. She was ninety-seven. That's a long life."

"What do you mean by gibberish?" Zasu asked.

"Nonsense. She wasn't making sense. She was already gone when she got here. If we can all be as lucky to get to ninety-seven." Mom looked at her mother solemnly, not without love. A life of antagonism, but Mom knew. She knew that we do this as one way of avoiding the crush of love, the fear it can produce.

"Tell us," Zasu persisted with the nurse, a completely forgettable face. "What was she saying?"

"She was delirious. Too far gone to perform the angioplasty. She was asking for a baby rabbit. We don't have baby rabbits. We tried explaining."

"For what?" I said, wanting to have the words repeated.

"For a baby rabbit. This is a hospital." Zasu wrapped her arms around me and held me. She held me for a long time.

And just like that, a life is over — the urgencies, the fights, the stories, the sweet peas, the rattlesnakes, the attempts to make something of it, bend it and stretch it and configure it with our wills, give it a narrative, a history, a story, to make it amount to something.

Her body was taken to the morgue, collected by a pair of morticians who wore Dacron suits. Jessie James and Jackson Jessie — those were their true names. They prepared her body for cremation, whatever that means, cremated her, and drove her remains to Rose Hill. Mom was alone at Rose Hill. She accepted the urn with the ashes and thanked the pair who sailed off again in their boatlike car, back to Lehigh Valley. Mom sat beneath the spires of the tulip poplars and rummaged her fingers around in Grammy's dust, feeling the softness of the ash, almost silken, and the sharp shards of bone.

12
MY STORY

"This is how it works," Gracie said, explaining Snapchat's My Story to Sam and me as we stood at the edge of the Hoover Dam. Zane and Mathilde, the French exchange student, were already conversant in the language of My Story, their stories under way. Zane, ten years old, found the great, bowl-like slope of concrete a magnificent half-pipe. "What a drop-in," he said. "I should have my skateboard."

"Oh man," Sam said. He was wearing his homburg hat; it made him feel like a hipster. "That's totally making me dizzy."

"Totally lit," Zane said.

"Dope," Sam said.

"Dad! You are *not* cool," Gracie said, cringing — my gorgeous girl with her sharp blue eyes, keeper of the family, her long Norwegian legs.

It was August. One hundred degrees. Loads of tourists, spilling out of the parking lot thick with RVs, then wilting in the sun-clobbered air. The Colorado River, stopped, blocked in a gorge, sluiced down chutes in thundering white foam jets below. Time had passed as it likes to do, picked us up in one moment and set us down in another, where we stared at a hydroelectric colossus in a desert.

How did that happen? we like to ask. Here I was now, a writer, a wife, a mother with two kids, traveling in a minivan on the great American adventure, wanting to show the kids, and the little French girl Mathilde, some history, some geology. We'd already been to Joshua Tree, had clamored up its peach-colored lithoscape, had an encounter with a sand-colored snake, watched satellites tracking through the stars of a desert sky. We'd followed Route 66 through the Mojave, stopped at a gas station in a dead town that had been purchased, lock, stock, and hotel, by a nostalgic hedge fund manager. We placed pennies on a railroad track and watched as a mile of tanker cars flattened them into hot coppery wafers, listened to the aftermath of that desert silence ticking in the heat. Looking down over the Pinto Basin, the air blistering around us, almost visible in its density, Sam said to the kids, "You just know, there is not a single human out there." At the Grand Canyon, Sam noted that John Wesley Powell, its discoverer, had built himself a raft and floated down the Mississippi River — when he was just fourteen. "What do you think?" Sam liked to ask after each piece of history, looking to Mathilde in particular, wanting to awe her with America. America was, simply, awesome.

Mathilde would offer him a smile, sweetly nod her head, and say, "It's good," in that French way that seemed to say, with a time-less European perspective, that many things in the world are good — that this was one of those things, but let's not get too carried away with it.

Then Gracie would interrupt the history lesson, "Dad! That was then, this is now."

Our western adventure wasn't completely unmoored from a sense of genuine purpose. From Hoover Dam we were headed to Las Vegas to meet Grammy's nephew, Slim Bennett. Grammy had ways, it seemed, of visiting me even some fifteen years after her death. Her emissaries arrived from the ether, little apparitions to keep her story go-ing: Glenna's favorite sister's grandson, call-ing to ask if we were really related to James Fenimore Cooper — he'd read an article I'd written; Grammy's firstborn great-grandchild, whose mother, my cousin, happened to be a witch, offering me a video recording of Grammy telling her life story on the occasion of her ninety-seventh birthday, the year she died — there Grammy was, sharp as a tack, singing the "Little Black Train's a Comin' "; Nancy LePine, whose life long ago Grammy had thought in need of saving, and who knew many (not always flattering) stories about my family that she wished to return to me — *They're yours,* she wrote, *I want to give them back. Well, thanks,* I thought, feeling very much on the receiving end of something far less generous than it seemed — a narrative loop for which I was just a stand-in, an extra in a movie that had come full circle but whose contours of regret I would never know; the present owner of Last Morrow, having read another article I'd written, tracking me down to let me know she was selling the house, did I want to buy it?

My favorite visit was with Slim. On the occasion of Grammy's death, he started writing me, telling me mostly about Glenna, eager for me to know who she really was. Somehow he thought I glorified her. *She was no hero,* he wrote. He wrote and wrote and wrote — colorful stories about Glenna's cruelty and his love for her; about his mother, Pat, weak woman that she was, surrendering her name; how he admired my grandfather with his polished shoes; the third-grade education of his father, a Los Angeles cop. Slim claimed he was dyslexic but that autocorrect helped him to appear otherwise. This was a man, who as the Quakers say, was moved to speak, a notion that, of course, I understood. In all his emails, he pleaded with me to come visit. He wanted to show me all the sites where Glenna had taught, many of them nothing now, just old rubble and fire hydrants, but he knew exactly their quadrants on a map and could show me if I'd come. *It's now or never,* he wrote. *The time's come. The deadly miasma is rising from the meadows.* Here was hyperbole straight from Grammy's playbook — and so we made our travel plans. When Grammy had mentioned Slim it was always to tell the story of how he, a dashing young sailor who'd gotten a girl pregnant, had helped her dress a dead Glenna at Mr. Moon's funeral home, dress her in a blue velvet gown, aiding him in the difficult task, her body stiff with rigor mortis. She never failed to mention that the girl's baby died, that the children they eventually had were all adopted.

Slim was eighty-six years old now, could

see the hourglass rapidly draining. He wanted to take us, he wrote, to Goldfield, Nevada, the town in which Glenna had died — a pilgrimage of sorts, which I had somehow sold to the children, throwing in Las Vegas and a ghost town for good measure. Gracie's idea was to document the trip, add it to her story.

"Her story! You can't say that," she chastised me. "It's *My Story.* Not *her story.*" I was having trouble understanding the form, so she was explaining, against the Hoover Dam backdrop, me feeling a little fleshy in a sundress and straw hat, readers on the end of my nose as I peered into her phone. Gracie, with oceanic patience, explained — once again — that with My Story you take shots, write brief captions, post, and the posts accumulate to tell the story of your day, and then all of it vanishes in twenty-four hours just in time for your next day. "So your story doesn't last?"

"It lasts long enough for your followers to see what's happening in your life."

"I'd say it's a scenic moment more than a story. There's no narrative."

"Mom," Gracie said. "The day progresses."

"And?"

"The photos tell the story of it."

"Where's the plot development? I'm waiting for that — and it doesn't happen. I feel misled."

"You're old school." She paused then added, "Your sisters aren't."

"My sisters?" I asked. "They follow you?"

"Yep." Gracie knew this would wake me up. My daughter — another channel for the ongoing sister conversation, what Sam liked to describe as a bygone narrative out of ancient Greece: a Greek chorus.

"There's a narrative angle," Sam piped in. "Sister rivalry — old story."

"The plot thickens," Gracie said.

"Nonsense," I said. "The sisters can't find their way out of a social media paper bag." But I thought about my sisters, how they were tethered to us from their four corners of the world, pulled up, then back down by satellites to Gracie's phone, watching us, along with us on our travels.

"Wrong," Gracie said.

"They don't speak your language."

"They follow me, Mom," she said, and rolled her eyes and gave the French girl a look. Mathilde smiled.

Sam started telling the kids about the dam: built in 1931, took five years to complete, put a lot of people back to work during the Great Depression. Epic WPA. Gracie had us all lean in, raised her phone, Hoover half-pipe framed behind us, said, "Selfie. One, two, three."

Goldfield was once the biggest town in Nevada, coming to life with the discovery of gold in the very early 1900s. It didn't last long, some eight years — the field was shallow — but as these things go, gold drew in some thirty thousand people, including eighty-seven lawyers, forty doctors, twenty-two hotels, seventeen cigar stores, five banks, three newspapers. Virgil Earp arrived, established residence, told his brother Wyatt that gold flowed here like wine. A young undertaker and his lovely wife set up shop on Euclid Avenue, just off Main Street, and did such a volume of business they were able to pass the shop on to their son, who would one day be the caretaker of Glenna's corpse.

The town also held claim to the longest bar in Nevada, the Northern, made by Tex Rickard, and that required eighty bartenders to serve its many customers. Rickard was a well-known oilman, owned sports teams, boxing teams, and arenas and cattle companies all across the country. He came to Goldfield for the gold, of course, and encouraged others to follow, populating the

531

town by promoting a prizefight for the lightweight championship of the world between Battling Nelson and Joe Gans. He offered what was at the time the biggest purse in the history of boxing: twenty thousand dollars. The fight was hailed as "The Fight of the Century," and the century had barely started. It was 1902 and journalists swarmed the town. The seventy-two-thousand-dollar gate was a record and made Rickard the winner after an astonishing forty-two rounds. With his winnings, he built a splendid home on the edge of town with a turret and Louis Comfort Tiffany stained-glass windows imported all the way from Tiffany Studios in New York City, adding a bit of glamour to this dusty desert town.

Buildings went up fast. On Main Street, The Goldfield Hotel was constructed in 1907 — 150 rooms, cost four hundred thousand dollars to build, flaunted circular banquettes upholstered in gold brocade, crystal chandeliers, a mahogany bar. The boom days created so much ore, miners sewed hidden pockets into their overalls, hollowed out pick handles, and made false heels for their boots so they could steal a bit for themselves, leading to factions and divides, civil unrest, miners against corporations, and the Goldfield labor wars. There was Theodore Roosevelt speaking to the masses and the miners from the balcony of the Goldfield Hotel, cautioning against anarchy — what it can do to a place.

By the time Glenna arrived in the summer of 1947, for her position as principal of the high school, the town had long gone bust, the gold finished, the town gutted by a massive fire and then another. She rented a little shack the town had in large supply, space big enough for a miner's bed, and she'd fixed it up as her home. The shack notwithstanding, somehow Glenna managed to have died in a room in Tex Rickard's home, which over the years led to the story that Glenna and Tex Rickard had been lovers. It didn't mean much. I had no idea who Tex Rickard was, only that Glenna had died in his bed — my grandmother stepping sideways into her fictions through the doors of collapsible and colliding time. Rickard had been dead a good twenty years earlier, but no matter.

We had set off for Goldfield that morning from Las, as Slim Bennett referred to Las Vegas, piling into our rented minivan at the crack of dawn for the three-hour drive. We'd spent the night before last in Boulder City, a few miles from Hoover Dam, in a well-kept motel with a glorious neon sign, a little pool, and vibro-massage beds that purred above the hum of air-conditioning — where time seems to have stopped in 1958. But now, in Vegas, the City of Lightbulbs, the kids were reluctant to trot back out into the desert, where you could feel yourself evaporating in the heat. The glitter of the city and all the beckoning shops kept them mesmerized. We had just last evening seen a Las Vegas extravaganza, Le Rêve — a triumph of the body as architectural extravaganza meeting a swimming pool. "Michelangelo would have loved this," Sam had said. Our hotel room, on the fifty-third floor, overlooked the strip, a sea of neon against the night, the world on view beneath the canopy of lights — the London Eye, the Eiffel Tower, the Leaning Tower, the Sahara, the pyramids, gondolas captained by gondoliers, floating peacefully through canals.

I had a professor long ago in college who was dying of AIDS, right smack in the middle of the epidemic. With his help, I read *The Divine Comedy,* visiting him at his home to do the work because it was more comfortable for him in his illness to be at home in his slippers. One day near the end, when we were reading in *Purgatory,* he told me of a grand idea he had. "Build a city in the desert that re-creates all the best monuments of the world, have the masses visit it rather than the real cities. Preserve the real cities for those of us who really care." Las Vegas: Professor Brogyani's vision realized.

The kids stared at it from the hotel plate glass windows, floor to ceiling. The Grand Canyon was spectacular, but this, this was stratospheric. "You like it?" Sam asked Mathilde.

"Oh yes," she'd replied, enthralled, with none of that French perspectival nonsense. Planes circled Las Vegas in the night sky, a ziggurat of approach that never stopped, America a slot machine ka-chinging, the constant noise of cashing in. Sam shook his head.

We met Slim Bennett early in the morning, the casino alive with gamblers sipping Bloody Marys. Slim came walking toward us, down the gilded corridor of the Wynn Hotel. Tall, hunched, dressed in army green shorts, a white T-shirt, and black suspenders, his hair as white as Grammy's, his face as broad. He approached with his big, green Grammy eyes and a smile, knowing exactly the names of my children, introduced himself to Mathilde, gave us all big hugs like he'd known us all our lives. I recognized him immediately, startling myself with the apparition.

"I finally got you here," Slim said to me, holding me in an embrace that was somehow comforting and familiar and not at all like I was in the arms of a stranger.

"We're off to pay Glenna a visit," he said to the kids.

"She's dead," Zane said.

"Boo," Gracie said. She snapped a picture of us all and sent it up to the ether.

Sam arrived, pulling an ice chest with drinks and sandwiches, hauling it right through the high rollers, hungry-looking people pulling away on the slot machines, too busy to note the incongruity of this very dad-looking dad. At the valet stand, we piled into the minivan and headed off. Within minutes the city disappeared and there was nothing but dry, dry land. Out there you could be dead in a minute. A ghost in search of a ghost town.

Slim sat in the middle row alongside Gracie, narrating for us as we drove, same road of nothing Glenna used when going to visit Slim's family in Los Angeles. She drove a black Buick, sharing the front seat with her cat and dog both of whom she worshipped, allowing them to fight for space on her lap. She taught in Nyala near Lucille on the Extra Terrestrial Highway. She also taught at Warm Springs, just a pile of lumber now. Towns incorporated because there was water, little nothing towns that attracted the down-and-out — a restaurant, a gas station, a school, always a bar. People wound up in these towns by chance and then had no good reason or the gumption to move on. "That's no fact," Slim was fond of saying. "Just my memory or the way I see it." Las was nothing then, he told us, just a bunch of gangsters.

Slim liked to talk just as much in person as he did in his letters and emails. He lived in Hurricane, Utah, right up against the Nevada border, with his third wife, Giselle, a Mexican woman with whom he had no children. His children were with his first wife (divorced) and his second wife who died of liver cancer back in the nineties, but those kids, as Grammy said, were adopted. Even he seemed to label them. There were three of them, well into middle age with grown children and lives worth living, into real estate interests, like Slim, who confessed he'd never been to college. "A fact," he said. "That is a fact and a disappointment to both your grandmother and your grandfather." My grandfather, a man he admired and looked up to and spent his days as a child wishing somehow he could wake up to discover was his own father. He believed that because Grammy had his mother's name somehow Charles could have been his father, that it wasn't out of the realm of reasonable even if he knew it was a pipe dream. His mother, Pat, had stolen a silver pitcher from the HMS *Alexander,* the ship that had brought her from Seattle to Los Angeles and upon which she'd met Slim's father. She took the pitcher as a reminder, a keepsake, to mark the beginning of her life. "My life began when I met your father," she told him. And the pitcher sat on their dining table across Slim's childhood, the prettiest thing in their home: stolen. Slim had spent a good deal of his time trying to understand what had come before the *Alexander* ferried his mother away and into the arms of her beloved Hank, what could have been, if only. Imagining the impossible was easy for Slim, and you could see him concocting right behind his emerald eyes, a parallel narrative that both haunted him and kept him going the way dreams can do.

As a young man he was a liberal, now he was a libertarian, took a stand against the government at the Bundy Ranch, standing out there on the highway with the rest of the heroes, as he called them, fully armed and ready for attack, ready to choose liberty over government. His email signature always included: *Life without God is like an unsharpened pencil, there is no point to it! A gun in hand is worth 2 Cops on the telephone. There's nothing more effective than an armed protector to prevent an armed attacker from doing harm.* He always packed a trim little .32 at his ankle, hidden in his sock. "A fact," he told the kids. "I carry. Have a gun right here in my sock," terrifying them. He made me curious; I knew no one like him.

It was having been a liberal that embarrassed Slim before my grandfather; the idea of disappointing his Uncle Charles diminished Slim for himself. But he'd made up for it. He'd done well. He'd found investors and developed property all over Utah. "The Mormons covet money," he said with a conspiratorial wink. He owned a little Cessna that he liked to fly over the Grand Canyon when the authorities weren't looking — whatever that meant — and over southern Nevada, looping above the towns in which Glenna had taught so long ago. He could spot the towns from fifteen thousand feet. Dry Lakes, Nyala, nothing much to see from up there but the oily silver of mirage, towns once occupied by Russian railroad gangs and Basque sheepherders, the children of whom Glenna taught.

"Uncle Charles would be proud of me now," Slim said. And it struck me that he'd probably devoted a large portion of his life to making the dead proud — Glenna, Charles, Grammy. He was my first cousin, once removed, tethered to me by all that blood running downstream from Mary, Queen of Scots, and Nancy Cooper Slagle — stories fed to us by our respective grandmothers — Glenna, Grammy. I didn't know Slim, but I loved him. There was something immediately between us, a shared story of make-believe and other stuff that had made us, he a western man, me an eastern woman, of the same originating ore. Two sisters at the divide: one went west and the other east, and now, here we were, their representatives. My mother, she hadn't cared enough, but somehow Slim and I did. I was curious about this journey, this adventure. Even if I didn't entirely understand its importance, it felt, yes, mythic, and part of me really hoped that something mythic would happen.

Glenna averaged fifty miles an hour, driving to Los Angeles. Because of the war efforts the limit was forty-five. Her hair was long and dark, red and gold — gorgeous, not a bit of gray. Grammy clipped off a hunk of that hair in Mr. Moon's funeral home and tucked it away in an envelope that floated down to me — a weird practice to save a person's hair. Scarlett said, upon seeing the hair, "You've got her DNA; you could clone her." My mother saved my baby hair, my sisters' hair too. I saved my babies' teeth, storing them in the various boxes that held my jewelry, no distinguishing now Zane's from Gracie's. But all those little teeth remain, calling back their toothless smiles, their little six-year-old selves. Who will those teeth float down to?

After an hour, we were thick into alien territory in the Amargosa Valley, where, as it also happens, prostitution is legal and aliens freely roam.

- Angel's Place
- The Shady Lady
- Dennis Hof's Alien Travel Center
- Area 51 Alien Center
- Cat House
- Warning: Alien Brothel & Bar — Girls Welcome, Free Tours
- Nude Girls
- Bikinis

"A lot of the brothels are abandoned," Slim said. "Lost their business in the sixties with the women's liberation movement. They became sort of obsolete. But Nye County is open and Esmeralda isn't."

Puff clouds against a blue, blue sky.

Empty landscape, just power lines running into the blue-gray distance. But something was happening out there beyond the glittering mirages: Mercury Test Range, Skunk Works, Area 51, Star Wars, former atom bomb test sights strictly off-limits to humans and trending slowly toward a half-life nobody will ever see, Apex, Nellie's AFB, Yucca Mountains, Yucca Flats, Indian Springs, where the drone pilots train. Somewhere OJ Simpson languished in his prison.

When we were in Joshua Tree, guests at the 29 Palms Inn, we had dinner with other guests on the green oasis lawn. The couple sitting nearby warmed to us when they learned we were New Yorkers. They were New Yorkers too, transplanted peacefully to Los Angeles. The man and his wife leaned toward us. "New York and LA. You get on the plane at JFK and step off at LAX and just fucking forget everything in between. It doesn't exist. Mississippi? What? Nevada? Huh? Never heard of them. They don't exist." That night at the 29 Palms Inn, a man stood up after dinner and began telling a story. He was funny and winning and the kids loved him and it seemed like we'd all just won an after-dinner prize — and then came the big reveal: Jesus loved us and we were all angels, and so on and so forth. The kids kept smiling politely. I looked across the table at Sam, who smiled and shrugged. The LAX couple mouthed the words "Fly-over."

And my great-grandmother had lived out here, my grandmother had lived out here. They knew what to do with a snake. We didn't. We knew nothing. I told Slim about our encounter with the snake, showed him the video we'd captured on my iPad, close up, zeroing in on its diamond-shaped head, its coiling body. You can hear me ask, "Is that a garter snake?"

"I don't think so," Mathilde says on the video.

Sam asked Slim, "What kind of snake do you think that is?"

"Ever heard of a diamondback rattle-snake?" Slim answered, and pointed to the rattle at the end of the coil. "The only reason it didn't strike was because it was too early in the morning. It was cold; the snake hadn't warmed up yet."

"You could have killed us," Gracie shouted.

"I didn't have my glasses on," I said.

"Out-of-sight," Zane said.

"Who speaks like that?" Gracie said.

Mathilde observed.

Driving long distances with Slim through the Nevada desert soon led to talk about drones and A-bombs and rocket propellants, and all of this got Slim talking about his own involvement in the war. Gracie and Zane didn't have a grandfather. Both had died before they were born. Here was this guy, very grandfatherly, speaking the way grandfathers spoke, about things that happened a long time ago, that were part of a larger, abstract memory only they could make concrete with stories. Slim was narrating about being on a ship in the Pacific, a signalman on the bridge of a vessel 290 feet long during the Battle of the Philippines. It was called the LST 1123 and was able to fuel off-tankers in the middle of the ocean. Big ships would just come alongside, sliding in side to side, like they were mating. The LST 1123 could also run up on a beach and open its front like a big mouth and let out jeeps and ten-wheeler trucks and three hundred troops and their artillery.

Slim had been eighteen years old, responsible for navigating, steering, signaling with flags, lights, radio while Japanese dive-bombers took out ships all around him. It was like the gods were booming and exploding all around him while his LST poked along, completely exposed. He was just one among so many targets for the Japanese to choose from, with nothing to do but just keep steering the ship forward, trying not to wince when something blew up nearby. Bad for morale. Their job was to help out ships that called Mayday.

"Did you kill anyone?" Zane asked, his big brown saucer eyes widening.

"Zane," Gracie said, and whacked him.

"Mostly what we saw were the kamikazes," Slim said. "We'd put up flack like everyone else. The Japanese would fight to the death, but they were interested in the bigger ships, so we just sat out there like some hellish taxi cab waiting for a fare."

Slim pointed out the window, to round out the conversation about the war — what he was doing versus some other folks. "Celebrities came out here to get arrested for protesting nuclear events. Such high security you can't see a thing, but it's there all right."

■ ■ ■ ■

Family, all these tentacles of us. Gracie, on her phone, sent her evaporating messages to my sisters in the clouds, reporting to her My Story, spreading the word. She had always cared. As a young girl she'd ask me endlessly to tell her stories. "Tell me something else." And so I told her the stories that had been told to me, passed them right on down. She knew Grammy and Glenna, Pat, Nancy Cooper Slagle, even the dizygotic twins, Maid Marian and Mary, Queen of Scots. She'd made a family tree in the fifth grade that reached all the way back to Scotland. She'd seen a family tree I had made in the fifth grade, beneath glass at Rose Hill, a beautiful and colorful drawing, but I'd failed to include Zasu on the tree even though she'd already been born. Gracie had noticed, did the math, and asked. "I was stupid," was my answer. Gracie made sure Zasu was on her tree and that Arthur was too — she didn't care what the teachers said or asked. She had loved this project. Sam was from Glendive, where Grammy had lived for some time on a farm with Pat as girls. They had been left with strangers while Glenna went off to teach in

Ekalaka. Gracie had her own theory. "You see," she explained to us back then when she was in the fifth grade. We were relaxing in bed. Gracie, all wise smile and her father's Norwegian blue eyes, brought a dry erase board bedside, a marker as a tool. She drew an elaborate diagram, dated it 1910, and proceeded to explain how Glenna and Rasmus, Sam's grandfather, had known each other in 1910 in Glendive. " 'Known' each other. It was a tiny town," she said, lifting her left eyebrow suggestively just the way her Aunt Scarlett could do. "Maybe they even had a baby. Glenna was a flirt." We laughed.

Sam looked at me and said, "Uh-oh, we're related." And he kissed me.

"I'm just saying." Gracie winked.

The other thing about Goldfield was the ghosts. For those interested in such things, paranormal activity in the town registered off the charts, attracting shows such as *The World's Scariest Places, Ghost Hunters,* and *Ghost Adventures.* In Nevada, the town was ranked the most haunted in the state, and many of these hauntings occurred at the Goldfield Hotel — big and spooky, perfect setting for a haunting or two. Elizabeth was a prostitute from the town's tenderloin, favored lover of George Winfield, who owned the hotel. Elizabeth became pregnant with his baby, and fearing for his reputation, he ordered her chained to a radiator in room 109, leaving her there to die, which she did upon delivering the baby who, himself, was immediately disposed of by being thrown down a mine shaft. You can imagine, right outside the window, the town thriving, people busy with their earthly instigations and negotiations, collecting that gold hand over fist in one way or another. As it happened, of course, death didn't stop Elizabeth from roaming the town in search of her baby, the long corridors of the massive hotel, working to stir fear and other emotions in those she'd been forced to leave behind. *I'm still here,* she seemed to be saying, *and I want my baby.* Cold spots, odd noises, ghostly figures and orbs had been spotted and felt over the years, along with the misty figure of a woman in a white gown. There were other ghosts: George Winfield himself, tormented by Elizabeth, pleading with her to finally leave him alone; a plutocrat who'd lost his fortune, shot himself in his room at the hotel, but that didn't stop him either from taking up residence there, puffing away on a Cuban cigar, the scent scaring off prospective buyers.

Then we arrived, come all the way out here to find our own ghost. What to say? We emerged from the minivan eating sandwiches plucked from Sam's large cooler. The outside air that day was cool, actually, for a summer day in southern Nevada. We stretched our legs. Zane threw the football to Sam, who went long. Mathilde continued practicing her irregular verbs, something she had started back in the Mohave, Gracie correcting her. Slim and I took in the scene. No one was around. Our arrival had increased the town's population exponentially.

Shacks everywhere. Tiny. Falling apart. Some of the shacks were on wheels, so small they could be towed liked a small RV, dragged away by a miner in search of the next boomtown. "Just as I remember it," Slim said. He emerged from the minivan as Slim pointed out the schoolhouse — the old one and the new one, which was new in 1947 and where Glenna would have been the principal, K–12, had she not died. The group of us walked the streets, taking in all the junk, which was everywhere. The desert is a graveyard for cars, old trains, and decommissioned military equipment. Here in Goldfield, the sun was baking and preserving old fire trucks and old mines and old stores and old saloons and old mining buckets and car parts, all dismembered and abandoned and casting shadows onto rattlesnakes curled into desert mandalas in the scrub. Only after taking this all in did anyone ask, *Why in the world are we here?*

"Why are we here, Mom?" Zane said.

"Because our great-great-grandmother died here," Gracie said. "You already know that." He offered a perplexed look, trying though to understand.

"She rented a two-hundred-square-foot home, very primitive, and then died before she even had a chance to start her job as principal. That job would have been the pinnacle of her career," said Slim. "That's what I recall, but that is no fact. She died of the same disease I have, but progress has mended my heart, at least for now."

A gridded town, replete with all the necessary historic buildings — fire station, hotel, school, saloons. The Esmeralda County Courthouse, jail and archives of documents preserving records, the *Goldfield News* and the *Weekly Tribune* in microfiche, saved by those same folks who had preserved the town — those who understood that once Goldfield had mined everything it could from the ground, it could continue to mine its own past — claiming status for it with the National Historic Registry. The locals, population three hundred today, tried mightily to hang on to history. Even so the town was being reclaimed by the desert, which advanced from the margins.

Slim was on a mission to find Mr. Moon's funeral home, and we set out on the quest, passing buildings labeled with plaques numbering them, ordering them: Historic Building no. 53, no. 82, no. 91. Some of the buildings had mannequins posing in the windows — a sheriff, a businessman, a pair of lovers in the high window of an apartment building, ghoulishly looking down to us on the street. "Here's your ghost town, Zane," Gracie said. He wasn't impressed. More dummies in position behind the plate glass windows of the Goldfield Hotel, the piano, the bar covered by a film of dust. The kids peered into these desolate scenes for a vision of what the town once was. Then we'd see a for-sale sign, an actual sticker price. Pool some of our retirement funds, we could buy the entire block — for what?

Slim, hunched over from a snaking spine, walked around pensively, continuing his search. We traipsed after him, hunting for Mr. Moon as if finding him would reveal something big, that mythic event I longed for driving out here. Diogenes of the Desert. In our search, we passed Tex Rickard's house. Slim pointed it out, the stained glass windows — loveliest house in town. I perked up, but for Gracie and Zane the house, a little bigger than the others, was also just a dump. They weren't wrong. "They weren't lovers," Slim said, "unless she loved a ghost. Rickard was long dead, but your grandmother liked to imply. She sure liked to imply."

At one point, on the edge of town, Slim pulled his little .32 pistol from its hiding place in his sock and let Zane hold it. My eyes popped. Gracie and even Mathilde shot me very disapproving looks. Fear ricocheted through me. I hit Sam for him to say something. But we were both struck dumb not wanting to be rude, the gun glistening in our boy's hand. Gracie took a picture with her phone: Snap. Click. Post. *I don't approve.* "Glenna always carried," Slim said. He took the gun back and once again it vanished.

The sky darkened, making the light beautiful and dull so the colors of the town and the red earth surrounding it sharpened. Rare earth mines surrounded the town, extracting elements and compounds that were useful for batteries and transistors, and now chips and solar cells. Volcanic ash used for making roads. Little Star Mine, Lode Star Mine, Diamond Field — mine shafts and mounds of tailing piles and shaft heads. The air smelled of chemistry, processed ore, arsenic and leaching. Beautiful toxic pools, a surreal blue.

We were all entranced, even Mathilde, searching, not sure for what, but searching all the same, for some link to the past, trying to hang on, save, a whole generation of seekers like us wanting to understand the true and scientifically verifiable stories of their DNA. While at the same time, it occurred to me, the next generation is erasing their stories almost instantaneously.

An Italian friend came to mind. Her mother had the manuscript of a great and distant aunt who'd traveled from Genoa to Chile with her husband in the early 1800s on a merchant ship. Adventures ensued. The ship was ravaged by disease, plundered by pirates. She was the only woman, dressed each day elegantly in Italian lace and dainty leather shoes. She wanted simply to see the world. My friend's mother gave me the manuscript. It was handwritten and in Italian. She thought I might like to write a book about this woman — this being the kind of woman I liked to write about. I took the manuscript with curiosity, started reading, struggling, I admit, with the language and the penmanship, when my friend called me to ask for the manuscript back. Her mother had changed her mind. She urgently wanted the manuscript back. It was her story and she had decided she did not want it told. My friend's mother died not long thereafter. She preferred the story to die with her than for it to be told — a simple story of a woman's bold adventure — while the rest of humanity, or Americans anyway, are desperately hunting to resurrect and save and carry forward and announce and declare and share theirs, however impermanently.

And here I was in Goldfield continuing Grammy's work, stories that she sang and that I transcribed, that were held in the moments of *dead and gone,* contained in the black box she filled with important documents and letters. All those ancestors were alive in Grammy's box: Charles's letters to his mother, genealogy charts connecting us to the War of 1812 and the Civil War, birth certificates, death certificates, a letter from Glenna to Pepperdine seeking acceptance — these "our papers," our proof that we have been here, that we have a trail, a tail, making a stand against the inevitability of time. I could hear my grandmother, her raspy bedtime voice, the one that would put me to sleep with my prayers along with one of her songs — *As you are now so once was I; as I am now so you shall be. Prepare for death and follow me.*

Close your eyes. Imagine our historic moment, all that it entails. Imagine a thousand years from now what someone would write about it. Would it fill a sentence? A paragraph, at most? One sentence tells the history of us gathered here today, our lives now so rich in detail, filled with love and hate and joy and dramas. We, all of us, are reduced to a sentence, crushed and overpowered and hidden behind the flimsy weight of that sentence. We are sentenced. Permanently erased — until some Herodotus comes along and with all the technique of a storyteller unearths us from that sentence, placing us, restoring us in a Technicolor biopic epic movie extravaganza.

In the larger scheme of things, how different were our attempts, mine and Slim's, at record keeping from My Story — here for a nanosecond then gone?

Gracie announced that Emma and Zasu had responded to her My Story, wanting to know if we'd found any documents: Glenna's death certificate, news articles about her death, her being hired, records from the school. Just like my sisters, they wanted facts. Later, Zasu would drive out here from Los Angeles, where she now lived with her wife and babies. They too would come to visit the town in their own minivan filled with snacks, learn that it wasn't just the Goldfield Hotel that was haunted but also the high school, by a former schoolteacher Zasu would believe was Glenna. She'd send me a picture of a woman in a high-necked dress, auburn Gibson girl hair — the image enhanced with painted-on color. *This is Glenna, right?* she'd ask. *She's the teacher who haunts the school.* The picture looked so much like Glenna, not quite, but close enough to believe.

When Emma came, she would spend her day in the archives digging and reading microfiche until she uncovered a news article from 1947, learning that Glenna died on July 7. She would drive up to Carson City, find more archives there and hunt until she produced Glenna's bona fide death certificate, which she'd duplicate for herself, an expedition that launched her own adventure to visit every town in Nevada, Idaho, and Montana in which Glenna had taught.

Scarlett requested we all send her any documents we found regarding our family. She had come up with an idea after cleaning the basement, after collecting the family antiques. (She was the one with Nancy Cooper Slagle's Cantonese wedding bowl.) Her ambition was to create her own family archive — a room at Rose Hill completely devoted to our family history, our own personal archive and library, facts verifiable, ordered, and arranged. It would take some doing. It would take some money, she said, but she also had come to her own realization — that all of us had enough money now, more or less, but not enough time.

In one way or another — I with my book — we were still shaking the family tree, *continuing the fight,* as Glenna had written, whatever fight that might be in whatever century, continuing the work of the ancestors who on occasion seemed to dwell within us and make their presence known as we walked under the unremarkable Nevada sun in the northeast quadrant of the Milky Way.

Semitrailers plowed through Main Street, one after the next, making the sidewalks vibrate, startling us.

Then I saw it. "Look," I said, pointing to a dilapidated barn near abandoned Union Pacific railroad tracks. An elegantly carved sign nailed into corrugated tin just beneath the sloping point of the roof read: Goldfield

Hearse Barn — Jack Noone, Proprietor. It was as if I had found a pot of gold, suddenly understanding why we were here. "Look, look," I said again. The others collected around me, Gracie squinting to decipher the importance.

"Hell's bells," Slim said. "You don't say."

"It was Noone, not Moon," I said.

"That's it," Slim said. "Hot diggity dog." I could feel Slim bursting forth, like this was all real, an inexorable truth. I too felt strangely more awake. How to explain: that Glenna had actually died, here in this town, in some approximation of the story that had been carried down for some seventy years. Was that it? It was so small, yet it felt exponential, large — an obvious equation that was somehow hard to get to. I could feel Gracie's discerning eyes on Slim and me, trying to add this up for herself. I could feel Sam's smile, his understanding, that he got this moment. Slim had been alive with Glenna, his grandmother, he'd been out here, seen her dead body, dressed it, maneuvered it, worked with it, watched Grammy clip a hunk of its hair. But even so he needed confirmation too that a story he lived had actually existed. This simple sign of Mr. Noone's, its gentle corrective — "Noone, not Moon" — showed how history actually worked over time, how things both vanished and how things were preserved, how the truth of things could be kept and held against vanishing, even if it meant the truth was slightly skewed, or even warped quite a bit. This wasn't my mythic moment, nothing hinged on this, but I could feel it palpably, history's liberation from myth; its attempt to escape the sentence. The sign of Mr. Noone lent a potent sense of confirmation to our time in Goldfield. Slim's body was bent, but he seemed to stand taller, his face suddenly more youthful.

In the video of Grammy recorded on her ninety-seventh birthday, she laughs her toothless laugh, smiles flirtatiously at the camera as my mother asks her about stealing her sister's name. "Tell them the story, Mother, of taking your sister's name," Mom says. And then we, the viewers, receive Grammy's miraculous smile, even without teeth, the teeth resting on the edge of her plate on the table along with the remains of some birthday cake.

"Oh that one," she says, mischief in that smile of hers. "That one," she repeats. When I watch that clip I see all that Avon product spilling from the drawers and bathroom closets of Last Morrow, Pat coming forth best she could. *Oh that.* And then Grammy pivots, launching instead into a tale of eating a box of her mother's chocolates and upon being discovered getting a beating. *Oh that* — after a lifetime just a joke, just another clever step forward among so many that managed to carry us: Slim and me, on our quest to this desert town.

"You know what?" Gracie said. "I'd like it a whole lot if seventy years after my death a bunch of family came looking for me."

A storm followed us back to Las Vegas. A high ceiling, dark and ominous, broke open releasing a waterfall so violent and unrelenting it seemed the Hoover Dam had burst.

"When it rains like this we get a bar of soap and wash ourselves in the street. Rain is like gold," Slim said.

When the rain stopped, the fields, gray just a moment before, turned green and the high desert Joshua trees seemed to bloom before our eyes. A sliver of blue sky and a shot of sunshine teased the gray clouds. A Technicolor blast. We passed a field of wild donkeys splashing in puddles. All the dry lakes filled with real water, rising and rising some more, water swirling torrentially at the edges of the road to biblical levels. On the highway, same one Glenna had used to get to Slim's childhood home in Los Angeles, there were suddenly cars bunched up and slowing to a stop.

"Glenna did damn well whatever she wanted," Slim said, sitting once again beside Gracie in the middle row of seats.

"It's Glenna," I offered, liking the notion that she was there. I'm not a superstitious person, hadn't thought myself an eidolist, but the weird weather accompanying us away from Goldfield made me think twice. "It's Glenna haunting us. It's Glenna doing what she damn well pleases." My enthusiasm was potent; it seemed possible this was Glenna. "She's speaking to us," I said. "She's thanking us."

"Now that's a good notion," Slim said.

"A ghost story," Zane said.

"*Quoi?*" asked the French girl.

"She was born too early," Slim continued. "Stifled by her time. Desperate to be her own person in a world that made that hard for an ordinary woman of small income."

A motorcycle whizzed by the stopped-up traffic, the two riders soaked in their black leather. "Those guys are about to find out about life," Slim said.

The traffic began to move. Up ahead, a highway patrolman redirected the long line of cars into the Yucca Mountains because a flash flood had washed away the road. Our minivan passed the motorcyclists in a ditch, wheels encased in thick mud, unmoving as the remains of the flood ran in torrents around them.

We followed the divergence up into the cooler air, where the entire piñon forest had opened up to release its aroma, petrichor: the smell of earth after rain. The air changed around us, an organism responding to the rain — the forest, a living thing — and the air was scented now with pine and sage while the sky continued doing dazzling things. We traveled the crest and then awhile later descended once again. Las Vegas rose from the flats in the distance, offering all the promises of Oz.

The winter before Grammy died, my sister Celia, in New York from Paris on sabbatical, had a baby shower for our sister Scarlett, who was pregnant with her third child. Emma was there. Adeleine was there. Grammy had been staying with me because Mom had been in Jamaica visiting Arthur, but she'd come home for the party. It was a happy occasion, all the cute clothing and bright food and wine, wrapping paper and ribbons everywhere, and Scarlett presiding like a queen. I was just pregnant, but I wasn't yet sharing the news. Grammy was in a wheelchair because she couldn't walk the distance from my apartment to Celia's rental even though it was only ten blocks. The arthritis in her hip was too painful. Emma suggested surgery; Scarlett said she was too old. We all always seemed happy when we were together, even if we fought. And because there were so many of us, these occasions happened more than infrequently.

At the end of the evening it started to snow. Celia's apartment looked out over the Hudson, above Riverside Drive. We were reminded of the apartment we grew up in thirty blocks south, how we loved to sit in the windowsills and watch the snow sprinkle down over the river.

"Imagination Jersey City Hall," Grammy said when we emerged into the snow world from Celia's building on our way back to my apartment. The snow was coming down softly and beautifully, a dry yet heavy fall. It was supposed to be a big accumulation, ten to twelve inches. Grammy had taken to repeating the *Imagination Jersey City Hall* phrase because she'd married there, perfect iambic pentameter so easy on the tongue, in her old age. She would say the phrase while with her right hand she'd make a circling gesture at her temple. All this indicated that she was seeing the world in a crazy yet fantastical way, like this was all a big laugh. Coming out of Celia's warm and glowing party, celebrating yet another life, and into the fast-dropping snow — so beautiful and clean — was crazy magic. And it was. I am a small, slight woman. She was a big, robust woman, seated in her wheelchair.

"It's snowing, Baby Rabbit. It's snowing." Mom too loved the snow, that it covered over everything to make it pure and clean. "Glenna knew weather," Grammy continued. "She could read it, smell it. 'It smells like snow,' she'd say." I was pushing Grammy now, around the corner from Riverside Drive to 113th Street, which contours a hill, a significant hill if you're pushing a wheelchair filled with some 160 pounds of grandmother. The wind was blowing off the river, sneaking inside our collars, but the street wasn't yet slippery. It was about midnight and we were the only two people out there. I was pushing her, using all my strength, back bent, arms outstretched. I didn't feel that we were alone. The wind from the river seemed to help even as it occurred to me, halfway up the hill, that if I stumbled, lost the strength, it would be a bumpy ride back to the bottom.

Grammy started telling a story about Glenna in Montana in a snowstorm, about tying a rope from the schoolhouse to the outhouse so they could get to it in a whiteout. Just follow the rope. But it wasn't Glenna I was thinking about as I pushed the wheelchair and Grammy up the hill. It was Nancy and her children, crossing the Alleghenies, how of all of Grammy's stories that one had remained constant. I could see Nancy traveling on foot with her seven children, carrying the Cantonese bowl that had been given to her as a wedding present, little Theresa dying along the way, buried in an unmarked grave and with little ceremony — how she just continued. Then I thought about my little baby dividing away inside.

I kept pushing, one step after the other, stronger with each one, an invisible force helping me. We were almost to the top, the snow falling faster now, sticking in our hair and on our lips, the wheels of Grammy's chair cutting through that thickening snow, two tracks marking my effort, filling in with more snow, a palimpsest.

As we reached the top, I bellowed, "We did it, Grammy."

Grammy started to laugh her magnificent laugh, and said, "You and I, Baby Rabbit, we can do anything."

ACKNOWLEDGMENTS

I would like to thank the following people for their help with this book: Andrea Chapin; Elizabeth Gaffney; Sara Powers; Beka Chase; Rene Steinke; Debbie Stier; my grandmother, who told me stories to keep our narrative alive; my mother, who, among many other things, encouraged me to write everything down and she also gave me the title; my father, who always listens; former dean Bernard Firestone of Hofstra University for being generous with his support of this novel and all of my novels and also for his patience; Dick Rein and Pat Newman, who understood my quest long before I did; Sally Howe; Sarah Chalfant; Jin Auh; Dr. Allison Lomonaco; and — always — Mark Svenvold and our children, Livia and Jasper.

ABOUT THE AUTHOR

Martha McPhee is the author of the novels *Bright Angel Time, Gorgeous Lies, L'America,* and *Dear Money.* She is a recipient of a National Endowment for the Arts grant and a fellowship from the John Simon Guggenheim Memorial Foundation. *Gorgeous Lies* was a finalist for the National Book Award. She teaches fiction at Hofstra University and lives in New York City.

The employees of Thorndike Press hope you have enjoyed this Large Print book. All our Thorndike, Wheeler, and Kennebec Large Print titles are designed for easy reading, and all our books are made to last. Other Thorndike Press Large Print books are available at your library, through selected bookstores, or directly from us.

For information about titles, please call:
(800) 223-1244

or visit our website at:
gale.com/thorndike

To share your comments, please write:

Publisher
Thorndike Press
10 Water St., Suite 310
Waterville, ME 04901